A Maid Again

David A Dunlop

Front cover painting by David McDowell
'Nostalgia' /Oil on Linen/2020
Photography - David A Dunlop
Cover Design - David McDowell

Copyright © 2020 David A Dunlop

All rights reserved.

ISBN: 9798645874513

ACKNOWLEDGMENTS

In the process of writing this story I have very much appreciated help and advice from the following;

Dónall Mac Ruairí and Máire Nic Cathmhaoil regarding Irish language phrases and west Donegal idiom. Further thanks to Máire for her guidance in the final stages of editing.

Séimidh Ó Dubhthaigh, a fount of knowledge on Rosses local history;

Trevor Martin regarding legal proceedings;

Thomas Boyd whose practical hands adorn the front cover picture;

David McDowell, a former pupil, now a very accomplished artist, who designed the book's cover, including his beautiful miniature, 'Nostalgia', a painting of the Windsor Hotel in Cape May, New Jersey;

Finally, deepest gratitude to my wife Mary whose constant encouragement, insightful criticism and painstaking proof-reading of the text has been invaluable as always.

In addition, I wish to reference the following;
- "Castlederg and its Red River Valley", by James Emery and Canon Harry Trimble (2005), an excellent pictorial history of the area;
- "Living With Partition: The Irish Borderlands 1920-1950"; M L Dennis, Phd Thesis 2008;
- "Partitioned Lives: the Irish Borderlands"; C Nash, B Reid, B Graham, Farnham:Ashgate, 2013;
- "The Rule of the Land - Walking Ireland's Border"; Garrett Carr, Faber and Faber, 2017;
- "Unapproved Roads"; Peter Leary, Oxford Press, 2016;
- www.irishborderlands.com
- "Border Country - When Ireland Was Divided" RTE 2019;

For the Brothers Dunlop

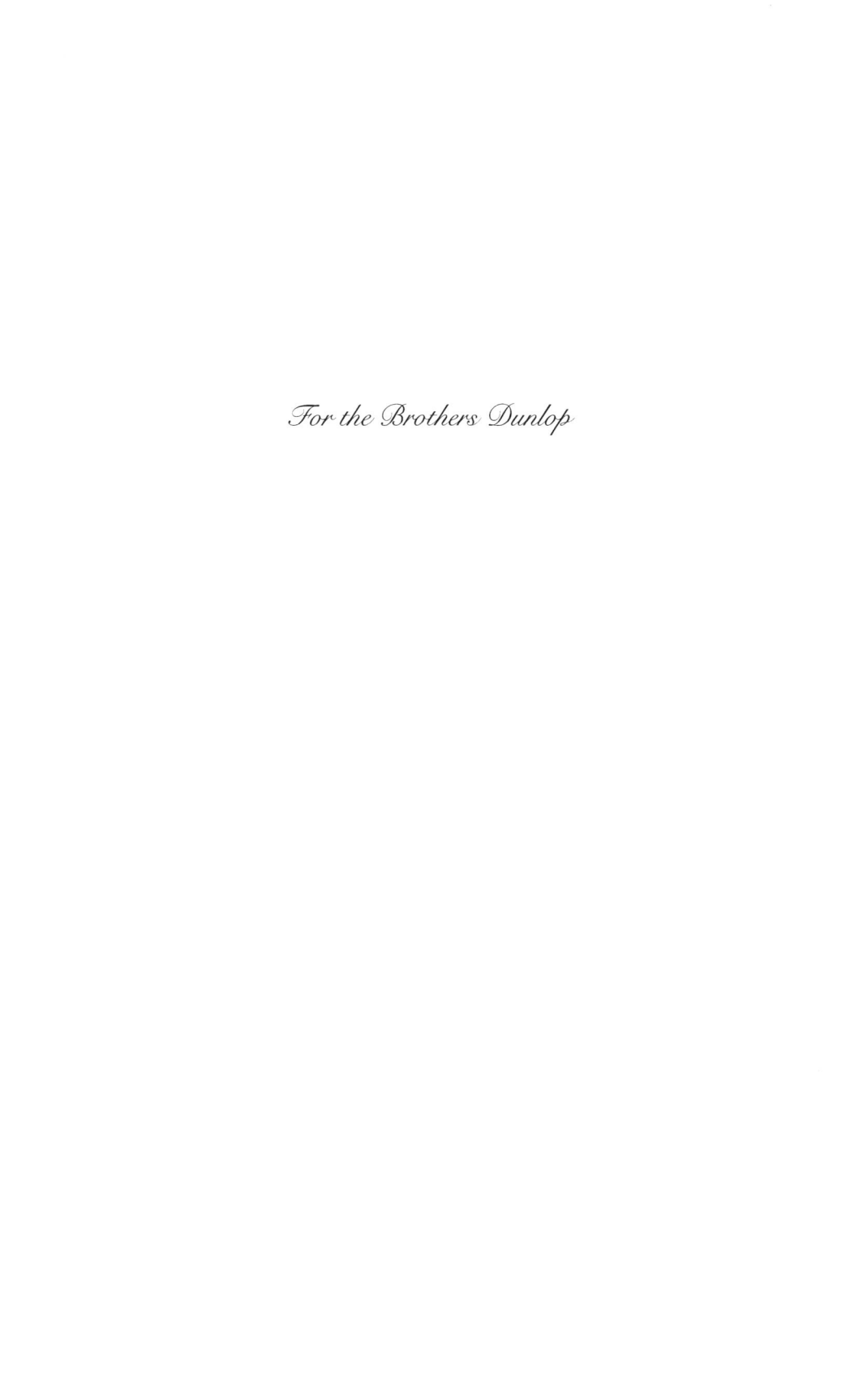

A Maid Again

Chapter 1

Matthew Henderson

I will go to her in the morning.
    It may be the most foolish thing I will ever do. Not, though, the most foolish I have ever done; no, nothing will ever come close to some of those big mistakes that I made in the course of my life. There are one or two dismal chapters back there that can never be bettered for folly.
    I have her letter in my hand. It's dated 22nd June 1945. That was Friday past, just a few days ago. I have her address. I have my car ready, filled to the brim with petrol for the first time in years.
    And I have the memories. They walk the floor with me manys a night, these ghosts that mock of lost opportunities, these prosecuting counsels who stand in line as I pace the darkened bedroom, echoing each other as they remind me of the weaknesses in my character.
    And I am still walking the room. Sleep will not come to me tonight. It is not a new feeling that, but this night, when I really could be doing with a decent rest, my mind will not shut down. Thoughts flit this way and that, like bats through the back yard at twilight. One minute my head will be lost in the middle of those memories, sweet ones or bitter ones; the next minute I will be thinking in amazement about what I am planning to do tomorrow.
    I am not a natural at this. I am not what you would call courageous; I haven't much of a silver tongue. Never had. What on earth am I going to say to her? Will I just stand there like a dumb bullock and feel the slam of the door being shut in my face?
    That is if I can even find her home in the first place. I do not know that part of Donegal. I have never been over in that western area, never been any further in that art than the town of Ballybofey. I don't have a map. All I know is that her address has the name 'Kincasslagh' in it. I believe that it is somewhere on the west

coast, from what I remember her telling me. My idea is that I will stop in Castlefinn or Stranolar and ask somebody, maybe a Guard. I am fairly sure it will be a long drive. I need to get on the road as early as I can, before seven, because I have to be back over the Border by six o'clock, otherwise it's a fine from the Customs men and I want no more truck with those boys. I am hoping that the meeting will go well enough to be worth a fine if it comes to that.

What is it that I am hoping for from this meeting, from this…I was going to say 'this girl', but of course after all this time it will be 'this woman'? And what am I hoping to be able to say to her in the first place?

I need to tell her how deep is my regret for all that happened between us, especially at the end. In her letter she has been very generous in asking me to forgive her; the truth is that, for the most part, it is the other way around. I need to be begging her pardon. I was far too hard on her. I listened to the wrong people, took the wrong advice and ended up misjudging her, pushing her away when everything inside me wanted to bring her closer.

When I do tell her that and ask her for forgiveness I have no idea what to expect in return. In some ways it will be enough to see her, maybe hear her say, "That's alright. It's water under the bridge. Go on back home to Lismore." It will be better still if she can smile at me, maybe offer me a cup of tea, sit at her fire and hear her talk about her life since we parted.

At the end of it all I will have to judge whether I just get up and shake hands, leave her with an "All the best to you," or maybe something different. I never had much success in gauging how a woman is feeling. I have had nothing but bad experiences when I have strayed into those dangerous waters. Back in my time with Alice Porter I nearly drowned altogether. If anything, it is this uncertainty that is mostly responsible for keeping me awake tonight.

How will I know?

Just play it by ear, you might advise me; but though I have a grand ear for music I seem to be tone deaf when it comes to knowing what is the right note with a woman. That is one of the reasons I have fixed up my father's old fiddle this evening. It has been hanging here on my wall for over twenty years, a stray string running down its face like a tear, its bridge twisted in a bitter, lopsided smile. Now it is looking a lot happier, the reddish grain of the wood shining through where before you couldn't see it for grease and dust, the strings tightened up to somewhere near the right pitch. My intention is to take the fiddle with me, have it in the car and, if the conversation with her appears to me to be going well, I will bring it in and present it to her. My fingers will be crossed that I will sense if that is the right thing to do, and that she will accept the gesture in good faith, a sign of my regard for her, my sorrow for times past and as my attempt to atone for the time in between.

I suppose the worst thing that could happen would be if she responded like she did the last time she saw this instrument; maybe I should just keep hold of it in case she rares up at me, grabs it out of my hands and flings it against the wall, the way she did back in that terrible year of broken things.

If I could just put it all out of my mind now and get over into sleep. Even if I do, I am fairly sure these thoughts will form up into some ugly smear of dreams, a nightmare of angry faces, pointing fingers, shouted words, gunshots, fear and rejection.

Chapter 2

Matthew Henderson

The big potato face of the Customs man beyond the car window.
 This is a window that has long since ceased going up and down like it should. So I have to open the door to talk to him. It's stiff, and he rips impatiently at the handle before I have it fully open.
 I don't recognise this man, heavy set, tall and flabby-jawed. I haven't seen him before at this crossing; a new hand, I think. Younger than the usual ones; round glasses that make him look more like a Sabbath-school teacher.
 Before he speaks I get in a friendly, "How's things the day?"
 He ignores my effort to be civil. Well-trained nowadays, these new men; they don't be put off by pleasantries.
 "You are early on the go this morning, sir," he begins. Not a local accent, more Down or Armagh maybe.
 "I am that."
 The low early sunbeams are lighting up his rosy cheeks, like you would notice in an old-style oil painting, and casting his long shadow on the gravelly road ahead.
 "Where are we off to then?"
 He holds out his spade of a hand for my papers.
 My passbook has fallen off the seat beside me, so I rummage around on the floor for it amongst the other junk.
 "Aye, I'm early alright," I say to the floor of the car. "You know what they say about the early bird? It catches…"
 "What is the nature of your visit, sir?"
 "Agh, just taking a wee scoot over, see how things are. Haven't been over in a good while so…"
 "Have you got a pass book or not?"
 "I have surely; it's here somewhere," I say. "I was down in the station yesterday for it. Ah, here. Ye see! Everything in order."
 He snatches the pass and brings it into focus, skellyin' through his specs at it. Behind him the Customs hut stands dark and solid as a well built peat-stack.
 "You need to get those specs looked at," I say. "It wouldn't look well for you if somebody sneaked over the Border after you not able to read the pass, would it?"
 "Never you mind about my spectacles," he says, checking the paper. "You haven't told me the nature of your business in the Free State yet, Mr …Mr Henderson."

We all still call it the Free State, in spite of the changes back in Thirty-Seven.

"Business," I tell him. "Like you say yourself."

He stares at me through the misting glasses, takes them off for a quick wipe as he waits. Then bends down in my direction and lowers his voice, as if he is warning a spoiled wain, quietly intimidating.

"The nature of your business?"

I take a second to ponder his question. It clearly annoys him. "Well? You're not going anywhere until you tell me," he says as he shuts my pass book and makes as if to put it in his inside pocket.

"The thing is, it's not really business the day. I don't know if I will do a deal or not...you see, I'm going to see a man about a dog."

This last bit I say in more of a whisper, sort of as if to bring him into my secret. In our part of the world 'going to see a man about a dog' doesn't mean the obvious. I am not sure if this fellow will understand the code and take the hint.

As he ponders this in the early quietness of the morning, I can hear a thrush singing its beak off on some nearby tree.

"A man about a dog?" he says, a puzzled look before I see a smile behind his eyes. It's only a very quick smile though, and fades into another frown almost before you'd have noticed it. "At this time of the morning? You trying to be smart here, Mr Henderson; nobody goes..."

"Ah-ha," I interrupt, "you think at this time of the morning I should let sleeping dogs lie, do you? Well you might be right. Can I have my pass back now and be on my way?"

As I am speaking, I see another official in uniform come out of the Customs hut, a small whippet of a man, a good bit older. He disturbs a crow which has been dabbing at the carcass of some dead animal splatted on the road. The bird rises in a squawking black flurry and flies off resentfully towards the Donegal bogs. The new man watches it lazily. He is obviously not long awake, stretching himself and wiping a yawn off his morning face. He turns in our direction. As he approaches our conversation I think, 'Agh God no!'

This one I recognise, a cagey older Customs man by the name of Bamford; I have come across him before, and not in the most auspicious of circumstances.

"Who have we here?" he says reaching for my pass from his colleague.

"He says he's going to see a man about a dog," the younger man explains, "but I don't believe him; like at this time of the morning..."

Bamford holds up his hand, sort of to silence the younger officer, and examines the pass. His eyes bounce up to stare at my face, suspicion hardening them I think.

"Henderson? Matthew Henderson?" he says slowly. "I shoulda recognised his oul banger o' a car."

I say nothing, going back into my shell, tapping the steering wheel and staring at the road ahead, at the rickety bridge over the Finn river and into Donegal. I can sense him smiling down at me, waiting, baiting.

"Matthew Henderson, I'll be damned. I haven't seen you since the court case, and that must be seven or eight years ago. Where have you been? I missed you out and about."

"I haven't missed you," I mumble into the back of my hand.

"How was it in Derry gaol anyway? Cold was it? Not the best o' grub, was it? Damp a bit, eh? An' you'd miss the animals, the pigs and the sheep an' all?"

I let him have his fun. No point in antagonising him this morning. I just want to go.

"What was it you got? Two months was it? There are so many of you cheating scoundrels I can't keep track of the sentences. Was it two, was it? Shoulda been more anyways."

"It was just one," I tell him through clenched jaws.

"Ah, just the one eh? Long enough maybe; you weren't the worst. A good, decent, God-fearing farmer, well-respected in the community, weren't you....until you got caught out. So hopefully you learned your lesson; what would you say, Mister Henderson? No more dodgy stuff for you since, eh? You didn't get involved in any of that nonsense during the war, eh?"

I just want to get away here. I say nothing more than, "Naw".

"And now it's over, there won't be such good opportunities for men like you to be making money on the black market, eh? Men like you are probably the only ones that are regretting the war's over. You'll have to tighten your belt now, eh?"

He shakes his head in disgust at me and I say nothing.

"Chancers! Using the national emergency to get rich quick. You're as bad as the rebels, and you a..."

"That's not fair," I protest. "I haven't used the war for anything. If I'd got rich do you think I would still be driving a car like this?"

"Maybe not, but you didn't join up either, did you?"

"No, I didn't join up. Farm..."

"No, of course you didn't," he interrupts scornfully. "Just thought you wouldn't be the type. Not got the guts, eh?"

"Anyway, I lost my father in the first war....so I sort of feel we did our bit as a family."

"I didn't know that," he says after a pause, a different tone.

He seems to be examining my pass again.

"I can't say I've seen you at this checkpoint before, have I? Mind you, I'm only here the odd time so maybe…"

"You musta missed me," I say.

"So you do use this crossing a fair bit, do you?"

"I have done, surely," I tell him. "My place isn't far away, as you know, so if I have to go into Donegal I always cross either here at Clady or on the back road to Castlefinn."

"Except that, as I remember the case, you don't always be using the official approved crossing points, do you? You seem to know one or two others that we weren't aware of."

"Your loss," I mumble so he can't hear.

"And are you always back over in time, when you're on these… visits, before the post closes?"

"Aye."

"And yer off into Donegal this morning?" He checks his pocket watch. "At a quarter past seven? You're going to have to give me a decent explanation for that, Mr Henderson. What's going on?"

From behind him the other officer butts into the conversation with a reminder.

"He says he's going to see a man about a dog, sir."

A short-lived smile and a faint shake of the head as he thinks about this. He folds the pass and taps it on the palm of his hand.

"At your age you should have more wit. Anyway, what's wrong with Northern Ireland lasses that you have to be going over to Donegal for one?"

I say nothing, just try to hide the annoyance that rises in me, the wince at the side of my mouth.

"Right," he says, stamping my pass, "don't let this be any exception. Back here by six o'clock or you'll be paying our overtime for us."

"What if I come back on the other road? Is that not alright? If I am on time and all?"

"Why would you want to come on the other road?"

"Just," I say. "It might suit me better, save me a lock o' miles to come back over by Kilclean."

He thinks about this.

"It might suit you but it doesn't suit us," he says, handing me my pass. "Don't be late now."

The two of them stand back, one glowering, the other with a half smile of triumph playing around below his moustache.

The old Austin belches and splutters as I hit the pedal; I drive past them very slowly, foot on the clutch and the engine revved up so as to create a grey cloud of fumes around the pair of them. The car is sixteen years old and burning oil like a tractor. In the mirror I see Bamford go into a fit of coughing, doubling up and waving his hand in front of his face to beat the smoke away.

"Have a lungful of that, ye sour oul reprobate," I say to myself as I start to slow up for the second Customs Post, this time the Irish one, just on the other end of the narrow bridge.

The Donegal official would seem to have had a better night's sleep than his opposite numbers in the north. He even nods at me in recognition as he studies the car, and raises his hand.

"'Mornin'," he says. "What brings you over today, Mr Henderson? There's no markets on anywhere."

I explain, as with the other men, and there doesn't seem to be a problem.

"Just need to check if you're carrying any goods," he says, standing back as I anticipate and push the door further open. "A wee check in your boot."

The boot creaks open. He gives me a quick look. There are two items in there that he did not expect to see.

"You are carrying petrol?"

"Aye. Just the one wee jar," I say. "In case I need it on the mountains."

"I thought it was still scarce over there in the north."

"It is. It's still rationed and will be for a good while, I imagine."

"So how did you come by it?"

"A neighbour. He owes me a good turn. If I don't need it I can give it back to him," I tell him.

"Ok, but don't be tempted to be selling it," he says, looking at the other item. "What's this then?"

"It's just a fiddle case," I tell him.

"I can see that. And is there a fiddle in it? You're not trying to hide some contraband in there, are you," he says, pleasantly enough.

I reach for the case and open it for him. "It's an oul fiddle of my father's," I tell him. "It doesn't have any value really. Just the sentimental thing of it being his. I'm not intending to sell it or anything."

He twangs the strings, as if to check they are in tune. By this stage they're not, nowhere near.

"So you don't play yourself then?"

He didn't have to be too sharp to work that out.

"Not a note," I say.

"And you're not for selling it?"

"I'm not."

"Petrol and a fiddle," he says, puzzled. "Can you open the bonnet for me?"

I do that and he takes a quick look.

"Alright," he says, "and you're not carrying any other goods? No flour or sugar or anything? What's in the back seat there?"

"Not a thing...well, I have a bit of lunch packed for myself. Here," I say, showing him the basket.

He laughs, having a quick fumble through it.

"What's wrong with Donegal food that you have to bring your own? Do you think we'd be trying to poison you or something?"

"Not at all," I say. "It's just I have a wile long drive to the far side of the county and I might need a bite along the road."

"Where is it you're heading?"

I fish in my inside pocket and bring out the letter. He might be a help in trying to find this place.

"All I know is that it's away over to the west," I say, showing him the address. "Look; some place by the name of Ranahuel..."

He studies the address. "I never heard of it," he tells me, "but I know Kincasslagh. I'd be from Dunfanaghy myself but I have been down that way; they call it the Rosses down there."

"And how do I find it?"

He thinks a second. "It's a hell of a drive," he says giving my Austin a doubtful look. "From here...well, you know your way to Ballybofey, of course?"

"I do."

"Right, well you'll need to turn right at the end of the main street there and just sort of follow the valley, along the side of the river all the way to a village called Finntown. Then another right turn towards Doochary and Dungloe. You could ask somebody the way from there. The roads will not be too great now, so take it easy."

"I have no choice," I tell him.

And he's right. At twenty to thirty miles an hour it takes me to near dinner time to reach Kincasslagh, and that after getting lost a couple of times and finding myself halfway up a mountain rodden. That is the trouble. With some of the roads it is hard to work out what is road and what is mountain track; potholes you could fish in and bends that leave you thinking you must be going back where you came from. The local folks help though. One old man with not a tooth in his head keeps going back into his Gaelic to describe things to me, then he realises and says something like, "Agh I'm right sorry, but it's a pity you don't have the Irish."

9

I think to myself, 'He's not far wrong; if I had had the Irish I might not have been needing to make this drive today.'

I notice a scattering of tumble-down cottages on this huge stretch of bogland. They look like some of them old pencil drawings from famine times. The poverty here must have been fierce. I wonder does her house look anything like these hovels. Later, when I am driving down to the narrow plain between the mountains and the sea, I am surprised to notice that there are far more houses here. This area seems to have a lot more folk living in it, far too many for this land to give succour to; scrawny wee fields between stone dakes and whin bushes. Hardly a decent beast to be seen. What do they all live on, I wonder. How do her people survive in a place like this? That's why she came to the hiring fair, of course, as I recall. And I remember her saying once that whatever cows they owned had to have their horns cut off, so they could get their heads in between the rocks to graze. Funny the things you remember.

I can recall a bit of a row with her one day when we were at the turnip thinning. Her notion was that people like me were someway to blame for the people in her neck of the woods being so poor. I thought she was talking nonsense of course, but she had a whole string of things that she said had happened in the history of these parts. The land had been 'stolen' from the natives, whole areas of good land in Derry and Tyrone given to Protestant landlords from England and Scotland, she argued.

"I suppose you think I am one of them English landlords?" I had laughed at her.

"No, but even your name gives you away as a man who is not of Ireland," she told me. "And the people who were forced to move from your good fertile countryside had to go somewhere. That is why there are so many of the native Irish crowded into the west and up to the mountains, on to the useless land that the planters couldn't be bothered with."

I often wondered how she knew so much. For somebody who claimed to have had such a poor schooling, and whose folks couldn't afford books, she knew about a pile of things, the kind of things that backed up her strong opinions anyhow.

Sally Anne is in every other thought as I drive.

What will she look like? Will I recognise her? What will she say?

Not long after leaving the town of Dungloe, I arrive in a quaint village that I have been directed to, Kincasslagh, I believe. I am tired and famished. I stop outside a pub in this village, park the car and take my basket of food for a short walk down towards the sea, a long estuary of some sort. It's a beautiful place this, wild and rugged like something you would see in a postcard. The sky, pure blue like a forget-me-not flower, with a few shaggy clouds blowing slowly across it, the dark rocks of some headland opposite topped off with the greenest of grass, the light reflecting off the channel of rippling sea-water between it and me. Seagulls are swirling all around me and a flock of some other sort of bird dabbing and picking along the edge of the surf, black and white but with bright orange beaks. Across the strand wee swirls of dirty sand pimple the surface, likely the result of some worm or shellfish down below. There's a bit of a smell in the air; thick brown seaweed is strewn all over the grey sand; the whiff of decay is rising off it, just the usual smell of the coast that I remember from being at Magilligan once, years ago with Alice. Not the best of a memory to be coming into my head at this particular time. Lord but I've made some terrible messes in my time.

    I sit on a flat rock and open the picnic, the gulls keeping a close eye on me. Millie's split soda bread farls with cheese between them go down well. So does the flask of tea, even without the sugar.

    Sally Anne's letter.

    Out of a grey Tyrone sky this letter had arrived. It landed in on me like one of those hand grenades you see in the war pictures, and blew to smithereens any bit of peace I had managed to pull round myself.

    I take it out of my coat pocket again for another look. How many times have I read it since Thursday? But I read it again. I near enough know it off by heart.

Chapter 3

Ranahuel
Kincasslagh
Co Donegal
22nd June 1945

Dear Matthew,

It is a strange thing to be writing to somebody that I used to know and who might no longer be alive, for all I know.

You likely have no memory of me and I could not blame you if that is the truth.

I was hired on your farm twenty three years ago, in the year that disaster struck your friend, Joe Kearney, God rest him. At the same time, I am thinking, how could any of us not remember that night?

You are probably wondering why you are getting a letter from me after all this time. Well, I am sailing to America in a couple of weeks and I just felt the need to tell you. That and some other things.

I often wonder what became of you. It was a very tough time that you went through.

I feel bad now that I did not stay to help you in it. I cut myself off and would not even talk to you when you needed help, because of how I felt after what happened between us. I suppose I was carrying a big hurt but that is no excuse. So that is another reason for me writing to you now, to say sorry that I left you in the middle of it all, sorry that I never even came to bid you goodbye and thank you for the work and for the times you were kind to me.

Over the years I have often thought that, if the truth be told, it was as much my fault as yours that Joe died. If I had not persuaded him to go to your aid that night the tragedy would never have happened. You would not have had to be carrying such a terrible burden for the rest of your life. I am sorry for that; not for encouraging him to help his old friend but for letting all the blame of it fall on your shoulders.

It would be great if we could only remember the good times. If there had only been the good times, who knows, I might be still around Lismore. But it seems to me now, looking back on it, that those terrible things that happened were somehow out of our control. We were just like characters in the play that was written for us and we could not change the course of those events.

I often wonder if you had not met that Englishman might Joe still be alive today. If he had not taken his father's gun to carry for him that night, you might have seen the shape of him rather than the glint of the gun in his hands.

I will never forget the details of that night. In particular I can still see you and Anthony walking, so slowly, inch by inch, across the street towards us, you in your suit and tie and the grief in you twisting your white face. It is an image that is stuck in my mind and I wish I could shift it. I have often wondered what made you change into your Sunday clothes to come down to look at poor Joe.

And I have often wondered what became of you after that night? I wonder did you ever get married yourself. I wonder about the twins and your poor mother. How did Anthony and Monica get over the death? And old Tam. Is he dead or alive? He thought a lot of you. I recall him telling me not to be too hard on you. I still sometimes wonder if he really had heard what he said he heard or if that tale was just a silly old drunken nightmare of his. Maybe there was no plot at all. If that was so it would make Joe's death all the more tragic. No, nothing could have made it any more tragic, I am thinking.

I hope this letter finds you and, if it does, that you are in good health.

Yours sincerely,
Your old hired hand,
Sally Anne Sweeney

Chapter 4

Matthew Henderson

What a lovely letter! I am still wondering at it.

As I finish reading I get the feeling that I am not alone. I look up to see a figure approaching across the strand; an elderly man is picking his way through the piled seaweed near the high-tide mark and coming in my direction. I fold the letter and slide it into my inside pocket again as I watch the stranger approach. There is something about his bearing and the blackness of his garb that immediately makes me think, 'Clergy'. Sure enough, as he comes closer, the white flash of his little round collar confirms my instinct. I lever myself off the rock to meet him.

He speaks to me in a friendly way…in Irish; it sounds like 'Jee A Ditch'. I should remember some of Sally Anne's words but I haven't a notion what this means. It is most likely a greeting so I respond with a shy 'Good morning'. Maybe I should have added 'Father', but I always feel a bit awkward saying that word to a stranger. From the fleeting look behind his eyes, I think he expected it too. There is just the slightest hesitation in his stride, as if he has just thought better of stopping for a chat.

"Ah, you are a visitor to these parts? Good morning indeed, a very fine day," he says and makes as if to move on towards the village above without a backward glance. He is maybe twenty yards away from me when a sudden thought strikes me. This man may very well be Sally Anne's priest; he may be the man who knows more about her than anyone else I could meet in this village. I am missing the chance to speak to the best person who can tell me how to find her house.

Now the word seems to come easily to me. "Father," I call, hurrying after him, "You wouldn't know how I can find a place by the name of Ranahuel?"

He stops and turns around abruptly. His dark cloak floats out like a flag catching an unexpected gust of wind.

"A stranger looking for Ranahuel?" he says. "Now that doesn't happen very often. Why would a stranger be wanting to find a God-forsaken place like Ranahuel, might I ask?"

I am taken aback by his tone. What has Ranahuel done to deserve this clergyman's scorn? It must be in his parish, I'm thinking, so, if it's God-forsaken, is it his fault? But of course these fleeting reactions stay in the safety of my cynical mind and I reply with all reverent meekness.

"I am trying to find somebody that I once knew."

As soon as I say it I realise my mistake. Now he will demand to be told which of his flock I once knew, how I knew her, when I knew her, how well I knew her and what brings me now to try to find her. I have landed Sally Anne in the muck and I can see no way to avoid it.

"Who would that be?" His eyes seem to twinkle with curiosity.

I am sure he senses my hesitation; likely reads too much into it.

"A girl that used to work to me," I say.

"A girl that used to work to you? And who might she be, this girl?"

"Her name was...her name is Sally Anne Sweeney."

"Sally Anne? Well she's not a girl now. Must be in her forties. So when did she work for you?"

"Agh, it was a long time back," I tell him. How I wish I had waited and asked someone else, anyone, anyone who is not a priest. "I think the year was 1922."

"1922 was it? That was a year never to be forgotten."

You can say that again, I am thinking.

"And where was it that she worked for you? You don't seem old enough to have been employing a maid in 1922, if you don't mind me saying so."

We are getting into too much detail here, I think, but how do I stop it? How do I get away from this dark interrogator?

"I have a farm in Tyrone. She was the maid in the house, helping out with my mother. It is a long time ago. She was a good worker," I add, as if that might explain why, all this time later, I would be coming looking for her. Sure enough, the clergyman picks up on the comment.

"A good worker she must have been if you are after driving from Tyrone to meet her again. So she has kept in touch with you over the years, has she?"

So this is what it is like in the confessional, I think to myself. It's not just a case of going in with a list, rhyming it off with a 'Father, I have sinned' sort of thing. You have to go through an inquisition before you are allowed off the hook.

"Well, not exactly kept in touch with me," I tell him. "I just remember her, that's all."

Why, in God's name, am I feeling guilty and me not even a Catholic? These priests! There is no way I am telling him about her letter to me. She'd likely have to do penance for a month in that Lough Derg place to cleanse her soul.

"You remember her, and you remember her town-land, twenty-three years later, and you come looking for her? She must have made some impression on you I'd say. What else do you remember about her?"

Now there's a question that, should he put thumb-screws on me, I will never answer. I remember everything about her, but I choose something without much consequence, just to have any sort of an answer for him.

"Agh now, it's a long time ago and I don't remember very much," I lie. "One thing she told me was that her mother couldn't talk, as far as I can recall."

He nods as if satisfied with this snippet of detail.

"That would be true alright," he says. "Poor old Annie has never said a word in all her life. Sally Anne looked after her for years, looked after her more than well; and manys a neighbour too, if truth be told. The best of a woman; heart of gold."

I hear the 'looked after her'; the past tense. I wonder if the old woman has passed away. The priest has a great way of sensing what I am thinking. Maybe it was the shape of the wee frown beginning on my face.

"She is still alive," he says. "But the other sister is looking after her now, Mairead that is, now that Sally Anne is going away."

He is watching me like a hawk to see how I react to this. But I am just as clever as he is and I give nothing away.

"Oh right?" I say with an air of surprise. "She is heading away somewhere, is she?"

"America, I believe. She'd have a couple of cousins somewhere about New York, or maybe it's Boston. I think she sails next week."

There's a sense of relief in me for two reasons at this. She has some relatives who will look after her in the new world; she won't be on her own. More importantly, she is still in Ireland. I will see her soon, if this priest ever lets me go.

I pretend an air of disappointment for his benefit.

"Ah, I see," I tell him. "So there's no point in me offering her work then, if she'd set on going to America?"

"That's what I would be thinking," he agrees.

"But...if you could just tell me how to find her place Father, I'd be very grateful. Just to wish her safe travels and all the best for her new life," I say.

He takes a deep breath, seeming reluctant to be obliging me; his motivation may be good of course; I have to give him that. Watching out for a 'vulnerable' member of his flock. Who knows what she has told him in the secrecy of the confession box? Maybe he knows a lot more about me than I can imagine; maybe he's been doing a good job of hiding it in this conversation. For all I know, at this minute he could be recalling old stories from Sally Anne, putting a remembered two and two together and thinking, 'So this is the killer farmer who near enough seduced my precious little parishioner and left her mentally scarred for life? I owe it to her to send him packing back to Tyrone with his Protestant tail between his legs.' I am almost waiting for him to tell me to take the road home when he speaks.

"You have a car, I take it?"

"I have."

"Well why don't I come with you and show you the way. Ranahuel wouldn't be the easiest place to find. It's up in the hills," he says with a wave of his hand towards the sun.

Oh Lord, save me from this interfering clergyman. How can I get out of this one?

"Not at all Father," I say far too quickly. "I would never take up your time doing that. Thanks all the same. Just tell me the way sure..."

I have no more chance of dissuading him than I have of stopping the tide that is starting to creep up the strand towards us. In two minutes I am putting my basket into the back of the car, then sitting beside him, almost praying that the engine will come to my rescue here and fail to start. Or that some other miracle happens and I get rid of him.

The prayer is not answered. He is a priest after all and his prayer likely trumps mine. Either way we are soon climbing a very rough and winding lane into the hills, between whins and rough stone walls, himself blabbering on about who lives in this or that cottage and which of their children sends home the most money from Glasgow or England, America or Australia. And who owns that donkey that stands in the smallest field I've ever seen. How he remembers all this detail I cannot imagine. Now a story about a young fellow from that cottage on the hillside who was killed while working on some tunnels in Scotland. And soon a story I remember reading about in the paper a couple of years ago. 'So-and-so who lived in that cottage was killed in the mine disaster at Ballymanus.'

"I read about that," I tell him. "Was that near here?"

"Just down there behind us, over those sand-hills we saw," he says.

"Is that so? Must have been terrible for the area."

"The whole parish was cut to pieces by it," he tells me. "You wonder how the community will ever recover from it. Between it and the emigration, we have our work cut out for us in this parish. What about your own area?" he asks. "Were yous badly affected by the war?"

While he was talking I was concentrating on staying on this narrow, rutted lane. All the time I was thinking less about his stories and more about how this long-imagined meeting with Sally Anne was going to be polluted by his presence. Now I could barely put two thoughts together to answer this question about the war.

I told him briefly about a few men I had heard of from Castlederg and the surrounding district who had gone to fight, and those who had not come home. I thought I might as well refer to my own father so I told him about how he had died in 1916 in the 'Great War'.

"Not so 'great', was it?" he said when I had finished. "Quite a few lads from around here went as well and the few who did come back might as well have stayed away. They were not the heroes they expected to be. The whole atmosphere of the county had changed and they were not exactly welcomed home. Strange how times change and history….ah, hold on now. Here we are. This would be Sally Anne's home here on the right, if you turn in just beyond this tree. This is Sweeney's place."

My heart is racing as I obey his instruction and let the car roll down the short street. Hens scatter from us as I pull up in front of the cottage. A very small cottage it is too. Maybe three rooms, if that; whitewashed walls that need a new coat; thatch needing replaced; a dank-looking midden just across from the front door; a collie dog yapping at the car as it runs beside us; a chicken balancing on the half door. Such a puny wee place. It's all so different from my two-storied house in Lismore. How strange Sally Anne must have found it to be living with us, her room up in our attic back then was likely a lot grander than anything in her experience before hand.

Sally Anne.

'Look out over that half-door Sally Anne, and see I have come to you. Please just ignore this priest. Let me watch the surprise on your face.'

I sit watching the half-door.

No sign of her looking out though.

There can't be too many times a car drives into this yard.

'Come on, Sally Anne!'

The priest steps out and waddles to the door. I stay where I am in the meantime. Afraid? Aye, you could call me that alright. Now, for a second, I am glad of the priest. The dog is still yapping beside the car so I open my door and speak to it. Like most collies, it becomes friendly straight away and comes to my outstretched hand. I wonder does it smell the scent of my own dog, Jess, from my clothes.

Eventually a figure appears, looking out over the door at the car. My heart jumps but it is not Sally Anne; a different woman; Sally Anne must be still inside.

I listen to the conversation; it is all in Irish and I can't make any sense of the words. I can make sense of the body language though, and what I am sensing is a dagger to my heart. She is not here, at least that is what I am gathering from the woman looking out, pointing towards the sea away to the north of us. After a few minutes the conversation seems to be drying up and the priest begins to edge backwards towards the car again. He raises his hand in farewell and the woman disappears back inside. As he returns to the car, a sort of smug flicker of a smile is playing about his eyes.

"She's gone," he says with finality as he bangs the door shut.

"What do you mean 'she's gone'?"

"Left for America," he says light-heartedly. "You missed her."

Something washes over me like a cold wave of sea-water. It's a very tangible feeling, like you've just heard of a death in the family. It can't be...surely not? After me making this journey and feeling it was the right thing to be doing, sort of like a destiny decision I had made, the right decision, for the first time in a long time.

"How come?" I say. "She couldn't have gone already? She said in two weeks time."

It is out of my mouth before I thought about it.

Madness!

He turns to stare at me. Now he knows that somehow I was aware that Sally Anne was leaving.

The silence is a long one. Then he speaks, slowly, in a hard merciless voice.

"How did you know?"

I say nothing, just stare away at the mountain.

"Take me back to the village and then drive back to your own place as quickly as you can."

I drive.

"You were not truthful with me. You hid things from me. I do not appreciate that, so drop me in Kincasslagh and get to hell out of my parish."

The journey down was silent, apart from the creaking of the springs of my old car and the odd outburst of language from his reverence, language that was anything but reverent.

"God is good, my friend," he says at one point, "and it is just as well that she is already on her way. I hate to think what transpired between you two back in the day and what might have happened if she had been here, but I cannot think it would have been of any lasting benefit to her. You are not even of the same faith, I am guessing, are you?"

"What faith is that, Father?" I say, aware of the insult but not too concerned about it. He can sit there and stew in his own self-righteous indignation.

I grind the car to a halt on the rough stones of the village street and he opens the door, stops there a second but fails to find the right words to rebuke me further.

"Thank you for your help," I say as drily as I can, revving the engine to encourage him to get out. He does with not another word and slams the door so hard it rings on in my head. I watch him stump away up the street. When he turns into the village shop and out of sight, I reverse the car into an alleyway so as to head back the way I've just come. Now I know where Sally Anne lives I am going back for a proper chat with that woman at the door. I am guessing it is Mairead, Sally Anne's sister that he mentioned earlier. Either way I am going to try to find out what has happened and where my old maid has gone.

I have come too long a journey to be giving up now.

Chapter 5

Matthew Henderson

I let the car run quietly down the slope into Sweeney's street again. No need to be annoying folk with the roar of the engine so soon after my last visit. The collie welcomes me like I am a regular, tail-wagging and body squirming for attention. I hope the lady of the house is as enthusiastic.

She meets me at the door and keeps the bottom half firmly shut against me, her eyes full of suspicion, maybe even fear. Not unlike Sally Anne in looks, I think. If I was to guess her age I would say somewhere in the middle thirties. When I get closer though I am struck by the lines of her face, the wrinkles that speak of lost weight and of recent worries. Her eyes are pools of pain, enough to ring a bell of sympathy in me right from the start...and I know nothing about her.

"Are you Mairead?" I ask.

"I am."

"I was here with the priest."

"I know that."

"You'll be wondering why I have come back."

She looks away from me to the whin-covered hills across the valley.

"He was asking about Sally Anne," she says softly. "I suppose it would be the same with yourself."

"It would," I reply. It is an awkward enough conversation and I don't want to be too rushed or forward with my questions. After a few seconds she looks back at me, studying my face for clues I think.

"What do you want with my sister?" she says. "Who are you anyway?"

"It's a long story," I tell her, "and I have come a long way today to try to see her. I thought she would still be here. You see, she wrote me a letter."

I take the letter from my pocket and show her. She stares at it.

"Look," I say, "there's her name at the bottom. And there's my name, you see?"

"You're Matthew Henderson?"

"I am."

I watch her reaction to this. If there is shock or dread she hides it well. At the same time she is finding it hard to meet my eyes, looking past me again. This must be so hard for her, especially if she has any knowledge of what happened between her sister and me. I give her time, and silence spreads between us as she ponders how to handle this situation. After a bit I try another sentence to see if I can smooth down the fear and uncertainty she must be feeling.

"It was a lovely letter," I say.

She meets my eyes again and slowly moves back from her defence of the door. Turning inside, she says, "Maybe you should come in."

"That's very kind of you," I say, following her. There is no hallway and we are in the kitchen right away.

The room is murky dull and, coming in from the bright sunlight outside, it takes my eyes a minute or two to adjust. The first thing that strikes me is that there is very little furniture in the place. Around the hearth two chairs; to the side, against the back wall, one of those settle-beds that you used to see in all the cottages. A rough looking table stands against the small window with a couple of chairs, one at either end. Beside the door there is a press that holds various dishes, pots and pans. That's about it as far as furniture goes.

I am looking around the walls for any photographs but there are none. I had half-hoped to see a recent picture of Sally Anne, just to see if she has changed much. The only decoration I notice is the Sacred Heart picture by the window, exactly the same one that hangs in the same place in Kearney's house. Jesus has that same sorrowful look in his eyes too, as if he has just arrived at your mother's wake and is offering his condolences. A bedraggled cross of rushes hangs above the door. If its job has been to collect dust it has been good at it.

My eyes light on a very dilapidated looking fiddle hanging high up close to the hearth. It looks in even worse shape than the one I have in the car. It's covered in grime but even with that, the darkness of the wood strikes me. It reminds me of smoked pork that has been hanging too long by a turf fire. Smoked fiddle, I think to myself. I wonder has she given up playing it. This is something I want to find out from her sister.

Drawn up to the hearth sits an older woman, her feet almost in the ashes. There's not much of a fire burning, it being the height of summer, just enough to do whatever cooking is needed.

Out of basic manners I go forward to her and stretch out my hand to greet this lady.

"How are you?" I say. Nothing back, apart from the blankest of stares. She neither reaches to shake hands nor smiles; just looks hard at me or through me, I'm not sure which. Mairead comes to her rescue, and to mine.

"This is mammy," she says. "She doesn't talk."

"Ah right," I say, thinking about something else Sally Anne had told me. Should I ask about it? Why not.

"Does your mother still play the tin whistle?"

She looks at me, curious, surprised.

"How do you know about that?"

"I just remember Sally Anne saying about her mother, years ago when…"

I'm not sure how to go on. When I brought her to work as our maid? When she and I were lovers…of a sort? What do I say?

Mairead helps me out.

"When she worked for you," she says simply, turning away.

"Aye," I say. "She worked at our place twenty-three years ago. She was…she was a great worker."

It sounds so lame, so pathetic.

"She likely was that," says Mairead, her back to me as she pulls the kettle around to the hearth and starts to fuss about, nervous. Then, "You will need a cup of tea before you go again?"

"I will not say no to that," I say. "I'm glad to hear yous still have tea in this part of the world. We don't always have it in Northern Ireland. It's still rationed you know."

"Aye? It used to be hard to get here too but there were some local men who used to organise a boat to Scotland every so often. They weren't supposed to be bringing in goods from there but they took the risk. Brought in stuff that we had trouble getting around here, tea and sugar and things. You'd have to walk all the way to Burtonport for it."

"I'm sure it was worth the walk though?" I say.

"It was. It tasted all the better for being illegal."

She is going past me and getting a teapot from the press, then stops and looks at me, a bit sternly I think.

"Father Devine will have told you that Sally Anne has left," she says, "so why did you come back to us?"

Why indeed? I sigh as I think how to answer. The mother turns to stare at me as I stand between her and the one tiny window in the room.

"I suppose I came back to find out why she had left so soon. You see, she told me in her letter that she was leaving to go to America in a week or two. That letter just arrived with me the day before yesterday, that's why I came. But she's gone already?"

"She is. But not to America. Not straight away. She took the bus to Derry yesterday; she was for catching the Glasgow boat."

"Yesterday?"

"Just."

"And Glasgow? She never mentioned Glasgow."

"No?"

"Nothing about that. So I just missed her?"

"You did." After a moment of silence as she puts tea leaves in the pot and pours boiling water on top she continues. "I knew she was writing a letter the other night. I just didn't know who it would be for. Then you turn up on the doorstep, so it must have been you."

"Why Glasgow?" I ask.

"Well, we have a cousin there... well, a sort of a cousin. She's my father's sister's grand-daughter, Nuala. Nuala was married to a Scotch fella and he went and joined up during the war. He was a sailor in the navy, you see, and his ship never came back. Sunk with no survivors, we heard. That was just a year or so back. And he has a baby son that he only saw once on leave."

"Sorry to hear that."

"That is why Sally Anne was for Glasgow. She wanted to spend a week or two with Nuala before she sails on to America. Give her a bit of a hand. Nuala is on her own. None of us have seen her since."

"I see. That is good of her," I say.

And it is, typically good of her.

A silence then that is only broken by the mother coughing, clearing her throat and spitting into the embers of the fire. I look around the room again, as if for inspiration. It comes to me in the form of the hanging fiddle.

"Sally Anne used to play the fiddle when she was with me."

There is a wee delay in the sister's answer and when it comes it does in a wry tone, subdued.

"Did she now?"

"She was good at it too," I say.

"Maybe she was."

"Did she not think of taking it with her, to America like?"

She glances at me, a shade of annoyance in the look as she pours tea into a tin mug.

"It is still here, is it not? Do you take a drop of milk?"

"I do, if you have it," I reply.

I study the forsaken-looking fiddle as she splashes the creamy milk on top of the tea. "So maybe she hasn't been playing for a while?"

"That she has not," says Mairead. "She used to play all the time when I was a wee girl. Not so much after she came back from you. Just an odd time."

This is like a punch in the guts to me.

"She once told me something about a fiddle at your place," she says. She pauses, remembering. "She had drink taken. Not that she ever took much of that. When she did she would get sad and cry a bit."

I want to hear more of this but I do not want to seem too keen. I just sip my tea, thinking it's a pity there is no sugar in the house.

"She talked about a fiddle, did she?" I prompt eventually.

"She did. She told me she had smashed it against the wall. That stuck in my head, for like....Sally Anne loved fiddles. It had something to do with a friend of hers getting shot, that is all I could make out from what she said. It was very mixed up. Something about 'poor Joe', and then she would be cursing. That was the only time I ever heard her talk about it."

Again the pain of regret rises in me and stops the flow of my conversation for a bit.

"Did she happen to mention my name in that story?"

Mairead looks at me long and hard.

"I don't know, maybe she did. I don't recall if she mentioned your name. But I know about you anyway."

I wait for more.

"You are the man that broke her heart," she says. "Would you like a bit of soda bread?"

How do you handle something like that in the situation I find myself in? Not easily, so I just sit silent and let it soak into me.

A broken fiddle to even up a broken heart.

She must have been so deeply hurt. God but I wish I could see her now and try to put it right, try to fix her brokenness, even after all this time. But it's useless to think about it; this whole journey has been such a waste of a day, a day when I should have been saving the hay crop. Am I not completely mad?

My head is in my hands without me realising it. I squint up at this Mairead as she stands watching me, waiting.

Then I remember the soda bread offer, and I remember the long journey home and the Customs men looking at the clock. I remember that our Millie will be struggling to milk my fourteen Shorthorn cows on her own this evening; John Sproule turned me down last night when I went to ask for his help, for he had 'a prayer-meeting to go to'. I wonder what he is praying for me now. I have long-since quit going to his mission hall meetings? He'd have an Orange fit if he knew the real reason I was going into Donegal.

"Aye, I'll take a bite o' soda bread if that's alright."

Before I leave these two women I have to know if there is any point to today's happenings. Where does it go from here?

"Will she write to you, Mairead?"

"She might."

"And you can write back?"

They are both staring at me again, eyes that are tired and dull but still able to throw me a question.

"If she puts an address on it," she says, "I suppose I will."

"Good," I say, "and will you please tell her that I was here, I was looking for her."

"I could do that, if you like."

"Please do," I say. "And she can write to me again, whenever she lands, when she gets settled and all."

"Aye," Mairead says. "She might do that too. You never know with that one. You never know."

Before I leave I stand beside my car looking down to the coast below. It is a beautiful day and this is a beautiful place. I see green islands out on the flat blue of the sea, steep headlands and long beaches running away to both sides and the wide stretch of the horizon beyond, where the sky meets the ocean. This kind of scene is not something I have seen very often, maybe three or four times in my entire life. It would be lovely to have the time to drive around down there; maybe climb some of those sand-hills and knock a few limpets off the rocks along the shore. But I don't have time. And I am alone…again. Even the dream has deserted me.

I drive away from Ranahuel, bumping down that bendy road and begin my journey home, trying hard to hold on to the hope in Mairead's words.

You never know with that one.

Chapter 6

117a Sandybank Street
The Gorbals
Glasgow
30th June 1945

Dear Mairead,

I have arrived safely with Nuala and Frankie here in Glasgow. There was no problem on the journey, a calm sea all the way across, thanks be to God. I hope it's as good next week for the voyage to America. Some nice folk at the docks here showed me how to get buses to Sandybank Street.

You have lived over here and you know what it is like. But for me it is the biggest shock, to see so many people jam-packed like fish in a barrel into these tenement houses. Everything in this city is grey and dirty. You have to look up to see the sky and when you do you be surprised that it is blue.

I am missing Ranahuel already. Oh for another walk on An Trá Bhán in the fresh air, with the seagulls calling above.

I hope Mammy is alright. It is hard to know if she will be missing me or not.

Nuala is still in a bad way. It is hard to watch her suffering so much and her so young. Wee Frankie is not the age to know anything about his father; he'll likely never miss him but Nuala misses him all the time. She has spent a lot of time crying to me since I got here and I am worried for her. How will she be able to make ends meet without her man and with nobody nearby to look after the boy? The neighbours in the tenement are very good, giving her bits of food and clothes for Frankie, but they have so little themselves. I never expected to see poverty like this in a big British city. We don't have much to call our own in Donegal but we know how to work things and how to survive, but these people have next to nothing. And from what I see the bottle is their only comfort. Nuala takes a brave drop of drink herself and who can blame her, but it does nothing to help her for she is even worse in the morning. I just don't know what is to become of her and I don't know how to help her. Maybe I will be able to send her wee bits of money when I start earning.

You'd think her in-laws would be more of a help but there is a whole story behind that, I have discovered. Frank's folks are from a village away outside Glasgow, maybe twenty miles away. They never really approved of their son marrying Nuala for they are staunch Protestants you see. They would have put a stop to the whole thing, Nuala says, except that she was pregnant at the time with the baby. This must have been a hard area for her man to live in, with the religious difference so important here. Maybe he was glad of the chance to get away and join the navy. It's very sad that he will never be back.

The worst thing about it is that her own mother can be of no help to her. Musselburgh is so far away and anyway, according to Nuala, Mary-Anne wouldn't be fit to do much for her or the child.

At night here I sit and think about what I am doing, going to America and leaving you all when maybe I should be staying with Nuala. But I have my papers all sorted and the ticket so

I must go on with it. I feel so guilty but then I tell myself that the opportunity will be there for me to make good money and send it back home to you, and now some to Nuala as well.

When I get to Boston I will write to you and give you the address of where I am staying, so you can tell me about mammy.

Le grá

Sally Anne

****

  I don't know where it comes from but I have this need in me to see what America is like. I have only ever seen two of those American movie films in the travelling picture house that came to Dungloe an odd time, so it can't be that. I wouldn't be reading stories from places like that either. Maybe having heard so much about it, in the letters from Uncle Dermot over the years, it has got me curious.

  It will be great to finally meet cousin Roisin, Dermot's youngest daughter. From what I read in her letters she sounds like a very different kind of woman from what you would have around home. For a start she is divorced. Thirty five years old, married, no children, a business woman and now divorced from her man. You don't get many like that in Donegal.

  If it wasn't for her I would not be starting out on this adventure, for it was all her idea and it was her paid for my passage. Money seems to be no object to her. She has travelled all over America and seen many different parts, mostly to do with her work in the hotel business. She says she will be able to get me a job with no bother at all. That is one of the things that worries me about it. It could be any sort of job and I might have no notion of how to be doing it. The only other work I have ever done has been stitching carpets in Annagry factory when I was thirteen, the six months I spent working on Henderson's farm in Tyrone when I was eighteen and the many years since when I have been knitting *geansaíthe* to order, for the COPE and different shops about the place. Not the sort of experience that is going to help me get a job in a place like Boston I imagine.

I have this fear that I will stick out like 'a crow among the peacocks', as we say about home, the backward Irish girl in the middle of these confident American relatives. It is not just the want of experience of work, it is the want of experience of life. What do I know about the world, stuck out in the middle of the Rosses? The wireless that Uncle Johnny brought us that time he was home from London never seems to have batteries in it. When it does they never last very long, for Mammy would be switching it on to listen to her tunes from Athlone, Radio Éireann as they call it now. The time was that I would be glued to it, listening to those tunes myself, trying to learn them but after all that happened in 1922 I more or less lost interest in music. To be honest, the tunes did something to me after that. It was like a damp mist sweeping in from the ocean and blotting out the sun when I heard that music. I struggled to understand those dismal feelings. I generally went out to walk the bog lanes when she had them on the radio. The birdsong held fewer memories.

Sometimes I would get to hear a news broadcast but mostly me and mammy just seemed to be living in the dark. When the conflict between England and Germany broke out, we didn't hear about it for days. Mind you, we weren't as bad as some old fellow further back in the hills who didn't hear till months later. The joke around here was that, when somebody eventually told him about the war, he is supposed to have said, "Well, they're getting a good day for it anyway." It was just a yarn but it does sort of sum up our isolation in the west of Donegal. The world was hurrying along at a far greater speed than we could credit. They have made bombs that can burn cities to the ground and kill hundreds of people at the one go. From what I heard at the time there were even a few of these bombs fell on parts of Ireland. Dublin got one of them but Belfast suffered far worse. You would wonder what business the Germans had to be dropping bombs out of aeroplanes on Belfast. What was Belfast ever going to do to them? Dublin too, for that matter. Ireland wasn't at war; we just had an 'emergency'...at least that's what we thought until tragedy struck close to home.

Other times I would have heard about some of the troubles between England and Ireland, like the economic war in the Thirties. I would not be too clear about what was causing it or why it was called a war, for nobody was getting killed, so far as I can remember. No doubt the border had a lot to do with it. It has never left me that, back in 1922 when partition began, I was working right in the middle of it, right on the other side of their new border. I was back and forward over it near enough every day, going over to Kearney's, and it never cost me a thought. It was just a bit of a stream with stepping stones across it. Some international boundary that was!

It was strange seeing it through the eyes of the Protestants I was living with. They were all for it. It was a wall behind their backs to shelter them, defend them from the enemy, whoever that was supposed to be. I wonder is it still the same over there? Maybe worse than ever, for it was really only getting going back that year. I remember one night Joe Kearney's sister, Mary, ripping a soda scone in two in her father's kitchen and saying something like, 'You can't do that to a country.' Funny how that stuck in my mind, the tearing apart of a bit of bread. I wonder what she is at now, Mary Kearney. She was very strong in her views about the fight against Britain and, if I remember right, she was somehow involved in the struggle herself.

I so often wonder about that stage my life. It should have been just a stage; I should have been able to get over it and move on but it seemed to follow me around like a shadow that I couldn't step away from. Those people had come to mean so much to me in such a short space of time. I don't just mean Joe or Matthew. All of them. It was as if I entered their lives in a time of light and happiness and left in the middle of the darkest of thunderstorms. They had all become a big part of my life. I had taken on their concerns, their thoughts about life, their ideas and plans. They were so different to what I had been reared with. Different attitudes, different language, different faith.

And very much a different standard of living too.

We get by. They made plans.

It all affected me so deeply, especially the hurt of being rejected by Matthew and, at the same time, my own rejection of Joe. His death I blamed on myself for years upon years. I could not seem to rise above it. Between the two of them they doused any spark of human joy out of me and left me like a dried up stick, young and all as I was. I went downhill and was only interested in myself. I sat by the hearth and breast-fed my grievance like it was my precious first-born. By the time I came to my senses, nobody was interested in me. I cannot blame them.

The only person I could talk to during that time was a neighbour girl from Kincasslagh who had become a good friend. Ailish Ní Dhomhnaill was the name that was on her. I first met Ailish when I was going to the hiring fair in Strabane all those years ago. She had years of experience of going to work over in the Lagan and Tyrone and kept me right many a time. She had her own troubles over there too. I liked Ailish, for you could tell her anything and know that it wasn't going to blow like feathers around the parish.

She was the only person who heard the full story of Matthew and the tragedy I was caught up in over in Tyrone. Her eyes would be near standing in her head when I was telling her about how Joe died. She heard far more from me than my own sister did, for Mairead and I weren't that close a lot of the time.

Ailish was lonely too, for the man she married spent most of his time working in the tunnels in Scotland. When she needed company she would ride her bike up to me and we would walk for hours across the bogs and mountains behind us. We especially loved walking all the way to Burtonport along the railway track. We would always buy some fresh herring on the quay there. I had a sort of connection to that line for my father and my uncle Johnny had worked on it when it was being built at the end of the last century. Daddy was full of stories about it, some funny but others sad for there were terrible accidents. If he'd still been alive he would have been badly annoyed when it was closed down five or six years ago, for it had done a lot for us in the west.

So here I am, in a tenement slum in Glasgow, about to leave my Ranahuel life behind me and sail to America in a few days to try to find who I am and who I might become. I am amazed at myself. What brought me to this?

One thing was my father passing away in 1934. He was fifty seven and that was far too early to be dying. But none of us have any say in that, have we? He caught a dose that winter, out working in the driving rain. Nothing would do him but to work on, through the pain in his chest. The consumption took him after only a couple of months. We could do nothing for him. That was the end of Sean Bán, God rest him. I miss him more than I can say. A good and wise man.

On his death bed he told me things about my family history I had never heard tell of before, things that helped me to understand his relationship with my mother. My respect for him had always been great but that chat gave me a far better appreciation of him as a man who was kind and generous and loyal to his core.

I could have gone deeper into myself at that painful time but I will never forget what he said to me, in that hoarse, gasping whisper he had left. "Daughter, lift your head and live your life, for you only have the one go at it." I tried my best to take his advice, even though I had got badly out of practice.

Then two years ago we had our own local disaster. Nineteen young men of the parish were blown to bits. Some sort of mine that they found in the sea and were trying to pull ashore exploded on the rocks. I knew nearly all of them. Good lads who just loved a bit of fun and adventure. Their families will never get over it. It left us all in a terrible state of shock and despair. How could such a thing happen in our quiet parish, so far removed from the dangers of the war? Why would God allow this disaster? There was no sense to it, no answers. But it made me realise again that life is precious. It's as fragile as thistledown in a storm.

I still remember what Ailish said as we met at one of those desperately sad wakes. "When you see what has happened to these lads doesn't it make you want to grab what you can from life?"

I think that is what first put into my head the idea of writing to the man I held so many bad thoughts against, Matthew Henderson. What happened with that mine at Ballymanus was an accident, albeit the tragedy could have been prevented during the course of that day. And what happened on Henderson's farm on that fateful night was also an accident, one that could have been avoided of course, and I have my own share of blame for not seeing ahead and doing something to prevent it. I have some of Joe's blood on my own hands. I cannot keep on with the pretence that Matthew should bear the whole burden of it himself. That is what brought me to the point of writing to him, both for himself and for me, that I could put the whole thing behind me and leave the slate clean before I journey to a new start in America.

I would love to know about him, if he is still alive at all. If he is, I would love to have watched his face when he read my letter. I can imagine him getting halfway through it and throwing it in the fire. Maybe he did. Maybe his wife did. Or maybe he gave that sideways smile of his and thought, "That's alright then."

Either way, I will never know and I must put it from my mind. Such bondages have to go now if I am to be able to look the Statue of Liberty in the eye this time next week.

Chapter 7

Matthew Henderson

I have not held a gun in my hands since November 1922. I still have one but it is in the attic.

The very thought of holding it puts a creepy feeling up the skin of my back. Even now, if there is anything to be shot on the farm, a fox that has gotten into the henhouse, or the time my mare broke her leg, I get John Sproule to come up and do it. The same boy seems to enjoy it. It would be like that too when I'm killing pigs. I can't stand the squealing of them and the sloshing of blood when they get their throats cut. John doesn't mind at all.

It has always struck me as a rare thing, to be standing watching John at this slaughtering, the big sharp gully in his dripping hand and him blood-red to the shoulders...and in the middle of it all he starts preaching at me.

He goes on about lambs to the slaughter and the like. 'And as a sheep before her shearers is dumb, so he opened not his mouth,' he says as we lift the carcass of the beast up to hang on the lintel of the barn door by its hind legs. These pigs are anything but dumb, their squeals can be heard all over the neighbourhood.

There's not a lot you can say when John gets into one of these preaching fits. He must think the drama of his performance with the gully will have more effect on me than the many words he 'blesses' me with on a regular basis. It is kind of like one of those flannel-graph presentations I used to see in children's meetings, but with real sound effects and real blood.

"Matthew, you are a backslider, my friend. You need to come crawling back to God on your knees. When are you going to listen to the voice of the Lord?"

Generally I don't bother to answer these questions. There doesn't seem to be much point, for whatever you say he is only going to keep hammering away at it. I could tell him to stop but he is helping me out with things, so it would maybe seem ungrateful. Having to listen is the price you have to pay maybe.

"Will you ever forget the squealing of Bond's pigs that day of the fire? Thon was some han'lin'." I am dredging up a memory from years ago, unashamedly trying to divert him from this rant of his.

It fails completely. It's like I never spoke a word. He ploughs on.

"'Turn, O backsliding children, saith the Lord; for I am married unto thee,'" he says, repeating one of his favourite verses.

'At least somebody is married to me,' I think.

Aye, marriage! Now there's a story that goes all the way back to the aftermath of Joe's death.

****

I was never arrested for the killing of my old friend.

It was all smoothed over, nice as you like. Mind you, from what I heard during that troubled period, there were men who did a lot worse and faced no legal proceedings whatsoever, a relative of my own among them too. That was how the country seemed to work during those times, justice wise.

The day after I shot Joe I had a visit from the local RUC, a sergeant and a constable. They took me away from the dark grief in our house and down to the station in Castlederg. There they spent an hour talking to me, asking what had happened, where I got the gun, how my relationship with Joe had been.

I think they couldn't fail to see that I was half mad with regret. They had stood in my kitchen and they witnessed that the whole house was in mourning, the twins bawling their wee eyes out and my mother in a terrible state. Sally Anne was nowhere to be seen at that stage, and I didn't blame her. She was likely over at Kearney's.

Before the police left me back home they told me that I might have to be sent over to Donegal to be questioned about the killing. That put the wind up me. I wondered if maybe that was their intention. Why would they threaten this, for after all the killing had been done in Northern Ireland?

The day after the funeral the same two policemen arrived in the yard and asked me to come with them, back to the local police station. It was one of those days when you could do nothing; the chores about the farm had to be done and I did my best, but it was as if I was walking through some terrible fog of a dream. I was sitting on the milking stool in the byre, my head between my hands, when the police car arrived in. It was nearly a relief to see it.

I went with them to the station and there was some sort of senior officer there from Omagh. The three of them interviewed me, to get my side of the story again. At the end up this Omagh officer asked me, "Mr Henderson, there will be an official inquest into this whole affair but in the meantime would you agree that this was an act of self-defence and a case of mistaken identity?"

Of course I would agree. It was the truth.

But surely it couldn't be just left like that? I had killed a man in cold blood; there would have to be some consequence.

"You have a very good neighbour," the sergeant said.

"I know that," I said, "and Joe had been a very good friend. I should never have…"

"Joe's father wants nothing further to be done," the sergeant interrupted me. "That is what we have been told by the Garda's investigating officer. They have interviewed Mr Kearney."

I stared at him

"As I say, there will be an inquest but it is likely there will be no charges against you after it, that is what I am saying."

Something in me was almost about to say, "Hang on now, I have just shot my best friend. It can't be just that easy, can it?" At the same time there was relief that I wouldn't have to go through a lengthy trial in public. All I could think to do was mumble, "Thank you."

"Don't thank us. Thank your neighbour. And thank your lucky stars there are such decent people on both sides of the Border, in spite of all that is going on in this country," said the Omagh policeman. "Now, about this gun. You told my colleagues that it came from a friend who works in the security services in Belfast. Is that correct? A Stanley somebody?"

"Aye," I said, "Stanley. But don't ask me his second name. I don't think I ever heard it, or if I did I have forgotten it."

"And how did he come to be giving you a weapon?"

I tried to explain his connection to cousin Victoria and how he had got involved in a row with some nationalist fellas at the harvest ceili, back in September. "It was just for my own protection, living so close to the Border and all."

"And how did you learn to be such a crack sniper?"

I must have looked puzzled. "Who taught you how to use the S.M.L.E.?"

"I don't follow…"

"The rifle, Mr Henderson? Who trained you to be such a good marksman?"

"I am not a good marksman," I said. "I was just lucky, that's all."

"Or unlucky, as it turned out."

"Aye, very unlucky," I said.

"It's just a pity that it wasn't Duggan in your sights. We would have one less IRA scoundrel to be dealing with. You see, Mr

Henderson, with skills like that you should be joining the 'B Specials'. You ever think about joining up, protecting your country?"

"I have thought about it," I told him. I didn't tell him how short a time it took me to get over the thought.

"Good," he said. "Well, we are letting you go here, no further action against you, alright? So don't be wasting any more time thinking about joining up, you hear me? Be a good citizen, get your papers in and join the rest of us in fighting the real enemies of this country, instead of shooting your friends, right?"

So this was the expectation. I was getting off, sort of on condition that I would become a 'B Special'. I resented this kind of blackmail right from the start. Never try and push me too hard in one direction for, as sure as day follows night, I will push back the other way. Stanley had suggested I join up as well. It only annoyed me. My father had joined the British Army and that did not end too well.

I would stay as I had been.

Except that something in my conscience kept waking me up at night. My dreams were so real and be times desperately troubling. I missed hours of sleep, re-living that night in my mind. Why had such a disaster happened to me? I was carrying so much guilt, not only about the shooting but about the fact that I had fallen out with Joe a couple of weeks earlier over the head of my servant maid. He was my rival for her affections; at times I thought I was winning and that he had no chance. Other times I was aware that she was more drawn to him, as a fellow Catholic and as another Irish speaker. They shared so many jokes and secrets, talking to each other in Gaelic. I was always left out of that and it scunnered me the way they went on together. Her identity and his were closer than mine could ever be to either of them and, no matter how much I tried, it annoyed the life out of me.

On top of these feelings I was more than conscious of the great hole in my life since I had lost her. I missed Sally Anne far more than I would admit, even to myself. She had been like a drink of cool, pure water from a mountain spring when she came into my life, until those events turned everything as sour as buttermilk.

These kinds of thoughts weighed me down and I felt like I had become a different person as I dragged myself around the farm that winter. The days were short and so was my temper, my spirits as dull as the weather. Christmas in our house was like a wake. My sister Emily came home from Belfast for a few days but she kept herself to herself as always, a complete wet blanket. It was the worst Christmas ever, well certainly since the one in 1916, when we spent Christmas without my father, and he spent his in the bowels of the Somme.

I started to notice that some neighbours and farmers around the district seemed to be giving me a wide berth. People would see me in the street in Castlederg and cross over out of my way, or find something to examine in a shop window. Whiles I even saw in the distance folk elbow-nudge each other, nod their heads in my direction and turn away. Maybe it was their embarrassment at not knowing what to say to me, whether to sympathise with my predicament or to tell me bluntly that I should have done time for the shooting. I am fairly sure some of them were thinking that, by the look on their faces.

A few people stood out as being different from the rest. One was a distant cousin of mine, Norman McKinney. Another was John Sproule. Yet another was Alice Porter.

Big Norman, as everybody called him, was a cattle dealer from down in the valley fornenst the Spamount estate. He was built like the side of a byre and had a couple of sons who were going to be even bigger. Bigger and maybe thicker, for Norman was one of the thickest customers you could meet. He was a fair bit older than me and I always felt bullied by him, even though he never really did anything to me. He just had that air of intimidation about him. His taunting smirk always made me feel a lesser man. I never had much to do with him but I did see him at fairs and markets the odd time.

The one event that sticks out in my mind from that time was a chat I had with him and one of his young fellas, Sammy I think, when trying to sell him a few heifers in the Castlederg fair, maybe a couple of months after Joe's death. The Sammy lad was the dead spit of his father, even down to the same sort of sneering smile on his boyish spotty face.

Norman asked about my mother first but it was one of those questions that you could tell he wasn't bothering to listen to the answer. He seemed a wee shade impatient for me to finish telling him about how bad mammy's doting had got.

"You've had a bit of excitement since I saw you," he said, grinning down at me in that way that I never knew whether he was being friendly or taking the rise out of me. For that reason, I couldn't think of any safe reply, so I just stayed quiet.

"If you want my opinion, son, you did right. You must be a hell of a shot too. Fair play to you, that's all I can say."

I was so taken aback by this I stood with my mouth open. I had shot my best friend. Did he not realise this? Not a thought for how I might be feeling, or for how the tragedy was affecting my neighbours who had lost their son. My voice, when I spoke, squeaked at him in disbelief.

"Norman," I said, "maybe you haven't heard the right way of it. Joe was a good friend to me. I killed my friend and…"

"Agh surely," he said, still smiling. "But you can't be too careful living up there right on the Border. It's dangerous territory like. I know it was a neighbour you shot but it coulda been worse."

"I don't see how," I said.

"Look, what I mean is…you shouldn't be hard on yourself about it. You were trying to kill that IRA bastard. You didn't know that it was young Kearney."

"I wasn't trying to kill anybody," I told him. "Just scare them off. That's the thing."

"Well like I say, if it had happened the other way around do you think young Kearney would be in a bother about it? Not a bit of it. He'd be thinking, 'One less Prod', too bad!"

"That's nonsense, Norman. You didn't know him. Joe was a sound chap. He would be just the same as me if it was the other way around. And, just so you know, his father told the police that he didn't want any prosecution for me. Nothing at all."

Norman thought a second.

"Just right too. Sure it was an accident. You were trying to shoot a rebel. You just got a Catholic instead. Anyway, look, these are three fine heifers but you're asking far too much for them. Come on, how much will you take, how much now? And we'll get a drink after in Ferguson's," he said, spitting on his hand and holding it out to me, palm up in the traditional gesture of the cattle-dealer.

That ended his views on the event that had driven me round the bend over the last while, though I knew that if I went for a drink with him I would have to listen to more of his nonsense. I wondered long about his opinions and this rough, don't-give-a-damn attitude he had.

John Sproule, on the other hand, was an old friend who farmed a mile further down the road from me. He was a lonely sort of chap and to my mind he spent far too much of his time with his own thoughts and imaginings. His parents had been older folk when they had him. They had passed on a good while back, leaving him to work the land and make his way in life very much on his own terms. That may have led to that bit of oddness he had about him. You could say he even looked a bit odd, his head as square as a block of wood and his curly hair dark with grease, but a great worker for all that. Living alone with his sheep and pigs and cattle, with no wife to keep him balanced, John needed friends but wasn't always the best company.

Be that as it may, he often took it into his head to come up to ours and sit with me of an evening. Mostly he would be talking to me about cattle or machinery or crops. An odd time we had a joint venture, generally to do with harvest or buying land. Being a bit uncertain about things, he depended on me for business advice. Whiles though we'd simply play a game of Draughts. He didn't say much, but he was there to listen if I wanted to talk. Generally I didn't but, when I did, he would start to tell me about how he had found God by going to mission meetings around the country. I paid little heed to this at the start. The last thing I wanted was to get tied up by some religious tripe in this my time of weakness. I was struggling enough with normal, day-to-day thinking and I didn't need to be trying to understand sermons and the like. But to keep the peace I tholed it, for want of anything better to be doing. I let John chat on, though most of the time my mind was elsewhere.

Over the next few months it tended to be on Alice Porter.

Alice was the daughter of our local bank manager. She wasn't from around here but, for a stranger, she had made her mark quickly on the town of Castlederg. She had a way with her that would make you feel you were the most important person in the world, the best-looking, the most interesting. Her smile just took you captive, making you feel that you and her had some special understanding, a special bond. The very way she moved, how she held her body, flicked her hair, used those dark eyes, all designed to appeal to your male instincts. She wouldn't have been the tallest; I was about six foot two or three and when she stood beside me she was a full foot shorter, maybe more. That didn't matter though, for she made up for that want by being more than well endowed in other directions. She had a different way of standing out in a crowd, if you know what I mean. You couldn't help but be attracted to her, and I was not alone in that.

The problem was her age. Around the time when Joe met his death and Sally Anne left for home Alice would have been something like sixteen. It sounds very young for a fellow like me to be fascinated by her. I was coming twenty-two. But, if her birth certificate said sixteen, the cut of her and her way of going on said something very different. In many ways I felt, as I got to know her better over the following months, that she was a few years ahead of me, a brave few years.

She was still at the studying in Strabane that year. I heard people say that she was the school star, on the stage and in the classroom. I heard other things about her but I couldn't repeat them, much less believe them. You see, Alice sang in the church choir and taught a class in the Sunday school. Watching her in church she always gave the impression of being a sincere Christian girl. It was only afterwards, when she made her usual beeline for me, that I could see the other side to her. While Sally Anne had been around the place I had had the strength to fight Alice off, but after all that happened I have to confess that I took some comfort from Alice's attentions. Her interest in me seemed to be genuine compassion for what I was going through then, not like the flirtatious stuff that had scared me off earlier. Now, as time went on, I found myself taking solace from it, enjoying it and eventually looking for it. I suppose it is always nice to be flattered by someone, especially by a girl with all the personality and charm of Alice. It helped as well that this time I was getting involved with somebody from my own side of the house, and a Methodist into the bargain.

It began to become a relationship one Sunday during the following summer when Alice begged me to come for a walk with her along the Derg, our local river. She had asked me a wheen of times before but this time I gave in, for the day was warm and sunny. She made no secret of her affection for me by hooking her arm into mine right from the start. In her eyes, it seemed, we were a couple. To be fair to her, she was great to be with, funny and chatty, and I felt my mood lighten in a way that it hadn't since the previous summer. I did have to fight the temptation to be comparing this walk with the many times that Sally Anne and I had walked together and worked together on the land. The main difference was that this girl was so intimate in how she touched me. Sally Anne was never like that. There was this mixture of ownership and temptation in every touch. I found myself going along with it all in a way I never expected. When she pulled off her shoes and hitched up her dress to paddle in the river I couldn't resist joining her. She started kicking water up at me and I gave her back as good as I got. We both managed to soak our Sunday best clothes. She didn't seem to give two hoots, and if she didn't, then neither would I. That is the kind of hold she was having over me. If anybody had been watching us they would have found it hard to believe I was the same fellow who had been so under a cloud of sadness just a few months ago, the same fellow who was generally so shy and reserved.

One thing puzzled me. It would be true to say that Alice and I had always flirted but what happened with me shooting Joe seemed to change her attitude to me. If anything it did the opposite of what I had expected. Whereas everybody else seemed to be looking at me with suspicion or dread, it did not have that effect on Alice. In past times I had got the impression that she found me a bit dull; aye, handsome maybe, and well-built but more of an interesting specimen of manhood to be toyed with, played like a fish on a line. But now? Now I was anything but dull. I had an edge to me. I had used a weapon in anger. There was an element of danger in who I was. More of the stallion, less of the tame oul mare. I had the aura of 'warrior' about me, like it or not. It was something I did not see coming but it was definitely there from the very first Sunday after Joe's funeral. She looked at me with a very different spark in her eyes, whereas I could hardly lift my head to look at a soul.

Over the next while we got closer and before long we were a courting couple. I never brought her home to Lismore though, for I had the feeling she was not the sort of cutty my mother would be wanting me to be with. In September that year she headed off to a brand new college in Belfast. It had only started up the previous year and it was the place to train teachers for this new country of ours. Alice took to it like a duck to water. She loved it and, when she came home on the tram from Victoria Bridge the odd weekend, she was full of the place. 'Stranmillis this' and 'Stranmillis that.'

I suppose it was for that reason that I started to get concerned that I might lose her. Belfast was a big exciting place with a lot of entertainment. There would be other fellas around this college of hers and they couldn't help but be interested in her. Compared to the excitement and attractions of the city, I did not have much to be offering her. How could I bind her a bit closer to me? I didn't want to lose another one.

The obvious answer was to put a ring on her.

I found a right decent one in the wee jewellers in the town and made a plan. I would have to chat to her father first, then find some sort of romantic place to take her to put the question, providing the father gave the go ahead.

Sure enough, Mr Porter had nothing against the marriage. I had had several dealings with him over the last few years, getting loans for various bits of machinery around the farm. He knew I was a safe enough investment. And yes, of course I would put the farm in our joint names as he asked, as soon as we were married and as soon as my mother passed away, it being still officially hers by law.

I couldn't wait to ask Alice. I dressed up well, picked her up in the new car that I'd bought with one of those loans from her father that summer past and we drove down to Lough Erne. We pulled in somewhere near Castle Archdale and went for a walk by the lake shore. Alice must have known something was coming for she was very quiet on that walk. I judged that she had guessed, or that her father had let the cat out of the bag. Anyway, when I eventually asked her to marry me she said 'Yes', jumped on my knee and more or less smothered me in kisses. Her hair fell around her face and she was so close in to me I couldn't see her eyes. I got the impression though that she was crying. Sure enough, when she pulled away there were tears in her eyes. I pulled the ring out of my pocket and slid it on to her finger. Luckily it fitted perfectly.

I have made one girl very happy, I thought to myself.

"We will get married the day after you finish in Stranmillis," I told her. "What do you think?"

"That'll do," she said quietly.

Chapter 8

C/O Roisin Sweeney
142 Lanyon Street
South Cove Boston
Massachusetts
28th July 1945

Dear Mairead,

I hope and pray to God that everything is alright at home with Mammy and yourself. I am well now but it has taken a week for me to get over the travelling.

Did you get the short letter I wrote to you from New York about my sea journey? I hope so. It was a great experience to be on that ship and feel the size of the ocean and the boat rolling about in the big waves. Thank God we saw no icebergs but I am told they can be seen on this stretch of water later in the year. The train journey up to Boston from New York was simple enough, once I found the station, bought my ticket and found the right platform. That station is a huge place.

I slept a good part of the way on the train and that passed the journey more quickly for me. It took so much longer than I could ever have imagined and my main problem was that it was stifling hot. I wanted to change my clothes I was sweating so much but I couldn't be doing that in public, nor in the lavatory for it was so small and smelt worse than a midden.

At the minute I am staying with Roisin. Over here she calls herself Rose, even though she was christened Roisin. She says that she got sick of everybody pronouncing it Ro-i-sin. They don't have the Gaelic here of course, so they wouldn't be knowing how to say it. My name seems to work alright for them. Roisin has her own house. Well, it's not exactly a house. They call it an apartment here. It is like a house in the middle of a pile of houses, all stacked up on top of each other. Her's is half way up to the top. You could climb the stairs but I am getting used to taking the elevator. It is like a mechanical box that gets pulled up and down.

I've met Uncle Dermot twice. He has seen better days, God love him, well into his seventies, and is in a place where they put all the old people together to make it easier to look after them. Each one or each couple has their own wee house but they get their food all together in a big room and can sit and talk to each other all day or listen to music or watch one of those televisions in the corner. Dermot is so like our father it would put the heart across you when you first see him. The only difference is his hair because it is long and white. Seán Bán never went in for that sort of thing but then sure he was nearly bald at the end. Dermot even talks the same way, although his is a strange mixture of our kind of English and the way the Americans here talk. He can still remember a good bit of his Irish and just loves to talk in it, likely to show off to the Yankees here.

"An bhfuil tu go maith, a iníon?" was the first thing he said to me. Then he asked about life in Ranahuel. "Cad é mar atá an saol i Rann Uí Thuathail?" He gave it the old Gaelic name too.

He has been in America since he was twenty and only made it back home the once. That must have been before we were born, I am thinking, but he did remember mother, and her mother too.

"I am sure Maggie Dan is long beneath the sod," he said. "She was a tough old boot, that one."

I sympathised with him about his own wife passing. He said she was better off out of her pain because the cancer is a terrible thing to have to deal with. She was a beautiful woman too. He showed me their wedding picture and I was surprised to see how brown her skin was. That is likely where Roisin gets her complexion from, and there was us looking at the photos Roisin sent and thinking it was down to the strong sun they be having here.

Roisin has never been to Ireland but once the war is over she says she would like to come and see what her father's home place was like. The Americans are still fighting the Japanese, even though the war in Europe is finished. If she does come she will be in for some surprise. I don't think she finds it easy to imagine life in a place like Donegal. Even the very shape of the place will give her an eye opener. You have to see America to believe it. There is so much of it for a start, so much space. Everything seems to be so much bigger than at home. This city is covered in trees, all sorts of them, like nothing you would ever see in Donegal. Amazing tall trees and bushes with flowers on them, and lots of lawns and play-parks for children.

Everything is so well laid out, lovely streets and houses, all so well off, it seems to me. The parks, the buildings, the advertising boards, the smiles on the faces, the horizon itself, all so stretched out. And roads are so straight of themselves, I suppose because the countryside is very flat. You can't walk anywhere for it is too far.

Food is different too, both what they buy in the shops to bring home to eat and what they get when they are out in a restaurant. I can't get over the idea that they eat out of their own houses half the time. Roisin even took me out for breakfast to what she called a 'diner'. They had a list of stuff that would have fed the people of the Rosses for a week. I had the strangest thing to eat. Roisin ordered it for me because I couldn't make up my mind. (I didn't like to tell her that half the food on the menu I had no idea about.) So I got a thing called a 'waffle' set down in front of me. I hardly knew whether to eat it or play it. Round and flat with a pattern of holes and ridges in it, nice and brown and sort of crispy on top and you covered it in honey or blueberry jam, with some whipped cream. It tasted a bit like a sweet pancake, very nice indeed. Now I know what to order the next time. "Blueberry waffle, le do thoil." That will throw them.

I have met a few of Roisin's friends but none of her brothers or sisters. They are all married and living in different parts of America. She never sees them. It is so far to places like California and New Orleans. You can understand why families here might not be so close as at home. We live in each other's shadows. Here your friends and work mates seem to be closer than folk in your own family.

My big news is that I am not getting a job in this Boston city after all. Roisin has been offered a new job managing a hotel in a different part of America altogether. She has been next thing to manager where she works now but is ready to step up, she says, and take on this new challenge. (I am starting to sound like her.)

It will mean that she has to move house to a place called Cape May in the state of New Jersey, a long way from Boston. It's the same distance as going from one end of Ireland to the other. I like the sound of this place for it is more like home, right on the shore. She is going to drive the whole way down in her car, a grander big motor you never saw. She says it could take us two days so we will have to get a room in a hotel (or motel, she calls it.) We might have time to stop in New York and see some of the sights.

Her idea is that she will be able to get me a start working in the hotel, maybe in the kitchen or as a cleaner or washing bedclothes. Chamber-maids they call them here. I think I can manage any of these kinds of jobs if they show me.

Roisin says she is glad to be getting out of Boston. She says there are too many Irish ruffians and gangsters in the city. I was shocked at this but she has filled me in on a lot that has been happening here since their Great Depression. A lot of the Irish hate the Jewish people and do terrible things to them. These Irish folk call themselves The Christian Front but they don't sound very Christian to me. A man by the name of Charles Coughlin is their leader and he is always on the radio stirring things up, blaming the Jews and the other races, according to Roisin. I am a bit scared by it all. You think these things only happened with Hitler in Germany but it is here in America too. I hope there is none of it in Cape May.

When I get settled down there I will write again and give you my new address so you can be telling me the news from home.
Le grá,
Sally Anne.

Chapter 9

A long-legged girl in a tight black skirt stands in dim light. She hugs an electricity pole, one knee bent out towards the passing cars. She is guessing that the time is just after midnight. If nobody pulls up in the next twenty minutes she will give up and go home to bed. She wishes she had put on her warmer coat but this one isn't as threadbare and looks a bit more appealing. She sinks a little deeper into it and flicks her hair to clear the raindrops.

Men seem only to have football on their minds tonight. The green and white of Celtic can be seen through steamed up windows as car-loads of fans wend their drunken way from the pubs towards the suburbs. She hears the sounds of their victory chants above the noisy roaring of their engines. Groups of men don't stop for business; they may slow down to wolf-whistle or shout abuse through half-open windows but they are heading home to their patient wives or sleeping parents. It has been a fruitless night.

A ginger cat appears from a hole in the fence behind her, mouse in its mouth. It scurries past in a nervous, arcing run, as if afraid she might want to compete for this evening's catch.

"You hae had mair luck than me the night, Tabby," she says through chattering teeth. "I must be mad altogether, standin' here at this time o' night, in this weather. Mad or desperate."

She watches as the cat pads around the corner beyond. It's then she hears the squeal of brakes as a car that had almost passed her makes a sudden decision to take an interest in what she is so obviously offering.

"Great," she thinks. "Just in time."

She cat-walks slowly forward towards the blue Ford, high-heels scraping on the paving stones. The window doesn't open as she expects; instead the driver pushes open the passenger door. Looks like no negotiation will be necessary. She has definitely pulled.

Into the front seat, rear-end first, followed by those long spindly legs. Closes the door and waits. He hasn't said a word yet. She turns curiously to look at him.

They stare each other in the eye.

"Martin!" she breathes.

He shakes his head, slowly, sadly.

"I just caught a glimpse o' you oot o' the corner o' me eye. I had tae stap."

She looks away. So does he, both silent for a bit.

"I'm right sorry tae see ye like this, Nuala," he says. "I had nae idea."

She can't think of anything to say. Her head goes down against the dashboard and she begins to sob quietly. A full five minutes pass, the car engine still running, Martin's hand rubbing the back of her head gently.

"Can I take ye hame lass?"

After a moment he sees her nod and lifts his foot off the clutch. The car moves sluggishly forward towards the Gorbals.

"What aboot the bairn?" he asks.

"He's hame in his bed."

"An' who's lukin' efter him?"

She cries again, shaking her head.

"Naeboodie," she says eventually. "He's sleeping."

"What if he wakens up?"

"He'll naw," she tells him. "I put a wee drop o whiskey in his milk always."

"Ah fer God's sake Nuala. Ye'll turn him into a wino afore he's weaned."

"I hae nae choice, Martin. I ken that ye despise me for this but I hae naethin'. This is aal I hae left."

He thumps the steering wheel and looks away to his right.

"Frank Wilson was a guid freen o' mine, lass. He deserves better frae ye than this. If he kenned what yer at he wud turn in his grave."

"He disnae hae a grave!" she screams at him. "He's rottin' somewhere in the bottom o' the sea, remember? Feedin' the bloody fish! He's naw comin' bac' Martin. I ken that he wud hate me for this but I hae nae choice."

The car pulls up in Sandybank street. Nuala sits on. Martin switches off the engine and waits. The city is silent for a moment, listening.

"Will ye come in?"

"Naw, I won't bloody come in. Your Frank was a guid mate o'..."

"I didnae mean for....I didnae mean...," she protests. "I just mean...I am lonely, Martin. I hae naeboodie. I cannae even taalk tae wee Frankie."

He takes her hand.

"I ken aal that, Nuala," he says, "but I hae me ain lass, and I dinnae want tae....ye ken?"

"Aye, I dae. I'm sorry."

She opens the car door, ready to leave him now.

"Stap a minute," he says. "Ye say ye hae naeboodie but that's wrang. Ye hae yer mither, dain't ye?"

"Aye, I hae a mither but she's naw in my worl'. She's readin' hersell Mills and Boon love stories in bloody Musselburgh."

"I ken that yer bitter about her, lass, but if she saw what I saw alang the street there she wud surely tae God stap readin' lang enough tae help luk efter her ain kin."

Nuala says nothing, so Martin pushes home his point.

"Ye see, yer far too proud Nuala. Too proud tae ask for help. Ye'd rether go oot on the street and sell yersell than let yer ma ken that yer in bother."

Martin puts his hand in his hip pocket and pulls out a pound note.

"Here, take this tae get yersell and him a decent feed the morra."

"Naw, I'm naw takin' charity aff ye, Martin."

"Agh for fuck sake woman! Ye'd rither open yer legs tae some dirty oul bastard who lakely has the crabs than taak a gift frae a freen? Here! Take this. Dinnae be daft.

A passing police car slows up beside them and two officers peer out at them. Martin hides the pound note below his legs briefly and waves friendly-like to the coppers. After a minute they decide that this is a normal domestic situation rather than anything to do with the business of the night and drive on.

Martin retrieves the pound note, grabs Nuala's closed fist, prises the fingers open to receive the money and folds them closed again.

"Thank ye," she whispers.

"Ye cannae go on lik' this lass. Yer only gan tae go lower an' lower tae ye hit the bottom and then they'll taak the bairn frae ye an' stick him in some sorta hame and ye'll nivir see him again. He's Frank's bairn an' he deserves better than this. Do ye no ken that yersell?"

"'Course I ken that, but I dinnae see any money growin' on trees aroun' here. I hae nae choice Martin. We hae tae eat."

"An' drink?"

"Whaat? 'Course I taak a drink. Everyboodie needs a drink."

"They dinnae need tae be on the bottle every day in life when they cannae afford to buy a loaf o' breed for themsells, dae they?"

Nuala slumps into the seat again.

"There's naethin' for me but tae jump in the Clyde," she whispers.

Martin looks at her, takes her hand again.

"Dinnae you even think about that," he says. "Luk! I'm thinkin' here. I hae a plan. You get up the morra and paak up whatever bit o' stuff ye hae and I'll take a day aff work and drive ye o'er tae yer mither for a while, just tae ye get yer heed straightened oot."

Nuala laughs.

"Me heed straightened? She drives me heed roun' the bend althegither. She wudnae want the two o' us landin' in on her."

"Well luk lass, I'm naw takin' no for an answer here. Seein' you oot there the night....an' thinkin' what might happen tae ye. Ye hae nae idea. There's some rare boys aboot, ye ken. Girls on the street ir fair game tae them."

"I can luk efter mesell."

"Naw ye cannae, Nuala. Ye cannae guarantee ye'll naw get up the skite again. Ye cannae guarantee ye'll naw get some dirty disease aff yin o' them. Ye dinnae ken who's pickin' ye up. Ye cud easy finish up wae yer throat sliced open if ye got in the wrang boodie's car."

She sits silent, defeated. Then pushes the door further open.

"Fer yer ain sake and fer the bairn's sake, God Almighty lass, fer Frank's sake...let me help ye here. The morra? Aboot twelve? I'll be here fer ye. So get yersell sorted and be ready for me, a'right lass? Please."

She doesn't say anything, just pulls off her high heeled shoes, gets wearily out of the car, pulls her skirt down towards her knees and shuffles to the entrance to the building.

"I'll be here," he calls after her.

Chapter 10

Ranahuel
Kincasslagh
Co Donegal
10th August 1945

Dear Sally Anne,

    I got your two letters from New York and Boston. I am glad everything is alright. It is nice about the new job. Mammy is the same as usual so it is fine here. I have no news to tell you except for one thing and it will be a surprise to you. When you read this I think you will be glad you were away out of the country.

That man from Tyrone that you used to talk about came here to the house. Henderson he said his name was. It was a few weeks ago, not long after you left but I had no way of telling you till I got your last letter with the address in Boston on it.

The way it happened was this. This car came up the hill and into our street. It was the priest, but not in his own car. He was looking for you. I told him you had left for Glasgow. That seemed to please him and he got back in the car and went back down the hill.

Then before the hour had passed the same car arrived back in here and this man got out, asking for you as well. I told him you were away but he knew that from the priest. He just wanted to know why and what had happened to send you on your way so quick. I made him tea for I was sorry for him after him driving such a long way to get here. He seemed sad

that you were not here. He met our Mammy and he asked about the fiddle and all. I told him you did not bother much with it now, that is why it is still hanging where you left it. He made me promise to write to you and tell you he was here, as soon as I got your address. So that is what I am doing.
I have no other news.
It is sad about Nuala and her baby. God look to them.
You sister
Mairead

Chapter 11

Matthew Henderson

It was Mr Porter himself who drove up to Lismore to break the news to me. He picked his way through the cow dung on the street, for we had just been shifting cattle, and came to me at the byre door. I was clabber to the knees and my hands were covered in filth from cleaning out the calf stalls. Regardless of that, I went to shake hands but he ignored it. I was sort of shocked when I looked closer at him. He had pain on his face and a letter in his hand.

"Matthew," he said, his voice sounded high, sort of broken.
"What's the matter, Mr Porter?"
"It's Alice," he said.
God above, I was thinking, has she died or fallen ill or what? Her father was quaking before me here, and him a bank manager.
"What about her?"
"I don't know how to tell you this son. I am afraid you are not going to take it very well," he said.
"Well try me and see," I told him.
"She has…Oh Lord…she has…how can I tell you this? Alice… she has forsaken you, forsaken all of us," he stammered.
"How do you mean 'forsaken me'? What has she done?"
"She has broken her contract with you."
"What? What contract are you…"
"She has met another man."
That was a blow alright. What came next was even worse.
"She has run away with him."
These words seemed to come to me in echoes, like you get in an empty church.
'Run away. Run away.'
"Run away? Where to?" I asked, my heart missing beats.
"She sent this letter before she left," he whimpered, waving the envelope. "By today she will be married. Married to a man we have never met, a man who has never asked my permission to have her hand…Lord above, I never thought I would live to see the day a daughter of mine did this to me. The little tramp that she is!"
"Ah, hold on now sir," I said, instinctively rising to her defence. "That is not the kind of thing you should be saying about your own daughter. She has maybe just made a mistake here and…"
"Made a mistake? Made a mistake, did she? Yes, my poor friend. She has made a dreadful mistake. The reason she is rush-

ing off to Scotland, to Gretna Green to be precise, is that she is carrying this man's baby. She is having to get married. Having to, you understand? We are disgraced altogether."

Carrying a man's baby? For a second or two I couldn't work out what the problem was with this. She was carrying someone's baby. I had a mental picture of her holding a baby in her arms, smiling down at this wain that belongs to some man she has....Oh my God! Was her father telling me that Alice was pregnant? Was pregnant with a baby to some man or other? Some man other than me like?

But it was only six weeks until our wedding day.

A baby? But not my baby?

She was away to some woman called Greta, Greta Green was it? Why? To have this imaginary baby taken care of? No, no! Mister Porter had said she was getting married. But not to me obviously, for I was still here in Lismore and I was in my working clothes and filthy as a pig, and the wedding day was still a good while away. What will people think of me, my good grief? How was I going to tell Alice....no, no, no! How was I going to tell my doting mother, the twins, everybody who had been bringing presents for us? The clergyman. He would have to be told. Told to sort this whole mess out. A baby? Belonging to somebody, some man?

My head seemed to spin for a fair number of minutes. There was a voice droning on in the distance somewhere and when I looked up I saw the bank manager still mouthing away silently at whatever he had been saying.

"Sorry," I said, "what is it you are saying? I lost you for a minute there."

"Matthew, my wife and I are completely shocked and mortified that you should have to suffer this terrible indignity, this further wound to your reputation," he said.

"A further wound? My reputation?" I said, puzzled.

"After what you went through some years ago when you killed..... when your friend got shot. This is the last thing you deserve, my boy."

"Ah right," I said, still wondering how he was linking the two things, and to my reputation. The whole thing was a massive shock and a terrible blow but I still didn't see it as affecting my reputation. How could Alice running away with somebody else affect that?

Then I started going over in my head. Words like 'Friend killer, failed lover, deserted bridegroom, hopeless farmer.' That led to 'lonely, bitter-twisted oul ejit on the hill?'

Was that what was ahead for me?

I wanted to read this letter he was now stuffing back into his pocket.

He had little choice but to give it to me. I would have ripped it off him, so mad was I getting.

****

Stranmillis College
Belfast
15th May 1925

Dear Father and Mother,

This letter will come as a surprise to you. I hope you are not too disappointed in me and will continue to love me.

During the course of this academic year I have made an acquaintance who has become very dear to me, as I to him. He is a young man (though some years older than me) by the name of Albert Morrison and he comes from the town of Comber in County Down. By profession he is a representative for a linen company in Belfast and he has the privilege of travelling to various parts of the world to market our fine linen products.

I met Albert at a ball in the city centre and we fell for each other straight away. Obviously I could not bring myself to tell Matthew Henderson. He would have been so hurt, I am sure, and would not have understood. Matthew is also older than me by several years and it seems clear to me now that he took advantage of my youthful innocence when he proposed to me and put undue pressure on me to accept him. He could barely wait until I was finished my training here to have me tied down in marriage and living on his farm in the back of beyond, having many babies and looking after his animals.

Albert, on the other hand, has promised to take me with him on his travels and show me the world. He is a fine man with good prospects and I am absolutely sure you will love him.

The thing is, dear parents, that I have got myself into a position where I am in the family way. I know this will hurt you deeply and I beg your forgiveness. It happened entirely by accident on a single night when I was forced to stay with Albert in his hotel room due to an extremely violent storm which had blown up while we were dancing. It was not going to be safe for me to get back to the college so Albert gallantly allowed me to sleep in his bed for the night. I had not foreseen the consequences. So congratulations, you are going to be grandparents.

The other piece of news is that you are going to be the parents of a married daughter. Albert has been very honourable. When I was sure of my condition he immediately proposed to me and of course I accepted. He is taking me this weekend for a quiet wedding to a place in Scotland called Gretna Green where such things are performed in a very discrete manner. The ceremony will be on Monday next, the 18th May. It is all entirely legal and above board and we will be just as married as the next couple. I am sorry of course that you will not be present. It is just the delicate circumstances I find myself in. Yes, a big wedding in our church in Castlederg would have been lovely, with a big spread in some grand hotel afterwards but it might not have been without its problems, not least for the clergyman when he learned of the circumstances. So this way will spare you any embarrassment and that is my sole motivation.

It would be nice if, when we return to Northern Ireland, you could visit us at Albert's lodgings on the Newtownards Road in Belfast. Obviously I will not want to be around Castlederg for a good many months. When our child is born we intend to call it for you mother (if it is a girl) or Wilbert, for you father, if a boy is born.

I would ask you to do a big favour for me. Please go to Matthew and explain to him what has happened, though perhaps not about the baby. It has not been my wish to hurt him. I send him my apologies. He is a good man and will find it inside himself to forgive me and move forward with his life.

Finally I wish you well. Please do not hold it against me that I am this kind of daughter. I cannot help what has happened now but I will try to make the best of my life. I send you all my love.

Your daughter,
Alice.

****

It took me weeks to face the outside world again after that. I felt like I had had my teeth kicked in, it hurt so much. I felt so alone, so betrayed, so naive. What a fool I had been. The sleekit wee bitch!

John Sproule came up often to sit with me. That was nice of him but it didn't help when he said one night, "It's all for the best Matthew. I mean, can you see thon wan feeding your pigs, can you?"

The answer was 'No' but that only made me feel more stupid.

"You are at a wile low ebb in your life Matt," John told me a few times. He didn't need to be spelling that out. It was the truth. He didn't stop there though.

"You know, Matt," he said, "God has a plan for your life."

"Oh right," I said. "And when does it start, this plan, for it hasn't been great up to now?"

"That's my point. It starts when you surrender yourself to him and get saved."

This was not new news to me. I had heard it preached from the pulpit in my church and from street preachers in the fair in Castlederg. Castlederg was safe; they'd have been stoned out of Strabane fair.

John wouldn't give over about it. In the back of my head I knew full well that he was taking advantage of my weak state of mind but anyhow, I eventually gave in to his gerning. I started going with him to various missions around the country. Sometimes these meetings would be in a big white tent, sometimes in a wee wooden mission hall and more often than not we would find ourselves in an Orange Hall. John preferred these I think, and it wasn't just that they were usually warmer than the draughty tents. He liked being surrounded by the paraphernalia of the Orange, the red, white and blue of the flags, the banners showing King Billy on his white horse crossing the Boyne in victory. For John, this was at the heart of who he was, this was his sanctuary. He very much saw himself as a 'saved' man, chosen by God to be given the gift of eternal life.

And he saw me as needing to be the same as him, rescued and brought into the fold. I was in the Protestant fold already of course, but that wasn't enough. To be truly Protestant, in his view, I needed to be 'born again'.

So night after night I would find myself listening to hymn-singing, lively and warm, with maybe an accordion player or a pedal organ at the front. Somebody from the congregation would tell their story of being 'redeemed by the blood', a 'testimony' as they called it. Some man in a suit and tie would preach for half an hour, generally with plenty of thumps of the Bible or the pulpit to emphasise his point. An odd time it would be a woman. I enjoyed those better, if enjoyed is the right word.

Over time it wore me down. You got used to the language they were speaking; it was sort of like their own dialect. Say the right code words and everybody understood and agreed and said "Amen." Sometimes shouted it too. Looking back on it I suppose it was inevitable that I would find myself putting my hand up at the end of one of these meetings and going for a prayer with the preacher afterwards.

"Pray the prayer. Ask God for forgiveness and He'll wash your sins away."

So I did. Lots of people waiting to shake hands with me after. I had 'passed' over into their clique. I was accepted as one of them. But even from the start I wasn't sure I wanted to be one of them.

Still, I had followed a very dodgy path in my life; in their terms I had 'committed sins', a heap of them. This was a sort of cleaning up of the mess I had made, inside myself at the very least. The sins were 'washed away'. That was how I felt anyway. And this plan that God had for my life could begin now, rather than me following my own unrighteous paths.

Alice was behind me. What I had had with her was washed away.

Joe was behind me. My killing of him was washed away.

Sally-Anne was behind me. My affair with her was washed away.

And those are only the bits I am owning up to.

I could move forward now and see if I could find this Divine Plan.

Chapter 12

Windsor Hotel
Cape May
New Jersey
United States of America
12th August 1945

Dear Mairead,

Yesterday we finally arrived in this town where I am to live and work, Cape May. I am very excited and nervous as usual but I can't wait to tell you of my first impressions.

First of all, our journey. Roisin is a great driver. She knows how to get the most speed out of her car, that is for sure. All the same it seemed to take us ages to get here. We went through part of New York City, but I wouldn't be on for staying there too long. Far too many people, too many cars and buses and trams and lorries. America has a smell all of its own, hot and tarry, and it is hard to get used to.

The coloured lights swinging above the street for telling you whether to go or stop had my head turned. And the height of them buildings. You never saw the like of it. How they don't fall over in a storm is beyond me, but nobody else seemed to be in a bother about it. Roisin just laughed at me when I said to her. I saw the Empire State Building and Brooklyn Bridge, those are the only two names I remember, for there were so many sights. Roisin would be laughing at me if she knew that is all that stayed in my head, but I was more concerned at the amount of traffic than to be listening to her every word.

We stayed all night in a fancy motel in a place called Newark. Roisin treated me to a grand dinner. She knows how to eat, and how to hold her liquor too. I was tipsy just watching her knocking back those glasses of gin. She didn't rise in the morning till near eleven o'clock. I was dying to be on our way.

Another four hours in the car, all the way down these fancy roads with people flying past you like you were stopped, and her doing near fifty. We had to stop in at various towns, just so she could get a look at them and show me what the coastline is like. I told her it is not a patch on the Rosses. Neither it is, Mairead, it's all low and flat and boring, strand after strand, miles of them, with not a ridge nor a hill nor a spink in sight anywhere. It is the funniest looking country I ever saw. Bits of it are covered in bushes, hardly high enough to be called trees. Other bits are like swampy marshland, with a lot of rivers and lakes in them. I lost count of how many bridges we crossed.

Another thing has struck me about America so far. The colour of everything. The grass and the plants would not have the same tone as around home. It's as if the strength has been bleached out to a dull straw colour. Maybe that is why they seem to paint their houses in bright, striking colours. In the towns and villages you see a blue house, then a red or green or pink one. If you painted your house in Kincasslagh some of these colours people would think you were off your head. Whitewash does us fine.

We went through a big fancy place called Atlantic City, then Ocean City, Stone Harbour and Wildwood and others I forget. But haven't they all the loveliest names. We have no names like that at home, just Braade and Mullaghduff and the like.

Final stop Cape May, which sounds a bit of a come-down from nearby Wildwood, in its name at least, but it is a lovely town, in a quaint sort of way. A lot of the houses are very grand and Roisin tells me they were built over a hundred years ago. (That's not half as old as most of ours but I didn't like to tell her that.) She says they are in the Victorian style, mostly built of wood. They must have a host of expert carpenters about here. Looking at these tidy streets, I do not see a lot of brick or stone work, though the church I went to for Mass today is a grand stone building. It's called Our Lady, Star of the Sea. The houses all seem to have verandas and some are so pretty they look like something from a picture book or a fairy story.

This hotel that Roisin is to manage, The Windsor, is such a beautiful old building; it is the shape of an L and has three floors. It's a timber building and is painted white except for the top floor which is red, a great contrast. I still do not know how many bedrooms it has but no doubt I will know soon enough when I get tired cleaning them all. From what Roisin told me at breakfast all the rooms are full. This is their busiest season, with all the visitors on holiday from the big cities nearby. Roisin takes over as manager tomorrow, a great experience for her. This will also be some experience for me, meeting all these strangers, but at least a chamber maid does not have much talking to do to the customers, not like a waitress or the girls at the front desk.

My room is right on the top floor and is at the end next the sea so I can look out and see the ocean. I did that as soon as I woke up this morning, pulled the curtains open and there it was, fifty yards away on the other side of a beautiful beach, the same Atlantic Ocean that I could see from our front door every morning. It is amazing that, and it helped me feel not quite so far away.

So now I am to try on their maid's uniform and get my instructions for what to be cleaning in the morning. It is into work straight away and I am ready for it, and the dollars I will earn. I have a fair bit to pay back to Roisin before I can be sending any home.

Write to me, now that you have this address, for I heard nothing from home when I was in Boston. Let me know how mammy is and if you have heard any more from Nuala. If you see Ailish at Mass tell her I was asking for her and I will write to her as soon as I get settled.

Le grá,
Sally Anne

Chapter 13

Musselburgh!

Nuala hated the very rasping noise of the word. She always felt it sounded as if some old drunk was clearing a throatful of phlegm from his tubes and spitting it on a wall. She hated most of her childhood memories of the place, but here she was, in the back of Martin's car, coming into the town on the road from Edinburgh, wee Frankie crying on her knee. Rain sloshed against the car's wipers making it near impossible to see the road. Frankie had been sick twice on the journey and Martin had had to stop by the roadside and pull some wet grass to try and clean up the vomit. He got soaked to the skin in a matter of seconds. The car stank of boke, so he had been driving with the window half down, just to get air and avoid puking himself. He was so wet already that it made little difference.

She directed him up the wee puddled streets to the house on Eskeside Road and he stopped outside, jumping out with more eagerness than was polite. Nuala struggled with the child as he opened the boot and pulled out the one case she had. A glance at the house, Nuala's former home, spoke to him of grim decay. Dark grey stone, flaking paint and a quarter pane of glass in one window replaced by a splintering slate. Rain gushing out of a drainpipe which was broken in two, halfway to the spouting, a fan of green slime on the wall below.

"Go on an' knock the dour an' see if ye can get me mither up oota hir bed."

Martin did as he was told, then turned to help Nuala as the shower eased back in ferocity.

"Lord but he made a right mess o' hissell, didn't he?" Martin said, trying to hold Frankie at a distance and diverting his head.

The green door grated open and the old mother looked out. Not so much old as old-looking, she had let herself go years ago and had never reclaimed any self pride. Her long hair was an unruly besom of white and grey strands sticking out behind her triangular head.

"Oh dear God! What ir you dain' here?"

It was not the warmest of welcomes and Nuala didn't dignify it with a reply, pushing past her mother into the house.

"I need tae wash the bairn," was all she said.

Martin stood watching, unsure of what to do next. He had driven all afternoon and hadn't eaten since he had a late fry about eleven o'clock. A cup of tea and a bit of grub would be great but he didn't like to ask. So he just stood and looked. The mother gave him a long suspicious stare, didn't break breath to him but turned inside and scraped the door closed behind her. Rain dripping off him, Martin jumped back into the car. He didn't start the engine straight away. He waited and his wait was rewarded as Nuala rushed back to open the door and shout out at him.

"Where ir ye gaan? Come in here for a bite o' dinner before ye go."

"Yir mithir…"

"Daenae worry aboot her. She's naw right in the heed. I might hae tae go an' scrounge up some food frae somewhere in the toon but ye are naw gaan' withoot grub, Martin. Come in tae…"

Martin did, and waited an hour before Nuala served him 'taties' and sausages. She'd had to strip and wash the baby before running to the corner shop for the food, while he watched as her mother made a clumsy attempt to dress Frankie in clean clothes. The wait was worth it though.

"Ye wor very guid tae me daughter, son, and I thank ye for it. But hoo am I tae manage noo, lukkin' efter the pair o' them?"

There was no real answer to this and Martin just kept his head down and his eyes on the disappearing food.

"It's naw fair what she haes pit me through," the mother continued. "I can barely luk after mesell, nivir mine her. And noo anithir bairn tae feed. Ye shudnae a broght them here."

Martin had had enough. He stood up and faced the old woman, his heckles up.

"God Almighty but it's the right heartless woman ye are. Nuala is yer daughter, yer ain flesh and blood. The bairn tae. If ye'd seen what I seen in the Gorbals the ither nicht ye would ken that I had tae dae somethin' for hir. She needs you tae luk efter the bairn while she goes oot tae earn money tae feed themsells, dae ye naw see? She haes naeboodie else. How the hell is she meant tae survive an' rare Frankie if she haes nae help?"

Mary Ann Quinn had not been spoken to like this for a very long time and she was speechless in shock, falling back into a low couch and grabbing a cushion, almost for protection. Nuala looked on wide-eyed.

"Luk here you," began her mother, "you ir a stranger here. Jist because ye ir tryin' tae help the lass daesnae mean ye can miscaal hir mither. Keep a civil tongue in yer heed son."

"I'll say what needs sayin', Missus. Her Frank was a guid mate o' mine an' I promised him I'd luk efter hir if anythin' heppened tae him, so that's what I'm daen'. Nuala needs tae get oot an' get a job and meet some dacent young fella. She's only twenty, for God's sake. She haes a whole life in front o' hir. So you need tae pull yer weight here woman an' take care o' the bairn fir a year or twa, tae she gets hersell on hir feet again."

The mother got up from her chair, turned away from them and slunk out to the kitchen at the rear.

"At my age I dinnae see mesell rarin' anithir wain," she said, her voice a grumble of bitterness.

Nuala came to him and they hugged.

"Thanks fer tryin' but it's nae use taalkin' tae hir," she said.

Martin took his leave of her, kissing little Frankie on top of his head but ignoring the old woman in the kitchen.

He drove back towards Glasgow, unable to shift the thought from his head that what he had done out of duty to Frank and an effort to show kindness to Nuala, might turn out to be anything but kindness. How, in God's name was she going to survive a woman like that?

Chapter 14

Windsor Hotel
Cape May
New Jersey
24th August 1945

Dear Mairead,

I hope you are well and Mammy too. How is the weather at home? You should feel the heat here. At times I am just dying for a breeze of cold air to be blowing across the sea from Ireland. Mostly I want to sit in the shade but these Americans are out in the middle of it, as few clothes on them as they can get away with, all trying to soak it up like it might not appear again till next summer.

I have begun my new life as a chamber-maid. I start early in the morning, a quick breakfast at six o'clock, then the work begins at a quarter to seven, (or a quarter off seven as they say here.)

It's not hard work, just very constant. Cleaning corridors and bannisters first, then the bedrooms, changing bedclothes, then carting all the used sheets to the laundry room. They have to be kept very clean for these sweaty Americans.

After lunch I am flat out getting the washing done and sorted. Thank God they have these big machines that do most of the laundry, rather than us having to stand half the day with our hands in hot water. The machines do make a terrible racket though. After the linens are washed we put them through big mangles to get the worst of the water out. Then we have to hoist the wet sheets up on very high clothes lines in a drying room. Those rooms are so hot you could nearly cook in them; you be dying to get out of them for a breath of fresh air. When we finish, generally about five in the afternoon, we all hurry to get out to the beach across the road.

In the late evenings you hear this noise from all around you, a chorus in the background of constant chirping sounds. I had no idea what it was at the start, but somebody told me it is the sound made by millions of crickets that live in the gardens about here. You hear it as a continual buzz when you are trying to sleep. It reminds me of the hearth crickets we would have behind the fire at home, but about a thousand times louder. I am not sure if it is the same insect here.

Then when you are out walking at night you see these wee flickering lights in front of you. These are called fireflies and we have nothing like them in Ireland. I don't know how they manage it but they can light up their bodies. I like them, but the ones I hate are insects that can bite the blood out of you and without you ever knowing at the time. They are very small and light of themselves. I'd call them midges, but here they are called mosquitos and they leave me very itchy with red blotches on my arms and ankles.

I haven't seen hint nor hair of Roisin (Rose!) since Saturday. She never came to Mass and she must be very busy getting to know the ins and outs of the hotel. But I haven't been lonely, for I have made a friend. She started here last year so she has been able to show me the ropes. She is called Caroline, which I think is a lovely name, and she is the first person I have ever talked to in my whole life who is not the same colour as us, for

she is a 'bean dhubh', a negro is what they say in English, I believe. We have become good friends already. There are only two of her colour working in the Windsor, Caroline and her father, who is a top-class cook, she tells me. That would likely be how Caroline got the job I imagine. She is only a cleaner in the corridors and stairs and lobbies. She tells me she is not allowed to be in the bedrooms, which is strange. I find her so funny to listen to, her way of going on and her accent which is so different to Roisin's. We go to the beach together but she can't swim either, so we stay on the sand. Last night we walked the Boardwalk and heard great music coming out of a big hall called Convention Hall. Caroline says it is called swing music and she tried to show me a few of the moves. You would have laughed at the pair of us, spinning round together out on this street of wooden boards. I wasn't very good at it and nearly fell over a few times. A few passersby let me know they didn't approve of my attempts at dancing with this black girl. Caroline said, "Pay them not a bit of notice Sally Anne. They is just jealous." We giggled like girls at that.
I asked Caroline if she wanted to go to Mass with me tomorrow morning on our day off but she turned me down. She told me she is a different religion. She goes to some kind of Pentecost church. I don't know if that is Protestant or Muslim or what but Caroline tells me I should hear how they sing in their Masses. Maybe I will go someday.
Some of the other girls are nice enough as well. I find that Americans can be all over you with friendly chat and make you feel sort of special, that's the impression they give you. It can get to be a bit much though, all the smiling. They are curious

about me, that's 'for sure', but some of them hardly know where Ireland is. A maid called Amy said to me at lunch the other day, "You know Sally Anne, your English is really good." I thought she was joking me but no, she was serious and was giving me a compliment. You'd think that English was their invention. I wasn't going to bother her with a history lesson about the English language, nor about how it has nearly wiped out Gaelic in Ireland.

I am sending you a share of my first wages which I just received this morning. This is a Five Dollar Bill and you should save it up until you have a few of them and then take them to the bank in Dungloe, for the man there to give you our money in exchange. Next time I intend to send the same to Nuala in Glasgow. I hope it gets to her safe. Please don't mind me sharing with her; it is just that she is in such desperate straights at the minute.

Le grá,
Sally Anne

Chapter 15

Matthew Henderson

Mary Kearney has been a friend since childhood. Our two families have lived and farmed side by side for years of course, us in Lismore and them just across the Border in Gortnagappel. Our fathers were always great friends and Anthony was the last person my father ever spoke to as he lay dying on the battlefield at the Somme.

Even after childhood Mary and I still talked a good bit when the two families were 'morrowing', helping each other out at farm work. We had manys a good yarn when working at the turf, manys an argument as well, for Mary was a feisty one. Her views would always have been very Irish.

I remember after Easter, back in 1916, she was mad at the British for executing Pearse and the rest of those rebels. Nothing I could say would change her mind. As time went on she talked less and less about politics, but when she did it was plain to me that she was on the side of the rebels during their independence war. Then after that, when the negotiations about Ulster were taking place in London, she was all on edge; she was mad against the idea of a border, like so many others of her persuasion.

I have a clear recollection of the night she arrived in her father's house with a newspaper in her hand. Michael Collins had just been shot and she seemed to be delighted, much to her father's annoyance. The rumour then was that she was friendly with my former hired hand, Kevin Duggan, a ruffian who was in the IRA.

Then came Joe's death. It was a terrible blow to Mary. Even though she had moved away to live and work in Strabane and wasn't as close in to her family, she mourned her brother's passing very deeply. It was not a nice thing to watch and near tore the heart out of me, especially with it being my doing. She couldn't look the way I was on for a good while after that and I wondered would we ever be able to talk again in the way that we had done in times past.

As it happened, it seems she really wanted to talk to me about everything that had occurred.

It came about like this.

Some weeks after Joe's funeral I had reason to go to speak to Anthony about a wheen o' heifers he wanted to bring over to my bull. Him being so lame, it was always easier if I took a dander over to him. These conversations weren't easy, especially at the start, but I have to give Anthony great credit for how he was able to lift his face and look at me and chat as normally as you could imagine in those tense circumstances. He managed his grief well. We stood talking in the yard for half an hour that day. As I turned to head back across the burn that separated the two farms... the two counties, the two countries...I heard Mary's voice call me from their door. I hadn't even known she was in the house.

I turned and waited for her.

"What about a walk up to the mountain?" she said. I noticed she was wearing a pair of black trousers, could have been Joe's, and she had her boots on.

I had nothing better to do on a Sunday afternoon. The weather was crisp and cold, it being early March, and the surface of the boggy lane was hardened by the frost. We climbed the hill that ran along behind the two farms, picking our way between the whin bushes that grew so keenly and threatened to close over the lane in places. I loved their deep yellow flowers and the strong, sweet smell that rose from them but their sharp spikes were not the easiest to work with.

"These need cutting back," I said, the first words after five minutes of walking. Mary continued ahead of me where single file was the easiest way to avoid the barbs sticking out at us. Still she said nothing. I was starting to wonder what this was all about, this walk up into Donegal where our common-land bog lay. Eventually we reached the highest point where, looking east, you could see the fertile valley of the Derg river stretching out in front of you. She stopped and stared at the puffs of cloud scudding towards the Sperrins. I stood beside her, waiting. When she spoke she sounded a bit tense, her face tightened and determined, her eyes full of emotion.

"You are likely wondering what I have to say to you," she said.

I didn't deny it. This was the first conversation we had had since Joe's death, other than passing condolences at the wake.

"I am," I said.

"You think I hate you...for what you did?"

"Likely," I said. "You have every right."

There was a long pause before she spoke again.

"Well, I don't, if it's any help to you."

"I don't see why you wouldn't," I said.

"After I heard how it happened, when I thought about it, well... I know it wasn't your fault. You thought you had shot Kevin."

I stood waiting. She was right about that last part. This was taking the breath from me.

"Look, I was as much to blame for what happened as you were."

"No, not at all, how could you have been? You weren't there."

"But I should have been there. I could have been there," she said. "I could have stopped it. Joe would still be alive. I tried, God knows I tried to stop it. I should have gone home that night."

I was shocked to silence by this. I said nothing, just waited while she tried to get her sobs under control. I had always thought Mary was as tough as oul leather. Now she was showing me different.

"Me and Kevin had a fall out that night. He had been staying with me, in hiding, sort of. I knew he was going to try and shoot the Englishman you had staying with you, but he said he wanted to have a go at you as well. I wouldn't hear tell of that. I told him you had nothing to do with anything, you weren't a 'B' man. He wouldn't listen. You were 'harbouring a Brit'. We fought and he left. I should have got the bike out and ridden home to warn you."

This was news to me. The nonsense of it all got into me and my mouth hung open, without a word able to fill it.

"You told me you were sorry...sorry about what happened, but I have to say sorry to you," she said. "It is my fault that you were in that situation, so it lies at my door as well. It is my fault too that Joe is dead. I miss him so much. I will never forgive myself."

"I miss him too," I said. "He was so funny and so good."

"He was. I can still see his silly grin..."

It was terrible to see her like this, so broken, but I knew that she had a point. I was sorry for her but at the same time I was pleased that she was wanting to share the heavy load of blame that I had been carrying. Still, something in me protested.

"I pulled the trigger. It was me killed him, despite what you say."

"But you shot in ignorance. You didn't know who you were aiming at. I could have told you."

"Alright, maybe," I said, "but would you really have warned me that Duggan was coming to shoot me? Your friend Kevin? Would you have told me that and watched me set up to shoot him? I don't think you would, Mary, no matter how much you wanted to save me. You didn't know that Stanley wasn't at our place, did you?"

She could see the strength of my argument but she still protested.

"Maybe not. Maybe I wouldn't have told you about Kevin, at that stage, but I could have stopped Joe being daft enough to take a gun and wander into the middle of a firing zone, couldn't I?"

She cried again and I found myself hugging the sister of my victim, telling her it would be alright. I never said a sillier word in all my life. It would not be alright, not now, not ever.

She got her tears quenched and then she gave me another layer of truth I had not known.

"You know, he was nearly arrested that night? Kevin, I mean."

"I didn't know that."

"He and the others were coming into Clady on their way to yours. Some man waved them down at the side of the road and told them there was a B Special patrol searching cars just around the bend. So they got turned and escaped. I don't know who that man was but he saved the lads, that's for sure. Kevin went on the run that night, for I was so mad at him I put him out of the house. I haven't set eyes on him since."

"You haven't seen him since?"

"No, and if I never do it will be too soon."

"I'm sorry," I said, thinking that I wasn't sorry at all.

"Don't be sorry," she said. "I thought I loved him and he loved me, but he was only using me, I can see that now. My father was right. I was a fool, but I won't be a fool again. There has to be a better way of fighting your battles than the way he was going about it. Trying to kill somebody here and blow up a building there."

"You won't have to talk me into agreeing with that, Mary," I told her.

We talked many times after that chat, that strange 'first confession'. She went up in my estimation as a brave and kind girl, one who still argued fiercely with me about the Border and the other political issues of the day but one who had turned away from the violence that, at the end of the day, had been responsible for the death of her brother, even though it was me who pulled the trigger.

We were to become closer still, Mary and I, as time went on. Not in any romantic sense though; I had my fill of that after the Alice affair that next year. No, it was more in a business sense that our relationship blossomed and by coincidence that bog lane played a large role in the partnership yet again.

Chapter 16

Sally Anne Sweeney

I have been doing so well, loving this new 'adventure', if you want to call it that, and not missing home too much. I suppose if I am honest I would say that I haven't had time to miss it. I have kept myself busy, both with the work itself and chatting to Caroline and the other maids and an odd time with Roisin.

The hotel is nowhere near as busy now as it was at the height of the summer. There seems to be a lot less people about since Labour Day. In the summer it was mostly husbands and wives, but I notice now that it is more men that are about the town and a good few of them stay in the Windsor. I have been surprised to find out that, on top of what you earn here in wages, most of the guests will leave behind a tip for you, for cleaning their room and doing the bedclothes. It can be anything from fifty cents to five bucks if they are staying here for a longer time. Bucks! I found it hard to get used to saying this word, but it is what they call dollars here. I intend to try and save these tips and see what amount I can put past me.

With the hotel not so busy some girls have been laid off, so those of us who have permanent jobs have more work to do. There is a great deal of cleaning to do in various parts of the place. All this furniture for example. These wicker chairs in the lobby and bar are the devil itself to clean. We have to use thin strips of cloth and pipe cleaners to get into the wee dusty gaps. You might as well be trying to clean one of our turf creels back in Donegal. The Windsor is a very old hotel and has kept all the old styles. There is a lot to be said for that, but the people who designed all this fancy furniture had little thought for cleaning staff like me.

At night I have been going to bed early, I am so tired and sleeping the whole night through without a bother. The only thing that wakens me up is if a mosquito has beaten the screens on the window and got into the room. You hear the wee faint buzzing of them around your ears, so there's nothing for it but to get up, switch on the light and try and find the wee beast, to put both it and me out of our misery. They seem to have a special liking for Irish blood, for none of the other girls complain much about them.

I do have the oddest dreams at night. The thing about these dreams is that, while you might think they would be dreams about home, they are not. They are about what I am doing here and what is going on around me. I woke up laughing the other morning because I suddenly thought, 'I have been dreaming in Irish. The people in my dream have been speaking Irish to me...Caroline, this black girl from New Jersey, talking to me in Irish, but Irish with her strong American accent.' I have a feeling that at the start of the dream it was Ailish I was chatting to but she turned into Caroline half-way through. I just found it all so funny. It didn't bother me either, it hadn't time to, for I was at work half an hour after I wakened, still laughing to myself.

I have been on the lookout for other ones from Ireland here in Cape May. In Boston you were tripping over them, Murphys, McBrides, O'Donoghues, even Sweeneys, but the Irish don't seem to have found the same attraction to this part of America, as far as I can make out. Maybe it was too flat and swampy for them. We like a good mountain behind us. I remember Matthew Henderson saying something like that about his farm.

"You canna bate a decent hill behind you, sheltering you frae the west win'."

"That and a good hard border," I said. "Protect you from all us rebel heathens in Donegal."

He had laughed at my sarcasm.

"Ah naw," he said, "but you know where you are with mountains."

'And borders,' I thought.

Them and their borders!

Only one Irish person has crossed my path and even then I am not sure if he would consider himself Irish. He works part-time in the bar here and he says his name is Carson Bill. Yes, Carson Bill! I looked at him when he told me that, waiting for him to turn it round for me sort of, but no, Carson is his Christian name, Bill his surname. When he told me he was from Belfast I thought to myself, 'Ah, that maybe explains it.' I didn't bother trying any Irish on him.

He gets made fun of by customers I hear.

"Ya got the bill there, Bill?"

What has brought me my first tears since I got here was so unexpected that I hardly could credit it. After work one evening, Caroline went for a long walk with me out along Lafayette Street to where the first bridge crosses the canal. We were looking across the bay to where there are some huge buildings and cranes and things. Caroline tells me that it is a famous American military base. Some of the men staying in our hotel work there, she says. The base had something to do with the war. I am not sure if it was the war in Europe or the other one against the Japanese. Anyway, that is all over now, since the atomic bomb was dropped on Japan and the Japanese surrendered back in September. From what I can see though, that military base still seems right and busy.

We walked on along the bay. The sun was low in the sky by the time we reached a lovely grassy park and we stood watching it sink towards the October horizon. It was a very still and peaceful atmosphere, just the distant sounds of some seagulls and the odd car crossing the bridge.

In the quietness, I started to hear sounds that puzzled me and interested me, more than interested me. I looked to the far end of the park where a couple of young fellas were exercising themselves. I listened to their calls. *Tchí Dia mé!* They were talking in Irish. And they were thumping a *sliotar* to each other across the park, *camáns* in their fists, and they speaking Irish.

I was off like a greyhound to them. Poor Caroline was left sitting on the park bench for a minute, wondering what had come over me.

"*Cad é mar atá sibh?*' I shouted to them and they paused in their pucking and stared at me trotting over the grass to them. They must have been a bit confused; this woman old enough to be their mother, and her laughing crazy and shouting at them in Irish. I think they must have thought they were going to be told it was time to be in the house, hang up their hurls and get ready for bed. We must have talked half an hour, all in my own language.

*Is ola le mo chroí é an Ghaeilge a chluinstin ag na stocaígh sin....*it was a joy to my heart, there was no effort in it at all. I suddenly thought, 'It's the having to say every damned thing in English has me so tired here.'

I said this to these lads and they agreed with me.

They were cousins from Clare, a village by the sea called Lahinch. They loved their hurling so much they brought the sticks with them, and not the sticks alone, for they were delighted to be speaking in our native language to a stranger from home. They told me they had jobs as engineers in some works over beyond Wildwood. They were mechanics, repairing boats and the like. A distant relative had started a business there years ago, and the families had kept connection.

"Not unlike myself," I told them.

Their Gaelic sounded a fair bit different to mine, more like what you would hear on the Athlone radio station, but we had no bother understanding each other. At the same time, they didn't understand everything. One of them put his foot in it badly. He saw Caroline hanging around a few yards behind, waiting for me.

So, half-joking he nodded towards her and said to me, "*Tá tú ag déanamh gnoithe maith agus do chailín aimsire féin agat.*"

What!? How dare he say such a thing, and in front of Caroline? I was mortified that this fellow had somehow got the impression that she was my maid, or at least was ready to joke about such a thing. I looked at Caroline, but she didn't seem too bothered. Of course she wasn't bothered. We were talking in Irish. She hadn't understood a word he had said. I gave him a telling off all the same. It was a brash insult from this lad that I had just met and I was disgusted that my friend and equal was being thought of as my servant. I never expected to come across this sort of ignorant attitude from fellas who were Irish. I was disappointed in them.

Caroline did sense something had upset me though. When we left the two lads and were hurrying back to the Windsor, she asked me about it. I tried to make up some other story but she was not having any of that. She kept insisting and eventually I had to tell her the truth. I thought it would annoy her deeply but she just laughed it off.

"Sally Anne," she told me, "if that was the worst abuse people like me have to take then the world would be a heavenly place."

We turned left down Madison Avenue past a row of very fancy verandas and on to the Boardwalk, just to be beside the sea again. I loved this time of night, the heat having seeped out of the day, the light starting to thicken around us, the crashing voices of the waves breaking one after the other just like they would be on Mullaghdearg Strand and the cries of the seabirds, as familiar as if they had been calling in Irish rather than American. It was all so normal, so like home.

It was then, looking out east across the Atlantic, that the first tears started to find their way down my cheeks. I was a long way from Donegal.

Chapter 17

Matthew Henderson

Mary Kearney found herself a husband sometime around the end of the Twenties. A fine man he was too, a farmer from out beyond Castlefinn. His name was Liam Coyle and he and I got on grand. Anthony and Monica were happy with the match. I suppose they were greatly relieved that Kevin Duggan had never shown his face again.

After she was married Mary visited her parents near enough every Sunday, driving Liam's wee car. It meant crossing the border twice though, because she had to come into Tyrone at Clady and then drive a few miles to our road before turning in her father's lane and crossing back into Donegal as she did so.

It was a terrible handicap for a farmer like Anthony to be sort of land-locked in like that. I was always a Unionist and I believed the border was necessary, but I would have to agree that it did not work for people like Anthony. It cut him off from so much that he would have considered to be normal living. The thing was, and Mary said this to me often, that there he is standing in his yard in Ireland but to get to the rest of Ireland he has to go out his lane into Northern Ireland, drive a lock o' miles to an approved Border checkpoint and cross back into his own country. At times the officials manning the checkpoint could get awkward with you and make you sit there for ages; that could be true for both sets of Customs men. It made no sense at all.

What eventually did make sense to Mary was that it was quicker for her to drive her car up the backroads, in Donegal but close to the border, reach the western edge of Gortnagappel bog, leave the car by an old derelict cottage up a short lane there and walk a couple of miles over a mountain track to join our shared bog rodden. That brought her down to her father's yard in no time. If the weather was half decent at all she could do it in less than an hour and avoid the hassle of the checkpoints twice over. All she would have to contend with was the clabber and the whins.

After a few years she had a couple of children to be carrying with her. That made her walk a lot harder but it wasn't the only thing getting harder for her. Politics had reared its ugly head yet again.

In the thirties the Governments of Britain and Ireland had a big fall-out. It had something to do with De Valera trying to cut all ties to Britain and refusing to pay Land Annuities to London that Ireland was supposed to pay, millions of pounds. So Britain got back at the Irish by slapping a huge tariff on Irish beef being brought into the UK. Well, the upshot was that people in Northern Ireland and Britain were no longer going to be buying Irish beef, for this tariff made it far more expensive.

Liam had beef cattle on his hill farm. Suddenly he found that he couldn't sell them, not into Northern Ireland, not in Donegal either, for suddenly there was a glut of animals that all had to be sold in the Free State. His cattle were next to worthless overnight. Anthony Kearney was in the same boat but at least he wasn't depending on beef alone. I was right sorry for them. If I had been living a few hundred yards to the west I would have been in that situation too.

Liam was distraught at times and Mary was very worried about him. There was nothing he could do. He was preparing for the day he would have to slaughter some of his animals just to save the fodder.

But, if Liam could do nothing, then Mary could.

It came about like this.

Sunday afternoon was a time when I had a habit of slipping over for a yarn with Anthony and I often saw Liam and Mary there. On one particular Sunday Liam seemed very low, with no chat at all out of him. He seemed distant, Mary too if I'm honest though she at least had the wains to distract her.

She went to the door at one stage and looked back at me, giving me the wink to follow her. I did.

We talked in Anthony's barn.

"Matthew, I am going to ask you for a big favour. We are in trouble over there."

"I know, Mary."

"He is going to have to slaughter the bullocks. Nobody is buying. All the butchers he has tried have their suppliers signed up already. He is stuck and we have barely two pennies to scrape together to buy food."

"What can I do for yous?" I asked her.

And that was the beginning of my career as a criminal, a cross-border cattle smuggler.

It was the least I could do for her and her family after all that had happened ten years earlier. I had already sold one of Anthony's bullocks in the Castlederg market, passing it off as mine with nobody any the wiser, so Mary knew I couldn't refuse her.

How we worked it was that late at night Liam would drive a couple of his bullocks up along the country roads to Gortnagappel and I would meet him at the top of the bog. If he was stopped and questioned by any Excise men he was not breaking any laws, he was still in the Free State and could claim, rightly, that he was only taking the cattle across the mountain to graze on his father-in-law's ground.

The whole scheme worked really well. I could slip a couple of his bullocks in among mine to graze and after a week or two sell them on at the local markets. A good lot of the cattle I was selling in Castlederg were being bought by big Norman McKinney, the cattle dealer, and he didn't seem to suspect that there was anything questionable about it. The cash I received I gave to Mary or Liam the following Sunday and they always insisted that I take a couple of pound out of it for my trouble. I tried to turn them down on this but they were adamant that it had to be a joint thing. So I made a few quid from smuggling during what they called 'the economic war'.

I even cut back those whins that were clogging up the back lane, just to make things less painful.

At this time I was attending gospel meetings, sometimes once a week, sometimes more. So how did I square my smuggling with me being what people called 'good-living'? In my own mind I didn't have any problem doing that.

I was helping out a friend in need.

I even heard a sermon one night that set my mind at rest. It was about the bit in Luke, to do with helping a neighbour. 'And who is my neighbour?' Jesus was asked, so he told the parable of the good Samaritan.

My neighbours might not be Samaritans but they had always been good to me.

I was doing the needful, helping a neighbour.

Mind you, I didn't bother to tell John. The way his mind worked I was sure he would find some objection to me smuggling to help some friends, Catholic friends, on the other side of the Border.

His idea of 'neighbour' didn't always square with mine.

Chapter 18

Sally Anne Sweeney

The wee white card is hanging on the door handle.
 'Room available for cleaning. Thank you'
 I open the door and reverse in, backside against it, pulling my laundry buggy after me. The door springs shut and it is then I hear the voice. A man's voice.
 "Excuse me!"
 I spin around in shock and I get an eyeful of him.
 He is naked from the waist up, a towel wrapped around his bottom half, thanks be to God. A man of about 50, I'd say, but very fresh of himself, dark hair on both his head and his chest, and a thin moustache, like you would see on some of those film star men and, to be honest, every bit as handsome as them.
 He is looking at me but it is not an angry look, not even an annoyed look. There is more of amusement about his eyes than any sign of rebuke. I get the feeling he is about to laugh at me.
 I am caught between open-mouthed gawking at him and being completely affronted. I don't think I've ever been so embarrassed in all my born days. And the English language deserts me altogether for a minute.
 "Gabh mo leithsceál," I mumble, my gaze tearing itself away and falling to the floor. "Agh...I am sorry."
 "That is quite alright," he says, pleasantly enough. "Don't reckon I hung a card out but maybe I did. We all make mistakes."
 He is grinning at me. God, let me out of here!
 Still, I defend myself as I turn to escape.
 "There was a card hanging on the door itself, or I wouldn't have come in."
 As the door shuts behind me I hear him say, "It's not a problem honey. Call anytime."
 I leave my buggy in the corridor and rush to the staff toilets to settle myself. I am nearly in tears at the whole disgrace of it. Maybe he will report me and that will be the end of the job. As I am about to go into the toilets I hear laughter from behind me.
 I turn to see Caroline and Amy in fits of giggles.
 "What?" I ask. "Did you..."
 "How'd you get on with Mr Clifford? Was he still in bed?" Amy asks.

"Yous hung that card out, you skitters?" I say.

"All part of the initiation," Caroline says. "Y'all had to go through it at some stage. We was guessin' ya was ready for it at last, so now ya a fully fledged chamber-maid Sally Anne."

I am cross for sure but they giggle so much that I get over it and soon I am laughing with them. Playing tricks like this is part of life wherever you go, but this is my first time to be the victim, certainly in America.

"But what if he reports me? I could lose my job. God above, he was wearing nothing but a towel."

"That ain't gonna happen gal," Caroline says. "Sure he is just delighted that ya got to see him looking his best. Ya is one up on the rest of us now, seeing him like that."

"Who is he anyway?" I ask.

"Oh ho, so she is interested!"

"I am not interested. I just asked who he is."

"He is Mr Clifford, that's all I know, 'cept that he come to Cape May quite often, something to do with the naval base," Caroline tells me.

As I work on the rest of that morning I find these things hard to get out of my head; the sight of a man in that state and the idea that I could be the subject of a practical joke by these American girls. At the same time there is a feeling of being accepted, of being one of them and in a sense I am warmed by it.

I had a similar feeling last week and again it was down to Caroline. There was less of a shock involved it it but it was something that affected me deeply. Caroline had asked me a couple of times to go with her to her church service. I was not really keen to be doing this. I am a loyal Catholic to the backbone and I knew that whatever church this was, it was not Catholic. But Caroline kept on at me, saying we could sit at the back so I could slip out at anytime I wanted. I wouldn't have to take part in any of their service, I could just listen to the songs without having to sing them and I didn't have to put any money in the collection box.

She has been very kind to me and is a good friend, up until that trick today. Now I'll have to watch her, maybe think of some way of getting even.

Anyhow, I gave in to her and we went last Sunday evening.

It was a small low down building, nothing like a church really, and certainly not a patch on Our Lady, Star of the Sea. We went in. It was bright inside, with a wide platform at the front. No sign of an altar though, which I found strange. I thought I'd better genuflect anyhow, just to be safe, but half-way through I noticed that Caroline wasn't bothering so I just pretended I was fixing my shoe and followed her into the back seat. They had a choir off to one side of the church and a band at the other. A band, yes, a band, with an organ, a guitar, drums and a few brass instruments that I didn't even know the names of. This was my first big shock. The second was the people.

I don't know what I expected but it had never struck me that I would be the only white face in the place. I must have stuck out like the Arranmore lighthouse. This was a church for black folk. What, in God's name, was I doing here? Caroline had never said that it was a blacks-only religion.

We weren't right sat down when I whispered to her, "I shouldn't be here." To be honest, 'whispered' is wrong; I had to near enough shout above the noise of the band warming up.

"Why not?" she said.

"It is obvious. I am the only white person here."

"Sure y'are, but that's ok, ain't it? It's not like church is just for black folk, yeah?"

"No but..."

The priest was getting up to start the thing proper. I was too late. What she said got me thinking right from the start and it stayed with me. 'It's not like church is just for black folk.' I'd never thought of that before, that these people might see everything, including church and religion, as being all about their colour. Maybe I was the same, come to think of it, just the other way round.

Did I enjoy it? I did, but it took a good while to get over the strangeness of it all.

There were so many differences between this and mass at home that I might as well have been on a different planet.

The priest was dressed the same as the other men, no collar nor robes nor anything.

The band was like something you'd hear on the radio, and every bit as good.

The people were all singing and not singing alone, clapping and swaying their bodies. There was a lot of this singing. I had never heard any of these happy sort of songs before.

When the priest was talking he was very excited and shouted a fair bit, waving his hands and walking about...and some folk in the audience thought it was only fair to encourage him. They were calling out words I had never come across before. The one word I did understand was, 'Amen', sometimes they added in 'Brother'.

"Preach it brother!"

Lots of them were shouting this.

I was thinking he must be from a big family.

I stuck it through to the end, but I was glad to get out of there. It was all a bit exhausting. After Mass I would usually feel relaxed and calmed, but this had me wound up like a spinning top. Maybe it was all the people shaking hands with me afterwards. I know they were being friendly and making certain I knew that they didn't get many white folks at their meeting and that I 'sure would be welcome back any time,' but it was all too much.

On the way back Caroline asked me if I would go back.

"Give me a while," I told her. "I need to let that one sink in for a week or two first."

The last thing I expected was that anybody would be annoyed at me going to that service. But that is exactly what happened.

I don't know how Amy and a few of the other girls, white girls all of them, found out about it but I got a bit of a talking to from them and a few cold shoulders. It wasn't as if I had been converted or anything. I had gone to one service.

"I can't believe a good Irish Catholic girl would be at a thing like that." That from my supervisor, a middle-aged woman who isn't even a Catholic, I gather.

Amy said, "I wouldn't be seen dead in a place like that Sally Anne. Just you let Caroline go to her things on her own. Stick with your own kind."

I was soon noticing that people gave each other wee sideways glances when I was around their conversations. Sometimes they would shut up when I walked in on them, or change the subject in a way that let me know I was the reason they were changing the subject. There was something just under the surface that I couldn't see clearly. I was getting the feeling that things were not as simple and straight-forward here in America as I had imagined.

I thought I should mention this to Caroline herself. We had a good chat about it, though it was bit awkward to begin with, maybe because of how I started the conversation.

I told her that a lot of years ago there was a *'fear gorm'*, or as we say in the Rosses, a *'fear dubh',* a black man, washed up on *An Trá Bhán,* that beautiful long beach between us and the place we call 'The Point'. "My father told me that his body is buried in an unmarked grave just below a place known as Braade," I told her.

"That sure is sad," she said. "Why in an unmarked grave?"

"I'm not too sure."

"I guess your country is just like here," she said. "He was a black man so he couldn't be buried with white folks."

I had never thought of that before. Maybe she is right. Maybe it was prejudice. But then I remembered my father's explanation.

"I think my father said it was because they didn't know his name or anything about him. He was likely a sailor washed overboard off a ship. They didn't know if he was Christian or not so they couldn't give him a Christian funeral, nor bury him in a church graveyard. It was the same for white men that were washed up. My father told me about finding a body on *An Trá Bhán* himself, long before I was born, and that man had to be buried on an island, a special place where babies and strangers were buried," I told her.

"Ya sure it wasn't just 'cause he was black?"

"I am sure, yes."

"Ok, that's good," she said, "'cause I guess round here white folks take every opportunity to remind us that we are not like them. We is kept in our place. I'm sure y'all noticed that Sally Anne."

"Yes and have you noticed that some of these white girls we work with have been strange with me since I went to church with you?"

"'Course I have. Daddy said I shoulda warned ya that this would happen if you came to our church. Give ya a choice. But I told him ya is a strong gal. I had to survive those white gals. When I started working here, I was the only black gal front of the kitchen, still am. I had to listen to their snide comments that I only got the job cause daddy is their top chef and they can't do without him. It wasn't nice at the start, having to listen to them and say nothing, seeing their despising looks. I had to become very strong inside; not just now, I had years of it. So I guess ya strong like me, gal."

"Thank you for that," I told her. "I hope I am strong enough alright, but it is complicated."

And things were to get even more complicated for me as the weeks went on, especially after my first experience of walking in on a guest wearing nothing but a towel.

Chapter 19

Matthew Henderson

It was a full ten months after I had started selling Free State bullocks that I had my first visit from the authorities. The RUC and the Customs men were carrying out an investigation all along the Tyrone border, the Derry one too, 'tightening up on things', as the sergeant said. My farm was 'not the only one being looked at', they assured me.

I wasn't so sure about this. I started to wonder if Norman McKinney or some other of my neighbours had begun to suspect the numbers of cattle I had about me and had dropped a quiet word to the authorities. I wouldn't have put it past big Norman for, even though it was no skin off his nose to be getting a bargain, buying these fine beasts and selling them on for beef at good profit, he would not have been happy to hear they were Free State cattle.

I had tried to be very clever about how I moved the animals on, and had made good money out of it, both for my neighbours and for myself. I would use Castlederg market this month, driving the cattle down the hill with the help of Millie and my two great dogs. The next month, I would send for a lorry and take the cattle to the Omagh or Strabane markets. A couple of times I drove them on foot all the way to Newtownstewart. Maybe it was this very fact that got the tongues wagging around the neighbourhood, the fact that I seemed to be going out of my way to change my normal pattern of doing things, which would have been to go to Castlederg fair where I was well known. How the suspicion got to the police I could only guess, but here they were in my yard anyway, peaked caps on their heads, notebooks in hand and suspicion deep in their eyes.

I was not being accused of anything, they told me, just routine checks being made.

They went around all the fields, counting the animals and writing notes in their books. I followed along behind, keeping my dog from biting the legs off them.

"Are these all your bullocks, Mr Henderson?"

We were standing in the fort field looking at seven bullocks and two heifers. Three of them were Liam's, but I wasn't going to be admitting to that.

"Well, not all of them are my bullocks," I told the young official.

"How many are yours then?"

"Well, you see....all the bullocks are mine," I said.

It was a bit of a white lie, of course it was.

He looked at me very puzzled.

"Which one is it? You are contradicting yourself," he said, getting a bit testy.

"No, I am not contradicting myself," I told him. "You asked me how many bullocks were mine and I told you they all were. So they are."

"Aye, but before that you said they weren't all your bullocks?" he argued.

"And that is the truth," I told him. "Only seven of them are bullocks. The other two are heifers."

With that he just turned away in annoyance, city boy that he was. It had the right effect though, for he seemed to lose interest in what he was counting.

After they left, I felt fairly confident they had not got any evidence that I was involved in smuggling. Millie quizzed me up and down about it, but she wouldn't have had the wit to know how to deal with the truth, so I spared her the details. She was a great girl, Millie, more than useful about the place, both inside and out. I could never have run the farm without her but, God love her, she had a wee want about her. Her twin sister seemed to get all the brains. She had missed Jane a lot, especially in those first few months after Jane married and moved to Drumquin. My mother, who was ailing badly at that stage, didn't know what day it was, so there was no point in talking to her about it. Millie would not give up though. At one point she asked me, "What would daddy say if he knew the police had been here about our cattle?"

That was a good question and one that troubled me all night afterwards.

I knew in my guts that he would not have been happy with what I was doing. Helping out neighbours, aye, he would not have been behind the door in that, but I had pushed on beyond that. Now it had reached the stage where I was helping myself.

The whole thing was so easy and I was perfectly placed to buy in a few extra animals from across the border, far cheaper and generally with Liam's help, fatten them up on our good Tyrone grass and sell them on for a decent profit. While a lot of farms were struggling in those depression years, especially in Donegal with the economic war, I was doing alright, thank you. I just had to be careful and not raise any more suspicion with the authorities.

My father's ideas of right and wrong were great for his generation but this was now. These were fierce difficult times and we had to do something to survive. If that included chancing your arm with Free State cattle, then so be it. Anyway, my father had given his life in fighting wrong, as he saw it, and died for it too. That was why I found myself running this farm before my time; it was hardly my fault that I didn't have him to be giving me advice. I would have to stand or fall by my own counsel.

The RUC and Customs men were back on my land ten days later.

Straight out to the same field and another count of the cattle.

"There were nine beasts in this field when we were here before, Mr Henderson. Seven bullocks and two heifers, as you were at pains to point out to us. Today there are eleven. How do you explain that?"

Easy, I thought. I had my lines well prepared in advance.

"Lord, would you look at that," I said in surprise. "A couple of Anthony Kearney's bease musta broken into my land again. Let me see. Aye, those two over by the stone dake look like his. I'll have to put them back across. You couldn't watch them and Anthony isn't fit to be out working at his fences you know..."

The policeman interrupted me.

"But hang on there, before you go blaming anybody else. You were in Castlederg market on Tuesday past and you sold two bullocks, is that not so?"

Goodness, these boys were serious. And they were well informed.

"I was indeed," I said, telling them the truth, "but those two bullocks had been in the shed up the back when yous were here. I never thought to mention them to you."

They looked at each other and back at me.
"Show us this shed."

I took them round the back to the shed. They took a quick look in it, presumably looking for and finding cow dung that was fairly fresh. I kept mumbling on at them about the weather, the price of pigs, the hens, anything to distract. It seemed to work.

"Aye, well, there seems to have been cattle in here recently," one of them said. "You should have shown them to us when we were here."

"I never thought," I said. "I'm sorry about that. I think it's because you just headed straight out to my fields when you arrived."

Which was true, though I was fairly sure they wouldn't remember the details.

"Right, Mr Henderson, get those stray cattle back across the border to where they belong, you hear me," said the sergeant.

I gave him a thumbs up and away they went, still looking very skeptical. I breathed a sigh of relief and then had a bit of a laugh to myself.

If they had looked a bit more carefully they would have noticed that, of the eleven cattle in the field that day, five were heifers and six were bullocks. So a sharper policeman might have been asking me the question, "So how come one of the seven bullocks that were here the last day has turned itself into a heifer?"

A question I would have struggled to answer.

Thank God for city-boy coppers, I thought.

Chapter 20

Ranahuel
Kincasslagh
Co Donegal
1st November 1945

Dear Sally Anne,

Just a letter to say that mammy is not well at the minute. She has a bad cough and has taken to her bed. I have had Nappy McHugh over. She has the cure, as you know. She gave me poitín and says to warm it up in water and feed it to her at night. She made a hot poultice to put on her chest to see if whatever is causing this cough can be shifted. Mammy is off her food so I am going to get vegetables to make a broth for her to see if that will help. Ailish is coming up to mind her while I am away. (She sends you her love.) I will call in with the doctor and see what he says. I have your money for any medicine he gives me.

We are burning more turf than usual and I think that if the frost doesn't clear soon we will not have enough in the stack to see us through winter. I might have to ask some of the neighbours if they could spare us a load. I might get the priest to come up and say prayers for mammy. He hasn't been next nor near us since that last time he brought that man here and that was near six months ago. Some of these priests are more in a habit of visiting the people who can afford to give them a glass of whiskey or a feed than folk like us in Ranahuel. I was to tell you that your old friend Johnny Mhici Bhrid passed away three weeks ago, God rest him. He had left his youth long be-

hind him but still could play more tunes than any other man in the county. It is always sad to see the old ones passing.

I have no word about Nuala. I hope she is alright.

I have not had a letter from you for three weeks.

Le grá,

Mairead.

Chapter 21

Windsor Hotel
Cape May
New Jersey
18th November 1945

Dear Mairead,

I got your letter and I am sorry to hear about Mammy. I hope by the time you get this that she is starting to feel better. Try and keep her warm. I know you are doing that already. The poitin might work for her, please God. But if not go back to the doctor and buy whatever you need. I've heard nothing from Nuala or Mary Anne either. I have been sending her money but she has never written to say it reached her safely. Maybe it didn't. Maybe I should stop sending till I am sure she is getting it. I hope she is ok.

I am very sorry to hear the sad news about Johnny Mhici Bhrid, God rest him. He will be missed, especially at the ceilidhs. He taught me many a tune back in the day. If you come across any of his people pass on my sympathy and tell them I will be saying prayers for his repose.

It is a great coincidence that you mention him in your letter today for I was thinking about him just the other night. I found myself in a very unusual situation here because I was taken out to a bar in a nearby town. As you know I would not be greatly on for going out to bars but I was invited by this person and I went along so as not to give offence. The coincidence was that in the corner of the bar there were three men play-

ing Irish tunes. I couldn't believe my ears nor my eyes. They played so many tunes that I knew that I felt as if I was back in Donegal. I asked the man playing the bosca ceoil where he was from and he said Roscommon. He told me that the flute player was from Antrim but the fiddler was an American. An American playing Irish tunes on a fiddle, as good as anything you would hear at home! He had a very different style to us though, the same tunes but his fingers and his bow seemed to slide and slur over the notes in a way you would not hear much in our way of playing. If you closed your eyes and listened closely you could imagine that 'The maid behind the bar' was slipping and skidding about on spilled beer.

They sang a few Irish songs as well, mainly the Roscommon man. He had a great voice for singing in a pub, rough as a rusty barn door. He could change it though when he needed to, like when he sang 'Slievenamon'.

'But I never will forget the sweet maiden I met, In the valley near Slieve Na Mban'…it would have put a tear in your eye. Later on the American fiddler sang one that we have back in Ireland, 'The Butcher Boy', but I noticed they have some different words to it here. 'In Jersey City where I did dwell', for example. All the same I was able to join in here and there.

'I wish, I wish, I wish in vain,
I wish I was a maid again,
But a maid again I n'er shall be
Till cherries grow on an apple tree'.

I took very little to drink, but whatever I did take must have given me a bit of courage for I found myself talking to the fiddle player after it was all over. I asked him if he had ever heard of

Johnny Doherty, Donegal's famous fiddler. He hadn't but he played me a great jig he learned from some Dublin fiddler. Next thing you know I had his fiddle in my hand and was playing 'The Donegal Reel', just to stand up for my own county. Whatever drink it was that I had been given, it turned back the years and turned me into a performer again. I just played the one though, for it was very late and I didn't want to leave Caroline too long on her own with this other friend. As usual she got a few stares in that bar from white faces but nobody said anything to her and she survived the night. She was amazed at me, able to take that man's fiddle and play a reel. I was slow and stiff at the start but it came back to me very quick, even after all this time. I was thinking it must be twenty years since I played in front of people. It was as if the fiddle had looked at me and said, "Where ya bin?" (it being an American fiddle.)

It was a great night's craic.

I hope you get the turf sorted out before too long. You don't want mammy to be sitting there and the house freezing. And you are right about the priests, but don't be too hard on them for you will need them at the end up to look after mammy when she goes. You say he brought a man? Who was that? I don't remember you mentioning it before.

We are nearly into winter here. The seas are getting bigger with more storms forecast. It is very cold at nights. The good news is that Roisin is taking me up to Boston for Christmas. I will see Uncle Dermott again.

Love to mammy.

Le grá,

Sally Anne

****

It really was the strangest of circumstances that had me at that bar in Stone Harbour. I couldn't be telling Mairead exactly how it happened, for she would think I had turned into a wild and loose woman. Believe me I haven't, but it still amazes me what has happened.

It was after Mass one Sunday morning and I was on my own, down by the beach. I walked out along the breakwater, well muffled up against the breeze from the north. I stood listening to the ocean for a while, looking out to the east, towards Ireland. The sea had lost its blueness and was more the colour of a slate, but with constantly changing ribbons of white froth and foam. It was cold here on shore, but I would have hated to be out in a small fishing boat.

When I turned round and walked back towards the safety of the sand, I saw a strange sight. There was somebody swimming in the sea. I couldn't believe my eyes. It must have been so cold in there but this swimmer was going across the bay as if he was being chased by one of those shark fish that I hear they have around here. I never saw swimming like it. When he reached the breakwater he stood up in the waves and started wading out towards me.

Gabh sábhála Dia muid, if it wasn't the same man I had walked in on, the one in the towel. My head told me to run and get away from him before he recognised me but for some reason my legs weren't listening. I stayed on, standing staring at him like the last time. The same hairy chest but this time dripping wet with cold Atlantic water. What a sight he was and not an ounce of shame on him at all.

I turned away and started shuffling towards the hotel, but he wasn't letting me escape that easy.

"Hang on there, lady," he called after me.

What made me stop I do not know, but stop I did. I still didn't turn around, for I had had more than enough of a view of him to do me a lifetime. He came up beside me, pulling a big towel around his shivering body. I saw this out of the corner of my eyes but I wasn't for meeting his.

"You must be fed up seeing me like this," he laughed. "Next time I promise I will be dressed, but you probably won't recognise me with my clothes on, eh?"

This was funny and I couldn't help but laugh at him.

"Great," he said, "I've got a smile out of you."

"You must be mad to be going into that water," I said.

He stood back a bit as if to look at me.

"My oh my!" he said, "I just love your accent. Irish, I am guessing, right? I thought I caught a whiff of it when you came barging into my room the other day."

"I am sorry about that," I said. "I didn't mean to barge in. The girls put that sign out to play a trick on me."

"Ah sure," he said, still grinning, "and I guess, having seen me like that once, you couldn't resist having another look? I guess you told all your friends?"

These guesses were nowhere near the truth and this was all very annoying. He was very confident of himself and so mad keen to be making an ejit of me. I just shook my head and looked away but not before he had seen a bit of a smile at the side of my mouth. I risked a cheeky answer; after all I was off duty and off the hotel property.

"You must be very disappointed then that I am the only one to turn up for a look."

"Ha, ha," he said. "I dig your spirit, lady; hey look, I can't go on calling you 'lady'."

'He "digs" my spirit?' I thought. 'What sort of word is that?'

He stuck out his hand to shake and I just looked at it.

"My name is Bob," he said, "Bob Clifford. And you are?"

I took his hand. It was cold as a dead *breac* that the boys at home would be catching in the Crolly river but it didn't leave my hand as quick as one of them.

"I am Sally Anne Sweeney."

"Hello, Sally Anne Sweeney," he said. "I am very pleased to make your acquaintance."

'Oh God,' I thought. 'What am I doing here?'

We had reached the rear entrance to the hotel by this stage. He said something about being in touch later and 'headed off for a hot shower', as he put it. Me, I needed to get up to my quiet room for a bit of a think to myself.

****

The next I heard from him was in a short note. There was a plain envelope in my staff pigeon hole the next morning.

Hi Sally Anne, Want to come to a night of Irish music in Stone Harbour on Friday? Bring any of your friends. Meet me at the rear car-lot at 8.00pm. I will be the one wearing clothes. (I do have some, honestly). Please come. Bob

Irish music? Here in New Jersey? I took the bait.

Caroline owed me a favour after being the one who landed me into his room that morning, so she had little choice but to come. I'm glad she did. I would never have consented to go otherwise. We both had a great night, the best since landing here.

Mr Clifford drove very slowly on the way back to Cape May. I couldn't understand that, for he had driven like a mad man to get there. Caroline and I had been sort of hugging each other in the back seat, half-scared that we had been captured by a maniac who was going to terrify us to death, like you see in some of those movies.

His car was very modern and far bigger than any car I have ever seen in Ireland, a Cadillac something or other, red like a cherry with a shiny chrome front, a cream-coloured top and white wheels. Very grand altogether and here I was getting driven around in it, and me not exactly used to being in any kind of car. I was in the front on the return journey, Caroline having pushed me into that, but she might as well have been in the front too, for her curious head was forever stuck through between the seats.

He wanted to talk about Ireland.

I found that very odd, all the questions he was asking. Like what part of Ireland was I from? When I told him Donegal he laughed so hard I wanted to ask him what the joke was. Donegal was as good a county as any other in the country and what did he find so funny? But I didn't want to be cheeky, after him giving up his night to take us out to the music bar, so I kept quiet.

"Well, what do you know?" he said. "Donegal. That place was one of my majors."

I looked at him for clues, for I had no notion what he meant by this. His eyes just laughed back at me, loving my ignorance.

Then he asked me if I had heard of Fermanagh. Of course I had.

"Lough Erne, you know where that is?"

I had heard of it but never had been at it.

"Ever hear of Castle Archdale? No? Killadeas?"

"Never heard of them," I said, puzzled that he should be talking to me in such detail about these places.

"And you are from Donegal?" he repeated, smiling away. "You ever see any aeroplanes flying over your part of Donegal?"

I had maybe only seen one or two aeroplanes in my entire life. I didn't want to admit that though.

"I have," I said.

"Well, guess what, I might have been in one of those planes.

This left me speechless for a bit. I could not begin to imagine what he was talking about. Was this just a bit of American boasting to try to impress me? I said nothing, just waited for him to explain.

"You see, during the war, 43 and 44 to be exact, I was stationed at Castle Archdale in County Fermanagh. I was part of a flying boat crew that was based there."

"Seriously?" I said. "You have been in Ireland?"

"Northern Ireland, to be exact," he said. "But we used to fly over your county all the time."

I could not believe this. I could not take it in. Ireland was not in the war. What would be taking him into Donegal?

He saw doubt in my eyes.

"You think I'm kiddin' you?"

"I don't understand. Ireland was neutral in the war. You couldn't have been flying over County Donegal for we were not in the fighting or anything. Maybe you were lost? Maybe you are mixing it up with County Derry or something. I think Derry had some military base..."

He interrupted me with a bold laugh.

"No, no, we flew over Donegal, on every one of our sorties," he said. "I know, I know, you are right that Ireland did not join in the fighting, you stayed neutral, but there was a quiet agreement with your government that the US Air Force could fly their planes over Donegal to get more quickly out to sea, out to the north Atlantic where the German U Boats were sinking Allied ships. The British Air Force flew over Donegal as well you know."

"Are you telling me the truth?"

"I sure am," he said. "We would take off from Lough Erne..."

He caught my doubtful look again.

"Yes, from Lough Erne. You see we had these flying boats, Sunderlands and Catalinas. They could take off from water and we'd fly directly west from Fermanagh on our missions. That took us over south Donegal. I could look down and see places like Slieve League. We saved many ships, lives as well, on missions like that."

"I have never heard of this before," I told him.

It felt so strange to be schooled about my own country by this man who knew so much more about what had been going on than I did and me living there.

"We lost a couple of planes in Donegal you know. You never hear any rumours about planes coming down? One crash was up in the Blue Stack mountains, a Sunderland from my base. Happened just last year. Half the crew killed."

I had never heard of this. It must have been hushed up at the time, because, of course, Ireland, being neutral, could never admit to any knowledge about things like that.

"I am sorry about that," I said. "And you knew these men?"

"Sure, though they were RAF."

I felt stupid. I didn't know what RAF meant. I'd never heard of any of this. I felt my own ignorance but I was also beginning to feel quite a bit of awe for this man. He was starting to fascinate me. Maybe that is what he wanted to achieve. If so it was working.

But it wasn't a one-way street, as they say here. He kept going back to talk about the way I had picked up that fiddle in the bar and played that reel. It was little or nothing to me, but both himself and Caroline seemed to be charmed by it. They wouldn't have known, of course, that music used to be something right at the centre of my life. It was sort of who I was, during my early years. When I laid it down I would say I was in the middle of becoming a different person, a more serious one, certainly a less joyful one. Those tunes tonight stirred the memories of a happier me.

"How could you just play it so fluently without the notes in front of you?" my American friend was asking.

"The notes?"

"Yeah, the music."

"It's in my head, I suppose. The notes are what I play."

This seemed too much for him.

"But you must have learned it from a score?"

I think I must have looked blank at that point, for he just laughed and said, "You are something else, Sally Anne Sweeney."

He was 'something else' himself, the same boy.

At that very point I had a very vivid flashback to another time, another place and another tall handsome man who had been taken by my fiddle playing. It was the oddest thing to think that, here I am with a black girl and a middle-aged American military man, travelling slowly through the dark swamps of New Jersey in his amazing car... and to be suddenly back in Lismore in 1922, on Matthew's knee in my attic bedroom, playing a tune on his father's fiddle. Nineteen and so innocent, so fragile. Oh the memories! They die hard. I wondered briefly if he had ever received my letter.

Bob Clifford was reaching across for my hand. "Show me those fingers, see if I can figure how the magic works."

Caroline hooted with laughter from between us. I pulled my hand from his and looked out the window at the passing shadows, my neck suddenly reddened.

Chapter 22

Matthew Henderson

In the end up it was not the smuggling of cattle that landed me in trouble with the law.

A different practice altogether and again it had to do with Mary Kearney, Mary Coyle... I find it hard to get used to calling her that.

We chatted often on a Sunday. Shortly after my mother passed away we had a great argument. I suppose it must have been in August 1935, for my mother's funeral was on Monday the 13th. I remember that time well. There had been bother at the local Royal Black parade on the Sunday and everybody at the wake was talking about it. From what I heard, a few nationalist fellas objected to the march past their Gaelic pitch during a game. Castlefinn were over from Donegal playing the local team and a few sticks and stones were clodded over the hedge. One man was injured when his bowler hat was knocked off but the marchers passed on with no retaliation, the Royal Black Institution being a very dignified branch of the Orange.

Big Norman had been marching that day, being a member of that Lodge as well as the Orange, and he was not impressed.

"You'd think they could just ignore us. We were doing them no harm, just marching past on our way to the church. The band was playing hymns, for God's sake. But then I suppose those bloody heathens wouldn't recognise a hymn," he said.

Mary was there too. Her husband Liam was a great Gaelic player. Her opinion was different to Norman's of course. "They got what they were asking for," she said. When I stood up for the Black men after what Norman had told me, she rose to the bait and we had a good oul barney about it.

"They had no business to be marching past the field when there was a match going on. It was all so obvious," she said. "You should have heard how loud the band started playing going past us. And they slowed away down to make sure we noticed. It was provocation, pure and simple."

"Never," I said. "Not the Black men."

"Black men is right," she laughed. 'Every last one of yous, all black."

Though she was joking, this jibe hurt me a bit.

"We are not all the same," I said, "and you above all people should know that."

"I do, of course," she said. "By the way, I read in the paper that one of your high up Orangemen has come out and said that any member of the Orange Order being caught smuggling will be turfed out of the thing. Did you know that?"

"I heard it."

"Just as well you never joined," she said, smiling. "You'd be facing an inquisition in some dark wee Orange-hall somewhere."

I said nothing.

We were sitting around her parents' hearth on a quieter Sunday afternoon; Millie had left us and gone home. The old folks were in bed for their usual nap and, for a bit, all you could hear was the ticking of the clock on the mantlepiece. Into that silence, though I wasn't aware of it at the time, there came an idea that was to lead me into deep trouble. It arrived like a sycamore seed, floating and spinning down from the tree and finding a good spot to land and take root. Needless to say Mary Kearney was its parent.

"Matthew, Liam and I have an idea."

"Another one," I said. "What's this one?"

"You know how there's a lot of things we are very short of in the Free State?"

"So I hear."

"Well, we have this contact in Strabane. He's a good friend, a cousin of Liam. He's a businessman."

"Right," I said, wondering where this conversation was leading but at the same time knowing full well that it wasn't going to be down the narrow path of righteousness.

"We have been getting one or two parcels from him, supplies that people can't easily get over there. He makes a few bob out of it and we make a few bob out of it and nobody is any the wiser. The people buying the stuff are just glad to be getting it, so everybody is happy and no harm is done."

"Right."

"Trouble is, the Excise men are getting far too clever and they have shut down our routes, if you know what I mean."

I didn't know what she meant, but I pretended I did and just nodded.

"So people are going without essential things, just because of this bloody border and the row between the governments. It is not fair on..."

"What is it you want from me, Mary?"

She waited, looking at me.

"I am trusting you here, Matthew," she said. "We go back a long way and we owe each other a lot, so look, if you don't like this plan just forget about it and say nothing to nobody. We never had this conversation, right?"

"Right."

"Our idea is that we could use the back lane to get stuff over the mountain."

"I see."

"Sort of like the cattle trade in reverse," she said. "Our Strabane friend isn't allowed to deliver goods to my father, for he's in the Free State, but he could deliver to you. Maybe you order something from him, all above board like, and when he delivers your order he can slip you the other goods. Then at night we can bring the stuff down the back lane to daddy's. Later we will work out a way to get it up over the bog."

"What sort of goods are we talking about?" I asked.

"Mainly things like bicycle parts, tyres, tubes, chains, that sort of thing. You can't find some of these things for love nor money since the blockade," she said. "But other wee items sometimes, just what he can get. He got us a few packets of...of stuff; like things that a woman would use."

"What things that a woman would use?" I asked, being a bit innocent then about such matters.

"It doesn't matter what, you don't need to know the details," she said and hurried on to another example. "We got a box or two of candles from him one time. And tea can be hard to get with us, that and white flour, white bread. The flour in Donegal is all the rough brown type and people get sick of it. They pay well for white flour."

Goodness, I am thinking, this could be some size of a racket. Do I really want to get involved? Cattle smuggling is one thing, and the local peelers are already watching me over the head of that scam. Due to their curiosity we had had to slow up on the cattle end of things for a while and the cash coming in from that 'cross-border trade' had dried up. I did miss the extra money but I didn't miss the hassle with the police and the nervousness about being caught.

Now this new plan. Why does she want to involve me in this as well?

I sat thinking about it, Mary watching me like a hawk.

"I don't know, Mary," I told her. "There's too many risks in it for me."

"Like what?"

"Well, what could I be ordering from this Strabane man that I don't usually get in Castlederg, for one thing? How do we get the stuff down the lane in the dark? If I start a tractor in the middle of the night around here people are going to get suspicious."

"Alright, but if we can answer those questions you wouldn't be against helping out? You'd be doing ordinary folk a great favour and there will be good money in it for you."

"What sort of money?"

"Well, wait to we see. For every hundred pound profit we make after we pay the supplier we are thinking of a seventy-thirty split. We do the transporting and the sales on the other side of the border so we take seventy percent. You are taking in the goods, storing them and managing the crossing, so thirty percent. How does that sound?"

Now I am 'managing the crossing'.

"I'd be taking a wile risk here, Mary," I said. "It would need to be fifty-fifty."

"Naw, naw. We are taking a big risk too," she said. "There's risk in the transport but there's also risk in the sales; people get caught with women's stockings or something and they spill the beans and we end up losing everything. You are just the storage, that and a bit of transporting."

"Alright," I said. "But I won't do it for less than forty percent."

We agreed that she'd talk to Liam and see it that was alright with him.

As I walked back across the march to my own land I was thinking, 'Lord above, what am I getting myself into now?' I had no excuse really. It felt like another step away from my father's principles, from all that I had been brought up to think. But I found Mary to be a very powerful influence. She had something about her that held me; it wasn't a romantic hold...she was a fine-looking woman but a married one...it was just that she had a presence and a way of getting into the kernel of me and taking hold there. In some way I felt strangely honoured that she would be trusting me like this, maybe flattered that she thought me a good partner in crime. The whole secret aspect of it, the intrigue of getting one over on the authorities, stirred something in me as well. And of course the money. Things were tight enough, trying to make a living on a wee hill farm in border country. There were very few men making money and those who were, you had to suspect that they were at some game or other. The place was rife with smuggling. We were border folk. It was an accepted way of life here and I was more and more accepting of it myself.

The next time I saw Mary I was into the scheme. Liam had agreed my forty percent if I would help carry over the mountain as well. I was part of their smuggling ring.

****

It all began well enough. On two occasions, I had a small load of goods landed on me, once by lorry and once by car. I had next to no conversation with the driver who was as nervous as a kitten and was in and out of my street in no time.

Millie saw the lorry on that first delivery. She was curious. "Agh, it's just a load of stuff I ordered from Strabane," I told her. Farm stuff." But her interest got me thinking that I needed to put the goods under a lock and key until the time was right to deliver. That was awkward. Millie had never seen a door on our farm locked before and would not stop asking about it. I had to make up all sorts of lies. This smuggling thing only led to more and more deceit.

Another outcome of this was that I had to make sure that Liam and his brother only arrived in our street after Millie had gone to sleep. Then we spent half the night carrying bags of goods down the back lane and up over the mountain rodden to Liam's car. We did three sets of carries, each one took an hour and a half. We couldn't have done it except that the moon was up and we could see clearly where we were walking. You couldn't be using any lamp during these escapades. I have to confess that I felt a sense of excitement during these night-time treks. There was that strange mixture of nervousness and fear, the sweat from my exertions meeting the damp chilly air of the mountain. The craic was good too, but you couldn't be laughing out loud at the black humour, or when one of us tripped on a root and fell on our mouth and nose on the bog dirt. I would never have done this on my own. It was all about the feeling you get from being part of a gang of fellas, the bond of being a secret group able to outwit the authorities.

Anyhow, the first two or three ventures worked well and I eventually got a few pound out of them. It was good money and it encouraged me.

The next load of goods was where it all went wrong.

We had made one trip from my place up and over to Liam's car, the three of us, carrying heavy bags of flour. We had maybe two more journeys to make. On the second carry, we arrived at the old derelict cottage where Liam had parked, Liam opened the car door and we were putting the bags into the back seat when...

"Stop right there! Put your hands above your head!"

The hard voice behind us had a southern lilt to it, but it was a voice you didn't argue with. We froze on the spot, dropped the bags and did as we were told. Three Excise men had us covered with revolvers. You did not want to make any false move.

We were loaded into their van at the bottom of the lane and driven to Lifford Garda station.

That was the end of my smuggling career for the time being.

When it was discovered the next morning that I was from Northern Ireland, I was driven back to the border at Strabane and handed back in handcuffs to the RUC.

****

The upshot of the thing was that I was fined twenty-five pounds, all the remaining goods were confiscated and I was bound over to keep the law for two years, on pain of imprisonment if I should fail to do so. Liam and the brother got similar sentences across the border.

In the past the shooting of Joe and then Alice running out on me had brought me cart loads of shame and derision but they were nothing compared to this new disgrace. The local newspaper ran the story, my name included with other notorious smuggling gangsters in west Tyrone. I even made it into a sermon in the church in Castlederg; the clergyman did not use my name of course, but there wouldn't have been a single sinner in the congregation who didn't realise who he was referring to.

"'Render therefore unto Caesar the things which are Caesar's and unto God the things that are God's,'" he preached. "And what that means here in our society in 1935, is that you don't cheat on taxes, you don't try to steal from the government and you have nothing to do with smuggling, whether as a buyer or a seller."

I would have been deaf and blind not to have been aware of a few sideways glances, throat clearings and under-the-breath mutterings. The worst experience was when I encountered Wilbert Porter. I should have had the wit to stay away from the bank, but I only realised that too late. There I was standing in the bank queue about to make a lodgement of cash that I had earned legitimately after selling half a dozen young sows. Porter happened to walk along behind the counter, saw me and stared like he had just witnessed a hanging. Out he came from behind the counter and, instead of the usual warm handshake, he caught me roughly by the elbow.

"Am I ever glad that my daughter chose to break off her engagement to you, young man," he said in a voice that was meant only for me but carried throughout the whole of the hushed bank. He looked at the wad of pound notes I had in my hand. "Tell me honestly now, can you guarantee that this cash is not the product of another smuggling run, can you?"

I mumbled a faint protest. "Of course it's not," I said. "I earned this from selling pigs at Strabane market last week."

"Hmmph," he said turning away. "I hope they were pigs you reared yourself and not the litter of some Free State outfit."

With that he disappeared into an office behind and I heard a shuffling of feet as other customers moved east or west of me, and not because I was smelling of pig manure either.

Jane and her man landed in on me one Sunday with their squad of wains. They had read the report in the paper and Jane wanted to tell me how disgusted she was with me. There was very little I could say so I just sat and looked at the fire in the hearth while her anger burned itself out. They only stayed an hour or so, for a couple of the children were coming down with the cold. The noise of them coughing and crying would have put you out of the house. The way my head was then, with the sound of gerning wains and the truth that Jane was hammering me with, it was a relief to see them drive out the street.

"The good name of Henderson is in the dirt," she had said and she wasn't far wrong.

Chapter 23

Sally Anne Sweeney

I had never heard of this Thanksgiving thing that everybody's been fussing about for the last week. Today we are right in the middle of it and I have a new job. I am a waitress in the hotel's dining room. Only for today though, just to be an extra hand. Roisin told me there would be so many guests that she needed more help. She also wanted me to be part of this Thanksgiving party, to see what it's all about.

I am not sure I understand the reasons for this celebration, but Caroline says it goes away back to the first people to set foot in America, the first white Christian people anyway. She says they feasted on wild turkeys to celebrate their first harvest in this new country. These modern Americans know how to celebrate too and the poor turkeys are still the main thing on the menu, God love them. Nothing much has changed for the turkeys.

I am serving a few dishes that I never heard of, like sweet potato casserole, cornbread stuffing and roasted sprouts. Then a pudding called pumpkin pie. I can't wait to taste these things after the party is over, if these folk leave us any.

The hotel has put on a big spread for a whole crowd of people from the town, the poorer people, to be fair, the ones who maybe can't afford to have turkey and all the other stuffings as well. It is good of the hotel owners to do this and the atmosphere in the place is great. It is an even bigger thing here than Christmas, I am told.

The top table seems to have a few of the town dignitaries, the hotel owners and a couple of special sponsors of the event. As I am serving, I am more than surprised to catch sight of Bob Clifford sitting there at the far end of that table. He winked at me and I nearly spilled the gravy on a poor woman's lap. I thought he was back home in Philadelphia, but here he is, large as life, the heart and soul of the thing. How come he is back so quickly? He told me his business with the naval base was finished until after Christmas.

To be honest, that thought had saddened me a bit. He wouldn't know this, but I have looked forward to him arriving back into the hotel, as he has done quite regularly. He has a way of cheering everybody up, so the thought of him not being around for the next five or six weeks put a shadow across me. When I realised this, it puzzled and annoyed me, because I like to think of myself as not needing anybody, especially any man, to make me happy. I have become content in my own mind about how I handle the world and I am sort of proud of that independence, so to think of me looking forward to the brief meetings and conversations I have with Bob Clifford, well it gives me an unusual and complicated feeling.

Anyhow, here he is back in the hotel to confuse me some more. I try to avoid that area of the dining room, almost to the point of turning my back on it so that I do not meet his eyes. I notice myself moving around between the rows of tables in a sideways manner, keeping my head diverted from that end of the room.

'Why am I doing this?' I ask myself. 'Just be normal. I mean nothing to him, apart from being someone whose accent he likes to hear, someone he can make fun of to amuse himself.'

When I hear his voice calling 'Waitress' in my direction I pretend not to hear and, sure enough, another girl goes to wait on him. But eventually Roisin sends me to collect plates from the top table and I have no choice. I begin at the end furthest away from him, leaving his corner to the last. By the time I get to him I have so many plates piled up that I can barely see over the top.

'Sweet Mary, please do not let me drop this pile of plates on him,' I pray.

I needn't have worried. Just as the pile was getting too heavy for me, doesn't he get up and take them from my hands.

"Here honey, you look like you're gonna struggle with that. Let me help," he says.

I have no choice. I can't fight him off and tell him to sit-down and mind his own business, not even if I wanted to. He gives me a great white-toothed smile, in front of everybody at that top table of special people. They all see it, they all see me go the colour of the cranberry jelly as Bob carries my pile of plates safely to the serving table at the back of the dining room, me following him like a pet dog.

"There you go, Sally Anne," he says with a grin as he passes me on the way back to his seat. "Anything else I can do for you? Just let me know."

"Thanks," I whisper.

"No problem. Can I see you after the dinner, maybe a walk on the Boardwalk?"

I give him a quick embarrassed nod that turns into a shake halfway through. It could mean anything. I run to the kitchen.

Later, when I reappear in the dining room, isn't the whole roomful of people listening to Bob Clifford making a speech. Why is he talking? There is enthusiastic cheering and clapping when he finishes and sits down and then I understand why; the hotel owner gets up and thanks him for helping to fund tonight's dinner 'for these citizens of the borough'. Goodness, he must be made of money, this man.

When it is all over, I make my way to my bedroom on the top floor. I sit for a while on my bed and have a think to myself. What is it I am doing here? This middle-aged man that I know very little about is asking me to go out for a walk on a cold November night in a strange town and I am considering doing it? I say 'middle-aged'. I am guessing he must be at least ten years older than me. I know he works as some sort of advisor to the military in the naval base up the road. I know he has been in Ireland during the war. I know he is from Philadelphia because he mentioned it a few times on our recent car journey. He didn't happen to mention whether or not he is married though. He is not wearing a ring of any sort, but I cannot believe that such a handsome and well-off man has been single all his life. But, I ask myself, why does this matter? It is no business of mine whether or not he is married. I am not in a bother about it, I tell myself. It is not as if he is interested in me for anything other than a bit of craic, the accent and the charm of someone from another country, a place where some of his ancestors apparently came from. And I am only interested in him because... well, because he is interested in me, I suppose.

Am I going to go and see if he is waiting for me down in the lobby or the bar? Why not? If he is, then fine, we can go out for a walk. If not, then I'll know it was just a bit of nonsense he was talking.

I have a quick shower. I need it, for it was hot work, that waitressing, in and out of that kitchen so quick I was scared I'd meet myself coming the other way. I love this shower idea they have here. At home you get a bath maybe once a fortnight, lukewarm water heated up on the open fire and poured into a tin bath in front of the hearth. The water would be used more than once, Mairead usually went first, then myself. We were lucky that there were only the two of us. In some families, the wee ones near the head of the queue got the best of the water, clean and at its hottest. After half a dozen of your brothers and sisters had been bathed, it was anything but. How different to be able to take your own shower everyday if you want one, nice and warm and private, and tonight I want just that. I want to feel clean and fresh and at myself.

I only have the one set of decent clothes, so I dress in them, brush my hair, pull on a coat and scarf against the cold of the evening and go down the stairs to the lobby. He is not there. I wait a few minutes and then decide to look in the bar. My heart is fluttering like a moth at the window as I push open the swinging door and go in, for I think Roisin said when I started here that the bar is only for guests. Ah well, I can be his guest tonight, if he is here. Sure enough there he is, a drink in his hand.

"Sally Anne," he says, bouncing towards me. "I was about to give up on you. Would you like a drink? Of course you would."

As he turns to the bar he must catch the hesitation in me.

"I am fine thanks, no drink please," I say awkwardly. One or two other men look in my direction at the sound of my accent.

"You sure? Ok, maybe we'll walk first and then pop in for a hot whiskey to warm us up afterward, how about that?"

"Ok, sure," I say. I am even copying his phrases I realise. 'Stay true to yourself, Sally Anne,' I think, then I realise, 'But that would mean going into Gaelic, wouldn't it?'

We go out into the chilly air and walk in the direction of the boardwalk; it seems to be the place for such walks. Bob chatters on for a bit about nothing in particular.

"I hope you didn't mind me relieving you of those plates," he says.

"'Course not," I say. "Thanks, but it did embarrass me a bit."

"And why would it do that?"

"Because! It made me look a bit of a handless *créatúr* that was about to drop them."

"A handless créatúr?" he laughed. "Is that Irish or something. It sounds so quaint."

"*Créatúr* is... It is just something we say. A handless *créatúr* is just a clumsy person, I suppose."

"You Irish have the gift of the gab, I'll say that for you," he says. "Fascinating."

I say nothing. Just walk on, head down against the cold of the Atlantic air. He notices and switches around to the inside of the boardwalk, walking closer to me and giving me a wee bit of protection from the wind.

"I want to hear more about you, Sally Anne," he says.

"Why?"

"Why? Why not? Here you are walking with me, talking to me, flirting with me and I know very little about you, except that you can play the fiddle and you talk with such a beautiful accent that you've brought with you from Ireland, and so I just want to..."

"I am not flirting with you, if that means what I think it means," I tell him.

"Why, what do you think it means?"

That shuts me up. I don't want to spell it out. Laughing, he hops out in front of me to try to see my reaction.

"Anyway," I tell him, "there is nothing to know. I am just an ordinary Irish woman who came to your country to find work and make a bit of money. And by the way, you are the one should be telling me about yourself, for I know very little about you."

"Ok honey," he says, "and what would you like to know?"

It is on the tip of my tongue to ask him if he is married, but I shy away from it. Maybe later I will have the courage to ask. Instead I play safe and ask him about the dinner tonight.

"I didn't know you were so well off, like giving that dinner for all those people tonight. That was nice."

"You think? It was nothing. Anyway I didn't pay the whole bill, I just made a generous donation, shall we say."

"Well, it was good of you. I didn't know you were so rich."

"I am not rich, not compared to some. But I have done ok," he says, "I got into the consultancy business after the war, using the experience I gained in your little country."

I don't have a clue what 'consultancy' means and he must guess that.

"Basically I advise the government about weapons and the like," he says. "It pays well and what is even better about my job is that it brings me down here to Cape May so often so I can see more of you."

This is too much for me. He is so forward, so sure of himself. I would rather he hadn't said that, or at least not said it so early in our conversations. He must read my cool reaction to his comment for he turns it into a joke straight away.

"Forgive me, I was going to say, 'So you can see more of me' and then I remembered you have seen more of me than most other ladies I know."

I must look puzzled again for he feels the need to spell it out to me. "The towel episodes," he laughs.

"Oh right," I say catching on.

Then after a bit he goes back to prying into my life before coming here.

I tell him a bit about life in the west of Donegal and he seems interested, surprised by a lot of what I say. Obviously you can spend time in an airfield in County Fermanagh but know next to nothing about how people around you are living in their cottage poverty, at least those ones who are living in the west. I talk him through what life is like during our various seasons, I talk about the local Mullaghduff flute band and the lads who play football on the banks and Kincasslagh parish. I describe my narrow little life looking after my mother in the isolation of Ranahuel mountain.

He listens well and I get the impression he is very taken by my story. Then comes the question that I should be asking him.

"So what about your love life?"

Just the very way he expresses this knocks me off my stride.

"I don't have a love life," I say, the annoyance clear in my tone.

"Sorry, I didn't mean to imply…I just mean do you have a husband, a partner, lover, anything like that?"

He is far too direct. I splutter to answer. In all my life nobody has ever asked me this kind of question or spoken to me so brazenly about such matters. I am shocked by it, but I get around to answering in a minute.

"I don't have much interest in that kind of thing."

"Come on, Sally Anne? You are kiddin' me. A good-looking lady like you? You must have had dozens of suitors tripping over each other."

"Well I haven't," I tell him and I am being honest.

"What? Absolutely none? You never been in love?"

I look away so I can think about this question. Was I ever in love? Only once, I think, that's if it was love and not just a passing fancy.

"I had a sweetheart once, but it was so long ago I can hardly remember," I tell him. He won't let it pass though.

"How long? How old were you?"

"I was eighteen, if it's any of your business," I say, too sharply. He pays no heed to my tone.

"And what happened?"

Now that's a good question and a long story of an answer.

"Ireland happened, that's what happened," I tell him and now it is his turn to look puzzled. Before he can ask any more I get my question in.

"Right, Mr Clifford. Now it must be your turn."

"What you wanna know?"

"I don't want to know anything but I think you owe it to me to even up the score."

He laughs.

"I like your style, honey. That was a neat put-down. Ok, I guess you want to know if I have any kids, right?"

"That will do, for a start."

"OK. I have two fine sons. Very proud of them. Robert Junior is twenty and Johnny is eighteen. I don't see so much of them now since their mother and I separated."

I know full well what he is telling me here, and why. I want to be sure I understand him though.

"Separated?" I ask.

"Yeah, divorced. Years ago."

"Sorry," I say, stupidly, for I am not a bit sorry.

"Ah thank you, but don't be. It's life. These things happen."

We have reached Convention Hall without really noticing how far we have walked or how chilly it has become. Bob takes my arm briefly and guides me into the cover of its reception area, just to get out of the wind.

"Look," he says, pointing to a poster on the notice board. "A Thanksgiving Dance on Saturday night. That's the day after tomorrow. What do you say if I hang on here for another couple of nights and we go dancing together?"

"You have never seen me dance or you wouldn't be making a suggestion like that."

"Ha ha," he says. "I bet you can. Irish girls are meant to be able to dance like dervishes."

"Not this one."

"But you will come? Please? I promise to teach you all you need to know."

"I'd like to, but I have nothing to wear," I plead. "These are the only decent clothes I have."

"My, my," he says. "What have you been doing with all the dough you're earning? All my generous tips?"

"Not much. Certainly not spending it on clothes. I send most of it home."

"I can believe that," he says.

Then he stands back to study me up and down, the way you would look at a pony you are buying, like men looked at me in Strabane hiring fair years ago. But he smiles at me.

"You'll be just fine, honey. Real fine."

I protest but it does me no good.

As we leave the protection of the hall he takes my hand and tucks it under his arm as we walk back, me walking in the shelter of him. The spray of the Atlantic smells so familiar and reminds me of home, walking Mullaghdearg strand with a big sea coming in. At the same time nothing about this evening is anything like home, not a single thing. I have never, in my whole life, walked Mullaghdearg strand with a man. Ailish was as good as it got, as far as I recall.

It feels tonight, for these brief moments anyhow, that I am beginning to belong, that the loneliness I have lived with for so many years might be starting to fade away. This is another life, one I have never believed would be possible. Somebody is showing me care, paying me attention, possibly even more than care and attention, but it is too early to think of such things. I am old enough to enjoy this without taking it too seriously, am I not? Yes I am, but I still hug close to him. It is a biting wind after all.

If you had told me before I left home that I would find myself in this sort of situation, out walking the street with an American man, his big muscular arm around me, I would have said you were mad. This is not who I am, certainly not who I have been over the past twenty years. What has changed me? Being in a different place shouldn't have altered my nature or left me vulnerable to this kind of circumstance, this flattery, this handsome stranger, but here I am and I have to admit that I am enjoying the thrill of it all. I know my limits and I am mature enough to be able to weigh things up and know where to draw a line when I see that pleasure might lead to pain. I have a feeling he and I are both in that stage of enjoying each other's company, even the physical affection I am getting from him, without much thought about where this thing is going.

To be fair to him, when we reach the hotel he leads me into the bar and we have that promised hot whiskey. Half way through, a couple of other men who seem to know him appear in the bar and he excuses himself from me, all very polite and goes off to speak with them. Later a cheery "Goodnight" from the alcove and a quick wave of the hand as I pass his group and head for bed. I don't mind at all. It was a lovely cosy walk and I am warmed by his company, almost as much as by the whiskey.

Friday afternoon I am stuffing soiled linen down the laundry chute when Roisin appears on my landing, a parcel under her arm.

"Hey girl, this is for you."

"What is it?" I ask, pausing in my work.

"No idea, but Mr Clifford seems pleased with himself. Open it. I'm curious."

I do as she tells me. In the parcel I find no less than three dresses. What has he done, the mad ejit? Three gorgeous dresses. Roisin's eyes are near popping out of her head.

"You've obviously made a big impression, Sally Anne," she says. "What brought this on? These are worth a fortune."

I am flustered as I try to explain and it isn't hard for Roisin to work out why. I have little option but to tell her the truth.

"We are going dancing tomorrow night. He wanted me to have something nice to wear, for I have nothing, nothing suitable."

"Well, what do you know? My little Irish cousin has caught a big one."

"It's not like that," I protest. "He's just a kind sort of a man, I think."

"I think so too," she laughs. "Just a kind sort of man who can't resist impressing his pretty Irish colleen."

"Oh Roisin, please don't make too much of it."

"I won't, of course I won't, but you be careful. My guess is that a man as handsome as Bob Clifford has got to be married," she says.

I am so glad I am able to clear this up for her.

"He was married," I say. "He told me this. He has two sons as well, but he is divorced now. He told me all about it."

"Ah, ok. So, go for it, cousin."

Later when I open the parcel properly and examine the dresses I am stunned by their beauty. They are each in a different style, different colours as well, but each one so grand and eye-catching. How can I choose one, how can I wear a gown like this?

I try on all three, Caroline advising with nearly as much excitement as me. Eventually I settle on the green one. It fits me perfectly. How could he have guessed my size so well? Apart from how beautifully it fits me, it is the colour I have always liked best. Green as spring grass, with a pattern of little white flowers all over it, a white collar that hangs down to my breast, quite tight at the waist, just below my knee in length and with short sleeves that stop half way down to my elbows. I have never, in all my born days, worn anything so 'glamourous', as Caroline calls it. Oh I wish I had somebody with a camera to take a photograph of this. I think I would send it to Ailish. She wouldn't recognise me at all like this.

"Look at your old friend," I would tell her. "The shabby Cinderella all dressed up to go to the ball."

The other dresses, a blue one and a red one, I parcel up neatly to give back to Bob for returning to the shop later.

My night's sleep is entirely ruined by the bubbling excitement inside. It is as if I am in my youth again, dreaming stupid fantasies and waking every so often to find they aren't real. Somehow the morning comes and somehow I work my way through the day to the evening, to dressing up and tripping down the staircase with a few whistles from my grinning workmates. I arrive at Bob's car in the parking lot, parcelled dresses under my arm. He is holding the door open for me.

He tells me I look 'fab'. The green one is a great choice, suits my complexion and my fair hair, according to him.

When I try to return the other two to him, he is having none of it.

"Keep all three, please. I will never have the figure to wear them myself," he tells me.

"But they must have cost you a fortune?"

"Lady, the way you look in this one, it was worth every cent. Just think of it as an early Christmas present, ok? Now let's get outa here."

The dance itself passes in a haze. Maybe I've had too many glasses of wine, making me feel giddy as a new-born lamb, but it seems to be over before it is right started. Bob dances with me from the start. He is very patient because I know very little about swing dancing, in spite of trying it with Caroline a while ago. He has a job teaching me all these strange steps and keeping me from falling over at the same time. I can handle the slow dances alright and I enjoy his manly arms around me in a 'real slow' close-up waltz, the scent of whatever he is wearing just about suffocating me. When I tell him I like his perfume he laughs so hard at me I think he is going to bust his waistcoat buttons.

"Not perfume, honey. It's called after-shave here in America. Don't say perfume or you'll have the bouncers on my case."

I am enjoying the band. There are trumpets, flutes, a piano, drums and a few other wind instruments. When the announcer booms out through his microphone thing that the next dance set will be the 'jitterbug', I think he is joking. That is one dance I have never heard of and one dance that I will not be trying, but everybody else is getting very excited about it and jumping out on the dance-floor. Bob tries to persuade me, but I hold my ground and tell him I'd rather watch him do it with someone else, rather than make a mess of it for both of us. He finds another woman and I watch in amazement at his energy in this crazy, mad dance. I'm laughing at him but I notice just a wee trace of jealousy deep inside me as he laughs with his partner, swinging her around as if she is his favourite rag-doll. I am exhausted watching them.

It is a great night altogether. I can't remember enjoying myself so much, not for a very long time. He drives me back to the hotel, very slowly again, I notice. We stop outside in the car park; he leans across the car seat and pulls me close. Maybe it is the drink but I find myself kissing a man for the first time since 1922.

Twenty-three years is a long time to have denied myself.

It won't be so long till next time, I promise myself.

Bob leaves for Philadelphia in the morning, telling me he will not be back in Cape May until the new year. I have expected this, but it is still hard to watch from a second floor window as he drives away. His goodbye wave as he turns out on to the street sends a rush of desire through the area where my heart used to feel safe.

Chapter 24

Matthew Henderson

I vowed to have nothing more to do with smuggling. The money side of the thing had been great, but I found that I couldn't live with the pressure that was coming at me from the folk I had to live with in my community. On top of the looks and nudges and abuse that I got in the town, I had neighbours who had always been good friends who were now barely able to speak to me, the Smiths and the Thompsons for example. To be fair to John Sproule, he kept coming up to the house. Maybe it was because Millie always made him a great fry, or maybe he still saw me as his mission in life. Part of me welcomed his visits but an even bigger part dreaded them.

His preaching started to wear me down. He was constant in this; he had this special divine commission to rescue me from the 'smuggling habit', as he called it. I tried to explain that it was not a 'habit', that I was only trying to help out my friends across the fence.

"Your 'friends'? Those people are not your friends, Matt. They are bad company for you, sent to tempt you off the straight and narrow. You have got to be done with them," he told me.

"I have done with them," I said. "Or at least I have done with the trade thing. No more smuggling for me, honestly. I'm done with it."

"You have to be done with them," he said.

"Not at all," I told him. "You're taking it too far, John. You have to be neighbourly."

"You have to be saved, my friend. Never worry about other people, especially that sort. They only want to lead you down the broad road to destruction."

I wasn't going to argue with him, but I did feel that this was a right selfish view of religion. It didn't strike me as anything like the man who started the whole thing off, but then I was no expert.

I kept my word too. I had plenty of opportunities to get involved again, plenty of contacts with yer man in Strabane and manys a chat with Mary and Liam Coyle. I never let them get the better of me, not once. I was determined to stay clean. Whether people in the area believed me or not, I didn't really care. I can understand their suspicions of course, but in my heart I was proud of the new leaf I had turned over. I had proved to myself that the leopard can change its spots. I was an ex-smuggler now. Sure, I would never turn away from doing a neighbour a good turn, but I would stop well short of anything that smelt of corruption.

It was all going well until Liam Coyle arrived at my door one Sunday evening, sometime in the early summer of 1937. Millie had been over the fields at Kearneys' place and she had told me that I had missed Liam and Mary and the wains. I was sorry about that but I had taken to my bed with a bit of a temperature; a couple of aspirins knocked me out for the whole afternoon until milking time but now I was reviving.

Liam wanted to speak to me.

"Matthew, come over with me till you see this bull," he said.

I didn't have any idea what he was talking about, but he explained as we wandered down the back lane to Kearney's. Seems he had come across this animal on some wee farm up in the back of beyond, near Finntown. He had been in the hills shooting rabbits and had got talking to an oul farmer he met. This man owned a mighty bull, but had given up on it for, though it was a fine animal, it was very hard to work with, never mind to feed on his poor mountain grass. It kept breaking out in search of richer pasture.

Liam bought the bull off him for next to nothing and brought it all the way to Gortnagappel with his tractor and trailer a few days later. It must have taken him hours. He had the divil of a job with the beast, leading it up over the mountain to Kearneys' good pasture with the help of his brother.

"If it hadn't been for the chain and the ring on its nose we woulda bin bate," Liam said.

"And what are you planning to do with it?" I asked. "Anthony doesn't need the hassle with a rough animal and he doesn't need a bull, for he can always bring his heifers over to mine."

"I know, I know," he said. "It's not for Anthony. I'll be trying to sell it on in the north."

I looked at him and he read what I was thinking.

"Naw, don't you be worrying Matt. I'll not be asking you to have anything to do with it. I'll get some dealer to come and take it off me some dark night. Maybe around the Twelfth, when the police and all are busy somewhere else. Might not get as good a price but I will still have a decent profit."

I was relieved. I didn't need this kind of business at this stage.

We reached the field with the bull in it. My eyes nearly came out of my head. I had never seen an animal like him. He was like something you'd see at the pictures. Black and shiny as a raven, with short, intimidating horns, he carried his head high and proud as if to say, "Have you ever set eyes on anything like me before?" I hadn't either. He was enormous. How on earth had Liam managed to lead him up that spongy path across the bog?

As we looked at him from beyond the gate he seemed calm. There were no other animals in the field and he looked like he had eaten his fill of Anthony's rich grass. He saw us and started wandering across the field towards us. You could nearly feel the ground quivering. Then he stopped and bellowed and I swear he could have been heard in Castlederg. That huge deep chest of his, the breadth and muscle of his rump, the way he carried his head, he was one impressive lump of beef, that was for sure. I was nearly tempted to make an offer for him there on the spot, but the thought of how I would explain his presence on my farm to John, to anyone interested, chased the notion out of my head before I could give voice to it. 'Still,' I thought, 'you have to marvel at a creature like that, as near perfect a beast as I have ever set eyes on.'

Would that I had never set eyes on him!

That was the Sunday. Sometime on the night of the following Tuesday, the same perfect beast invaded my land and had his way with a couple of my heifers that had been coming into heat. Now that might have been welcomed, except that to get out of the field to go to do the job, he had to demolish a sturdy stone dake that had stood on Kearney's land for generations, wade through the burn, fight his way through fences, bushes and barbed wire and jump another stone ditch into my field to get to my heifers.

What happened my own bull, you might ask? When I arrived out to survey the damage, he was lying in a corner licking his wounds and looking very sorry for himself. The visitor had bullied him out of his patch and taken control of his harem. It must have been some scrap, but my oul Shorthorn stood no chance against this brute. The black bull stood on a wee rise in the middle of the field, a picture of defiance. "I'm the boy!" he seemed to be saying.

I grabbed a good stout stick and climbed the gate. I have never been afraid of any animal and I had an urge inside me to test myself against this one. I had only walked ten yards into the field when he squared himself around towards me, lowered his mighty head and bellowed. There was no pawing the ground. He just took off. He was heading straight toward me at top speed. A thoroughbred horse wouldn't have kept up with him. He didn't seem to build up this pace, he just had it right from launching.

I was scared, I admit it. Fear got the better of me and I was back over that gate in a flash. Thankfully I had the sense to stand to the side. The bull hit my gate at top speed. It was a sturdy gate, well anchored and with good strong timber running left to right and at the diagonal. There was a crash of splintering wood. The gate held but some of the planks were wrecked. The bull's head came through. There it was, sticking out from the remaining planks like some of those trophy heads you would see on the walls of old-time castles. I had my chance. I hit that hoary head a couple of good thumps across the nose and the bull bellowed again, shaking its head loose and backing into the field. I had a sort of victory over him but, at the same time, I had the gate to thank for my life.

Later, I was to regret not grabbing that chain while I had the chance close up and tying it to the post at the side of the gate. Instead I made my way down to Anthony to tell him what had happened. I did not want this monster on my land for any longer than was necessary, especially after my history with the authorities.

Anthony was going to be of no help, of course, given his age and infirmity. He did advise me though, that I should drive over to Liam at once and get him to come and help get the bull into a secure shed or something. I followed his advice that afternoon. It was his responsibility, we agreed, and Liam had a great way with animals. He would know how to handle it. He had walked the bull all the way up over the mountain, after all.

I drove to Castlefinn using the Border crossing at Kilclean. There wasn't too much trouble getting through, I got my passbook stamped and promised to be back inside the hour. When I got to Liam's he was in the fields and I had to go looking for him. He was easy enough talked into coming with me to see what we could do with the bull and he set off following me in his car. We were fifteen minutes over the hour. I must have caught the Customs men on the northern side in a good mood for they let me through no bother at all. I drove on towards home, but a mile down the road I slowed to wait for Liam. He was nowhere to be seen. I sat for a while waiting, then I thought to myself, 'He can come in his own time, he knows the way,' and I drove on home.

It was ages later that he arrived into my yard in his wee car, but lo and behold, he was not alone. Right behind him was a black car. It screeched to a halt in my yard and out stepped three Customs and Excise men. One of them was by the name of Bamford, from Donemana or up that way somewhere. I'd come across him before.

"What the hell are they doing here?" I said to myself.

I wasn't long in finding out. They had interviewed Liam, him being a known smuggler and him being on the road with another known smuggler, myself. They must have put two and two together and thought that these two chancers are up to something. Liam's chat hadn't been able to bluff them at all.

He sat on briefly in his car and I saw defeat in his face. When he eventually did get out, he held his hands out to me as much as to say, 'Sorry mate, I have landed you in it.'

The officers made straight for the damaged gate and stood staring into the field where the bull was back on his command post and not looking any less menacing.

In my head I was thinking, 'Go on lads. Hop over the gate there and take a closer look at him, see how you get on asking him questions.' No such luck though.

"So, Mr Henderson. When did you smuggle this beast across the border?"

I was presumed guilty right from the very start of the affair. It was maybe understandable on their part. I was going to have a serious job of argument to do to convince these men of the truth. I was innocent. I had nothing to fear surely? Nothing except my reputation.

"That bull has nothing to do with me," I said. "It broke into my land last night from Kearney's. You can go down and check the fence down there. You'll see where he ripped his way through."

"I told them this already, Matt," Liam said. "They won't believe me."

"So another break-in, is it?" Bamford laughed, the sarcasm tripping him. "You seem to be a great attraction for Free State cattle, don't you? They all want to break into your land. What is it about your grass that tempts a bull all the way from Finntown, eh? Last time I seem to remember it was two heifers had made the crossing. That was four or five years ago, if I remember right?"

"Aye, maybe that."

"We have been waiting a long time to catch you again. The Donegal fellas caught the pair of you in the act of smuggling, but that was just a few bits and pieces of contraband. This is a lot more serious. This bull is worth a lot of money. We will be starting criminal proceedings against you; and we'll be taking possession of the bull, you understand?"

'All the best with that,' I thought. 'I can't wait to see how yous manage him.'

I could say nothing of course. They weren't going to believe me, not this time, not after the previous conviction. Liam neither. I knew he would be arrested and handed over to the Irish authorities.

And all because my heifer mooed over a few stone dakes to this black bastardin' bull.

One of the Customs fellas was looking around my yard. "Have you a shed we can put him in 'til we get a lorry up here for him?" he said.

"Surely," I said, trying to be helpful, but wondering how they were going to manage this. "That shed at the far end of the street."

Liam was smiling at them as he was being handcuffed.

"Yous just going to grab the bull by the horns, fellas? 'Cause if you do I want to be here to see it," he told them.

"Never you mind that."

"I have told you the truth, men. This is my bull. It was in my father-in-law's land over there. That is the Free State. I swear to you that it broke into Henderson's."

"And I came floating up the Derg in a bubble."

"It's the truth I'm telling you."

"Tell the court then. See if they believe you there. Now, stand there and shut up."

Liam shook his head, a smile on his face.

"I have to warn yous, you'll not be able to take my bull. He'll murder you first," he said.

Sure enough, as soon as the three men opened what was left of the gate and entered the field, the bull charged them, just as he had done with me. Back out the gate they ran and slammed it shut just in the nick of time. I thought they were going to dirty themselves with the sight of all that black muscle pounding down the hill at them.

The two of us stood laughing out of the sides of our mouths. That didn't go down well with the Customs men.

"So how would you catch him, smart Alec?" said one of them, turning angrily to Liam.

"Try him with a carrot; he'll eat it out of your hand," I told him with a smile.

"You keep your ideas to yourself," he glowered.

"I wouldn't be trying to catch him," Liam said. "Sure just let him be. He's doing nobody any harm. You'll never be fit to capture him anyway. You would need an army."

"We don't need an army," the man said. "We just need a butcher with a lorry."

I looked at Liam. He was staring in disbelief at this.

"You can't be serious," he said. "That bull has done nobody any harm."

"Not yet, he hasn't."

"Look lads, if you let me out of these handcuffs I promise you I can get hold of him for yous."

'That would be a brave course of action,' I thought. The officials weren't giving in though.

"Lads, if I give you twenty pound each, will yous let the bull live? Let me take him back over the border. You'll hear no more about it. Come on now, be decent. He's a fine animal."

"That may be true, but once we get the butcher here he's going to be a dead fine animal. Get into the back of the car till we deliver you to the Garda at Clady bridge."

Liam took a last look at the bull and I swear he had tears in his eyes as he turned away.

True to their word, they arrived back in the evening. Behind them was a green Foden lorry with a ramp at the back and a winch system. I couldn't bear to watch so I went inside and took my dinner. Half way through eating I heard the gunshots, two of them, then the lorry reversing from the yard into the field. After a while it returned and drove slowly out of our yard. The bull was on its way to the butchers.

And I was soon to be on my way to Omagh Courthouse, charged with the unlawful import of cattle from a foreign jurisdiction.

Chapter 25

47 Eskeside Road
Musselburgh
Dec 1945

Dear Mairead and Sally Anne,

I ken that Sally Anne might not be still in Ireland but Mairead can pass this news on.

Our Nuala is in a terrible bad way. It's her nerves. They are away to hell altogether and she has been like this for weeks. I can't mind how far back it started but ever since she arrived here way me she has been poorly. She would eat nothing and wasn't in a bother about feeding her bairn either. I could do nothing way her. She has got as skinny as a rake and there never was much to her even when she was at herself. She doesn't listen to a word that comes out of my mouth. We fight all the time, her and me, and if we are not fighting then she is in her bed and crying half the time like a baby with the toothache. She won't get off her arse and go out and look for a job, she doesn't go to Mass any more, she has lost any friends she used to have about here.

You try to bring up your bairns as best you can and this is the thanks you get from them. I can do no more for her or for the bairn. He sits greeting all day, every day. I took him once to see the doctor but he said there wasn't a thing wrong way him. Nuala won't go to the doctor. She says she is scared they will lock her up and throw away the key. In my opinion they could do worse for she is a hopeless case and that's no word of a lie.

If she's not on the drink she is just lying here in my road, gerning about everything. And if she's not doing that she is away out at nights and doesn't be coming in till the morning. I have no notion what she is at. Some man or other I think but she just tells me she has been away for a walk. Some walk she must be doing, all night on the roads. It's not good for the bairn to be so much on his own but there's nothing I can do. I am far too oul to be looking after him. Them folk that belong to her man never look near us. They have no thought at all for their grandson, now that their son is lying at the bottom of the sea. You would think they would come looking for the bairn, just to see if he has their family likeness if nothing else but not a peep out of them. Are they Christian folk at all, and them Presbyterians? I have a right mind to take the bairn to wherever it is they live and dump him on them for a month or two and see how they like it, hippocrits that they are.

Sally Anne was right and decent to our Nuala when she come over to her in Glasgow last summer, so Nuala told me. If she is in America I suppose there is not much that she can do, maybe she could send us a few bob sometime if she can spare it and I wouldn't be the begging type, but it would help feed the bairn.

I hope Aunt Annie is in good form. She must be a grand age now. She'll not be able to say it of course but I am sure she is glad of you about the house Mairead.

Your cousin
Mary Anne Quinn

Chapter 26

Sally Anne Sweeney

December. I am nearly six months into this new life of mine and it is back up north to Boston with Roisin, that long torture of a car journey, to spend the Christmas season with her father and whoever else from Uncle Dermot's family turns up. They are never sure of that, for travel can be interrupted by the wild weather that can hit them here at any time. You could have great plans to fly in from California or take the train from Chicago and find the place snowed in or flooded. Living in Ireland we have no idea.

For the first time since I arrived here I am feeling that bit homesick. It is strange, for I can't think of anything in particular that I am missing. Christmas in Ranahuel is usually nothing to write home about. I had been hoping that the celebrations here do give me something to write home about.

The way things turn out though, it is not the celebrations here that give me cause to be writing a letter to anyone at home. It is more the fact that there is a letter from Ireland, the strangest letter I could imagine. It is from my sister Mairead and, according to the date on it, she posted it in August, nearly five months ago. She sent it to Boston; it arrived well after we had left and for some reason nobody thought of forwarding it to me in Cape May, along with Roisin's mail. It is old news, very old, but it is no less interesting for that. I read it several times, trying to understand the information that she was sending me, trying to picture what had happened that day back in June at my old home.

That man from Tyrone that you used to talk about came here to the house. Henderson he said his name was.

Tchí Dia mé! I can't take in what I am reading.

After all this time Matthew Henderson had driven all the way from Tyrone and somehow found our house? He was looking for me? According to Mairead he thought I would still be there because my letter to him had mentioned that I was going to America in a couple of weeks. This is unbelievable for me and I am struggling to know how to react to it. It is all so unsettling that I nearly wish Mairead had not bothered to tell me but then....

He made me promise to write to you and tell you he was here, as soon as I got your address.

Mairead was only doing what he had made her promise to do. He wanted me to know he had come. And she had brought him into our poor wee cottage for a chat. Jesus, Mary and Joseph, what was she thinking? Meeting our mammy and her so... and seeing the poverty we live in? Oh Mairead!

He met our Mammy and he asked about the fiddle and all. I told him you did not bother much with it now, that is why it is still hanging where you left it.

Aye, he would see it hanging there like a relic and it would remind him of those nights of music in Lismore when I played his father's fiddle. Those happy times. But it would probably remind him as well of the bad times, when I had lost control and threw it against my bedroom wall.

I start to wonder how I would have reacted if I had been there when he landed in our street. It would have been mainly shock of course, but would I have been as generous as Mairead and brought him into the house? Or would I maybe have stood by the gable of the house with him and let him say his piece? What did he want to say anyway? Was it my letter that had brought him over? It couldn't have been anything else, of course it couldn't. Was he angry at me for writing and digging up all those terrible memories after all this time? Maybe he just wanted to see for himself the poverty that I had often described to him, the simple way of life we have out on the windy margins of Ireland.

Maybe he wanted me to go back and work for him, give me another chance at the job? Or maybe he wanted to say sorry as well and wanted to make things up with me? I could be guessing his motives all day and still might not hit on the real answer.

Should I be writing back to him to see if he can explain himself? No, I don't think so. There was a time, even since I arrived here in America, that I would have wanted to satisfy my curiosity. Now that I have Bob in my life I have enough to be curious about, like what lies ahead for us? Where is this friendship with him going to end up?

I do wonder though, what did Matthew look like that day he arrived, how has he changed since 1922? He'd be middle forties now, maybe just over his prime. I wonder is he as straight and well-made as he was, or have the years of work taken their toll on him and turned him into an old man. Oh I wish...I wish I had been there to see him for myself and understand why he...no, I can't start to think like that. I am here. I have a job. I have a new life. I have a man, a very exciting man who seems to dote on me; what a change for Sally Anne Sweeney. Forty-two and going on like a *cailín óg amaideach*. Ah well, at least I can laugh at myself.

What did I ask Matthew in that letter I sent before I left home? I can't remember. Maybe something about his family? The Kearneys, Anthony and Monica? Tinker Tam...probably. Did I have the nerve to ask him if he ever got married, or did I stop short of being so bold? Hopefully I didn't ask anything so daft, but the question is now back in my mind. How did life turn out for him after that tragic year? Does he still carry the guilt of it or how was he able to get over it and move on in life? Should I write back to Lismore to try and...to try and what? Satisfy my need to know? It is none of my business anyhow, but after all, he did make the effort to find me.

What was that about Father Devine in the letter?

This car came up the hill and into our street. It was the priest, but not in his own car. He was looking for you. But I told him you had left for Glasgow. That seemed to please him and he got back in the car and went back down the hill.

Then before the hour had passed the same car arrived back in here.

So somehow Matthew had arrived with the priest in his car? That is just so strange, the Protestant with the priest. I can't believe that Matthew has turned Catholic or something and enlisted Father Devine's help. But it is puzzling that the first time he arrived he had the priest with him, then drives away, then returns alone. He must have been determined to find out about me alright.

'Good for you, Matthew,' I think. 'You tracked me down and you didn't let Father Devine put you off the scent.'

Suddenly I think, 'What did I tell Father Devine in confessions all those years ago? Oh Lord no! I have a memory of confessing something to him about how intimate I had been with that young

Protestant farmer in Tyrone. Has he remembered all that and worked out the connection?' It would not surprise me if he did, for he is a sharp man, and, if I am right, that would explain him being pleased that I was already away from the house, away from any more association with that dirty heretic. God but don't you have to be careful what you confess to? I am just glad Father Devine is not around Cape May at the minute and listening to any confession I might make here.

It is funny, looking back on those long years of self-denial and self-banishment at home. In a sense Father Devine became my conscience during that period. He definitely had some kind of hold over my thinking, likely out of good motives on his part, wanting to protect me from any other indiscretions in the field of romance.

"You must deny yourself Sally Anne," he would be telling me. "When you pray the *'Ár nAthair'* you say, *'Agus ná lig sinn i gcathú, ach saor sinn ó olc'*. But you can't then put yourself into temptation, can you? You can't pray, 'Deliver me from evil' and then walk straight into it."

I took him at his word, too much so, I think now. I tried to live as a good and faithful Catholic in the way I went about my life. That meant staying away from men, obviously it did, for they were the big temptation. I suppose it was all a way of wrapping myself up in a cloak of piety and religion. It was a false comfort though, and it stopped me from dealing properly with the depths of my hurt and the blow to my pride. I can see this now with the benefit of distance and time. I am here in America. I am in a new chapter. I will not be trying to protect myself from every experience that this new chapter of life has for me. Father Devine is no longer my conscience, my moral guide, and I resent the fact that, from what I read into Mairead's letter, he is still interfering. What does he want from me? To go join some convent?

I am so tempted to write back to Matthew and find out what his visit was all about, but I think at the minute I will resist the idea. It might only complicate things and, despite my need to have the air cleared between us, I feel I have done my bit. He could have asked Mairead to send him my address if he had really wanted to write, couldn't he? It baffles me, but I will just put it out of my mind.

I have enough in my head already. I have this Christmas dinner to look forward to, all these new traditions that are so different from home, meeting these relatives for the first time and so on... and then eventually getting back to Cape May to follow this mysterious path into the unknown, this new territory of romance that I find myself in and whatever might lie beyond it.

Chapter 27

Matthew Henderson

Standing in the dock of the Petty Sessions Court in Omagh was not something I had ever imagined myself doing. It seemed that now I was becoming a regular visitor. Here I was again, in August 1937, nearly two years after the last visit and almost to the day from my mother's death. In some ways I was very glad that neither she nor my father were alive that day to witness the humiliation of their only son. If you believed in the old saying about people turning in their graves, then this was the day when they would both be spinning.

I had been brought up very strict by both parents. We were a fairly religious family. My father was known through the whole district as a moral and upright man. Nothing could ever have been said against him. He kept the Sabbath and worked hard on the farm he had bought out from the landlord a few decades before. He was scrupulously honest and owed nobody anything. People of all sorts looked up to him, especially in the local Methodist church in the town.

Now, for the second time, his only son and heir was standing in court in the county town, accused of smuggling. Only this time I was entirely and completely innocent. I honestly was.

The charges against me were read out. When the magistrate asked me how I pleaded I confidently replied, "Not guilty, my Lord." He looked at me blankly, as if to say, 'You ejit, do you think I'm as big a fool as yourself? Of course you are guilty.'

I had a solicitor but I might as well have had a talking bird. I don't think he believed a word I had told him in the interview, that this was all a mistake, that I was innocent. If your solicitor doesn't believe you, what are the chances of the magistrate believing you? There was no jury in a case like this of course, I just had to convince the man in the middle of the bench.

The prosecution lawyer rose and opened the case for the Crown. His preparation wasn't the best, I thought. He outlined the case against me. Part of it was that I had not been able to bring any witnesses who would testify that this bull was mine.

"The 1934 Finance Act requires such witnesses," he stated. "In the absence of these it must be assumed that this animal does not belong to the defendant and that it has been illegally brought into this jurisdiction."

All this I could completely agree with and I whispered as much to my lawyer. "He's right, it didn't belong to me. But it wasn't me brought it in."

All he could say was, "Ssh, just listen to the case against you."

I tried but it was so annoying. They were all barking up the wrong tree in this court.

The prosecution then turned to question the Customs and Excise men. As they talked about me it was like they were talking about somebody else. I did not recognise myself, so black and evil were they painting me.

"A known and convicted criminal, he is," Bamford told the judge. He went on to remind the court of my previous conviction and the sentence, which included being bound over for two years. Sadly for me, we were just short by a month of that two year period being over. Not that it would have made a pin of difference.

Then it was the turn of my lawyer. He mumbled away for a while about this being a terrible mistake; the bull was not mine and had nothing to do with me. It had been brought to the neighbouring farm next door and had broken in to Henderson's land, completely unaware that in so doing it was crossing out of one jurisdiction into another.

"My client was asleep in bed when this transgression occurred, Your Honour," he said.

I could barely hear what he was saying and me sitting beside him. The magistrate kept asking him to speak up and to repeat things. It was a hopeless performance. At one point I tugged at his sleeve and asked if I could address the bench directly myself. At that, he slumped down beside me and quietly read his notes. I stood up and gave my story as clearly as I could.

"I already had a bull, a good animal. Why would I go bringing another beast into my field, one that would attack my own bull and leave it lying in the corner? It broke into my land, I am telling you. I didn't bring it in. The thing is, my Lord, you can't expect a dumb bull to know where the Free State ends and Northern Ireland begins," I told him. "Around Lismore the border zig-zags all over the place. There's people living in my town-land who don't even know when they are in one country and when they are in the other. How can we expect a bull…"

"Is it true, Mr Henderson," he interrupted, "that this bull was in your field with your heifers?"

"It is. But it had no right…"

"Is it true that it did not belong to you?"

"Yes, my Lord."

"Is it true that the origin of this bull was the Irish Free State?"

"It likely was, but I cannot answer that, my Lord."

"And why not?"

I shook my head in confusion. All I could think to say was, "Because I never....I never checked his papers."

There was a titter of laughter around the courtroom, but the magistrate silenced it with a wave of his hand.

"I hope you are not trying to be funny, Henderson. It does not serve you well at this point in time. You already have a criminal record; this court remembers that and it remembers that you are still in a period of licence. The simple facts of the matter are that a smuggled bull is on your land, with your herd. That is where these officers of the Crown found it to be. It is therefore your responsibility. I do not have any reason to believe your cock and bull story..." (this brought more laughter at my expense, but this time it was grand, the man on the bench was the one being funny, whether he meant it or not), and I find you guilty as charged. Do you have anything to say for yourself by way of mitigation, before the court passes sentence?"

I shook my head in disbelief and frustration.

I had been found guilty of a crime that had not even happened. This was supposed to be a fair process, a fair, British justice system. I did not think that there was anything fair or just about it. It was madness. That bloody bull had broken into my land. It was dead and now I was maybe heading to Derry gaol.

It flashed through my head that the next two months were the harvest months, September and October. What on earth was I going to do to get the corn and the potatoes harvested, let alone the usual work with the cattle and the other livestock? The whole thing got the better of me and I stumbled in the dock. My face must have gone white for I heard someone say, "He's gone very pale, get him a drink."

I was sitting down when I sort of came too. My face was wet with something, whether tears or because somebody had thrown a glass of water over me. I heard the magistrate's voice again as if it was coming from a great distance away, sort of echoing.

"Are you alright now, Mr Henderson?"

I got back up to my feet somehow. "My Lord," I said, "I am sorry that happened, whatever sort of a dwamle came over me."

"It is not the first time something like that has occurred in this court," he said. "It changes nothing but I ask you again, have you anything to say in mitigation?"

I pulled myself together and cleared my throat.

"Only this, my Lord. I am a farmer. I live with my sister who is a thin waif of a girl who wouldn't be able to work the place on her own. If you have any knowledge of farming and seasons and how we operate on the land that feeds the likes of you, you will know that a farmer has to be on his land to bring in his harvest. The harvest starts in September and goes on for maybe eight to ten weeks, depending on the weather. If I am in gaol and if I can't do my harvest it rots in the fields, I can't sell my corn," (he raised his hand to stop me at this point but I ploughed on,) "I will have no straw for my cattle, there will be no income from the spuds and that's before I start to ask you about how my cattle and sheep and pigs and hens are to be fed and my cows milked and stuff taken to the market. And all because a bull broke into...."

I got stopped in my speech. I noticed that every eye in the courtroom was on me. A great hush of stillness had come over the place. Even the magistrate was quiet, his hand still raised like he was trying to stop a bus. Eventually he spoke.

"Alright, alright, Mr Henderson. You have made your point very well and, by the way, you are speaking to a farmer's son, albeit you are speaking without the tone I would expect you to use to the court. I will take five minutes to consider your sentence."

I continued to stand, waiting, looking around at the faces in the courtroom. Lo and behold, there in the back row I saw the face of John Sproule. 'Fair play to you John,' I thought. I had not realised he had been sitting there all the time. He must have slipped in after we started. He had given up his day's work to come and support me, in his own silent way, no doubt saying a prayer of some sort for me. As I caught his eye he stuck up his thumb, as if in agreement with my speech. I read his lips as he said, "It will be alright. It will be alright."

I knew then that at least John believed me. I also knew that my animals would be safe and that he, with Millie's help, would do their best with the harvest. 'Thank God for good neighbours,' I thought.

The magistrate spoke again. "I have considered the defendant's plea of mitigation and I find some merit in his argument. However, he has a previous conviction for a similar offence and received a substantial fine. This appears not to have been a sufficient deterrent. The accused is therefore sentenced to one month in custody at Her Majesty's pleasure and will be bound over to keep the law for a further two years. All rise."

My speech had had a good effect, I think. I was fearing worse. I had heard of smugglers getting three or more months. Maybe the judge half believed my side of the story. I would be out of prison by the middle of September, I could manage the harvest if the weather was kind and John and Millie between them could hopefully manage the animals in the meantime.

Lying in Derry gaol, there wasn't a day of that month that the thought didn't cross my mind that I am the man who shot another man and walked away scot-free; yet now, here I was doing time for smuggling a bull that I didn't smuggle. And the word from across the border was that somebody had pulled a few strings for Liam Coyle. He got away with a caution. I started to realise that this is a funny oul country, this Northern Ireland.

What I did not realise then was that my time in prison would bring about a change at home that I had not bargained for. When I arrived back in Lismore on the sixteenth of September John Sproule had his feet below the table and Millie was cooking him the best meal ever you saw and him smiling at her like she was a princess. Our Millie!

Goodness but didn't he have his hair cut and washed as well!

'I couldn't be away from the two of them for a month,' I thought, 'without oul Cupid firing a couple of crazy arrows in my own kitchen.'

I was down in Castlederg at the market the week after I got out. Nobody had been able to take any of my cattle that were ready for selling and that I could understand. I had three calves, maybe six or seven months old that I felt I should move on before winter. When they appeared in the ring, the old auctioneer gave me a long silent stare before he started taking bids. The whole place seemed to slow down. Suddenly nobody was buying. Eventually big Norman came to my aid, but it seemed to me he put on a ridiculously low bid, very reluctantly at that. Nobody followed him, not a soul.

In the quietness I heard a voice mumble, "Does he not have any stray bulls for sale?"

That brought a titter of laughter that grew and rumbled around the ring and I stood there, my face reddening, not able to do or say a thing.

When the laughter died down a bit, the auctioneer thought it was only right that he join the fun, at my expense.

"Are some of you maybe holding off for a few months, waiting for him to arrive in with some sturdy black calves, are yous?"

He got his laugh from the crowd and then thumped his hammer down. My calves had only had the one pathetic wee bid.

"Sold to Norman McKinney," the auctioneer boomed.

Later, my few pounds in my pocket, I called in the Ferguson Arms for a pint before heading home. There's always a big crowd of farmers in after a market. They stand around under their flat caps, dark pints in hand, puffing on their Woodbine fags or their favourite pipes. Without these comforts, how on earth would they ever be able to argue the finer points of cattle and prices? It is nearly as big a part of the market day as the auction itself.

Through the brown haze of tobacco smoke I saw big Norman and a couple of his cronies bent over their pints, their elbows leaning on the polished oak counter. I wasn't sure whether to go anywhere near them, but Norman happened to glance around and his eyes met mine. I sidled forward towards him, for want of any place better to go. He spoke first.

"You'll be wanting a pint, Matthew?"

'That is nice of him,' I was thinking.

"Aye thanks, Norman. A pint of the black stuff," I said, moving as if to pull out a stool beside the group.

"I didn't say anything about buying you a pint," he scowled at me. "Clear away off to hell and buy your own pint. You should have plenty of money after all that smuggling you've been at. A bloody disgrace! And you call yourself a Protestant?"

With that he turned his back on me and the cronies snarled into their drinks.

I heard one other voice from further up the bar. "Are you sure you're in the right pub, Henderson?"

I turned on my heel and left the bar, the sneering eyes of my fellow farmers following me to the street.

Chapter 28

Windsor Hotel
Cape May
New Jersey
7th January 1946

Dear Mairead,

I have arrived safely back in Cape May after spending Christmas with Uncle Dermot. It was a happy time and I was glad to meet a few more of the family. Uncle Dermot himself is in good spirits even though his health is not the best.

I was amazed to get two letters from you, especially the one you had sent to Boston back last August. I couldn't believe that Matthew Henderson had come looking for me after all this time. How was he? Why did he come at all? It is all very strange and I wish I had been there just to see what he was up to. You did right to tell me about this, but it's a pity the letter lay in Boston for all that time without me knowing. Ah well, there is not a thing I can do about it now; just let the hare sit. I have enough other things on my mind here.

But this latest letter you sent about Mary Anne and Nuala is very worrying. I wish to God Mary Anne had let us know earlier. Nuala sounds like she is in a lot of trouble in her poor mind. I wish we could do something for her but we are both so far away. I thought I was helping by sending dollars every couple of weeks to her address in Glasgow. I wondered why she never replied. Now I realise she has not been there and hasn't got a single penny of it. Whoever is living in that flat now has got it all and it is lost. It is only money though and it is far more important that Mary Anne gets help for Nuala and wee Frankie. Did you write back to her?

Things here are sort of slow. There are fewer people around the seaside at this time of year; no visitors at all, just a few men who are travelling salesmen or who work at the naval base. It can be a bit lonely at times without their friendly chat. The only good side to it is that, because there are not so many rooms in use in the hotel, Roisin has me training to do various other jobs, everything from waitressing to working in the kitchen. If I make a good fist of any of these I can apply to switch over to better paid work, with different hours. I wouldn't mind trying my hand at cooking full-time. My friend Caroline's dad is our chef and he is a great teacher. The only trouble is that Americans like different kinds of food and want them cooked in ways that we have never heard of. You would not believe how many different ways they can ask to have their eggs cooked. I had no notion what 'sunny-side-up' meant, for example, or 'over-light'. And steak! These men say things like 'medium rare, honey' and I just raise my eyebrows. Then there are things like peppers that we don't have at home. Peppers are hard to describe, they can be green or red and have hollow centres, so sometimes you get them stuffed with meat and rice. They can taste a bit spicy for me and I don't like them much but they are not as bad as a dish called ravioli, wee pouches of pastry with minced meat and vegetables inside and a sort of tomato sauce. They come from Italy I hear. My tongue is not at its happiest with these strange tastes.

I am glad to hear mammy is well and that things are alright around the place. Write again as soon as you hear anything about Nuala.

Le grá,
Sally Anne

****

Mairead's two letters do bother me, of course they do. And the winter weather now is depressing, very cold and wet most days now. And yes, you do miss what the Yanks call 'the buzz' about the place in this slow season in the hotel.

I am not going to confess to Mairead, though, that the real reason I am not in great heart at the minute has nothing to do with her letters, nor the weather, nor winter, nor the boring hotel work. It has a lot more to do with a postcard that arrived into my pigeon-hole this morning.

On the front of the card there is a photograph of a beach, a very sunny beach with palm trees and lots of good-looking people in bathing costumes, playing around in the sea and taking the sun. In the background, there are some modern-looking hotels stretching up to a cloudless blue sky. The writing scrawled across the top of the card reads, 'Corpus Christi Texas".

On the other side of the card there is a short message.

"Hi Sally Anne, greetings from sunny Texas. My work has unexpectedly taken me to the naval base here for a few months so I will not be back in New Jersey probably until Easter. Sorry. I will return, don't worry. Can't wait to see you then. All my love Bob xxx"

This is a bit of a blow. There had been no mention of him going anywhere when he left me after the Thanksgiving Dance in November. I have been looking forward so much to seeing him in the new year. I feel like something has been wrenched out of the centre of me.

Easter time! But that is three months away, more than that even. What is this next period here going to feel like without...agh Sally Anne, don't be thinking like that. You have had twenty years of waiting for your future to walk in the door, sweep you off your feet and bring a smile back to your heart. Surely you can wait another couple of months for...for what? For the feet-sweeping to pick up where it left off? And then what? Is it just a passing fancy of his, something to amuse him when he happens to be in Cape May? For all I know, he could have another lady-friend in this Corpus Christi place, maybe others in different cities, like the old sailors with a girl in every port.

There is no doubt that this postcard has unsettled me, it along with this strange news from Mairead about Matthew Henderson. I am caught between the devil and the deep blue sea, except that I sort of want the devil and I wouldn't say no to understanding more about the deep blue sea. Why, in the name of God, did Matthew have to come looking for his old maid? It is this question that most annoys me, the uncertainty of it.

I am the maid in the middle. What is it about these two tall, handsome, muscular men that they find Sally Anne Sweeney so fascinating? She is only a maid, for God's sake, the one in the dusty apron, the skinny one whose mousey-coloured hair needs brushing, her without a touch of make-up on her face, the quiet one who has managed to reach over forty years of virginity without any bother at all. What is it about these two men they find the humble Irish maid to their taste? *Ní thuigim!*

I study Bob's postcard again as if looking for clues. I even sniff it. Nothing. What was I hoping for? A whiff of his aftershave? Or a hint of a different scent to help me conjure up the shape of some dusky-skinned Texas lady? Suspicion and jealousy talk together in my restless mind. I do not like what they are saying.

But then the postcard in my hand seems to give me a new train of thought, a different notion altogether.

Postcards!

Behind the desk in our foyer I have noticed a display board which contains postcards of some local scenes, including a lovely picture of this hotel. I cannot send one of these to Bob because he has not bothered to include an address on his card to me. I have no way of replying to him and he must know that; indeed he must have decided to do it this way, to send a postcard rather than a letter which would have sort of obliged him to begin with his address at the top. He does not want me to write to him, for whatever reason.

But I have a feeling Matthew might.

The feeling turns quickly into an idea. I act on the whim, without much thought really.

I rush down the flights of stairs to the foyer; it is faster than waiting for the elevator. I skip across the foyer to the desk like a young thing. The receptionist's name is Joy, unless her name-badge is just referring to her happy disposition.

"Can I buy one of those postcards of the Windsor?" I ask Joy.

"You sure can," she says, her smile so wide that I wonder if she can read my mind and guess what I am up to. I think she has more teeth than I have ever seen in anybody's head, and they all gleaming like flint-stones. I have the strange thought that maybe in another life she was a horse.

The picture on the front is perfect, a lovely simple painting of the hotel, with some seagulls whirling around over the beach. On the front of the card I'm delighted to see in the top left corner 'The Windsor Hotel, Cape May, N.J."

There, I think, I don't even have to write my address as if I was demanding that he write back to me. The clue is there for him if he wishes. I scribble a few brief lines to him, filling the small space easily. I keep it clear and simple, always the best plan when dealing with someone like Matthew.

Later I am in the Post Office buying a stamp.

"You want airmail or just the normal service?" I am asked. I hadn't thought of this and I must look a bit confused for the clerk explains slowly, as if he is talking to some idiot from the bogs of Ireland, which he is of course.

"It will get there much faster than the normal mail," he tells me.

"Ah, right," I say, playing down to his opinion of me. "That's great, isn't it?"

I decide on the dearer airmail stamp, much dearer. Maybe the American way of doing things is making me more extravagant in my spending, but the airmail stamp is a strange choice, when I think about it afterwards. What is the urgency now, after twenty something years of no contact with him and six months since he came looking for me? I hand over the card for 'mailing', as the clerk calls it. I watch him read the address.

"Lismore, Castlederg, County Tyrone, Ireland?" he says, a question running through his tone. "Should that not be Northern Ireland?"

Oh my Lord. For a minute this annoys me, but then I think, "If I want this card to get to Matthew I suppose this fella is right."

I grab the postcard back out of his hand and write the letter N before the 'Ireland'. An N is as far as I will go.

"Sorry," I say. "And thanks. How did you know about...?"

"I may not have the accent any longer," he tells me with a smile, "but I was born in Bangor. This is your lucky day, ma'am."

It absolutely is. My card might never have found its destination if someone other than this fellow, with his local knowledge, had been serving me.

I am so flustered that I thank him in Irish. He just looks at me as if I am talking double-Dutch. I smile inside because something about his reaction reminds me very much of how another man reacted to my Irish many years ago, the very man whose name is above the address on the card.

Chapter 29

Matthew Henderson

Mary Kearney is forever arguing with me. Is it not enough that I did time, all on account of her and her man? Years have passed since they got me roped into their cross-border game but the taint of it all hangs around me like a foul smell.

What annoyed me about it at the time was that, while folk in my own community shunned me and gossiped behind their hands about this chancer of a farmer who had been caught at the smuggling, the Coyles seemed to find it all a great laughing matter. I suppose that, looked at from their point of view, the idea of the Protestant in gaol for a crime he didn't commit was just so full of irony. Whatever about their micky-taking, I took a good while to get over it and to forgive them for their part in it.

'Look at it this way Matthew,' I told myself eventually. 'They had no intention of landing you in trouble with the law. The whole thing was another strange accident. When you think about it Liam hadn't actually committed any crime, except maybe in his head. Just get over it. What goes around comes around. And, in my case, around and around and around!'

John Sproule had put it a different way in those days after I was released. In his sternest sermon voice he told me that my sin had found me out.

Found me out it certainly had, so I went to a few more meetings with John and Millie and did a bit of repenting about it. John was forever on at me about receiving the 'gift of saving grace'.

"Saving face, more like," was what Mary said. "You are just trying to get into their good books Matthew. Just accept yourself for who you are. It wasn't a sin, for God's sake. You had nothing to do with the bull so how could it be a sin?"

She always had an answer for everything. Still does. I could never win an argument with Mary.

****

We are talking in Kearney's parlour. Her wains are playing in the yard with their grandfather. God love him, he can hardly move now with the pain in his legs but he still sits on his chair and throws the ball for them. Monica is with us by the hearth but she is too deaf to listen to us now. Not that Mary's politics or her views on the recent World War would interest her much anyway; never did.

"I don't see why you are standing up for De Valera," I am telling Mary. "Ireland staying neutral was all wrong. Just plain wrong."

"It was not our war," she says. "Why should Ireland get involved in Britain's affairs? It had nothing to do with Ireland, nothing to do with Irish interests. It was Britain's war."

"It was never just Britain's war. What about America, Australia, South Africa and all the rest? All those countries came and did their bit against Hitler. Ireland sat on its hands."

"And England sat on its hands when our people were starving. And they fought us tooth and nail when it came to giving us our freedom. We remember..."

"Your freedom! Your freedom would have meant nothing to Hitler if he had decided to invade Ireland as a backdoor to Britain. You would have been just like France or Holland or any of those countries who thought they were free."

I think I am winning this argument. I have right on my side, so I plough on.

"Sure didn't some IRA man, Russell was his name I think, didn't he have talks with the Nazis about the IRA joining them in the fight against Britain? You can't tell me you agree with that Mary? Siding with a mass murderer like Hitler, just because you see it as a chance to get a slap at Britain? And De Valera sending sympathies to Germany when Hitler shot himself? That was just crazy. The Nazis had to be defeated, no two ways about it. Sure didn't your own father fight against the Germans in the first war?"

She is quiet for a minute. Then she makes it even more personal.

"So why didn't you go and fight them then?"

"Agh, come on! I did my bit at home here. Farmers were needed. Who else was going to work my land? Who was going to keep feeding people if farmers like me went to war?"

"Aye, alright," she says, "you had to be a farmer... and people had to fight Hitler. I get all that, but it does not follow that Ireland should have been involved. Ireland didn't know, nobody knew, what was going on in the concentration camps and how evil it all was. You can't hold us responsible for things we didn't know about. Anyway, that is not the point we were discussing."

"What point was that?"

"The point that Britain had no right to use Lough Foyle as a naval base. That's breaking international law. So was flying RAF planes over Donegal."

"So was smuggling butter, but you still did it."

She laughs at this.

"That's a different thing," she says. "The border made criminals of us all, didn't it? Anyway, this border I was crossing with my butter should never have been there in the first place. In my mind it doesn't exist."

"Agh, we are back to the border," I tell her, getting up from the hearth. "We'll never agree on that. But it's getting close to milking time and I must go back over the Border and chase a few cows into the byre."

****

When I finish the milking and the redding-up I make my way into the kitchen to get a bite of dinner. Millie has it ready for me as usual. I am very fortunate that she still comes up a wee while every day. She pedals her old bicycle up the hill from her new home with John, just to cook a decent dinner for me and whiles wash a few clothes, then she goes over to check on the Kearneys. John doesn't mind at all. In fact, way back when he raised the subject with me, the idea of marrying Millie, that was one of the things he made sure I would know.

"If she agrees and marries me," he told me, "you can rest assured that she will come up here every day and do whatever you need doing, cooking or whatever. She won't need to be working all the time at mine."

That was more than generous of him. He wasn't going to leave me to fend for myself entirely. I am not sure that he bargained on her looking after the Kearneys as well but the arrangement has worked out well ever since. It is good to see the two of them married and happy. I wouldn't begrudge that to anybody, least of all poor Millie, for she has not had the easiest of lives with the way she is. But when you think about it, the poor girl is now more or less running three houses and all without a word of complaint.

"The postman was here. There's letters for you, Mattue," Millie calls from the sink in the scullery. "On the table."

I pick them up, four of them, and have a quick look through. At the bottom of the pile is a bright looking card with a picture on the front. It shows a very grand building, white with a red top floor. There's a beach in the foreground, blue sky behind and an American flag flying. You don't be getting cards like this in Lismore through the post. I am more than puzzled. Who could be sending me such a thing? I turn the card over. There is a short message on the back. Oh Lord! I think I know this handwriting, cramped and all as it is.

God above! It's her again.

Dear Matthew, I have just heard from my sister that you visited her and my mother last summer. That was nice of you. I am sorry I had left by then. This is the hotel I am working in. I am a maid again. I hope you are well and all your family. Yours sincerely, Sally Anne.

****

For the next few weeks this card takes over my thinking. My work goes on as usual. It is ploughing time, breaking fallow fields to be ready for planting potatoes and sowing corn. The weather is good and dry for once, and I am working as hard as I can remember to make the best use of it. The Fordson tractor that I bought a couple of years back is proving its worth and the spring-green sod is turning over into brown, fertile-looking furrows at a great rate. Jonty, my ageing Clydesdale, is looking sadly over the hedge at this noisy blue beast that has taken over from him.

"Why the long face, Jonty?" I shout to him. "You can be happy now that you don't have to drag this plough around."

He snorts and shakes his head, as if he is disgusted.

The birds are happy, flying behind the plough and feasting away on the worms and grubs that I am turning up for them.

And I am happy too.

I am happy in the knowledge that I made a great decision back last summer after Sally Anne's first letter arrived, the decision to go and look for her. I realise that now of course, but it has been a very long wait for that truth to show itself. It had been like an ear of corn thrown to the wind, taking root in the unknown darkness and now poking its head through the earth, looking for light. For months I was wracked with doubt about that journey. All sorts of thoughts came to me and none of them did anything to argue against the stupidity of what I had done.

I imagined that Mairead had probably kept my visit to herself. I was the man who caused her sister grief, the 'man who broke her heart', isn't that how she had described me? Why would she be telling Sally Anne about my visit, especially now that she has made the break to a new life in America? The priest might even have stuck his nose into it all, finding out that I hadn't taken his advice and simply gone home that day, and maybe forbidding Mairead to tell her sister of my visit.

Even if that news had reached Sally Anne I could easily understand that it would be water off a duck's back to her. She would probably have felt, 'Well, I have done my bit, not for him but for myself. I have made contact and said my sorries and left Ireland with the slate clean behind me. Him coming to my home is twenty-three years too late, too little and too late.' She might even have laughed in scorn at the whole idea of me spending a day trying to find her. 'What was he thinking, the big-headed fool that he is, imagining that I would want to see him to say goodbye for the last time or something? What on earth would he want with me now, after rejecting me so heartlessly all that time ago? He has learned nothing over the years. He has little to be doing.'

I re-read that letter she sent me last June, still in a drawer beside my bed, of course. I could easily imagine her reasons for going to America for a new start in life. Let the past fade away, no more backward thoughts. I had come to accept it all, this chapter ending. Expect nothing from her.

But now! Now I start wondering if this card from her keeps the thread of the story going. Is that what this is about, this beautiful American picture, these simple words? Am I in danger of reading too much into it? Surely not!

In her wee note there is the strange line that says,

'I am sorry I had left.'

This I find very curious. I want to shout to her right now as I turn the tractor at the head of the furrow, 'I am sorry too, girl!'

The trouble is that she didn't write any address on her card, so I have no way of contacting her. I am desperate to do this, to write a letter, or send a similar card if I can find one, just to let her know that I appreciate her taking the time to write...to write on both occasions.

As these busy spring weeks pass I make a plan in my head. Come the wee break after I get the crops all in I might drive over to Ranahuel again. I know the way now. I can find Mairead easily. I will ask her for Sally Anne's address. It is that simple and it is that important.

****

Saint Patrick's Day has come and gone and for once I have all my corn sown and my early potatoes planted. I would not be superstitious at all, or at least nothing like Anthony and Joe used to be, but it is still a good feeling to have my earlies in the ground. A few more days with the disc harrow and the upper field will be ready to drill for the Arran Victors, the later spuds. I will have them in by Easter. It has been a great year of weather and it seems as if the brightness has sort of entered my soul itself. I have really enjoyed the work. And, in my imaginings I have been enjoying the sowing of plans for what lies ahead.

"I have a journey to make over to the far side of Donegal," I tell Mary Kearney as we drink a cup of tea. It is not often she calls in with me and I haven't seen her in a few weeks, but she has arrived in my kitchen tonight with a message from Anthony about cutting him a lock o' turf.

"What is taking you over there?"

"It's a long story," I begin. "You remember Sally Anne, the maid I had years ago…"

"Ah ha," she says. "Now this is my sort of story. Of course I remember her. Nice girl she was, a good girl too. Go on Matthew, tell me all."

So I tell her. I tell her more or less everything. She listens well and with a wee smile flitting around her curious eyes. When I get to the most recent bit of the story, the card from America, Mary is on the edge of her seat, slapping her leg and smiling like the morning sunrise.

"God Matthew, but aren't you the right romantic. An oul dark horse, you are! You know, I have looked at you over the years and wondered what the hell was wrong with you. Years ago, when that wee hussy threw you over, that seemed to knock the stuffing out of you. But my God, now this! 'The secret life of the Protestant farmer,' eh? Who would have thought?"

"Don't be laughing at me, Mary," I say. "And don't be telling anybody else, alright? Please? I just told you, for….I don't know why I told you, to be honest. I haven't even told anybody else."

"Alright," she says, "but let me see this card."

I run upstairs to my bedroom to get it. When I come back she is standing, back to the range and below the light. She takes the card eagerly.

"That's some place she is working in. Can I read what she says?"

"Aye, go on."

She turns and reads. I wait for her.

"What do you make of it?" I ask.

"Very nice of her to send this," Mary says, "and she obviously wants you to write back."

This puzzles me.

"What makes you say that? How can I when I don't have her address? That's why I need to go back over to…"

"Agh, Matthew," she says, "You silly oul man. Sure look! The name of the Hotel is there along the top."

She shows me.

"Sounds a bit of a royalist place for a Donegal girl to be working in. Windsor Hotel, Cape May, N.J. What more address do you want?"

I take the card and stare at the address.

"Do you think that would get her? Like, what's this N.J.? There's not enough…"

"N.J. is New Jersey. That's the name of the state. It's all you need."

"Agh, for goodness sake!"

It has been there all the time and for some reason I didn't realise that this is actually Sally Anne's address. I have to laugh at my own stupidity. Not for the first time.

"I think I just saved you another journey into Donegal," Mary says; then, with a smile in her eyes, she adds, "that is unless you want to deliver a car load of flour and butter to my house instead. What do you say, eh? There'll be a few quid in it for you. Sally Anne's address can be your cover story with the Customs men at the border."

I laugh at her. I don't think she really expects me to be taking her up on this offer and I am still laughing at the daftness of it all as she leaves.

Chapter 30

Ranahuel
Kincasslagh
Co Donegal
27th March 1946

Dear Sally Anne,

I hope you are keeping well and not working too hard. If the hotel is quiet in the winter you are likely not too busy.

Mammy is fair at the minute, no change in her at all. But the news from Scotland is not so good. Nuala has got worse and Mary Anne has had to get the doctor to her. She is so poorly she has been put in an asylum in a nearby town. Her mind is gone. I do not know what is to become of her or of her wee one, Frankie. Are you still able to send them money? I hope so for they are on the breadline altogether.

I am managing not so bad. I was able to sell that calf for good enough money, you know the one out of the white-headed cow with the bad foot. And I have been lucky with the eggs, for all the hens have been laying well. An odd time one of the Stewart boys will bring up a couple of fish that he has caught. It is very good of them out at the Point to still think of us but then our father was always big friends with the Jacob one, and Jacob still comes up the hill to see mammy if he gets the chance. You never know if she knows him but she sort of stares at him long and hard as if she does. He can usually get her to play him a tune as well and her 66 years of age.

Ailish was in with us on Sunday and her news is that she is starting a new job, working in the doll factory in Crolly. God love her but she needs the money, for times have been hard for that family during the war years. Seamus is away back to work now as well. She is very happy about the job and wanted you to know. "It beats the hiring fair," she says. Oh, I meant to say that Father Devine is always asking for you. I don't know what his special interest is in you, but he needs to know all about you. Maybe he is after a contribution to the parish fund from what you send home but I tell him as little as possible.
Write again soon.
Le Grá
Mairead

Chapter 31

Sally Anne Sweeney

Monday morning and the Windsor Hotel slowly shakes itself awake, reluctant to become too enthusiastic about the day ahead. I am to be in the kitchen all week and that is no bad thing. There's only so many times you can clean the foyer and the corridors and the stairs and the linen stores and still feel the joys of living.

Easter is not far off now and, while I am saddened by Mairead's news last week about poor Nuala, I am feeling a bit brighter in my spirits. It may have something to do with the lengthening of the days, the warmth returning to the air and the fresh growth of grass and plants in the gardens along the streets here in Cape May. It has been a dreary winter to be sure. The lack of people and the want of activity about the hotel leaves you feeling at a loose end. But Easter is coming and we are expecting an early influx of visitors, mainly from the areas up north of here, Philadelphia and its suburbs. Apparently when the schools get out for Easter vacation a lot of families head down this way to catch a bit of sea and sand and surf, so I am told anyhow. This should bring some excitement about the place.

Myself, I have my own reason for excitement and it has nothing to do with cooking these blueberry pancakes. After not hearing from Bob for six weeks I eventually got a letter from him. He explained that he wasn't able to be in contact earlier, due, he said, to 'security concerns'. I have no idea what he means by that because it is not as if I am the sort of person to be gossiping about him or his government contracts or what he is doing in this Corpus Christi Texas place. Maybe he will explain it to me himself when he gets here. The letter said a lot of very nice things about me, things I am not used to hearing, to be honest. He tells me he has been extremely busy with this big contract and I believe him; one of the results of the whole thing is that I gather he has come into a load of money from it. He must have, for he mentions getting a boat, some sort of a 'pleasure cruiser'. I have no idea what size or shape of thing that is, but he says he will take me for a sail up the coast in it when he gets here, so it must be a good enough boat to go on the sea, on the Atlantic Ocean even. Maybe we'll get lost and finish up sailing into Burtonport harbour. He said that he looks forward to me *reclining on deck in one of those pretty dresses I bought you, the wind blowing your hair back and your pale Irish face catching some good American sunshine.'*

He is a right sweet talker, but then a lot of Yanks are. They must get it from the movies or something.

He is to arrive on the Wednesday of Holy Week. I wonder if I can book a day off to go with him. Maybe not though, for Roisin tells me we are likely to be busy by then. I'll have to see if I can work something, for I have waited long enough for this sort of adventure in my life.

As I gather up the cooking bowls for washing I start to wonder what Mairead would make of all this. I hardly know myself, to be honest. I suppose it depends on how far it all goes and how it ends up. I am forty-three this year so it's not before time that I am thinking about a man that I might marry. Lord knows I was never going to be interested in it when I was looking after my mammy. There wasn't much temptation either, if I am being frank.

It is so hard to know how to work with this situation, whether or not to follow my heart and accept all Bob's advances. He is a fine-looking man, a 'heart-throb' as Caroline calls him, and I may never get a better chance with such a man, a man who has been so attentive and generous and loving to me. At the minute my attitude is to let the river flow and see where it takes me. I might be surprised and pleased by its course. And, if it looks like ending up in disappointment, well sure haven't I tasted that bitter cup before and survived. I have the past behind me to buffer me against any hurts or shocks.

****

I pride myself in being prepared for shocks, but the one I receive this morning is beyond anything I could have imagined. It is the proverbial 'out-of-the-blue' event that really stuns me into confusion.

We are on our ten o'clock break at the back table in the kitchen, eating doughnuts and sipping sweet, milky coffee which I am getting a real taste for by this stage though it took me a while. Roisin breezes in through the benches with a long-looking parcel in her hands.

"Sally Anne," she calls, "this came for you. It was too big to put in the pigeonhole so I thought I'd deliver it by hand." She holds it out to me, a broad smile on her face. "But you have to open it now, 'cause curiosity is just about killing me, you know. From the stamps and all it looks as if it has been sent all the way from Ireland. Somebody's broken the bank for you, gal."

Now the kitchen staff start to circle around us, people peering in from all angles, a few urging me to open this parcel. It feels quite light as I take it from Roisin, even though it is near enough three feet long and a foot wide. I grab a knife to cut the string around it and start to peel off the brown paper, sheet by sheet. A cardboard box greets me but still no clue as to what it holds.

I hesitate for some reason, I can't say why, except that I have some sort of deep spirit sense that finding out what is in this box could be somehow very significant for me. I find it hard to describe this feeling that rises from way down in the heart of me; I can't put words on it; it is just something I sense. Maybe it is the fact that this is from home. Home, where the person I am is a shy, thoughtful, lonely, self-critical but faithful, middle-aged woman. Home where I have lived a private life, with few friends and little fuss, where I don't think I count for very much, where I don't get surrounded by nosey people when I am opening a strange parcel.

"Come on, hurry up!"

"Open it, Sally Anne!"

"Let's go, girl!"

I look up at the eager faces of maybe eight or nine work-mates, friends now, who are wide-eyed, waiting, urging.

I take the lid off the box.

Inside is a violin case.

And inside the case, lying snuggly in its wine-coloured velvet casing, is a fiddle that I think I know.

Matthew Henderson's father's fiddle.

Oh sweet mother Mary!

Although I recognise it immediately, my first instinct is to turn it over to check the underside. Sure enough, there is the wee dint that it had gotten when it hit the wall in my bedroom all those years ago.

I do a strange thing.

Without thinking, I put it to my face to breathe in the wood smell. I bring it to my lips and I kiss it lightly.

Then, without warning I find myself dissolving into tears and I cry without any self-consciousness for a good minute. It feels like a dam has burst and I cannot help myself. Once again I am unable to put words on the deep emotions that are running through me. I hear nothing of the kind words and the soothing questions of these new American friends, I feel nothing of the gentle hands patting my back or of Caroline coming beside to hug me.

Roisin seems to take control.

"Ok everybody, give Sally Anne some space please. Let's get back to work, come on, off you go."

She sits down opposite me and waits.

It is too long a story to try to explain to her. I can't even explain it to myself, so what chance has she got?

"What's wrong honey? You have us all very worried?"

"I am sorry," I say. "It is just a massive shock, that's all."

"But...is somebody not being very kind, sending you something that obviously means a lot to you?"

"Yes, of course," I tell her. "And it is very kind. Very, very kind..."

I cry again but get the tears dried up more quickly this time.

"A long time ago, Roisin....this fiddle meant the world to me. I can't really explain it all to you, it would take all day but..."

I can say very little else so I fade out.

"The fiddle," she asks, "or the person who sent it to you?"

"Yeah, you're right," I say, "both to be honest. I was...I was in love with him. It's twenty years ago; he gave me this fiddle but then...then he hurt me, I suppose, and I took a long time to get over it. I thought I was over it, but him sending me this now, it brings it all back."

Roisin sits silent for a bit, thinking, maybe of her own situation, for all I know. I am still holding the fiddle, nursing it close to my breast like it is a long-longed-for infant.

"Here, let me take this for you," she says, holding out her hands for the fiddle. "You don't need to be reminded of things that brought you pain. He has no right to do this to you. Believe me, gal, I know what this manipulation is like. You gotta..."

"No Roisin, no," I tell her. "It's not like that. This fiddle....Lord no, this fiddle...you see I destroyed the music in it back then. I threw it at the wall and smashed it; I rejected it once, just to get back at him. I am not going to reject it a second time. He isn't trying to remind me of hurt you see. He is trying..."

"What is he trying to do, Sally Anne? You are here in America now. He has no hold on you, none whatsoever. Let go of the past and let go of him."

"Oh believe me, I let go of him a long time ago," I say. "But I was at fault too and now all I want to do is move on with my life. That's why I wrote to him."

"You wrote to him?"

"I did, yeah, I did but it was just to tell him about...I suppose to tell him I was ok and that things here are great and all that, you know?"

"So why would he want to send you a violin? Is that not some form of control?"

"How control? And it's a fiddle, by the way."

"Reminding you of your past, your past bond with him, your past fiddle-playing for him?"

"Maybe," I tell her, "but look, if I forget my past who am I?"

"Who are you indeed?" she says getting up. "Let's go gal. There's work to be done, over and above these international affairs of the heart."

As I put the fiddle back in its case I see it, a small envelope tucked in at the side of the velvet lining. I am desperate to open it straight away, but Roisin is watching and waiting for me, so it will have to wait until later.

I go back to work.

It is the toughest day's work I have done here and the work itself is not to blame. My mind is not on it, not one bit. It is far away at times, in a kitchen in County Tyrone, and all I can think of is what on earth has he said in this letter.

Chapter 32

Lismore
Castlederg
29th March 1946

Dear Sally Anne,
I hope you are not angry at me for sending this fiddle to you. I will try and tell you why and what put it in my head.
You know now that I went over to your country one day last summer. It was the least I could do after getting your lovely letter. I just wanted to talk to you about all the things you had said. It meant a lot to me that you wrote. I still have that letter. It is sitting here on the table beside me as I am writing.
The things you said I could hardly credit. You said sorry but you had no need, for it was never your fault in any way what happened. It was all mine. If I could have seen you before you left for America I would have been saying sorry to you and asking you to pardon me for all the things I did to you that were not good. You did nothing to deserve them.
But you were gone already.
Your sister was kind. And your poor mother was nice too.
I got tea in your house. And I saw a fiddle hanging up by the hearth. It looked very lonely and a bit sad of itself.
I asked your sister about it and she said you had given up playing it years ago. She said it was after you came home from working in Tyrone that you stopped.
This made me mad inside myself. You should never have quit playing the fiddle. I was so annoyed at myself, for it was on

account of me that you had turned against it. That is what I think happened to you. Your music put a light inside you and I snuffed it out. I think I am more sorry about that than I am about all the other things put together and we both know there were a lot of other things that I did to you that brought you sorrow. So when your wee card with the picture on it arrived, I knew I had to do something about it.

I don't know if you have any chance to play music there in America. I don't know if they have your kind of tunes over there. I know they have all that jazz music and dancing tunes. Maybe in some places there are ones that can play your Irish sort of tunes, like the fast tunes you played and the Kearney wains danced to and thon slow one about the woman Eleanor that I used to love.

(I would give a pile of money to hear you play that one again, but it is too late now for that, I think.)

Anyway, for old times sake, will you please see if you can get a tune out of my father's fiddle? I have no idea if it is alright or if it is in tune or anything but I tried fixing it up and giving it a bit of a polish. My father would be delighted that it has found its way to America and into the hands of the best fiddler I have ever seen. He would have loved your tunes. I wish you two could have met.

I hope you are not annoyed at me but if you are maybe just give it away to someone who can use it, like a school or something.

I hope that you are well. It is some big step to do what you have done. You are a brave one, always were. So I wish you well in your new life. But if you ever come back to Ireland I would love to hear from you and we could maybe meet. I can't help wondering how you have changed. I am certain you will not look anything as bad as me, for the years have taken it out of me and left me a grey old man before my time.

Thank you for the picture of the hotel. It looks a grand place. But I would like it if you sent a picture of yourself, just to see if I recognise you, for I still have the old picture from the newspaper, the two of us standing with the new binder all those years ago.

I asked Mary Kearney how to say this in Irish. I hope it is alright.

Slán anois a sheanchara, agus ádh mór ort.

Matthew

Chapter 33

Sally Anne Sweeney

It has taken me a long time to get over the arrival of this letter, it and the fiddle. Here I am, free of Ireland and all its tightness, free of the shadows and hauntings of the past, a new woman in a new country, with a new love in her life, and this fiddle lands on me, grabs my attention against my will and drags me back.

I have taken it from its case and nursed it, stroked its wood, tuned and twanged its strings, but, after four or five days, I still haven't played a tune on it. I haven't even taken the bow in my hand, nor put the fiddle to my chin. There is a fear on me. I feel it is too big a risk, a risk of what, I do not know. Maybe of falling again into the shape of person that I was before.

The thing is that, in our local folk lore in Donegal, the fiddle itself is sort of the guardian of our music. The ancient tunes have their home in the body of the instrument itself…that's where they live, every bit as much as they live in the mind of the fiddler. So to have broken this fiddle against the wall in Henderson's attic was to chase the music out of it, maybe for ever. It has often struck me that what I did then was to put a sort of curse on the poor fiddle, indeed on the home itself; for, if the fiddle could no longer be playing its tunes, then all the happiness of those ceilidhs that took place in Henderson's kitchen would be banished. I have a fear on me that, even if I try to play this instrument, it will somehow screech back at me in anger and revenge, and I won't be able to get a decent melody out of it.

Something will have to happen to break this spell. The girls who saw me open the parcel will not stop pleading with me to bring it down to the kitchen again and play a tune, especially since Caroline told them she heard me play the violin 'so bootifully' in that Stone Harbour bar. Little does she know how rusty I felt that night.

"What is wrong with ya gal?" they say. "Play the damned thing!"

Roisin stands up for me though.

"She will play it when she's good and ready."

And Caroline senses that, behind my hesitation, there is some reason. She comes into my room at times, asks me if she can take the fiddle out of its case but doesn't go any further in her questions. She just admires the golden brown tone of the wood and the ebony fingerboard and she sniffs its scent, but she has yet to ask me who sent it. That is sensitive of her for sure.

She knows that I have asked for a day off during Easter weekend and, when Roisin seemed reluctant to give it to me, she volunteered to work my chamber-maid shift, so maybe it will happen. I could not ask for a better friend here and I have no idea what gets into the heads of some of these other workmates that they seem to frown on our friendship. I just don't understand their resentment. I suppose every country has its own history and its own way of looking at things, but, for a place that prides itself in being the 'land of the free and the home of the brave', why do its people turn up their noses at me for being free and brave enough to be best friends with a black girl? What business is it of theirs?

The fiddle seems to stare at me from its open case, the f-shaped holes like two drooping eyes that hold an age-old sadness in them. I have never noticed that before. I take it out again and hold it long-ways on my knee like you would a baby. My hand goes to the bow still clasped in the lid of the case, but pulls away again as if it might be red hot. To lift out Matthew's bow, to play that tune he referred to, 'Eleanor Plunkett'...I cannot imagine what that would do to me. I cannot face that danger. A tune like that is not just a series of notes. It is a deep, deep connection with a particular time and place and person; it is a feeling as deep as the sea. I cannot take the risk of swimming in those waves. Not now. Not now that Easter Wednesday is only two days away. I have enough risk in my life, enough challenge in this new future of mine, without spoiling things with the music of the past.

I know I should probably write back to Matthew Henderson to thank him for his kind thought. I have sat down a few times and begun to do that. The crumpled pages in my trash-can mock me as they are joined by yet another version. So I have given up on trying. I don't know what to say. One of my efforts was so honest and straight that it shocked me when I re-read it.

'Matthew, I have turned a page and I am trying to write a new chapter in this life of mine, but every time I try to write something new there are words burning through at me from the other side of the page, reminding me of who I was and who I am trying to free myself from, so thank you for the fiddle but I will never ever play it again. Sorry. Sally Anne.

Of course there is no way I would send this to him but it may just be the most honest feeling I have written. Anyhow, if I can't be frank and if I can't, at this point in time, think of what to say I will not say anything. Sometime I may get around to writing again. He deserves it, of course he does, but it is all too complicated right now. Imagine if he learned that I haven't played the thing yet, that I may never play it? It would be like a knife to him and I won't do that to anybody, much less to somebody who has spent a good bit of hard-earned money to mail me this gift from the past. Somebody who has gone out of their way to find out how to translate into Irish 'Goodbye for now and good luck, my old friend'. He had no need to do that, but it was nice of him to respect my Irish language. I can't imagine that happening back when I first knew him. He despised the language then, suspecting it for being a means for Joe and myself to communicate in secret code behind his back, right in front of him as well, now that I think about it.

I wonder is he trying to tell me that he has changed. Is this a move in my direction? Or is it, as Roisin might put it, a clever bit of manipulation of my emotions, playing on my homesickness? That is another tune I am denying myself at the minute.

Chapter 34

Matthew Henderson

The day after I posted my father's fiddle to Sally Anne, I came in from the yard to the sound of Millie crying in front of the range.

"Look," she said. "Somebody stole daddy's fiddle when there was nobody here. You never lock the door when you go away."

Poor Millie. She would read the worst into the situation. I had to handle the whole thing gently for her.

"Naw, nobody stole it," I told her.

"What happened it? Where is it gone?"

"It is gone somewhere safe," I told her.

"Where is safe?"

"Agh, Millie. It's a long story."

"Go on and tell me. I like a long story," she said, sitting down at the kitchen table. I had no option but to try to explain.

"You remember Sally Anne that worked here?"

"Aye, I remember Sally Anne. I liked her. You liked her too, didn't you Matthew?"

"I did. She was a great worker."

"What has her to do with daddy's fiddle?"

"Do you remember how she played it? She was great at it, wasn't she?"

"She was the best ever. Far better than oul Tam," she said.

"She was that. Well, Sally Anne is in a far-away country, in America. She is working there and she is lonely and missing home and she doesn't have a fiddle of her own to play, you know what I mean? So I had this idea that I would send her daddy's fiddle for sure nobody here is playing it and it's like lonely too, hanging up there beside the fire with the dust and ashes gathering on it. So I cleaned it up and put it all in a nice big parcel and sent it off to her in America. What do you think of that?"

Millie took a while to think about this. I could see her mind working its way through what I had told her, forming up questions. When the first one came it sort of shocked me though.

"You still love Sally Anne after all this time? Same way I love John, but only it's for a short time that I love him?"

Goodness, that is a straight question alright, I thought. Do I indeed?

"Not at all," I told her. "She was a great girl and all but I don't love her, not like that. But that doesn't mean to say that I don't, you know, that I don't care what happens to her...."

"You still love her Matthew. And I never knew till now," she told me, smiling at me with that same divilish mischief in her eyes that she had as a wain. "Well then, you did a good thing, sending her the fiddle, for now she will know that you still love her and maybe she will get on a boat and come home to you from America. That would be good, wouldn't it? And I wouldn't have to ride up here every day to make your dinner, for she would be doing that...."

"Stop, Millie. That is not what this is about. I don't want her to be coming home. I just want....look, I hurt her feelings back then. You maybe don't remember that, do you?"

"I mind she was very sad after Joe died. I mind she disappeared and before she went she was crying. I didn't know it was you that hurted her."

"Well it was, so now I want to do something to make her happy, cheer her up, you know. That is all."

"If you say so," she smirked and turned to go about her cooking.

****

It is one thing to take the big step of trusting the fiddle to the postal service and paying such a sum of money for the price of my faith. It is another thing entirely to wait on a note or a letter or something saying that it has arrived where it was meant to arrive.

I have waited weeks now and I've heard nothing.

Either it has gone astray in the post or it has reached Sally Anne and she is not minded to reply to my letter. I don't think I said anything in that correspondence to annoy her. I was fairly straightforward about all I said. It needed to be said, for after the nine months since she first wrote to me, I had to acknowledge her letter and indeed her recent postcard thing with the address on it.

In my thinking, it is more likely that the fiddle has never reached her. For all I know she may have picked up that postcard somewhere and thought, 'Wouldn't that be a nice place to be working?' Maybe she has never even been to that Cape May place. Maybe she just sent that picture to me as a bluff, a blind to what her life is really like. I start to imagine all sorts of issues that could have arisen for her, dark opportunities that she may have been driven to as a result of things not turning out for her as she had hoped.

Agh, these depressing thoughts. And after me being so pleased with myself and the notion that had come over me of sending her the fiddle. Maybe I acted too hastily.

I am hoeing potatoes in one of what I still call Bond's fields.

The story of how I came to buy land that had belonged to my former neighbours goes back to when the last of the brothers passed away. There was nobody to inherit their land. They had slaved tirelessly at this ground all their days and built it up into a great wee farm. Hard workers they were, the Bonds, and good, decent, quiet folk to have as neighbours.

When their forty-seven acres came up for sale a lock o' years back John Sproule and me had a dilemma. The land lay in to both of us. His farm marched on the lower side of Bond's holding and mine marched on the upper side, to the north. I knew John would be interested in buying, but I also knew he likely could not afford the asking price. I was interested in it myself of course, but I wasn't wanting to be bidding against him. After all, he was my brother-in-law by that stage you see.

We eventually got round to having a chat about it.

I told him my dilemma.

"John," I said, "come the auction I am not for bidding against you, rely on it."

"But you have to," he said. "What happens if some ither boodie bids it away up on me? I can't go too high. I would have to pull out. Then where would we be? You never know who would get it. Maybe wan o' the ither sort."

"I don't care what sort they are," I told him, "but it would be a great chance wasted if neither you nor me got it. Look, what I was thinking the other night was this. Why don't you buy it and then you and me can do a deal. I'll buy the half that lies in to me and you keep the other half?"

John was delighted with this, Millie even more so. He had never thought of it. He only asked if he could have the Bond farmyard in his half, for his yard would be very tight and run down of itself. I agreed to that and we did the deal. It suited us both down to the ground, in more senses than one. I have never regretted it.

It is lovely rich soil for growing early spuds and I am knocking off the weeds and moulding the brown earth up around the green shoots. It is hard work but a great kind of work to be thinking to, like much of the work a farmer does. How you do the job is so bred into you that it becomes as natural as breathing, so you never have to think about it, you can get on with solving the world's problems in your mind. The world's problems for me, though, have tended to narrow down recently to the problems closer to home. Maybe 'problems' is too strong a word and maybe I am in danger of becoming too obsessed with times past. I do catch myself on whiles, dwelling on days long gone by, wondering what might have been, how life would have been different if I had made different choices.

I often wonder too what is to become of this farm when I am no longer here. I don't have a will made yet, unlike the Bonds who wanted their land to be sold and the proceeds passed on to their church. I know I should be getting round to doing something about my place but, for the life of me, I can't think who to be leaving it to. I have no son and heir and I have very little chance now of ever having one. The young lassies about here who could have been in the running to be a wife for me were never much interested. I had the complicated stink of murder and of smuggling and of tight religion hanging about me and, between these and other failings, I managed to put any would-be brides off the scent. Now, at this age, I have all but given up hope of a son.

I could leave it to Millie and John but they show no sign of producing any wains, so that would be another dead end. Jane has her own brood with her man over in Drumquin, five children but didn't manage to have a boy among them. And Emily in Belfast has no interest and has never been the marrying kind.

Next door, I can imagine Anthony leaving his place to Mary and Liam. That will be a great opportunity for them. With a new farm beside the border they stand a chance of making big money, if they can watch the Excise men. And they have a host of wains to be passing the two farms on to, the one near Castlefinn and this one beside me. No bother that way for them.

But for me grafting away at these spuds, I sometimes wonder what am I doing it all for. I have fought a losing battle to keep the place tidy, repairing the stone walls, draining any wet fields and keeping the sheughs flowing, trimming back hedges and keeping the street clean, all as my father would have expected. But who for? Who follows me into it?

I think about these things near enough every day as I work. It doesn't help though, for I am no closer to an answer.

Chapter 35

Sally Anne Sweeney

Bob is back!

He arrived as he promised on Wednesday, two days ago, and I went straight to him as soon as I saw him come in the main entrance. We hugged until I heard the receptionist clearing her throat loudly. Maids don't normally greet guests arriving in the foyer in this fashion; it's an unwritten rule, I suppose. So I pulled away and rushed back to my cleaning, but as I did heard him say, "Later, gal. When you finish work."

So we went for a walk that evening and again on the Thursday. The weather is lovely and mild at the minute, not unlike the temperature you would have on a nice summer day at home. I feel more like myself when it is like this, not the real stifling hot weather that we had last summer, when you couldn't get a breath at times and your clothes were sticking to you.

"This weather is perfect for what I want to show you on Friday," Bob told me.

"And what is that?"

"The boat trip. I told you about it. Don't tell me you've forgotten."

"No, I haven't forgotten," I told him. "I'm just not sure that you know what you are letting yourself in for. I am a hopeless sailor. If the sea is rough, I'll be sick all over you."

"Don't worry about that," he said. "We won't be on the sea. It won't be rough."

I was curious about that but I let it pass, for it suddenly struck me that I wasn't even certain yet that Roisin would let me off work. I told this to Bob.

"You leave Rose to me," he said. "She owes me big time."

I wondered what he was talking about, maybe that dinner he paid for back at Thanksgiving. Sure enough, when I approached Roisin later she said it was fine. Caroline would do an extra shift and I could return the favour next week. Roisin did give me a long stare though, a strange look, as if she was trying to read my thoughts.

"You sure you know what you're doing, Sal?" she asked.

"Sure I'm sure," I said, sounding so American I surprised myself.

"Ok gal, if you're sure. Go get 'im, Tiger!"

My knowledge of Yankie talk didn't stretch far enough to be understanding that remark.

When we were out walking I tried to get Bob to talk about his time in Corpus Christi but he kept changing the subject. Apart from vague comments about it being 'a remarkable place' and, 'You saw the picture, didn't you?' he would say very little. When I asked about his job, just a general question about how his business there had worked out, he stared at me as if I had questioned his honour.

"You know I can't discuss my work," he said, the only time I've ever seen him come anywhere close to anger.

"Sor-ree," I said. "I wasn't asking you for any state secrets. I was just asking how you got on. God above, do you think I am a spy for the Irish Navy or something?"

He laughed at this. "You know, when I was stationed in Fermanagh and flying over Ireland we used to have so many jokes about the Irish military."

"Oh yeah? Like what?"

"Ah, I don't recall half of them now," he said. "There was one though…something about the Irish Navy being the only one in the world where the sailors could go home for lunch."

"Not funny," I said. Now it was my turn to stare at him.

"Yeah and someone drew a picture of a guy in a rowing boat with a shotgun in his hand. The caption below said 'Irish Naval Destroyer'.

"Ha, ha," I said without a smile. "We have our jokes about Americans too, but I am in your country, so I won't dirty your carpet by telling any of them."

"Hey, I didn't mean to offend you, Sally Anne," he said. "I thought the Irish were meant to have a great sense of humour and could laugh at themselves."

"Yeah, we do," I replied, "but only if we are the ones telling the joke."

We left it at that.

Before we went out on Thursday night, I went to confession at Our Lady Star of the Sea. It was Holy Week after all.

Bob couldn't hide his amusement at the idea. He walked me to the church and waited outside.

"I can't believe you still go to confession," he said. "You're going to have a tough time in there, trying to dream up confession material."

"Don't you believe it," I said, leaving him at the door.

"I could maybe give you one or two ideas," he called after me, laughing.

I waited my turn in the shadowy silence of the side chapel. The Blessed Virgin stared down at me, a hint of rebuke in her icy-blue eyes.

In a few minutes the priest rammed the rebuke home a bit more.

"How long has it been since your last confession, daughter?"

Now there was a question. I mumbled something like, "A couple of weeks Father," but, when I try to count it back, I realise it is months. I have only been to Mass a few times since Christmas and not very often before that. I sort of got out of the way of going, for hardly any of the other girls seem to be religious at all, Caroline being the exception. Roisin doesn't bother with it and doesn't seem to miss it. Maybe it has just been laziness, or maybe you get like the people you spend your time with. Maybe it is the fact that I am so far removed from Ireland and the normal rhythm of the life that I had there. Is it that I am far away from the expectations of my community and that my loyalty to the church and to Father Devine has waned? Maybe a mixture of everything, but I comfort myself that I am observing Lent and here I am on Holy Thursday, doing confessions so I can take Mass on Good Friday morning.

It's not that I have given up believing...well, maybe my faith has faded a bit. The chapel certainly hasn't been playing as big a part in my life over the last while. Do I feel guilty about that? I suppose deep down I do, but not enough to have me make any great effort to change things. It is just that now, in this place and at this time in my life, I seem to have other priorities. Living in the here-and-now is just so much more exciting and colourful than any of the grey drabness and rules of the priests.

****

The roof is down on Bob's car as we speed up the road to the marina at Stone Harbour.

"It's a Cadillac convertible," he told me, "Of course it's got a soft-top roof that comes down. That's why it's called a convertible."

That's me told.

The moving air is blowing through my hair and making a tangled mess of it. Worse though is that it is playing havoc with my dress, the red one that Bob bought me and insisted on me wearing today. I have trouble trying to hold it down over my legs to protect my decency, so Bob slows the car and passes me his jacket from the back to wrap myself in. I feel a bit warmer and more secure with that around me.

Above us the heavens are as blue as a robin's egg. 'Wall-to-wall blue' as they say here. Except that out to the east, above the Atlantic there are some beautiful little clouds that look like scoops of vanilla ice cream floating in the morning sky.

Along the sides of the road the many shades of foliage have taken on a much stronger tone now that Spring has fed them with sunlight. The contrast of colours today amazes me. Anybody watching us from the roadside will be seeing an even nicer picture, this flash of bright red across the green background, like one of their Cardinal birds through the bushes, as Bob's car flies past.

The radio is playing Perry Como's new hit, 'Prisoner of love'. I have heard it back in the common room at the Windsor when someone put it on the record player, so I sort of know the words and sing along. Bob is grinning widely at me, the whiteness of his teeth bright against his dark moustache and tanned skin.

I love this song.

I love this day.

Maybe I even love this man; maybe he is the master of my fate.

> *'For one command I stand and wait now*
> *From one who's master of my fate now*
> *I can't escape for it's too late now*
> *I'm just a prisoner of love'*

We arrive in Stone Harbour and park Bob's car right beside the marina. I have never been to one of these marina places before and I am shocked by the size of it and the number of boats. Boats of all shapes and sizes, dozens of them. The people around here must have stacks of money to be affording these.

Bob takes a can of fuel and a large hamper from the trunk of his car, a 'cooler' he calls it. I raise my eyebrows.

He laughs at me.

"Guess you don't do this very often, honey," he says. "I don't intend to let my date starve on our cruise. You gotta have your own supplies on a trip like this."

"How long are we going for?"

"Long as it takes," he laughs. "You in a hurry back already?"

"Of course not," I say. "As long as we are back by tonight."

Bob's face falls, but his eyes are still twinkling.

"Aw shucks," he says, "I thought this was gonna be an all-nighter. Why d'ya wanna go back so soon to your lonely little bed in the Windsor?"

"It's not that," I tell him, "but I am working at six o'clock in the morning. Where's this ship of yours?"

He laughs over his shoulder as he leads the way along some sort of floating pier, me following behind like a faithful collie.

"Here we are," he says, stopping beside one of the biggest of these cruisers in the row. At a quick guess I would say it is at least ten yards in length, painted white but with a crimson-red cabin section on top, not unlike the colour scheme of the Windsor itself.

"You're not serious? This is yours? It's enormous."

"You're not meant to call it enormous, honey. Maybe 'beautiful', or 'stunning', or 'impressive', but not enormous. There are much larger ones further along. Anyhow, this is our home for the next...well, as long as you wish, m'lady."

Bob removes the protective cover, 'tarp' as he calls it, and we load the hamper on board. I watch as he prepares the boat, using his keys to open up the hatches and the door to the cabin below. Then, while he fills the fuel tank, I take a look inside. There's a small kitchen at the end and a table surrounded by cushioned benches. Comfortable looking.

Bob unties the ropes from the moorings above and jumps back down beside me.

"One more thing before we cast off," he says, disappearing down into the cabin and coming back with two glasses and a bottle of something in his other hand. He pours us two glasses of some sort of bubbly wine and gives me one.

"Here's to our first voyage together," he says, pulling me close. "Happy sailing, Sally Anne."

A lovely drink, this champagne. And it looks to be a huge bottle.

"So where are we going if we are not going out to sea?" I ask him when he untangles himself and goes to the controls.

"We can go north for miles on these waterways," he tells me. "You see, the Jersey shore here is a whole series of sandbars and islands stretched out north to south and behind these islands there's miles and miles of waterways that are protected from the Atlantic Ocean. You probably remember crossing lots of bridges on your drive down here? Today we will be going under some of those bridges, ok?"

"Ok," I say, but I'm not really sure what he means. He fires up the engine and casts off. We get underway and I find that it is a very smooth journey with no real waves to contend with. It feels at times that we are sailing along a wide canal, rather than being on sea-water. The banks can be close to the boat in places, but at other times we are in the middle of a lake. Along the sides are stretches of reeds, low trees and bushes that he tells me are mangroves. They look to me like they are fighting with each other for space, branches and trunks entwined like men wrestling. It isn't the most interesting scenery at times, but I am with the most interesting man you could ever meet and the amount of champagne he is giving me to drink makes everything seem more colourful and beautiful than it probably is.

We do see a lot of interesting wildlife, mainly birds of various types that you would never see in Ireland. I should remember the names he put on them but after a while I am giggling so much I just give up on even trying.

We meet a brightly coloured speed-boat coming towards us at a fierce rate. Our boat rocks side to side in the waves it throws at us when it passes. The one man in this boat is hiding behind a pair of huge sunglasses and doesn't so much as look at us, never mind wave. In Ireland he would have waved, I am sure, but then in Ireland he would likely have been rowing a curragh.

We go past signs pointing to the various villages and marinas. I remember seeing Avalon and Sea Isle City. That was before I lay back on a deck-chair thing, stretched out to enjoy the sun and, without meaning to, I fell asleep.

When I wake up the boat is not moving. Everything is very still and there is no sign of Bob. I raise my head and look around. We are parked, (I know that is not the right word for it,) in the middle of a huge lake. The shore seems to be miles away on both sides of the boat. Suddenly I feel very alone.

"Bob," I call. "Where are you?"

"Down here, honey," he calls back. "Fixin' some lunch."

He climbs back up with a tray of filled rolls and fruit and of course more drinks, this time beers.

"Where are we?" I ask, "and why is the boat not moving?"

"We are in the middle of Ludlam Bay, as far from the shores as we can get. We are not moving 'cause the anchors are down. Any other questions, just ask a deck-hand. This is your captain speaking. Over and Out!"

'For one command I stand and wait now', I sing again with a touch of mockery in my voice. Bob just laughs at me. Perry Como won't get out of my head. And he's right, I am *a prisoner of love.*

Later Bob takes my hand and leads me down the hatch to the cabin. We get very intimate at the kissing and he works at the buttons on the back of my dress. Then he asks me, "Are you sure you want to do this, honey?"

"I'd better be sure," I reply, "for your have just taken my dress off and just because you bought it for me doesn't mean you can do that."

I notice again that my words are heavy and slurred in my mouth and I know that, as much as I am a prisoner of him and of love, I am also a prisoner of alcohol. Bob just laughs at me, enjoying the view.

'I can't escape for it's too late now'.

Oh Lord, what am I doing? Is this really me? It doesn't feel like me; maybe it's the drink, but it seems like I have become someone else, someone that if I was back in my Donegal life I would have despised. But I can't seem to stop any of this. It's the curiosity. It's the power of this handsome man whose hands are pulling me down.

We lie on the make-shift bed that he has put together on the cabin floor. There is no swell, no waves in this bay to make the boat rock, but I am sure anyone watching would notice it rocking anyway. I seem to be happy in a giggly sort of way; then it hurts, and a wave of disgust rises in me; I feel so sore and almost sick, my stomach heaving. These feelings churn around in my body and I am more tired than I have ever felt in my whole like. Stop please. So sleepy now. Head spinning. Just let me be, let me rest.

****

I waken in his arms and am suddenly aware that the shadows the sun is casting through the cabin windows are nearly horizontal. The evening is closing in on us.

"Bob! Waken up, we need to be getting back. It's...Oh Lord, what time is it anyway?"

"You're ok, honey, it's six o'clock. Yeah, you're right. It is six o'clock and we have an hour and a half of daylight to get this thing back in the harbour."

"How long did it take us to get here?"

"Three hours, but we can do it faster on the way back....unless...unless you fancy staying here all night and making it back tomorrow? What d'ya think?"

"No, no. I must get back. I have to work tomorrow morning. Please. Just let's get going."

He hauls the anchors and revs up the engine and we begin a hectic ride back the way we came. The boat seems to raise its head in the water and leaves a white foaming wake behind. Birds rise squawking and swirling from in front of it and from the salt marshes beside us. We see very few other boats out on the water at this hour.

The sun has well and truly disappeared by the time we reach Stone Harbour but Bob does a great job of navigating us through the narrow channels and right up to the berth where his boat is moored. I am amazed that after the amount of drink we have drunk he has been able to get us back safely. By the looks of things he is far more able than me to hold his liquor, thanks be to God. At times on that journey I thought I was going to vomit but I kept my head down and somehow survived without making a fool of myself.

At the same time, back on land I am not exactly feeling great, my stomach churning a bit. The horizon seems to keep spinning, or if it's not spinning its wavering up and down like a rumpled carpet. I have to hold to the railings as Bob secures the boat and I am no help to him at all.

He helps me to the car, one arm around me, his other hand holding the empty cooler. I feel a bit of a disaster as I lean on him and stumble along. I keep apologising.

"Don't worry, honey. We'll get you home and into bed."

Home? Home, is it? Home is a long way away.

"You're not taking me home," I tell him. "Not home! Promise me?"

He doesn't get it, just gives me a strange stare, but I don't care and I don't explain.

In the car it suddenly hits me.

My mother fell pregnant on an occasion like this. Not that any of us know anything about the event, for she was never able to tell us. The result was a baby though, a baby who didn't make it. What if?

"Bob, what if I have a baby after today?"

"What?!?"

"If I am pregnant after...after what we just did?"

"You won't be."

"What makes you so sure? I am only forty-two? I could still..."

"No you couldn't," he says. "You couldn't because I have had a... a procedure, a medical thing that means I can't have any more children. See what I mean? So you are safe, honey, ok?"

"You have a proce...a pro-ceee-dure?" I say. God but it's a hard word to be trying to say after all those beers. "You never told me before. What sort of thing is that? A pro-ceee-dure?"

"Don't worry about it, Sally Anne. Just trust me, ok?"

"So no children?"

"No, no children. Now drop it."

"So after we get married, like when we get married I won't have any children?" I say quietly, half to myself.

"What are you talking about? When we get married? We haven't ever discussed marriage, have we?"

"No, no we haven't, I suppose. But we should, do you not think?"

"What makes you say that?"

I think about this and look at him for a second. His gaze seems hard as I look at him and he turns away to look out the window.

"Bob? What's wrong? I love you. You love me, don't you?"

"'Course I do, honey," he says.

"And you will want to make love to me again? Again and again?"

He reaches over and takes my hand. It feels good.

"Now you're talking, gal!"

"So, if we are married that's what you can do. Every day, as much as you want to, right?"

"Yeah sure, sounds good to me, but let's not push things too fast, ok?" he says.

"Today was pretty fast," I tell him, "And after what we just did today, I think we should get married as soon as…"

"Sally Anne," he says as we pull into the parking lot at the Windsor, "you've had a lot to drink today and it is affecting your judgement. You can't just ask a man to marry you like that. You need to wait, wait and see how things work out with us, you know? Don't rush."

"I'm sorry," I tell him. "I am just a bit con…confused, a bit drunk still. I had a great day, best day of my life, and Bob…."

"Yeah, what honey?"

"At least now I won't die wondering."

"Wondering what?"

"Wondering what it's like, you know…."

He gets out of the car with that. I'm not sure if I have offended him again. I get out anyhow and lean my rear end against the car door. I am still a bit dizzy.

"Hey, you need to move your ass so I can get this soft-top secured," he says.

I do as I am commanded. Again. I move my ass.

He hasn't spoken to me like this before. It's a new crudeness I haven't seen in him. Maybe it's because I am tipsy, or maybe hung-over.

"Here, come on. Take my arm and let's get you up to bed," he says, guiding me to the main entrance. "It's past your bedtime."

I wish I'd told him to take me to the staff entrance around the back. I really do.

I really, really do, for as we come in through the front door he stops abruptly. A sudden stop that nearly causes me to fall, or maybe I fall because he has let go of me. He is standing stock still. The swear words that are coming out of him are unbelievable.

"What the hell?"

And worse. What is wrong with him? What is he doing? I look up at his face. He is staring across the foyer. It is an angry stare, dark as the robe of a priest. What is he staring at? Why is he looking so shocked, so scared, so angry? I follow his gaze.

I see a woman coming towards us. She is tall, I notice. Tall and elegant and beautiful, hair the colour of ripe corn, everything about her gorgeous like the women you see in those Coca Cola advertisements, and she's youngish, maybe thirty something and so pretty in her fabulous clothes and high heels. So sophisticated, though that word doesn't sound right when I try to say it in my head at the minute. She is smiling, but even I can see that the smile is a cover, a poor cover for her cold anger, her icy rage. She walks slowly towards us, well, towards Bob anyhow. I don't exist. She reminds me of a cat for some reason, the menace of a cat stalking a mouse. Bob is the mouse, thankfully. Not me.

"Bob, darling! How nice to see you back. Back from your day of whoring, eh? Another great day of screwing," she hisses.

"What in God's name are you doing here, Melissa?"

Mel-issssa? Never heard that name before. Nice name, nice lady, but her voice is pure poison. Mel-issssa! Like a hissa! If her words could melt, poor Bob would be a puddle in no time.

"I am here, my dear husband, to check up on you. Surely that much is already obvious, is it not? And I have caught you out this time. My drive down from Philly today has been well worth it, well timed, wouldn't you agree? All it took was a phone call to Roisin here. She confirmed that you were in residence at the Windsor, but you had gone off somewhere today. So, all in all, I would say that I have caught you with your pants down around your ankles, yet again. Texas wasn't enough for you. You had to have a lover in Cape May too. My cheating bastard of a husband."

Beyond her I see Roisin, her face twisted with some emotion I don't recognise. Her hands are together at her mouth, as if she has remembered that this is Good Friday and she needs to pray.

My Good Friday has just turned really bad. Did that woman just say, "Husband"? I think she did. I think she is wrong though, she has made a mistake for Bob has already told me that he was married and has two children but that he is divorced. So what she means is "Bob, my ex-husband". That's what they say for such things around here. I hope she corrects herself.

I open my mouth to point this mistake out to her but Bob gets in first.

"Melissa darling, this is not what it seems. I am just helping this girl, this maid who works here in the hotel. I found her in a bad state out in the parking lot. She's Irish, you see and...the drink, you know?"

Melissa laughs. How can a person look so beautiful and so ugly at the same time, I think. She laughs long and loud at Bob's explanation, her pretty mouth wide open.

My mouth is wide open too, but I am not laughing. Again I try to speak some truth into the situation.

"That is a load of..."

That is all I get out. Melissa jumps in again. She is right up to Bob's face now and I back off a bit incase she looks at me.

"You are full of it, Bob Clifford," she spits. "When Daddy told me you had asked for the keys of his boat, I guessed that you were up to something again. Another one of your conquests. And here you are."

She puts her hand into his jacket pocket and produces the set of keys.

"And here is the evidence...these keys and this poor drunk."

She gives me a look that would freeze a boiling kettle.

"I'm no drunk," I tell her. But it doesn't matter what I tell her. I am not her enemy. I am a nothing here. This is all about the revenge of the cheated wife.

She turns to me.

"I suppose he told you he was divorced, eh? Well he was. Twice. I am wife number three, or if you want me to be more honest, I am fool number three. You, my poor friend, are probably bit-on-the-side-fool number twenty-three."

I am in shock here. The truth is slow to sink in with me. Maybe it is to do with all that champagne and beer and whatever else he fed me today. I look at him and I grab hold of his jacket. He can't meet my eyes and who could blame him. I hold on tight to him. My stomach is bubbling. Something is shifting down there.

"I trusted you," I tell him as I am gagging. "I believed you. I gave myself to you. I was your willing.... May you rot...." I don't make it to the end, for at that moment my body turns into a volcano and it spews hot, stinking sick straight on to Bob's shirt front. It runs down his trousers and on to the floor. A terrible smelling soup of ham and oranges and beer and bread and bits of corn and whatever. It slimes its way down this man's body and spreads itself on the Windsor's wonderfully clean wooden floor.

Melissa was quick to jump to the side. In my dark cave of embarrassment I hear her.

"Way to go, girl!" she says. "It's no more than what he deserves. I am sorry you had to be the one to go through this."

Bob just swears some more and stands there looking like a soiled toilet bowl.

Roisin is on the scene now and takes over, calling instructions to the night porter and another maid who was passing and got caught up, watching the row.

I am helped over to the elevator and up to the shower room.

In the shower my tears blend with the hot, healing water. I want to scream but I haven't got the energy. I feel hollowed out, like a halloween turnip. My stomach aches and feels empty now, but it is nothing to the emptiness in my spirit.

What a fool I have been. What a fool I am!

I think, with absolute horror, about the woman I was on that boat. Melissa was right. Nothing but a whore, a stupid, sordid trollop. I retch again to think about it.

And to vomit in public like that, in the main foyer of the hotel that I have a job in...that I had a job in, more than likely. To boke all over Bob, all over that man. That chancer! That bastard!

'Well,' I think to myself, 'if you were ever going to vomit over somebody in public you couldn't have picked a better man for it.'

When I finish my shower Caroline comes to me. As she helps me get dried and dressed for bed she just keeps saying a soothing prayer for me. And she cries, she cries with me, bless her heart. She walks me to the safety of my bed. I am dozing in no time and the horrors of this day of my crucifixion quickly fade as I bury myself in a deep sleep.

Chapter 36

47 Eskeside Road
Musselburgh
6th May 1946

Dear Mairead,

What am I to do Mairead? They let our Nuala out o the asylum for the weekend on Friday to see how she would get on and she only bided in the house a couple o nights before she took off.

She would do nothing but row and fight way me for the days she was here. She never looked next nor near the bairn and him crying all the time for her. She has no heart in her, that lass, and her me own flesh and blood and the mother o wee Frankie.

This morning I got up way the greetin o him from the other room. I waited for her to get him settled again but there was no settling o him, so I had to get up and go in to him. Where was his mother? Nowhere to be seen. She had took off sometime during the hours o darkness and left me way him again, and him crying the bit out. What is to become o her, or the poor bairn? I am lost to ken what to be doing. I wish wan o yous was here.

The police, I suppose. I'll take him way me and go to the police station and report her missing. I blame them doctors at the asylum for they shouldn't have let her out, not till she was better. You may tell your sister in America, not that it will do any good, for she is far away from us. She was to send us money to help out but damn the bit o money I seen all year till Nuala

went in the asylum. Then a couple o letters did arrive from America way a few dollars. Maybe Nuala always got her hands on it first before she went in the mad-house. That must be what happened. It never put a bite in our mouths all year. I will send you word if I hear any mare about Nuala but you may say a prayer for us all in the meantime.
Your cousin
Mary Anne

Chapter 37

Sally Anne Sweeney

I have the fiddle in my hand, my left hand, the bow in my right.
It has been a long time and the smooth neck of the instrument takes time to settle and feel at home in these rougher chamber-maid hands.

I am alone in my bedroom, the door is tight shut, the girls are all at work below so I am fairly sure nobody will hear me.

I have done my best to bring the strings up to proper pitch, but it has been an age since this fiddle was in tune and it is fighting with me. I wonder again if it really is cursed. When I get the D string up to what I think is pretty close to how a D should sound, the G protests with a twang and slips back to where it had been resting comfortably for the last God knows how long. But I keep arguing with it and I won't be beat in this struggle.

"Come on, you sinner. Stay in tune."

It's a thran oul Protestant fiddle this, as its owner might admit. But it is in my hands now. It is in my hands, after me having stared at it for the last couple of days and wondered if, instead of vengeance, it might have within it the magic to take me back to a time where life made sense. To a place where everything was simple and easy to understand, where nothing needed to be so complicated, so distressing.

I was told to stay in bed yesterday morning and I did. Little good it did me though, for I did nothing but fret myself and think back about the fool I have been. Roisin has been very good but very insistent that now I must do what she says and Caroline has made sure that I have tried to rest. She has also been a great listener and in the times when I haven't been able to talk she has just been there, handkerchief at the ready.

She took me for a short walk last night when no-one else was around. We strolled to the west of the Windsor for once, to an area along the shore that I had not explored before. Not much was said, but is was just lovely to be out of the hotel to clear my head, with only the sound of the sea and the gulls in my ears.

I say 'the only sound' but that is not the truth. There is a song in my head constantly and, while the melody of it is wearing a groove in my brain, the words are like a nagging toothache.

'I wish, I wish, I wish in vain. I wish I were...'

Today is Easter Sunday.

I didn't go to Mass. I couldn't face it, to be honest. Anyhow, for a girl who isn't even a Catholic, Caroline is a lovely 'priest'. I have talked more deeply to her than to anyone I can remember, but her powers of forgiveness are limited.

"Only Jesus can forgive," she keeps saying.

She is right and she is also wrong. Leaving Jesus aside, it's me who has the hard time forgiving myself.

And that thought brings the sob back in my throat.

What an idiot I have been!

I cannot face going down those stairs, seeing the faces, hearing the muttered comments.

But I should be back working. This is now three days that I haven't worked. I won't be paid for these days. More importantly, other girls are having to do extra work. I am letting Roisin down, after her trusting me, giving me this job, getting me trained as a cook as well. This has been the busiest time since Thanksgiving Day and here I am, stuck in my room, wallowing in the muck of disgrace and self-pity.

How did I fall for all that? For that man?

I paid no heed to Roisin's early hints about him being married. I am in my forties, for God's sake, not a frivolous teenager.

I like to think of myself as a fairly sensible person. I am generally clear-headed, nobody's fool. I don't have a high opinion of myself but I have always prided myself that I could see through flattery and falsehood. Way back in time, I had that whole experience of disappointment and betrayal, but I was only nineteen at that stage. And I was in a situation that was completely new to me, that crazy world of the North in 1922, where nothing was what it seemed and where there were so many unspoken rules and such strange ways of thinking and behaving. But this? This is entirely different, almost entirely anyhow.

And yet the similarities depress me, when I admit to them.

America is different, different to Donegal, just as the North of Ireland was different. Different customs, different ways of being, different expectations. Here there is a sense that 'anything goes', I suppose, with few limits of a religious or moral kind. In that way it is very much the opposite of anything back in Ireland, north or south. I did like this aspect of America at the start. Certainly I found the differences refreshing, up until now.

And in both cases, Tyrone and Cape May, I did fall for the man. I fell completely for his masculine appeal, his strength and shape, his downright good-looks; true both then and now. And to be fair, Bob was so loving, so generous to me. I thought he was in love with me, as I was with him, but to stand in that foyer on Friday night, after all that happened during the day, and learn that I was nothing more than his flousie... unbelievable! So devastating!

I wonder how long he would have strung me along for if his wife hadn't turned up? Maybe that would have been it, he'd made his conquest, proved and satisfied himself, so that would have been the finale. I might never have seen him again. Now I hope I never set eyes on him again. Roisin tells me that he has checked out and left, just after his Melissa did. I wish her well of him.

With Matthew it was different though. He never seduced me or forced me into anything I didn't want to do. We were close but he respected me enough to stop. I never felt, and I don't feel now, that he used me. Our break-up was less his fault, (though he was so stubborn and contrary at the end), and more the fault of those people in his family and in that tight community who had him under their thumbs.

I can't escape the fact that in both cases I was 'the maid', the one at the lower end of the social scale. Why am I an easy target for such men? I would never have thought of myself as naive or easily impressed. Or maybe it is that I am not an easy target at all? Maybe that is the point, that there is something in my personality, my self-confident nature, that is a challenge to the big strong man, something they have to try to master and tame? I struggle to work it out but, in the meantime, I have this gut feeling of being used and abused. How will I ever come to terms with this deception, with this deep feeling of defilement?

In my despair I have re-read Matthew's letter. Perhaps because of how low and vulnerable I am today, I am touched by what he has done. He has given me a part of his family, straight from his home hearth, a precious part of himself and, other than seeing it as a peace-offering, I can't begin to understand what to make of it.

Maybe the fiddle itself will speak the answer, if and when I get it in tune and get around to playing it.

So I do. I play Matthew's fiddle.

The shakes of me as I play that first long 'E', my heart thumping and me fighting back the tears blurring my eyes.

Slow tunes at the beginning. I can't find any part of me today that wants to be hearing a reel or a jig, let alone playing it. Far too joyful. But there are plenty of *foinn mhalla*, beautiful slow airs and waltz tunes that I used to love.

First I play a tune from down the road from my home, the townland of *Rann na Feirste*; it's a gorgeous old song called

'Méilte Cheann Dubhrann'. I follow that with a famous Donegal song, *'Coinleach Glas an Fhómhair'*. There are beautiful words to these airs of course, but they remain in my head as I play. The ornamentation returns to me as I delve into the soul of the tune, *spioraid an fhoinn*. I try the old trills and slides and, by the time I reach those lovely cadences at their endings, I am well on top of them.

I try a waltz, playing more slowly than the people at home would allow me to if I was playing in a ceilidh in *Halla Naomh Muire*. It seems to turn into a lament, or *'caoineadh'*, as we call it.

By the time I am finished this, I am crying again, but these are not tears of hurt and anger, this is a yearning for home and the past that cradled me, that succoured and protected me.

This is the scent of dry turf burning in my mother's hearth on *Grianstad an Gheimhridh*, the night of the winter solstice.

This is the rasping call of *an traonach*, the corncrake, in the long grass of Mullaghdearg banks of a July evening.

This is the fresh rain washing my face as I walk home over the soft, spongy *caonach* of Ranahuel bog.

This is the stooping shape of our *seanachaí*, Micheál Paddy Óg O'Dubhthaigh as he leans into an ancient tale of Lugh or Balor, *as Gaeilge* of course.

This is the lilt of our local dialect as neighbours sip *'uisce beatha'* and talk weather at a wake in Calhame.

Only once in my life do I recall my father telling me to stop playing my fiddle. I must have been about ten or eleven at the time. My grandmother, Maggie Dan Ní Dhomhnaill who lived just down the lane from our cottage, had passed away the previous week. It was a sad time; I had been very close to her and always loved her stories, for I missed that from my own mother. Anyhow, I was sitting on a tree stump playing a few tunes when my father appeared down the hill from the turf cutting.

"*Stad, a leanbh!*" he shouted at me. "Stop. Your granny is hardly cold yet and you are sitting out here in the open playing tunes like she is gone months ago."

The thing was that in our parish, and in others too I am sure, there was a custom that you didn't play or listen to a fiddle for a year after there had been a death in the house. I just never thought, but my father wasn't long in reminding me. I think it would have been alright if I had been in the house itself, but the tunes carried all over the countryside from our place up on the hill. So I had to honour the tradition and hold myself in, to wait out the months of mourning.

That was back then.

What I find interesting is that I have turned again to the music of the fiddle at a time of deep mourning in myself. I know there was no death involved, unless you want to count the end of my innocence as a death itself. The music speaks into me where words just bounce off. It would not be right to say that the fiddle or the tunes cheered me up, far from it. Indeed you could argue it the other way around, that they saddened me even further. I don't know. But I do know that there is something about the ordering that music does to me that I absolutely crave at this moment in time. I need it like I need fresh air. It straightens me out in my thoughts and puts a calmness and a harmony back in my head and this is of far greater importance than the dismal circumstances I find myself in today.

So thank you, Mr Henderson.

I owe you one.

But the other tune is hard to beat down and I find myself humming it, the lyrics a silent lament in my head.

> 'But a maid again I n'er shall be
> Till cherries grow on an apple tree'.

I need to chase it and start praying the Memorare instead.

Chapter 38

Matthew Henderson

"Millie, you'll never guess."

"Guess what, Matthew?"

"Mind you were cross at me for sending daddy's fiddle to Sally Anne in America?"

She puts her finger to her lips as she often does when she is going back in time in her mind. Her eyes flit up to where it hung since time immemorial.

"I was never cross that you sent it to Sally Anne," she says. "Just that you sent it away to America and didn't hold on to it, for daddy's sake."

"And you were scared it would never reach her in a big place like that?"

"Aye. Well, what?"

"Well this," I tell her. "It has reached her. She has the fiddle. It got there safe and sound."

She ponders this for a minute, suspicious of my joy.

"How do you know?"

"I know because…look," I say, producing Sally Anne's letter, wrinkled from having spent the day in and out of my hip pocket. "She wrote to say she got it."

"That's alright then," she says, turning back to pound the spuds in their pot.

"Do you not want to hear what she says?" I ask.

"Aye, if you want to read it to me."

So I do.

Dear Matthew,

I don't know how to say thank you for sending the fiddle. That was a very kind thought. But you know that I can't keep it. It would not be right nor fair. It is your father's and you must pass it on to the next generation, so I must get it back to you. I would never dream of giving it to someone else. It must have cost you a fortune to send it. But I want you to know that it has meant a lot that you sent it to me, especially now, for I have been through a rough time lately and it has brought me comfort to go back to playing tunes from home. The light of music in me that you talk about hasn't been completely snuffed out, you see.

It is a lovely sounding fiddle and always was. I generally only play it when nobody else is around to hear, but last night I got invited down to the hotel lobby to play for some Irish Americans from New York City. They were nice folk and one older man knew a lot about Irish tunes. He was from Mayo way back when he was young and he asked me if I knew certain tunes. So I played for him and it stole away years of my life to be doing it again.

You say that I am very brave for coming to America. Maybe I was at the start but now I am thinking that I was more foolish than brave. This is a strange country, with some strange people, and you can finish up getting misused if you are not careful. I have had to learn lessons but I hope I will be the stronger for it. Thankfully I do have some good friends who stand by me.

No, I am sorry but I won't be sending any photographs, other than the one of the hotel. I am no picture to look at now, at my age. You wouldn't know me if you met me on the street for I am hiding behind a crumpled page of wrinkles and my hair would be nowhere near the colour I had when I was young and working for you.

You never told me anything about your own life there in Lismore. I have often wondered about how things turned out for you. Anyway, I must go back to my work so thank you again

for your kindness. And for the words in Irish which was good of you too.
Slán go foill,
Sally Anne Sweeney

"What on earth does that mean?" Millie asks.

"Likely means 'Goodbye or something," I tell her and she looks at me with suspicion.

"Wait till I tell John that you can speak Irish... and Sally Anne is your teacher," she says. "That'll give him something to pray about."

Chapter 39

Sally Anne Sweeney

May Day is not much celebrated here in America, not like home where we feel the need to mark the important times in the circle of the year. No day is more important that the first day of summer. I tell Caroline all about our traditions as we walk the strand after work. It is a rich evening of colour out here, the green-blue stretch of the Delaware Bay as the big ball of the sun sinks over the rim of the earth in the west, leaving orange and crimson paths in the sky, like the pattern of a beautiful bed-quilt.

The chat is great. She always does me good, this lassie. Up ahead of us there seems to be a whole swarm of birds, excited about something. They are swirling around above the beach and the air is filled with the cries of them. I have never seen birds as crazy as this, all kinds of seabirds.

The light is on our faces and in our eyes as we are walking and, maybe for that reason, we don't see what we are walking into until we are on top of it.

The beach looks as if it is covered in some sort of strange animals. It is black with them, and they small and black themselves. I did not know from God down what I was looking at and there is a fear on me about them, for they look very odd, very foreign altogether. Caroline takes my elbow as we stop to stare.

"What are they, Caroline?"

"Ya never seen these before?"

I shake my head, mesmerised by this sight. A carpet of dark-looking objects that would remind you of those helmets that motor-cycle riders wear.

Caroline seems excited to be the one in the know and pleased to be my teacher.

"They is our famous horseshoe crabs," she begins.

"Horseshoe crabs? Never heard of them."

"Yeah, well that's what they's called. They appear all along this coast every year 'bout this time. Look, they is spawning, see the males getting all around the females. Just like a dancehall, ain't it," she laughs. "And all those birds feasting on the eggs that the females a-laying in the sand. Ya must have crabs in Ireland as well?"

"Not like this," I tell her. "These ones are amazing. They look so strange, like some creature from a nightmare. And they do remind me of horseshoes. There must be thousands of them on this beach."

"Millions, more like; on every beach north of here ya see the same sight during May and June."

"They look like nothing I've ever seen before. There's something creepy about them," I say. "Mysterious and ancient and evil all at the same time. I wouldn't like to be running along this beach in the dark and fall into the middle of them."

"Might be a bad omen indeed," laughs Caroline. "Some people say they are one of the oldest animals alive. Ya know, the science type of people, they say that the horseshoe crab could be millions of years old."

"I suppose it depends on whether you believe in Adam and Eve and all that," I say. "The whole thing about creation."

"Yeah, I guess," she says. "Like, were they in the Ark with Noah and all the other animals? How'd they breed without sand to be laying they eggs in?"

"Who knows," I say.

The birds are continuing to go wild for these crab eggs, swooping and swirling, diving and fighting and all the while creating a terrible din. I notice that most of the birds are of a certain type, about the size and shape of our *crotach*, the curlew, but without the long bill and having a nice reddishness to their breast.

"What are those birds?" I ask.

"They's red-knots and they feast on the crabs' eggs. Ya have those in your country?"

"Not that I know of. We do have a lot of different kinds of birds."

"Like what?"

"Do you know, I don't know what names are on them in English," I tell her. "But we have *an fháinleog, an fhuiseog, an chorr mhónadh agus an lon dubh*. That one's the blackbird. I could go on all night."

She seems fascinated.

"Sure is lovely to hear ya speak y'own language," she says. "It sounds so different. It is very musical. Ya must miss it?"

"'Course I do. I miss a lot of things about home."

"It always gonna be home, ain't it?"

"It will."

I want to change the subject but I am not ready for the direction it takes as we bypass the beach. Caroline, blunt as ever in that nice way of hers, asks me how I am managing to put the affair with Bob Clifford behind me. I hadn't thought that I was close to putting it behind me and I tell her that. It is still a very raw sore to be talking about, even to someone as easy to talk to as her and after all we have already said on the subject.

"I just have to try to let it go and get back to real life," I tell her. "The music has been a big help."

"Yeah, I get that," she says. "Y'all is so talented on your fiddle. So ya going to tell me about the person who sent it ya, this mystery fiddle? I think, whoever it is, they got a great connection to your spirit, you dig?"

I can't answer this question. We walk on in quietness for a bit. I think the length of the silence has allowed the question to float off into wherever unanswerable questions go in their afterlife, but Caroline has other views on that.

"I think that your silence means ya agree," she says, "and I would add that this person is not only tuned in to your soul's wavelength, I think they have a high opinion of ya, maybe even love?"

These questions are getting out of order, certainly beyond my ability to answer.

"Caroline," I say, "there are things that have happened to me just now and there are things that happened to me in the past and I find it impossible to understand these things. The person who sent the fiddle was part of those things."

"Ok," she says. "That why ya refused to talk about who sent it all this time? I'm guessing that he a guy, right?"

My silence gives approval as I look away across the Delaware Bay.

"Well, whatever happened, it should not be the label that hangs around your neck for all time, should it? Just like what happened lately with that piece of trash."

"But these things have happened to me because of me, because it's who I am. It was my own stupidity. I can't blame anyone but myself."

"So ya is determined to go through life wearing a great big sign that say 'Soiled Goods'? Ya can do better than that gal."

"I'm not sure I see how," I say.

"Bin back to see your priest yet?"

"I have, yes."

"How was that?"

Again I find this an awkward question, one I wouldn't be used to answering.

"It was ok, I suppose. He listened well."

"Was he angry at ya?"

"Not really. I expected him to be. But he was nice. In Ireland my old priest would have had a fit if I told him what I told this one." I laughed at the very thought of it. "He'd have burned the ears off me and have me doing penance for the next forty years."

"So what this one say?"

"Well, maybe he'd heard it all before, but he was very gentle, very understanding. He listened for ages first; he let me talk myself out. I cried a lot. Imagine crying in the confessional to a priest I barely know."

Caroline looks puzzled. She obviously can't imagine this scene, her being a Pentecostal and not having our Sacrament of Confession. I see this in her blank expression.

"Then he just talked very kindly. 'Gotta guard who we are when faced with temptation, when we are separated from our roots. There's three of us involved in this,' he told me. 'Me as your confessor, but I can't forgive you. Jesus as your saviour, he can, of course, and then there is yourself. And you must. You must try to forgive yourself because, after all, he does.'"

"Lovely," Caroline said.

"He seemed to be able to figure out what sort of person I am, maybe by the amount of crying I was doing. He even passed me his handkerchief, which I must remember to get back to him sometime."

"Don't!"

"Don't what?"

"Don't give him back his handkerchief," Caroline tells me.

"Why would I not?"

"Keep it and treasure it. Hold on to it as a...like a token of your sorrow. He won't mind. In fact I guess he be happy to have been able to help ya get some healing."

I think this is lovely, coming from someone of another faith. I give her a smile which she might not even see in the gathering dusk.

"Thank you, Reverend Mother," I say. "Keep it like a holy relic, sort of? I might just do that."

Chapter 40

Lismore
Castlederg
17th May 1946

Dear Sally Anne,

    Thank you for your letter. I am sorry to hear you have had a rough time lately. It must be lonely there and you are likely missing your mother and sister.

I am glad to hear that you got a tune or two out of the fiddle and that it lifted your spirits. That was the whole idea. I am sure if it could talk it would say something the same. You likely gave it a bit of pleasure too and cheered it up no end after hanging silent on our kitchen wall for years. I wish I could have sneaked into your hotel to hear you play for those Yankies. They are the lucky ones this time.

You ask me about my life since. There is not much to tell you. The farm is going well now after all the bother. My mother passed away back in 1935. She had lost all her wits by that stage and was completely doting. It hit the girls very hard at the time. Both Jane and Millie are married now. Jane has a whole squad of wains and Millie is married to a local man by the name of John Sproule. I don't know if you remember John, he was always a big help to me. Millie still comes up to me every day to make dinner, for you see I never got round to marrying. I was engaged at one time but it didn't work out, so I never bothered again.

Anthony and Monica are still alive and as well as can be expected for folk that age. Their daughter Mary, (you remember her?), is about their place a fair bit, for she is married to a farmer not that far away in Donegal. She has turned out a good friend to me and we often talk about Joe. Mind you, Mary and her man did entice me into a bit of smuggling over the years and that landed me in more than enough trouble with the law, but all that is straightened out now. The war was a terrible time of shortages but we got through it. I wonder how it was for you away over there. Likely just as bad. It was a great relief when it all came to an end last year. The celebrations in the Diamond in Castlederg were powerful altogether.

Poor oul Tam ended his days in Lifford Hospital. I saw him in there often and one of the things he told me was that I was a fool to let you go away back to Donegal. He said I should go and look for you. That notion stayed with me and that is why I did go, after I got your letter last year, so blame Tam for that. He had the right idea though and I am not sorry I did. Just sorry I was too late.

I hope you stay well. Don't work too hard for those Yankies. All the best for now, but let me know sometime how you are getting on.

Yours sincerely,
Matthew.

Chapter 41

Sally Anne Sweeney

Independence Day and what a day I have had. There is a real tiredness on me after it all and I could be asleep in no time if I lay myself down, but I must write to Mairead tonight.

Still, it was all so exciting. It gave me so much to think about, things about this country that I have maybe noticed in passing before, but, on this day, have really stood out for me.

The thing I found most interesting was seeing all those hundreds of strangers, individuals every one, but all brought together and focused on this celebration. It really struck me today just what a wonderfully strange thing this America is. It is as if God has had a crazy notion to himself. 'Let's draw all these people together from all arts and parts of the earth, stick them on this massive stretch of land and see if they can get on together and make a go of it.'

Studying that string of faces lining the quaint Washington Street, you see people of every shape and appearance under the sun. Most of them are white folk like you would see in Donegal, but even then you can sort of work out the ones that have likely got ancestors in places like Italy or Greece or Spain. They look that bit darker, swarthy skinned and mostly fatter in the face than the taller blond ones. I am guessing those paler ones are from a German background or from Sweden or somewhere like that. Then there are the Jewish ones, some very religious by the look of their beards and dark style of clothes, others looking more like the rest of us. And if you listen to the people talking, you get the odd foreign language, like maybe Spanish, for I am told there are people in America from some of those Spanish-speaking islands, Cuba and Puerto Rico and the like. A few people might be from somewhere around China or Japan. And of course there are some black folks like Caroline among them, people whose forefathers were brought here from Africa as slaves in centuries long past, but who are now here, waving their wee Stars and Stripes flags like the rest, in spite of how this country has used and abused them.

What I find interesting about all this is that there they are, all together in their Americaness, no matter what background they come from. They love this Independence Day thing, yet what they are celebrating, America's freedom from British rule happened a few hundred years ago and had absolutely nothing to do with their history or the countries they come from. But here they all are, singing the same anthem, proud to call themselves Americans. It is a strange and amazing feat of history.

And now I am part of it and, to be honest, while I loved being the outside observer today, it is hard not to feel yourself being drawn into it all. I am only a recent arrival, a visiting Irish immigrant and already I am starting to feel the faintest desire to belong and be part of it. For all its faults, and I see many, the country has a magic about it that pulls you in under its wing.

I have noticed in the hotel that Americans whose ancestors come from Ireland have been very warm to me. They always want to hear the accent, sometimes want to hear a bit of Gaelic, or a story from 'the oul sod' and I oblige, of course, because there's always the chance of a decent tip after it. Those folk are proud of their roots, their Irishness. They may be recent immigrants or they may be great-grandchildren of those who came out of the great famine, they may have begun their life here in the poverty of New York's worst slums or as better-off land grabbers from western states, they may be called O'Neill or they may be called MacNeill, but they are all Americans and proud of it. They belong here.

I often wonder is it the same for people who have arrived from other nations? I have my doubts. Maybe for Italians there is the same sense of motherland. I don't know about the others. I should ask Jan Piotrowski, (if that is how he spells his name), a lad who is a bellhop in the hotel. I have wondered what country his people came from, but he is a shy boy and I didn't like to annoy him.

There are a few girls who work in the Windsor who have names that sound a bit strange to me as well. Take Amy, for example. Her second name is Sherman. I made the mistake of asking her where that name came from and I could see that she was almost taking offence at my question.

"Why do you want to know?"

"No reason. I am just interested," I told her. "I don't think we have that name in Ireland."

"I guess 'cause it's German," she said.

"Really? Sherman is German?" I replied, only then thinking how funny that sounded. I must have smiled for she continued with a resentful frown.

"It wasn't Sherman to begin with," she said.

"Ah right. What was it first then?"

"Actually it was Schirmann originally, " she told me. She spelt it out when I looked a bit blank. "S-c-h-i-r-m-a-n-n."

"And why did it change?"
She smirked at me as if I was a bit slow.
"'Cause of the war."
"The war?"
"Yeah. My dad didn't want us to be having a German sounding name during the war, so he got it changed a few years back. I was born a Schirmann. Now I am Amy Sherman, easier for people to spell as well."

This struck me as strange until I thought about my own situation. Then, when I did, I told her, "You know, Amy, my name is not really Sweeney."

"What is it then?"

"It's *Nic Suíbhne*." She is puzzled so I spell it out for her. "That is the Irish name, the way it was at the start, originally."

"And did your father change your surname as well?"

"Not on your life," I laughed at the thought. "The change had nothing to do with us. It wasn't changed with our permission either."

"I don't understand."

"Well, away back in history, the English took us over and they didn't like our language and they didn't like our names. They couldn't say them, couldn't spell them, so they changed them into something they could get their tongue around. So *Nic Suíbhne* in Gaelic became Sweeney in English."

"Stick with Sweeney," she laughed. "I could never get my tongue around that other one either."

****

Cape May
4th July 1946

Dear Mairead,

How are you and how is mammy? I haven't heard from you for a few weeks and I start to worry that maybe everything is not alright. Have you heard any more from Mary Anne about Nuala? Has she turned up yet? I am praying to God that she goes back home to her mother for, even though they don't get on with each other, blood is thicker than water and she would be better living with her own folk.

We had big celebrations for Independence Day here today. The hotel has been filling up all week as the schools up north close and the summer rush to the beaches begins. Cape May has four times as many people in it now as a few days ago. Everywhere is buzzing, the shops and restaurants are full and the money is flowing. I notice myself getting far more tips than ever so that is good. It is as if everyone has forgotten the hardships of war that they were in last year. The weather is roasting hot again and the mosquitoes are out in full force.

You never saw anything like the events in town. The whole place was done out in colourful streamers for the parade, with American flags flying on every corner. Saint Patrick's Day in Dungloe would not be a patch on it. They drive floats up the street, lorries and carts pulled by horses and them all carrying people dressed up like in the old days, acting out bits of their history. At night the sky above Cape May was lit up with fireworks the like of which I have never seen. It was nearly worth coming to America just to see this alone.

I am more busy now than I have ever been. Mornings I do laundry and cleaning rooms, then I get a couple of hours off in the afternoon to lie on the beach. I am getting a bit of colour about me and I get into the waves to cool down when it gets too hot. Then in the evening I work again in the kitchen. The money is great at the minute, though you do end up exhausted after working twelve or fourteen hours in the day. I hope I can keep it up.

Write soon and let me know how things are in Ranahuel.

Le grá

Sally Anne

Chapter 42

Matthew Henderson

The last I heard from Sally Anne was back at the start of July. She sent me another postcard, all about Independence Day in that place she is working. The picture on the front showed a crowd of folk, all smiling and waving wee flags as they watched a brass band marching down the street behind their banners. It looked a grand colourful sight.

On the back of the card she wrote;

Hello Matthew, I am here right in the middle of Cape May's big day. You would feel right at home here, though it does make your 12th of July seem a bit drab. Funny that here they are celebrating freedom and independence from Britain in red, white and blue, but in your part of the world the same colours mean the exact opposite. I think it's funny anyway. Sally Anne

I struggled to make sense of this card, not so much the card but what was written on the back. It annoyed me for a while, so much so that I nearly wished she hadn't bothered to send it.

What was it she was trying to do, sending this and saying those things? It was a reminder of the differences between us, that is what I was thinking. Why could she not just let that rest? Since we started writing to each other I had not had a single thought about her being Catholic and Irish. I was just enjoying the fact that we were talking to each other again, sort of in the same way that we had always done...well, always done up until those sorts of things came between us. Now here she was reminding me of the difference, the fact that I would feel at home in the red, white and blue atmosphere, with the sound of the band playing rousing music. To me it seems she is saying, "You're a loyal Protestant, so you would be just at home in this sort of thing, the marching, the flags, the clamour of it all."

And then to be comparing what she was witnessing to the one and only time, to my knowledge anyway, that she saw anything to do with the Twelfth, back when she went with Joe Kearney to see a couple of bands marching down the road into Castlederg. That was not a fair comparison. That would have been a puny wee feeder parade. She would need to see some of the massive parades they have in Londonderry or Belfast to be able to make such a remark. They have thousands on the streets there I hear.

And then this comment about how the same colours mean exactly the opposite thing in the two countries. I found myself reacting to that, though I can't quite work out why. Does she have a point there? But our red, white and blue is to do with the Union Flag, their's is to do with their flag, the Stars and Stripes. Same colours of course, but different flags and different messages. The point is, why would she want to say that to me now, to draw attention to it? Why not just send the card itself and leave it at that? Was she not thinking how I might react to it? Had she a few drinks in her that maybe raised her old nationalist feelings?

I took it so bad that I have not written back since. It may be foolish of me, to be taking offence at something she may never have intended. My question is, should I ignore it, pretend it didn't get under my skin, or should I take her up on it? I could ask her what she meant. I could hint somehow that I had found it a bit insensitive and ask her what she was meaning. Maybe send her some sort of card or newspaper cutting showing the Twelfth of July celebrations in Belfast and say, "There you are, lass. What do you think of that?"

Then it strikes me how daft I am.

The point being that I was nowhere near the Twelfth of July myself this year.

I was up in Kearney's bog that day helping Mary. I worked with her and a couple of her wains to get a spread of footed turf put into clamps before the rain came, as was forecast on the radio. Mary had called over on the Eleventh night, mainly to say that Anthony had taken a bit of a turn and was in bed and would I mind coming over and giving a hand to help with the turf. I never thought twice about it. Of course I would come and I did.

Why then was I getting so defensive about Sally Anne's card and her comments that I imagined to be sarcastic?

I am not an Orangeman. I would usually go and watch, always have done, but only because it is a day out, a traditional day to leave the work and join the crowds...of both religions too, let me say, and watch the bands march and play. There was no harm in it and at the same time it wasn't something that was deeply important in my blood and my bones, at least not until Sally Anne got under my skin.

I read her card again.

What if I try to imagine myself standing beside her, watching this parade, the one on her card?

The glare of the colours in that bright American sun. Ice creams in our hands, melting before we get them in our mouths. The sound of the brass instruments loud in our ears. The strutting march of the players reading their wee music sheets. She turns and smiles up at me, that great flashing smile she has. And maybe she says, "This must make you feel at home, Matthew, the colours and the band and all; it's like the Twelfth, isn't it?"

I would probably say, "It's a damned sight better than the Twelfth in Castlederg, that's for sure."

And later we would talk calmly about the colours and the whole question of Britain's rule over places like America and Ireland, and the Americans way back then wanting to be free and not be governed by a power thousands of miles away across the sea. And she might say, "Same was true in Ireland in the Twenties," and I would say, "Yes but only part of Ireland wanted Independence," and she would argue back as she always did, but with that Sally Anne smile in her eyes and we would end the evening going for a walk beside the sea there.

The big questions about independence and freedom would be drowned in the sound of the Atlantic waves. Even better, the sound of her laughter would quieten the ancestral voices of my people back in County Tyrone.

It is all wishful thinking, of course it is, but at my time of life what else is left to me? Where would I be without imagination, without something to dream about?

Chapter 43

Ranahuel
7th August 1946

Dear Sally Anne,
      I have terrible news for you. Nuala is dead. I had a letter from her mother yesterday. It is heart-breaking. Nuala's body was found by a fisherman somewhere along the banks of the Clyde river near Glasgow.

Mary Anne says that, after she ran away back in May, the police did little or nothing to find her. She had not a word from Nuala in all that time. It was as if she had disappeared off the face of the earth. Her mother thinks that she must have somehow made her way back to Glasgow. She had no money so how she did that Mary Anne doesn't know. Maybe she got herself smuggled on to a train in Edinburgh, or maybe got a lift in a motor car or in a lorry with some man. Where she lived in the meantime is anybody's guess.

Mary Anne wrote this. "The police are not for saying whether she jumped into the Clyde herself or was pushed in by some son o' the divil, for I asked them."

So it might have been suicide or maybe she just slipped and fell or it might even have been murder. We will likely never know. Nobody has come forward with any information. The only way they knew that it was her body was that they found her name on a document in her purse. Mary Anne wrote, "The police wouldn't let me see her. They said she was too badly decayed. She was rotted, I suppose. She had likely been dead a long time. All they could show me was a purse they found in her pocket and a shoe that was still on her when she was pulled out o the river. I knew that shoe. It was one of my oul ones. I had no money to go to Glasgow to bring her home for a decent funeral and I have nobody to look after the bairn anyways, so the police said they would make sure she was buried, likely in one o them graves they have about the Gorbals for folk who cannae afford a proper grave."

So poor Nuala is resting in some pauper's grave, back near where she lived with her man before the war. It is all so tragic and pathetic. Mary Anne is a strange woman. Now she will have to rise to looking after Nuala's wee one. Frankie will maybe never have any memory of his own mother. I feel so sorry for him but what can I do? Not a thing. I would go across on the boat but there's nobody to look after mammy. (She is fine now, by the way. Healthy as a trout.) At least Mary Anne has that wee bit of money you send her and that will put a decent bite in wee Frankie's mouth. I hope it does anyway. She said to make sure I wrote and told you all about Nuala. Not so much as a 'Thank you' though, and her forever putting on the poor mouth. Ah well.

I hope you are well and have got over whatever that problem was that you had a while ago. Don't work too hard, even if the money is good at the minute. It's only money. I know I don't have to ask you to say a prayer for Nuala and for Frankie and the granny. Maybe get your priest there to say a Mass for her, God rest her.

Le grá,
Mairead.

Chapter 44

Sally Anne Sweeney

Mairead's letter tears the heart out of me. To think of that poor girl, so demented by whatever worries were going through her mind that she leaves her baby son, leaves the safety of her mother's home, flees to Glasgow and then throws herself in the river. It doesn't bear thinking about.

I know, and I suppose we have always known, that our cousin Mary Anne had a strained relationship with Nuala. There was no love lost between them, not even when Nuala was a child. It was as if she was always a burden to Mary Anne.

When I spent a few days with Nuala and Frankie last year, just before I sailed here, I could see that Nuala was under a lot of stress. It was understandable, given that she had just got word that Frank had been lost at sea. It wasn't just him was a casualty of that terrible war, it was those left behind, especially Nuala and the child. Grief, made worse by worry about the future, by unhappiness with the pattern of her life and by feelings of separation from those who should have had a care for her and the baby.

She felt totally rejected by Frank's family. The old religious bigotry in that area of Scotland was a big part of that, but so was Nuala herself if I am honest. I can well imagine that those in-laws found her very through-other and not all that reliable. Still, I can't forgive them for washing their hands of her and their grandchild. To disown their own flesh and blood and want nothing to do with Frankie is just so hurtful. It is inhuman, never mind unChristian, and I hope I never run across them or I will tell them exactly that.

Nuala must have felt so alone. I try not to but I can't help imagining her walking along the banks of the Clyde, or maybe hanging on to the railings of one of its bridges. All that pain she carried from her mother's attitude over the years, from the abuse she suffered from so many people, all that pain pouring down her face in tears. The poverty she lived in when Frank didn't come back and her living in that smelly tenement in the Gorbals with no money and no prospects and a baby to feed. The guilt of what she had to do to survive. Then lately, the treatment in the asylum would not have been nice at all and probably only made her feel worse. There is no way for me, from the position of my comfortable life here in USA, to understand the depths of her despair. It is impossible to see into somebody's mind and read the thoughts that drove her over the edge and into the Clyde, impossible. It darkens my heart every bit as bad as the feelings I had after my own foolishness back at Easter time. I was low then but in a million years I would never have considered jumping into the sea. Poor Nuala! How tortured she must have been to do that.

The problem for me, though, is not the past. The problem is not understanding all that led to Nuala's suicide. The real problem is the future. What is to be done for that poor wee lad in Musselburgh? If we just ignore it and let him stay with his granny there is a very good chance that she will treat him at least as badly as she treated Nuala. The poor boy can't be condemned to that as a life. She will destroy him as she has done his mother.

I am sitting with Caroline at the dinner table after our lunch break. My plate of spaghetti bolognese sits untouched and pushed from me to the middle of the table. I have never managed to like this pasta stuff with the spiced tomatoey meat on it. Usually I try but today I couldn't bring myself to put one bite in my mouth. I will be hungry later, I know, but no matter.

I have told Caroline what has happened with Nuala and, softhearted as she is, her tears join mine. The others have gone back to their tasks and, with no-one else around, she holds my hand. That is where Roisin finds us. She is taken aback by the sight of us.

"What's going on, girls?" she asks. "You still can't bring yourself to eat spaghetti, Sal? Can't be that bad?"

I have to pour it all out to her as well. Although she has never met Mary Anne or Nuala, Roisin is family. I am pleased to see her concern for the situation.

"Something has to be done," she says.

"But what? There is nobody close to Mary Anne who can step in to help. Even if there was, she might not welcome that."

"Child be better in an orphanage ya think?" asks Caroline.

I think about this. It is an option alright, for he is exactly that, an orphan. But it does not sit right with me. Frankie is family too.

"That would be a dreadful thing to have to do," I say. "No matter how bad Mary Anne..."

"And if we were to send her a bunch of money?" Roisin asks.

I shake my head. Money is not going to change the nature of the problem.

"It might help for a bit," I tell them, "but I have been sending some over the past months and yes, it might put food on the table, but it can't do magic. It can't turn Mary Anne into the sort of woman who will do a good job of rearing Frankie."

"And your sister? Can she help?" Caroline has never grasped the idea that just because Ireland and Scotland are 'over there' doesn't mean it is easy to get from one place to the other.

"She is with our mother. She is in Ireland, you see. Frankie is miles away in Scotland."

"Yeah, I get that, but what I mean is could your sister not bring the boy over to Ireland and raise him there?"

This has crossed my mind of course. It would be ideal, except for the fact that Mairead isn't really cut out to be the mother-type of person, that plus the fact that she cannot leave our mother to go and get the boy.

Roisin interrupts.

"Look girls, we are not going to solve anything here at this dinner table today. Why don't you go back to work and give it time? A solution may come in ways that you don't expect. Give it time, ok?"

We go back to the scent of our floor polish and the tourists' sun lotion, but my thoughts are across the ocean.

I imagine that wee lad crying for a mummy who will never return to him. I hear that Scottish accent shouting at him in angry tones to 'Gae me heed peace!' I see him crawling around on the dust of Mary Anne's kitchen floor in the stink of cat piss and decaying food. And I know it rests on me to do something.

Chapter 45

Matthew Henderson

There is nothing to beat the fresh smell of well-dried hay.
    The sun is slipping down the sky, for it is almost eight o'clock. Shadows are stretching themselves lazily, as if they are dog-tired at the end of a long day. Strangely though, I don't feel any tiredness this evening. I am aware of the swallows ducking and diving between the hay-ricks and through the orange shafts of speckled sunlight. Clouds of midges stir and swirl as the birds fly through them in search of their supper. There is barely a sound in the still air, just the odd low bellow of a distant cow and the happy chirping of some sparrows flitting among the greens of the hedgerow.
    I am over with John Sproule, helping him with the last of his hay today. Having invested in half of Bond's farm some years ago John would have very little capital left to be playing with. He never had a penny, it seemed, to be buying new machinery. His 'wee grey mare', that's what he called his old Ferguson tractor, was a crock and was for ever breaking down.
    That is what has happened today, some problem with the starter again. So I have brought my Fordson to shift his hay-ricks up to the stack at the head of the field.
    I am happy, as happy as I've been in years. John even remarked on this when we were sitting against the hay-stack eating the bite of food that Millie brought up to the field for us. My mind was away elsewhere and I could barely tell you a thing we talked about sitting there.
    "I heard you whistling on the tractor there," he says to me. "What's put you in whistling form the day, Matt?"
    I think my moods must puzzle John. He is for ever trying to understand me, maybe looking for some chink in how I am doing so he can be offering me the benefit of his spiritual wisdom.
    "Must be the weather," I say. I wasn't going to be telling him what was going on in my head. "And sure, in an hour or two we'll be finished the hay for another year."
    "Aye, we will that. 'The harvest is passed, the summer has ended and you are not...'"
    "Come on," I interrupt, sensing a sermon to follow the Bible text and standing up from the stack. "It's not over till we get these last few ricks in."

I head to my tractor, the rick-shifter hitched on behind. We'll make short work of these last hay-ricks. Then I will shin up the ladder to the top of the stack to build the last forkfuls that John will throw up to me. He has a few bundles of rushes cut and ready to thatch the peak of the stack and run the rain off. The ropes are waiting to secure the thing against whatever the west wind wants to fire at it during the coming autumn and winter.

It has been a grand year of weather, the year. Saving hay has been easy for both farms compared to manys a year. The growth of grass on most of my fields was as good as ever I saw it and I have a full barn of lovely, dry hay already stored away since July.

This is John's last field and this final stack is the crowning moment of the process; as Millie would say, 'The icing on the cake.' It feels good being a farmer when the weather gets behind you like this and you know you're not going to have any shortage of fodder in the hungry months of winter. You couldn't be doing a better job, that's how I feel tonight as we get into the final half hour of labour.

But for all the fulfilment that work brings me, my happiness today is for a different reason altogether. It all goes back to the latest letter that arrived this morning from America. Its message completely fills my head as I work this evening.

It had been weeks since I heard from Sally Anne, months more like. And even then it was only that silly card with the brass band picture on the front of it. I had started to wonder if I had said anything amiss in the wee note that I eventually sent her by way of reply. The letter that arrived today has set those fears at rest.

Sally Anne is coming home!

Windsor Hotel
Cape May
20th August 1946

Dear Matthew,

Thank you for that letter you sent a while back. Sorry it has taken me so long to reply. The thing is, I have been going through some troubles lately and it is only now that I feel sure enough about things that I can write. It is not that there is anything wrong with me myself. I am in the best of health and I have enjoyed working here this summer. It has been busy but I have not minded that one bit. It has been a great experience. But things have happened that have been weighing on my mind and I can't seem to settle here in America at the minute. So I have decided that I should come home, at least for the time being.

The problem is this. You might remember that I have relatives in Scotland. I won't take time to tell you in detail all the troubles they have been through. My cousin Nuala passed away recently. It looks like she may have taken her own life. She had been very ill in her mind for a good long time but it is still a terrible shock and a terrible thing to have done. Nuala's mother would not be in the best of health herself.

I have been talking to my boss here. Her advice to me is to finish work at the end of the summer and go back home for a while, just to see my mother who is getting older and also to see if there is anything I can do for the relatives in Scotland. I am going to heed her advice, for I can't seem to content myself here and I'm missing home. Then if I want to come back, maybe next Easter, she will have a job waiting for me, maybe even as a cook. I am to finish here the day before Labour Day, that is the 2nd of September. I still have to book a passage on the boat from New York to Glasgow but I will do that soon. After I visit my aunt in Scotland I will take the boat home to Derry. When I get settled and all this uncertainty is behind me I might write to you again, if that is alright. And don't forget that I have your fiddle and I am bringing it back to Ireland. It will be the most travelled fiddle in the country. I do want to give it back to you, but I can't think how to get it to you, unless if you are ever in my part of Donegal you could call in for it. It has

been great to have it and I have played many tunes on it since it came, so thank you again.
Yours sincerely,
Sally Anne

Sally Anne is coming home. She will land in Londonderry some time next month most likely. I can just see her coming down the gangplank, her hair blowing back off her tanned face. I see her standing on the dockside, looking colourful in her impressive new clothes, a suitcase and a bag of stuff in her hands and my father's fiddle case at her feet and she is staring around for a porter or somebody to help her get to the station to catch the train to Letterkenny. Then, when she gets there she will have to get off the train and hope there is a bus to carry her across the mountains to the west coast and her village. I picture her getting down out of that bus with all her bags, dragging herself along the road a few miles and climbing up that steep hill to her home in Ranahuel.

These are the imaginary pictures that have taken root in my mind as I have worked today.

But now, back on the Derry Quay I think I see somebody coming forward to meet her. A tall man with the cut of the farmer about him. He hugs her first and she smiles so happily, then he picks up her baggage and carries it off towards the train station as she walks beside him. But forget about the train and the bus and the long walk. He is opening the door of his car and she is getting in.

And his car looks a lot like mine.

This is what is in my head as the sun drops into the shelter of the hills to our west. I tie down the last rope on the haystack, throw the ladder and the fork on to the buck-rake and open up the throttle on the Fordson. She roars across the field after John and I see him look back over his shoulder as he goes through the gate. The expression on his face seems to say, 'Slow down friend. What is the hurry now? The hay is saved, you can relax, no need to rush.'

And I am thinking, 'Please John, just go in the house to Millie and don't be expecting me to wait around tonight for another chat, for I have a letter to write and post in the morning, first thing.' A letter that will struggle to keep control of itself and not seem too mad keen about the part I plan to play in this emigrant's return.

Chapter 46

Sally Anne Sweeney

My last experience in New Jersey is a really lovely one and I will remember and treasure it for a long time.

Caroline has asked me several times over the year that I have been here if I would like to visit her folks at their home in the nearby town of Wildwood. Eventually I have found the time to go with her. I already know her daddy of course. His name is Manny, and, though he is a chef and has taught me a lot in the kitchen of the Windsor, he is not cooking this evening. He says he is not allowed.

"Cookin' in my wife's house is all her job," he laughs. "She put me outa her kitchen double quick if I start messin' with her pots and pans."

Mrs Lee looks like a lady who enjoys eating her food even more than she does cooking it. She is one of the happiest people I have ever met and she has a great knack of making everybody around her happy too. She and Manny are well into their sixties, I would guess, and they tell me they have been living in this same little shack of a house since they started out together.

"Bin here since the big year," Manny says. "Nineteen Hundred. Year I lost my freedom to this good lady. Never got it back. Never even asked to get it back."

"Ya was free to go anytime ya want," his wife chirps back at him as she sticks some more fish on the grill.

"Couldn't do that, ma'am," he grins. "Even if I wanted to. Ya gave me six fine kiddies so I had to hang around and make sure they got a scrap to eat after y'all was finished."

The banter between them is something I have never heard before. It is all the best of craic. I can see where Caroline gets her personality from. These two are mustard together.

Something strikes me as I watch them. Caroline is obviously from a very happy home, but she herself has never mentioned any man in her life. She is the baby of the family but she is in her thirties, I believe. I wonder why she isn't married.

As we eat our way through a platter of all sorts of grilled fish, served with sweet potato, black-eyed peas and stewed vegetables, Manny tells me of his service in the American navy. He was a cook on board a destroyer and 'saw action' in the Pacific. I pretend to understand and throw in a couple of easy questions for him, not that I made any sense of the answers. When he came out of the navy last year he managed to get a job in the Windsor again, having worked there before the war. He is a lovely man and the atmosphere in the home is just so warm and joyful. It is a pleasure and an honour to experience it. All the more so because Caroline tells me later as we walk the Wildwood boardwalk that I am the first white person who has ever eaten at their table. I am amazed by this, but having spent a year here maybe I shouldn't be. The two groups exist in the same town but, from what I can see, they pay very little attention to each other, almost as if they are blind to people of the other skin colour. The attitude seems to be, you over there in your corner, knowing your place and your limitations, and me over here with my sort, calling the shots, as they say here. It feels like both sets accept this as the normal way of being.

"No point in upsetting the apple cart," says Caroline. "I did, once. Cost me dear."

"How was that?" I ask.

She stops walking and moves away from me to hold the rail beside the boardwalk. I join her, facing out to sea.

"It's ok if you don't want to tell me," I say.

"I do," she insists, "but I ain't really talked about it for ten years. And never to a white person."

"What's it got to do with me being a white person?"

"Hell of a lot," she says. "Ya see, long time ago, just after I finished school, I had a boyfriend. He was the best guy you could ask to meet. Ran track for his college. That's how I first met him."

"You were at the same college?"

She laughs. "You for real? We sure not at the same college."

"How'd you meet then?"

"Well, I did track as well in those days...yeah, I know it's hard to imagine now but I was a runner too. I kept meeting him at events and I noticed him looking at me a whole bunch, but we didn't really get to talkin' until I bumped into him by accident on this here boardwalk. We hit it off right there and then; kept meeting in secret for a while."

"What was he like?"

"He was strong and tall and very handsome. Fine Christian boy too, loved to sing in his church, played piano there. I loved him so much; he loved me too, I know he did. But, it didn't work out for us."

"Why not? What happened?"

She waits a bit and then, when she turns to look at me, the tears standing in her eyes, she speaks.

"This country, Sal. This country don't work for a couple who is like us. See John was white, I was black."

"Oh no!" I say. "But it didn't matter to you what he was, I'm sure it didn't."

"'Course it didn't. Didn't matter to him either."

"Who then?"

"His folks. His church. See his daddy was high up in that white church. I don't know, not a pastor but some other name I didn't understand. It just was never going to be possible for him to accept that his darlin' son John could throw his life away on a black girl from the wrong side of the tracks. She coulda bin the brightest girl in her school, the prettiest, the best athlete, a brilliant singer. She coulda bin the most Christian person in the state, didn't matter, 'cause she was black and it ain't ever gonna work out."

"But you loved each other? He loved you, so why didn't he fight to keep you?"

"There was no point. This is how it is in this country. He had to follow the family line. His people would never have accepted it."

"How about yours?"

"They had their fears about it too, 'course they had. My daddy met John's daddy, 'cause we was pretty far down the road to marriage, if ya get my meaning. That man told my daddy that the bible say that marriage between races ain't allowed. I never found that bit in my bible. My daddy told him he better start looking for another heaven 'cause as far as he knew there wasn't gonna be a segregated one for black folks. We all gonna be stuck in together, like in a mixed heaven. He didn't wanna hear that piece of news. Didn't make any difference though. This ain't heaven, this America and black girls don't get to marry white boys."

Caroline's story rings a bell for me of course. I am devastated for her and we stand together hugging each other and our particular hurts, then wiping away tears and memories as people walk around us on Wildwood boardwalk. We get a few stares, but thankfully nobody stops to complain.

Caroline's story leads naturally to me explaining my heart's history to her, the story of how I came to be Matthew Henderson's maid and then almost his lover in my distant past.

She listens to me describe how poor we were in the western part of Donegal, her eyes getting wider.

"Y'all was livin' in poverty like that? I never knew white folks had to live like that. Ya neva said before."

"I didn't like to be talking about it. It is just how it was. Ireland was always very divided, the rich were really rich, the poor were really poor and the west was worst of all. That's why people had to go to work in the east, children as well, young as nine or ten at times."

I find myself describing my first and only experience of being hired in a hiring fair. It left such a mark on me, that day in Strabane in 1922. When I finish she tells me, "Sounds to me that ya hiring fair was just like those slave markets in the Carolinas, down south where my folks come from. Sold like animals back then. 'Cept you guys weren't in chains."

"We weren't, and I was well treated and got good food and good money, but I think I was one of the lucky ones."

"Don't sound lucky to me, if that Matthew treated ya so bad. Sound to me like he was an evil master, he was so cruel to ya," she says.

"He wasn't cruel at all. Well, maybe he was at the end but...no, I don't think he was cruel, nor evil," I say.

"Treating you like ya was dirt? An' ya say he weren't cruel?"

"I think he was a good man and a kind man, at the start especially, but then things happened and he turned sour."

"Why that happen to people, you think?"

"I don't know. I just think he was like an apple in the wrong barrel and he got tainted by whatever was wrong with the others. His tribe turned him bitter. But at the bottom he was a kind man. That is why he sent me the fiddle."

"So he sent ya the fiddle? Same one ya done busted on him?"

"Same one."

"An' all those letters ya get are from him?"

"Some," I say, "not all of them."

"My Lord, this is some story gal. And will ya meet up with him when ya get back home? How far apart are ya?"

I am laughing before she has finished the question.

"The thing is, you know that letter that came a couple of days ago?"

"Yeah. That from him too?"

"It was. He wants to come to get me off the boat when I get back."

"You serious? How's that gonna work? Like, if ya is with your cousin in Scotland for a while?"

"Yeah, I know, but as soon as I know when I am taking the boat from Scotland I am to send him a telegram, so he can drive up to Derry to get me. He wants to give me a ride back to my home in Donegal."

"I can see 'xactly where this ride gonna take ya, Sally Anne. This guy clearly sweet on ya. Your romance is gonna take off again.

The spark is still there. All it needs is for ya to give it a bit of encouraging air and it'll be a mad flame in no time."

"Mad flame?" I laugh. "That's the trouble. I am not sure I want that. It is nice that he has been so kind and it is good that he is keen to meet up and wants to help me, but it can't be a romance. You see, in Ireland it is impossible. Different backgrounds, different religions, he can't even speak my language. It didn't work before and the bottom line is that nothing has really changed, even after all this time. Our two ways of life are so different. It's like oil and water."

"Oh Lordy," she says. "Don't ya just sound like John's father. Oil and water! At least ya got a chance. Y'all the same colour. Ya can do something about all that other stuff."

"It is not that simple. It is how he was reared, how I was reared. It's maybe not colour but it is every bit as deep."

"And if ya love him, can those things not be overcome?"

"Who said I love him? Maybe I did, but that turned to hate, after all that he put me through. I hated him with a vengeance and that went on for years until I somehow got over it. Then something told me, some small voice in my conscience told me that I needed to try to forgive him, especially if I was to make a go of this new life in America. That is why I wrote to him. It all sparked off from that letter, though it took a good while. But it is one thing to forgive someone. It doesn't mean I actually like him. Maybe when I see him my stomach will turn and I'll run."

"No way. I don't think so. You must have been in love back then."

"'Course I was, but I was a child, a maid of eighteen years. What did I know about love?"

"Maybe enough to know how it felt. It can grow again and this time it can do it in the face of all the issues between ya, not blind to them like before."

Sweet Mother Mary, I think, this girl is some counsellor.

"Enough of this love talk," I tell her. "Tonight is my last night off in America and here you are trying to organise my entire future. How about we go for a quick drink somewhere, before you have me married off?"

We do exactly that and an hour or two later the two of us make a very strange couple, rolling back arm in arm to Manny's house for a car ride back to the Windsor, tipsy as a pair of gypsies.

Chapter 47

47 Eskeside Road
Musselburgh
20th September 1946

Dear Mairead,

      This is just a note to let you know that I have arrived safely at Mary Anne's house. It was a very long and tiring journey. The sea-sickness hit me bad with that storm in the middle of the ocean, throwing the ship around like a cork. You likely felt the force of it in Donegal too. I had days of it and I was very low. It made me wish I had never set out on this journey at all, but at the same time I know it is the right thing to be doing, coming home. Then the train I took from Glasgow broke down halfway to Edinburgh. After sitting there for a long time, we had to be taken off and crammed into a wee bus for the rest of the journey. We were so late getting into the station that there was no transport out to Musselburgh and I had to take a room in a hotel, a dear business. Finally I have made it to Mary Anne's but I am exhausted and not in great health, to be honest. It is annoying, for I left America feeling grand and more than thankful for the whole experience of working there.

This house in Musselburgh doesn't help. It is so damp and cold, and Mary Anne will only light a fire if I plead with her. She has got so tight, the most miserable soul you could ever meet. It seems to have got worse, the older she gets. I have tried to clean the place, the dirt and rubbish is everywhere. I was going outside to the toilet in the middle of the night, with no light to see what I was stepping on and I cut the bottom of my foot on a tin. She just throws stuff out into the back yard. The rats must love her.

This is the situation that poor wee Frankie is being reared in. It is an absolute disgrace. I know that Mary Anne hasn't got over Nuala's death yet, but that is no excuse for the neglect that the boy is having to suffer. The smell is terrible and I can never find a nappy towel when he dirties himself. First thing I had to do was to go out and buy some new ones and some soap and powdered milk. The child is skin and bones. If you saw his wee face and it smeared with grease. The only white bits are where the tears have flowed down from his eyes. Something has to be done. I can't stay here for ever to take care of him but I don't see any way that Mary Anne can change herself and look after him better. I will go and talk to her priest, or maybe the St Vincent de Paul people to see if there is anything they can do.

I have just another week here, for I have booked my ticket to come home to Derry next Friday. I can't wait to see you and mammy. I will maybe arrive home late on the Saturday night, if I get the transport sorted right.

Le grá

Sally Anne

Chapter 48

Matthew Henderson

It is half past eight on a fine autumn morning. I should be at my breakfast after the milking, but I am not.

I am driving into Londonderry and there is some sort of battle going on between my brain and my heart.

My brain is finding it hard to take in the fact that this is really happening, that I am going to get Sally Anne. Is it a strange dream I am having? What am I doing? Playing the good Samaritan, yes, but getting tangled up again in this woman's life?

My heart is beating far more often and far stronger than it needs to. Whatever this feeling is, whether nerves or expectation or doubt, it has me tied up in knots. Last night and today it has been skipping around like a calf let out of its winter stall. Telling it to settle itself has had no effect.

Her telegram was short and to the point.

> Arrive Derry 9am 28Sept. Thanks SA.

This landed in Lismore on Wednesday so I had plenty of time to organise myself, get a shave and haircut and get my Customs book set right in Castlederg. I am hoping to have time to drive to the far side of Donegal, leave her off at her house and be back to do the evening milking, but just in case anything goes wrong, I have Millie on standby to keep an eye out and take over if I don't make it.

I nose the motor across the new Craigavon Bridge and turn right towards the docks. I am in good time but, as I look for a parking space along the road beside the quay, I see the big white ferry sliding into its berth, engine roaring and black smoke flying from it. It has made good time on its overnight crossing.

I get parked as close as I can, maybe fifty or sixty yards away from where it docks. I stand by the side of the car and watch as the crew and dockers go through their procedures, tying the ship to the bollards with thick ropes, guldering and swearing at each other with good humour.

My heart hasn't calmed down one bit.

The gangplank is slid slowly into position.

Now the passengers start to cross it, picking their way like hens coming down the tripper from their coop. Some scatter at once, some are hailing taxis and others are hugging relatives in huddled groups, blocking my view. I stare intently, for I am too far away to be seeing clearly. I haven't noticed anyone that looks like Sally Anne, not a soul. There's maybe fifty to sixty people have come down those steps, a fair few of them women too, but none of them look in the least bit like her. I walk a bit closer. That seems to be the last of them too, I think, as a thin lady with a bad limp is helped along the narrow gangplank by one of the crew. She is struggling because she is carrying a baby. The porter has her cases.

She is not Sally Anne.

She looks a skinny brown sort of woman, older than I imagine Sally Anne to be and a bit broken down, maybe crippled with pains or something.

I wait another five minutes, eyes fixed on that gang-plank. Nobody else appears.

I turn away. This is a massive disappointment. Sally Anne is not on this boat. Could I have got the day wrong? Could she have missed her connections? Could I have missed her among that first crowd of passengers who came off in a flock? Hardly.

She's not here. What a let-down!

I turn and wander slowly back down the street to my car. I sit there for a bit, my hands on the steering wheel, wondering what to do. Nothing for it but to turn and go home. I pull the starter and begin to ease out on to the road, turning around to head back along the river towards the bridge. One last look in the rear mirror at this ship of disappointment.

The crowd has cleared a bit. That poor woman is still standing there on the side of the road, her cases at her feet, her child in her arms. She's obviously waiting for help, maybe for somebody to… wait a minute? Could that be her? It doesn't look anything like her but that's maybe only the blurring of my mirror, that or the passing of time.

I stop and get out for a better look.

One of the cases at her feet looks very like a fiddle case.

The woman raises a weary hand and even from this distance and after all these years I know that wave. I lift my hand hesitatingly, still in doubt.

She takes a half-step towards me and stumbles, almost falling over, the child wriggling in her arms.

I am running towards her and my arms are out, as if to break her fall, or maybe to hold her, I don't know. I don't know…but as I reach her there is something about her frailty that stops me and I reign myself in. Grabbing her in my arms, which is my initial instinct, would be too vulgar, too boisterous. This lady is weak and frail and needs help, not clumsy hugging.

Our eyes meet though and her's fill with tears straight away. But again, it isn't hard for me to work out that this is probably less to do with seeing me and more to do with whatever is wrong with her, her and this crying baby.

This crying baby has me confused. Whose child is it? Surely she couldn't have had a baby in America and told me nothing about it? It is a fleeting thought and a ridiculous one. No, this must be the child from Scotland. I drag my eyes from hers to take a quick look at it. A little red-headed lad. What age could he be? He is small enough to be six months; no he must be older than that, despite his size. He looks more like a year, or maybe a year and a half, just the shape of his face and the way he is wriggling about. All this crosses my mind in a split second, as does the fact that I haven't spoken a word to her yet.

She beats me to it.

"Thank you for coming."

It is such a feeble sounding voice that again I have to ask myself, 'Is this the same Sally Anne that worked for me, the lively confident girl who, in any argument with me, could give as good as she got? What, in the name of God has happened to her?'

"Welcome home."

"Ok," she says.

'Ok'? That's not something she'd have allowed to cross her lips back in the day.

"I'm glad to see you," I say, "but you don't seem to be well. What...?"

"I'm tired, very tired," she says. "Need to get home."

"Sally Anne," I insist. "there's more wrong here than tiredness, even I can see that. What's wrong? What happened you? And you must introduce me to this wain?"

I reach to hold its hand but it pulls away and hides its face in her shoulder.

"Can we sit in the car, Matthew... please?"

Oh Lord, how inconsiderate of me. I turn and run to bring the car up beside her. She can't mark her foot to the ground and seems to be in great pain. I help her into the front seat, the wain on her knee, then load her luggage into the boot and climb in beside her. I don't start the car yet, just stare at her for an explanation.

"I cut my foot last week. It's sore still."

"What did you cut it on? Can I take a look at it?"

She takes her shoe and sock off, and even that wasn't easy for her. I see a very swollen, red-looking foot. The cut must be on the bottom for I can't see it, but the thing is obviously very sore.

"It's not looking good, Sally Anne," I tell her. "You must have cut it on something dirty for it seems to have gone septic on you."

"I did," she says. "An old, rusty tin."

"And you're not feeling well, are you?"

"I am not myself. I was sick even before the cut," she says. "The sea journey from America took it out of me. It was rough. Sorry. I must look a bit of a mess."

"Never mind how you look, I am just glad to see you. It has been a long time."

"It has," she says, trying to smile. "This is not the way I wanted to meet you either. I feel such an old cripple. I am sorry."

"Wheesht girl," I tell her, reaching out to hold the child's hand again, an instinct I didn't know I had in me. "Don't be saying sorry. But tell me about this wee lad here. What is his name?"

"Aye, that must have confused you too. This is Frankie," she says. "Frankie Wilson. He is my cousin's grandson. His granny can't look after him any longer so I am bringing him to Donegal to see how we get on."

I look at her in a mixture of surprise and admiration.

"And what about Frankie's mummy? Is she the one..."

Sally Anne holds a finger up to her lips and I stop. We shouldn't be talking about this in front of the wain, I am thinking. I can hear more of the details later.

I study her face. The skin is still taut over her forehead and her jaw, just as it was when she was eighteen. It is such a pretty face, older, thinner yes, but perfect in its shape and proportions. But there is something about the skin, the colour and tone of it. Obviously she has been in the open-air a lot, but the sun-burn is fading fast as her natural whiteness and freckles show through from below. It puts me in mind of a cup of tea that looked alright until someone poured far too much cream into it. It's a paleness that looks sort of grubby, soiled. For all that, she is every bit Sally Anne, just a very jaded version of herself, missing that old spark that I used to love, most of the time anyhow.

"Right, I think the first thing we have to do is get you to a hospital, if I can find one. That foot of yours needs looking at and quick too. An infection like that could spread; maybe it has already, and that's why you are feeling so sick of yourself."

She doesn't argue. I catch a wry sideways look from her.

"It wouldn't be you and me if there wasn't some drama involved, would it?" she says.

"No doubt about that," I tell her. "At least this time you didn't jump off the top of a fort and wreck your ankle."

"I never jumped. I was trying to run away from you, if you remember right."

"Well, you can't run now."

"Nope, not even if I wanted to."

With that she lowers her face to take refuge in the tousled hair of the youngster on her knee. She seems exhausted and distraught in a way I had not expected. I think she is crying.

I have no idea where the hospital is in this town, so I stop to ask a man pushing a wheelbarrow beside the road.

He takes a fag out of his mouth, then seems to sing at us through his nose. A funny wee man, his way of talking gives us both a smile.

"Ye go away up that road there till you get tae the Northland Road, know what I mean like? Turn right and ye canny miss it hi. The County Hospital."

I follow his instructions.

On the way Sally Anne fumbles in her bag, looking for something.

"Could I ask you another favour?" she says.

"Surely."

"I have an envelope here with money in it. A lot of money, all that I made in America. Would you keep it for me? It might be safer with you than lying in my bag in this hospital, if they take me in. I'll need it later to pay them."

"Aye, I'll take it for you," I tell her, happy that she is comfortable enough with me to be asking this. "There's a new car I saw in a garage in Strabane on the way up and they need a deposit, so... I'll take it for you surely."

She smiles very weakly but doesn't seem to have the energy to be bothered replying. The package, for it is far thicker than your normal envelope, goes into my coat pocket.

I nearly have to carry Sally Anne and the wain into the place, for she is yelping with the pain of it.

"Will you keep Frankie for me?" she asks as an orderly seats her on a wheel-chair thing, before pushing her away down the corridor.

'My Lord,' I think. 'I come to pick up this woman I haven't set eyes on for twenty something years and instead I end up looking after a youngster I have never set eyes on before. This is just ridiculous. What am I to do with this Frankie? How long am I to look after him? Will he need feeding? Help!'

Frankie doesn't take long to let me know that he has better ideas about how to spend the afternoon than sitting on my knee in a hospital corridor. He squirms away from me and crawls about the place. Nurses passing have to step around him and over him and I get a few critical looks from them. I decide to take him out to the fresh air.

We walk a few of the streets and I find some conkers for him below a huge chestnut tree along the Northland Road. He seems to enjoy playing with these, though I have trouble keeping him from trying to chew them. You never know what dog has pissed on them, so we take them to a public water pump for a bit of a wash.

A few minutes later I get a whiff of baby shit. Oh no, now Frankie will need the nappy changed and I have no idea where to find a clean one. Likely there's some in Sally Anne's bags but, here we are on a steep wee street in the middle of Londonderry, a good distance from the hospital. What do I do now?

I would not be the most experienced in things like this. Eventually the stench gets too much for me and I get the idea that this street pump would be a good place to give the lad's backside a wash, so I strip the nappy off him and pump a few gallons of cold water over his rear end. This doesn't seem to please him at all and he screams blue murder at me. A small crowd soon gathers around us and I get the benefit of some tasty advice from a few locals.

"Jasus, wud ye luk at yer man, washing the wain's erse un'er the pump!"

Some woman comes to my rescue, shooing the ruffians away and taking the shivering wain off my hands. She wraps him up close to her huge bosom with a pair of arms that could stop a galloping horse.

"What were you thinking man, sticking his wee, bare bum under a public pump? Have ye no sense?"

"He's not my wain," I tell her. "I have only just got him, so I didn't know what to do to clean him."

"Only just got him? You don't say," she says with that strong Derry sarcasm. "An' I thought looking at you that you were a dab hand. Where's his mammy anyway?"

Now there's a question. I have no idea of the answer but, if I start to explain all that, it will likely look as if I have just stolen this wain from somebody's pram, so I just point up the street at the hospital.

"She's in there."

"Well tell her not to be trusting you with him any more. Here, take him. I have him dried on my apron so pull those wee pants on him again and get him back to his mother quick, before you freeze him to death."

I leave her washing out the filthy nappy under the pump, my fingers crossed that he doesn't create any more mess till we get another one. I wander back towards the hospital, carrying Frankie and trying to keep him entertained. I point out passing dogs and cats, passing cars and bicycles, passing people; they must all be wondering why I am pointing at them, babbling away.

"Look, Frankie; see that man taking his hat for a walk. Look, there's a Morris Cowley, a green one. And would you look at that woman pushing two prams at the same time."

He stays interested most of the time. I buy him a wee bar of soft chocolate and that finishes up all over his hands and face. He doesn't ever say anything but maybe at this age they don't. Or maybe it is just the bad start he has had in life, with his mother and granny being a bit crazy from all accounts. Should he be talking already? I try him with a few words.

"Say da-da, Frankie. Da-da. No? What can you say? How about ma-ma? Can you not say ma-ma?"

Nothing but blank eyes staring out of a brown-smeared face. I give up on the language lessons, feeling a bit useless of myself. I have a brave bit to be learning about wains, I think.

My arms are starting to tire after all his wriggling. I feel like we are starting to bond alright. Then I worry that it's just that he has peed himself and, as a result, his bum is sticking to my coat sleeve.

We arrive back at the hospital and go in to check on Sally Anne.

The news there is not good. Her foot has gone septic, as I thought, and they need to keep her in the hospital to make sure the treatment they are giving her is working. The doctor tells both of us that her temperature is very high. It will take time for the penicillin to work. It would be too dangerous to let her out straight away, he says. Might take three or four days before they can be sure.

I am so glad I had the wit to bring her here. It doesn't matter what it will cost, it doesn't matter that I have been left with this wain in my care, all that matters is that, yet again, I have to do something to look after this girl, this woman as she is now.

This is what I think about as I start the drive on the long road to the west of Donegal. At the Border I have a serious bit of explaining to do about this child crying in a make-shift cot in the back of my car, a cot that I had begged from a grocery shop along the Strand Road, a cot that until half an hour ago had been a tea-chest. It's only when I show the Customs man Sally Anne's bags with the labels on them showing her address in America and in Donegal that they start to come around and believe me. They have to check through all the bags of course and that takes time. They still look doubtful, but when I tell them to contact the hospital and check on my story they finally decide to wave me through.

Frankie has thankfully gone to sleep, since I fed him some milk that the hospital kindly gave me for him. I had been doing my best to keep him in chat. But I have made the discovery that there's only so many times you can sing 'Old MacDonald had a farm' and stay sane. My e-i-e-i-ohs had started to sound like a drunken donkey. I had been running out of animals, ideas and energy.

"Frankie," I said at one point, "how would you like to come over to my farm some day and I could show you all these animals, eh? Isn't that a good idea? And we could maybe talk your...your new mammy into coming as well. Now there's an even better idea."

He didn't reply of course, and when I looked in the mirror he had disappeared into the bottom of the tea-chest. 'Likely asleep now,' I thought. 'Maybe dreaming about this new friend by the name of MacDonald and his farm of mad braying donkeys.'

The tea-chest is at least keeping him safe and in one place. This journey would have been a nightmare without it. Even worse if he hadn't given in and fallen asleep on my coat.

I'd thought of avoiding this Border issue by taking Frankie home to Lismore but how could I have looked after him and worked at the harvest at the same time? The only plan I could reasonably come up with was to drive him to Mairead and the granny. Apart from anything else, they would be worried if Sally Anne didn't arrive home as expected, with no way of finding out what had happened. At least now I can explain the situation to them and they can look after Frankie until Sally Anne is well and home again.

What is it about Sally Anne and me that brings about this kind of situation? There are so many echoes of the past. Yet Sally Anne looks so different, seems so different, so vulnerable. This is the woman who had the courage to travel to America on her own, to take on working in a new job in a hotel, learn to cook there, travel home to help her relatives. Look at her now, so weak, for whatever reason. The injury to her foot is a big part of it, but I just feel she is very needy at the minute. And I think this brings out the best in me, always did.

How glad I am that she allowed me to come to collect her.

Tomorrow is Sunday. I won't be working of course, so I can drive up again to see how she is. I could maybe bring Millie with me too. Naw; I will come on my own, I think.

Chapter 49

Sally Anne Sweeney

They tell me I have been delirious. I didn't know that word before. The doctor says it means talking nonsense.

"*Bhí tú ag rámhaillí*', he said.

That wouldn't be new to me, to be raving but how did he know I had *an Ghaeilge?*

"Sure weren't you babbling away in it all night," he says, his accent, now he's in the English, a sure sign that he is from Cork or somewhere far away down there.

"At least you understood me," I tell him.

"Not a word of it," he laughs as he unwraps the bandage they have put on my foot. "It may have been in Irish but you were swearing away at somebody called Bob and shouting to Caroline for help, whatever was going on."

"Oh sweet Mother Mary, don't tell me that. What did I say?"

"Ah don't worry, I won't tell anybody," he says, "but I am just glad I am not the Bob person. His ears must have been burning, wherever he is."

"Not hot enough," I whisper. Then, "Will I be able to get out of here today, doctor?"

"Not from what I see here," he says, poking gently at my foot. The pain shot through me like a needle. "You have a deep infection and it is going to take a bit of time to make sure it goes away. So you will just have to content yourself and rest it totally."

"So how long?"

"Couple more days at least," he says. "And then it will need you to stay off it for a while. What do you do?"

I tell him my circumstances and about my journey from America to Derry. He is a good listener.

"Well, at least you have the child looked after and this friend can maybe give you a ride home when we think you are ready. Now, take your medicine and drink water like you've never drunk before."

****

Matthew arrives late in the afternoon. He strides up the ward to the bed. In my doze I hear the click of his shoes on the wooden floor. My gluey eyes take in the fact that he is in a smart suit. Very Protestant looking altogether, but then it is a Sunday I remember. The tense expression on his face changes for the better as I give him a bit of a welcoming smile.

"How are you?"

He stands over me, big as a tree, his arms folded as if he is scared they might do something without his permission.

"I have been better, but I am not as bad as yesterday," I tell him.

"Still very sore?"

"Aye it is sore alright, but the drugs are starting to work I think, so it is just a matter of time."

"Good," he says. "I was worried for you."

"I know, I could see that. And thank you for all you did yesterday..."

He interrupts me with his hand.

"Don't," he says, "it was the least I could do. I am so glad you sent me the telegram. You were in no state to be trying to get home on your own, never mind having Frankie and all your stuff."

"I know that."

"And that money of yours," he says. "You're going to love this new car."

"Of course I will," I smile. "What about Frankie? You got him to Mairead alright? Are you not going to sit down?"

There is no chair. He looks around, then at the narrow bed. Carefully I shift my body over to the side and he puts a hip on the bedspread beside me.

Oh, the memories, the memories.

"Frankie is alright. He slept most of the way. In a tea-chest, would you believe."

I laugh when he tells me about that idea.

"And you explained to Mairead?"

"'Course. You should have seen her face when I got out of the car with the wain in my arms. She was a picture."

"I am sure. What did she say?"

"I couldn't tell you; it was in Irish for a start. She was more worried about where you were and what had happened to you. But once I got her to understand everything and that you'd be in hospital for a day or two she calmed down."

"Did she feed you?"

"Oh aye, plenty of soda bread and spuds. She was grand, after the start, but it must have been some shock to her to see me back again at her door a year later, but with the wain this time and your cases."

"My cases, yes. Did you take the fiddle back home with you?"

He looks me in the eyes for a minute.

"I am not taking it, Sally Anne. It is yours."

I shake my head.

"No, I can't keep it. It was a lovely thing you did for me, but it belongs in your home and you must take it back there."

He lets the subject sit on the bedspread between us. It's as if both of us are staring at it there. He gets a wee bit agitated, as if he has something to say but can't think how to put it, afraid to express what is in his head. When he does speak again it is as if he is making a veiled joke, as if this is just an after-thought that has come to him. I can read it though. It is no after-thought.

"It will only come back to Lismore if you bring it."

This is clever. He is watching my reaction closely. I give him a quick stare, then my eyes bounce away to look out the window, which is impossible for the glass is frosted. What he has said is both awkward and lovely at the same time. I have to judge my answer very carefully, so he will not read anything into it more than I have really said. So, after a few seconds, I slowly turn to him.

Quietly I say, "I would love to visit Lismore again."

The man may have aged, but his sly half-grin hasn't and his big, blue eyes are still as clear as a shallow rock pool at the end of Carrickfinn strand. I can read what lies behind those eyes with the same ease as I did when we first met.

My answer has pleased him no end.

To be honest, it has pleased me too, nearly as much.

"So, how was America?"

Suddenly I feel really tired, both tired and emotional. I snuggle down into the sheets a bit.

"It was…it was America," I tell him.

"Sorry, Sally Anne. Look, you are tired. I shouldn't have asked. I will go here and let you get some sleep."

"You can stay but maybe let me close my eyes for a bit. And I will tell you about America, when I have time and when I feel a bit stronger. Just need to put my head down now, sorry."

My eyes close at once. I think he stays.

If he didn't then somebody else has taken the liberty of stroking my hair as I drift off into sleep.

I haven't the energy to resist.

Chapter 50

Matthew Henderson

"You should not have paid that bill, Matthew. That is not fair. It was me was sick, for goodness sake. And I have the money. So tell me how much it was, will you?"

We are driving between Derry and the Border, on the way to Letterkenny, Sally Anne in the front seat. It feels great to have her beside me again. I don't answer her question, just a sideways glance and a tease of a smile.

"Please?"

"Can't remember."

"Don't make me angry. 'Course you remember. It was only half an hour ago. You're playing games with me and it's not fair. Me getting changed and you sneaking up to their office and paying."

"I couldn't very well stay there and watch you changing, could I? It was just manners..."

"Oh stop, will you! Just tell me how much it was and don't annoy me any longer." Her voice is raised to that pitch I remember so well.

I give her a 'calm down' look.

"Hey, settle yourself. I am only trying to help. And look, it was my doing to take you to the hospital, so it is my responsibility."

"It was my foot they treated, so I pay."

I let silence pacify her for a minute before going on in the argument.

"Why can't you just accept things....?"

"Accept charity, is it? Wee, stupid, Irish woman has to accept charity from big Protestant farmer who is trying to..." She stops short.

"Trying to what?"

"I don't know. I don't know what you are trying to do," she says and she does sound very exasperated, to be fair to her. "Look, it is hard for me, this. You send me that fiddle and it brought me back from the brink. Maybe I will tell you about that sometime. Then you drive up to Derry to get me and take me home. OK, I asked you to, but still. I did need the help, even more than I ever imagined I would. But you take me to hospital, you take Frankie all the way over to Mairead, you keep my money for me, you come up to Derry three times to see me, when you likely should be working. Then on top of all that you pay the bill and refuse to let me pay you back. And now you are driving me home. Can you see how unfair this feels to me?"

I don't answer. We are approaching the Border crossing and the conversation has to stop for the minute, much to her annoyance.

"My good Lord," she says, "even the border is on your side."

"Now you are starting to see the right of it," I laugh.

There are no problems at the check-points compared to what I had had with Frankie. Both sets of Customs men are easily enough satisfied when Sally Anne shows them her travel documents and explains about the hospital. The bandaged foot convinces them. The Free State man does take a look in my empty boot and below my bonnet but there is nothing there, so we are quickly waved on through.

"Right," she continues. "Answer me."

"Answer what?"

She clicks her tongue impatiently.

"Tell me what you are trying to do here."

Easy. "Taking you home, like you asked."

"Come on, Matthew. What is all this for? Why are you being like this?"

It's not easy to answer while driving, keeping one eye on the road and the other on her at the same time, so I pull the car into the mouth of a quarry area that we are passing.

I turn to face her and we look hard at each other across the car. I am furiously trying to think how to put this, how much to say, how far to go. She is only back here a few days, but I have seen her every one of them. At the start, there were long silences during those hospital visits, as we both struggled to know what to say, but slowly we got beyond the shy awkwardness and the distance between us. Now it feels like we have talked so much more than I ever imagined we would. She has had little choice, when I think about it, captured below the sheets of that hospital bed, her foot all bandaged and up in a sling of a thing.

I begin. "I suppose I am only trying to be the person to you that I should have been, way back then."

She doesn't answer this, just turns and stares out the left hand window as a rain shower begins to splatter against it.

"Do you understand that?"

"Yes, but you don't have to. That was then, this is now."

"This is now, indeed it is. But I have this need in me to finish off the 'then', if you know what I mean. Before I go on in the 'now'."

Quietly she says, "And how are you going to do that?" She is still watching the rain.

"That letter you sent me, back last year. It was just great. You have no notion how many times I have read it. Still have it too. And, maybe what you were doing then, all those things you said, maybe that is what I am trying to do now."

"Alright," she says, "but you don't need to do all these things to try to impress me. You just need to…to speak, you know, to talk."

"I suppose I am just trying to say sorry."

"Well say it then, but stop trying to sweeten me up all the time."

"I am not trying to…"

She turns to stare at me and I stop arguing. Right, this is it.

"Alright," I say and I clear my throat. "I am asking you to forgive me for being such a bigoted ejit. Forgive me for how I hurt you."

She tries to interrupt but I hold up my hand, for I haven't finished yet.

"Instead of loving you and caring for you like I wanted to do, everything inside me wanted to do that, but instead I turned away from you and closed you out. I was a fool and if you knew how many times I have thought that over the years, especially since I got your letter, you would know that I mean it."

After a silence she says, "And Joe?"

"Joe, of course. You don't have to rebuke me about that. I begged his forgiveness every night for years. It nearly drove me demented. Joe was dead and you might as well have been dead. The two most precious things in my life at the time and I killed them both."

"Not both," she whispered.

"Might as well have been. In my wildest dreams, and believe me I did dream about it, I could never have imagined a circumstance like this, you and me talking again. You writing to me. Me sending you the fiddle. This here. It is like a miracle."

"It is a bit of a miracle," she agrees, a soft look on her face.

"So am I forgiven?"

She just gives me a fleeting smile and says something quietly in Irish. It sounds nice and I hope that means what I think it means but I daren't ask any more.

Then, "Now can I pay you and can you take me home please."

"The second one I can do, the first one is my gift to you, so…I know you well enough to know that you will have the grace to accept a gift, just as you have accepted the fiddle."

"But I haven't accepted the fiddle," she argues again. "I want you to take it back."

"And we agreed in hospital that you will bring it back, didn't we?"

Her mouth twists into an unwilling smile of resignation.

"If I bring it to Lismore you will take it back?"

"I might." I get the stare. "Alright, alright, I will then."

"But how am I going to get to your place?"

I pause to wet my mouth with spittle, for it has gone suddenly dry.

"You could always invite me over some Sunday and I could bring you and Frankie back to Lismore for a day or two?"

There, I have said it. Is this another step too far? I try to judge her reaction but she turns away to the left again. She is great at avoiding the search in my eyes. But after a bit of thought she says, "If you like."

"Great," I say and then we both need time to think about what has just happened. We think in quietness, a sort of peaceful acceptance of each other, of this strange twist in the path of our lives.

In my case at least, I am thinking as well of how easily we have taken to this level of familiarity again. It amazes me. I wonder does she realise it too. In a strange way, it is almost as if this long passage of time has only happened insofar as we are both aged by twenty years. Any distance between us that I might have expected has melted away like snow off a ditch and we are chatting as we might have done in my kitchen in 1922.

The fields, the houses, the lanes and the bends seem to fly past on this journey. In no time we are climbing up a road towards the back of Errigal mountain. It feels more like a bog-lane than a road, a torture of potholes and puddles and worn-away grass verges. I have to slow down to ten miles an hour in places, but I don't mind, if I am honest. Sally Anne's chat is great. She has recovered from her sickness and fatigue during the last few days and she has got back her appetite for conversation. I am hearing more about America than I ever imagined wanting to hear. Funny too that as she talks about it I hear some expressions and bits of pronunciation that are clearly not her. She has picked up phrases and ways of saying things and she probably doesn't know it. If she goes on too much like this in the Rosses they'll be calling her 'The Yank'. Still, I don't mind one bit and I am really enjoying her enthusiasm.

When she goes too far too fast I throw in the odd question, usually about some of these people she has been working with. She seems to have got very close to this Caroline girl. She tells me again about playing my fiddle for some Irish folk in her hotel. This is music to my ears. Also her enthusiasm for the new work she was doing as a cook and the great money she was earning doing it. Then I hear a sentence I hadn't wanted to hear but probably expected.

"So when I go back next Easter I will be full time in the kitchen hopefully."

There is a bit of a pause after this. We are both aware of it. She may feel she has said too much, or maybe it was a deliberate piece of news to drop into the conversation, sort of to take the wind out of my unfurling sails.

I let it pass. There will be plenty of water to flow under the bridge before next Easter.

We have reached the other side of the mountain pass beside Errigal. The view below us is just beautiful and I pull the car into a gap, so we can look at it from outside.

"Do you want the crutches?" I ask. Last night I had made a pair of makeshift crutches from a couple of ash-plant saplings and she had been able to walk from the hospital to the car using them. Now they lie in the back seat.

"It's alright. I won't walk, just lean on the car," she says.

She stands on one leg, the other foot barely touching the ground. The colours of the forest and the purple hillside beyond the lake are reflected in its still water. There is a lovely old church below us, standing white and proud against the shimmer of the sun on the lake.

"Dunlewy lough," she says. *"Galánta."*

"That is the one word I remember you teaching me," I tell her. "It usually comes into my head when I look at that newspaper cutting, with the photo of us standing beside the binder."

"Lord above," she laughs. "I can't believe you still have that."

"Have surely," I say. "You haven't changed a bit."

"Now look," she scolds, "if you and me are going to be friends and if you are not going to go back to your old ways you have to stop telling lies like that, alright."

"You haven't changed, in my opinion anyway."

Turning away from me in a motion that I cannot fathom she says, "But I have. I have...and I wish it was not so, but I have changed. I will never be...."

I don't have a notion what she is on about but my instinct is to put my hand on her shoulder, sort of by way of reassurance, or of consolation, I don't know which. It is a natural response to her but she seems to lose her balance, stumble away from me briefly and sway back to lean against me. Her body gives a wee shudder as if she is crying, which I did not see coming. She only stays there the briefest of seconds, then straightens and moves away from me, turning back to open the car door. I am at a loss to work out what this is all about, but I sense I have touched some sort of nerve in her. It disappoints me that maybe I have been too forward of myself, but I can't think what I have said that would have annoyed her.

I get in beside her.

"Sorry, I didn't mean..."

"It's not you. It's me. I am not the girl you knew. I am somebody who thought she was in control of everything, nothing could ever hurt me again, but I was wrong. I am just a silly woman and nothing can ever be the same again."

"I don't understand. What makes you say this?"

"That's the thing. I can't tell you, I can't tell anyone."

I know better than to push the question now.

"Look," I tell her, "we'll not talk anymore now, right? But just let me say this. You couldn't tell me anything about yourself that would be worse than some of the stuff I have done in my life. So neither of us is perfect, remember that."

She stares ahead, silent and thoughtful.

"Are you ready to go home or what?" I ask.

"I am," she says. "It has been a long time. But, before we go home, there's a place I want you to see. In case you never get the chance again."

"Where's that?"

"A place near me called Carrickfinn; the boat strand there," (she had a name for it in Irish; it sounded to me like 'Tra Wadge' but I could be wrong.) "It's my favourite beach," she continued. "I can't wait to walk along that shore. It will be a while before I can do that, so if you drive me there first, just to let the shape and the sound and the scent of it seep into me. Please?"

"Why not?" I say and we drive far too quickly down the steep hill beyond the mountain and, miles later, turn on to a rough lane across the sand flats that she tells me leads to this special place of hers.

I have to admit she hasn't overstated its beauty. We stand beside each other where I pull the car up on a flat headland above a wee harbour and watch the waves break on the beach below us. The bay to our right is very pretty, the shape of a horseshoe and hemmed in by steep cliffs of light-coloured rock. To the left, a dark slab of an island seems to be standing guard, as if protecting a very pretty curving strand. The colours are lovely to look at, the greenish-blue of the water in the shallow bay, the pinky rises of rock, the fairness of the even sand, the various shades of green on top of the island and the sand-hills behind, while out on the distant horizon banks of grey cloud are easing their way in our direction.

Out of the corner of my eye I see Sally Anne making the sign of the cross over her chest. I turn to her and she sees that I am curious.

"My baby brother is buried out there," she says.

"What? You mean it's a graveyard, on that island?"

"Sort of," she says, "it's called ...." And again it is an Irish name that I haven't a notion about, except that it sounds like 'illan' something.

"Say that again," I ask her, so she spells it out.

"'*O-i-l-e-a-n*', means island; '*n-a m-a-r-b-h*'; it means 'island of the dead,'" she explains. "I'll get you learning Irish yet."

"So it is an island for burying folk?" I ask. "Seems a very sad place then. And your brother, you say?"

"He died at birth, you see. So, because he was never baptised he couldn't be buried in consecrated ground."

"Oh right," I say. "That is tough. How did your parents feel about that then?"

She just shakes her head. Enough said.

"Can you give me a minute to say a prayer for him," she says.

"Of course."

I stand back and take in the view for a bit. It is hard for me to understand these customs of hers, of her faith, of this area, but I am not going to let it spoil these moments.

When she turns back to me I decide to change the subject.

"Does the sea smell the same as America?"

"It does but that turf smoke in Crolly is like no smell you will ever find over there. I missed it, that smell. This is home."

She turns to me. "Matthew, I can't begin to thank you for what you have done and for how you have been to me today."

"This is thanks enough," I tell her.

"Now, come and meet mammy...again."

Chapter 51

Sally Anne Sweeney

What on earth have I taken on here, this pretend-mother role?

It is hard work, I am learning, something I should have known, but it's not until you commit yourself to it, with no escape routes, that it hits you.

The constancy of it.

And I have Mairead to help me. Now there's a thing.

Mairead and my mother were glad to have me safely back, of course they were. Mammy just stared at me, long and hard. No smiles, no words, no gestures, but deep in those dead eyes of hers I think I saw a little light of recognition, of love. I like to think that anyhow. It was the longest look I ever remember her giving me, that is for sure. And it wasn't long after I arrived in that she went to the drawer in the table, took out the whistle and played some old Donegal tune that I haven't heard for years. That was her word of welcome, I am certain of it.

I was struggling to keep my eyes open after my illness and the long day I'd had, but I thought to myself, how many more times will I get the chance to play with her before she is gone. I took Matthew's fiddle from its case and joined in for a couple of tunes before tiredness got the better of me. I think she enjoyed it, just by the look in her eyes afterwards, blank but motherly in that way that only a daughter with years of experience can recognise.

Over the next few days, Ailish called up a couple of times in the evening for a chat. She seemed very pleased to have me back home. She has a new lease of life since getting a job and her happiness shows in her face. I had so much to tell her, both the American tale and the events since coming home, but two things sort of spoiled the chance. I would start a story, maybe about the Windsor, or 'that man', but Frankie would be bouncing around the kitchen floor, wanting constant attention or needing food, so the story would be abandoned. I was dying to explain to her about how Matthew had come back into my life again. Her opinion of him would have been very low of course, because it was based on what she saw at the harvest ceili back in 1922 and on the endless litany of my complaints over many years, but I was getting no privacy to talk about this. Mairead was always around, so I could not open up my heart to my old friend as I wanted to, needed to. I longed for a walk up the mountain with Ailish, just so we could talk frankly. Mairead was not in a mood to offer to make that possible.

My sister was happy that I had come home, but I wasn't long in until I realised that this was less about me and more down to the fact that she wouldn't have to look after Frankie on her own any more, as she had while I was in hospital. A day or two after I arrived we were having a bit of an argument and her resentment about the boy started to surface.

"You didn't give much thought to how it was going to affect us, landing him in on us without so much as a warning," she said.

"What else was I meant to do? The child is an orphan."

"He has his granny. He has uncles."

"His uncles are in Australia, for God's sake, Mairead. And you know Mary Anne. She is not capable of rearing him. She wasn't capable of rearing Nuala in the first place. If you saw the squalor he was living in you wouldn't have left him there either."

"Well, just so long as you know that he is your responsibility."

"Of course I know that. But I am sure you will want to help too."

Mairead thought about this. I could tell she was trying to choose her words carefully.

"I will help where I can, but what I won't do is take over from you. You brought him and he is welcome, but he is your choice."

"That's grand then," I told her.

"It is until you decide you are going back to America. What will you do with him then?"

I knew this question would come up at some stage but this is very early. I didn't really have an answer either. So I tried the money argument.

"Alright, so why don't you go and get work? Go down to Crolly and get a job in the factory like Ailish did. Go back to Scotland and get yourself a good paying job there, if you can't get one around here. We can't live on fresh air. I'll mind Frankie and mammy and you make the money."

She didn't like the sense in this idea, I could see that. So I continued.

"This year, I slaved my guts out in America. I made good money, more than you could make here in a lifetime. I sent money to Nuala, half of which she never got. I sent money home here. I paid my fares both ways, which wasn't cheap. And we still have a fair pile left over for the winter. And you can't see your way to volunteer to help to look after Frankie if I get a chance to go back for next summer?"

With that she stormed off to our bedroom. Only for her head to appear around the door again seconds later.

"He's dirtied himself again. This place smells worse than a byre," she complained.

I understand. When you have reached this stage of your life without having to change filthy nappies every half hour you take it hard. But there are nicer moments too. Frankie is a lovely child, most of the time. He can be stubborn and cries for attention when there's nothing much wrong with him, but I suppose we were all the same. He just needs working with, patience and firmness. I am learning as I go along.

Father Devine calls up to see us.

Has this child been baptised, he wants to know.

"Do you know, Father," I tell him, "I don't rightly know. I am sure his mother had him baptised in Glasgow."

"You need to find out. The child should be baptised."

"How would I find out? His mother is dead. His father is dead. He was with his granny in Musselburgh and she is house-bound so she wasn't at it, if there was a baptism itself."

"What about the father's people?"

"They are Protestant. I don't know how to get in touch with them, even if I wanted to."

He rolls his eyes.

"Maybe I should contact someone in the Glasgow Diocese. The Gorbals area was where they lived, was it? Just to see if they have a record of any baptism for him. What's his full name again?"

"Frankie Wilson," I tell him. "His daddy was Frank as well."

He writes this down in a notebook.

"Maybe we should do him just in case?"

"That's up to you Father."

"It's up to you as well, you are his guardian now. You won't be able to officially adopt him but that doesn't matter, you will rear him as a good Catholic, won't you?"

"Of course."

"And this man who arrived here last summer looking for you? Have you heard of him since, for he was a right cheeky one, so he was. More than bold of himself. Typical of his sort."

I decide to give him something to think about when he is gone.

"Ah yes... Matthew," I say, open and brash as you like. "He's a good friend. He is the one that got me off the boat and took me to the hospital. Paid the bill and brought me home too."

"Did he now? That surprises me, but I want to tell you, Sally Anne, I warn you to have nothing more to do with him, no more letters, no more contact. You have this child to devote yourself to.

You pay heed to me now. Nothing more. Bring this boy up as a decent Catholic child who will respect his church."

"I intend to, Father, but I can't promise the other."

He storms away, raising the dust off the yard as he leaves.

Here he is, still trying to box me in, still judging me and trying to save me from this terrible weakness he sees in my character. He should have known better than to mention Matthew to me. It only gets my goat up and makes me more determined to follow my own head on this.

It is nearly two weeks since Matthew brought me home. I intend to write to him tonight. And, in spite of knowing that Bríd Mhicí Jinny in the post office will most likely pass the news of the letter on to Father Devine, I will post it without another thought.

What will I say to him that I haven't said already? What will I say that I know how to say, without seeming too keen? It might just be the hardest letter yet.

That first one I sent him last year had been building up in me for ever. I had had a very long time for it to form in me. It wasn't hard to write because I knew it was the proper thing to be doing. But now what do I say?

I can't go on thanking him. I can't just continue making small talk.

Should I write about how foolish I was when I was away, how I left my maidenhead in a New Jersey lagoon? Maybe I have said enough about it when we were standing by his car up the Errigal road and I was hinting how I had been changed. Might he have been able to read beneath the front cover of the book and guessed at the story inside? Would he have that kind of sensitivity? Maybe not.

Is it any of his business for a start? Why do I have this feeling of needing to tell him? What is he to me anyhow? A man I used to love? A person from my past?

Not any longer, I think. Not after his letters. Not after seeing the concern for me in his face when he picked me up in Derry. I just wish I could have enjoyed that reunion a bit better, without feeling so pathetic. It was nothing like I had imagined or hoped for. But it is how it happened and I can do nothing about it now.

Maybe I should just let the matter rest, keep the ugliness of my mistake hidden among the shadows of my mind? Bury it for years, like I did the hurt that he himself caused me, until something pricks at my conscience and I know it is right to tell him? By that time I might no longer know him anyhow.

I might no longer know him?

My mind stumbles and falls over itself on that thought.

No, surely no! There will never be a time, I begin to admit to myself, when I will no longer know him. These two lives are twined together like ivy on an old beech tree, for better or worse. The ivy may have been pruned off at one stage, but look how it is regrowing.

But I cannot write this in a letter to him tonight, this twining idea. He would likely take a hatchet to the ivy, put an end to it and that would be the last I would hear of him. And he might be the luckier for it too.

I must write something though. I promised him.

I won't mention my American fall. It can wait till the time is right.

I try to imagine us chatting away at his kitchen table, maybe I am telling him about Caroline and Roisin, or the food I had to make, or the horse-shoe crabs on the beach and then in the middle of it I just throw in a line about how that man seduced me on a boat. Hardly!

I cannot see how this conversation will happen. Yet I have this need in me to be honest with him. It is the only way, otherwise I have no right to expect him to be open with me about what is going on at present in his complicated head.

I feel the need to somehow dig below this facade of Matthew's, if that is what it is, a facade. He does seem changed, more fair-minded. He is less bothered about the differences between us. He seems more respectful of my language, even went out of his way to include a few words in one of his letters. If I thought for one minute that this is just a pretence to draw me back to him, I would turn on my naivety with a fury. I don't think it is though, for he has backed it up with generosity, with this eagerness to go many extra miles for me. I know it is all an effort to impress, of course I do, but there is nothing wrong with that, as long as it is coming from a changed heart.

Back in 1922, things between us had developed so quickly, so madly, that we were almost lovers. That was before the poisoned juices of his clan seeped into his bloodstream, undermining everything and sending the whole thing to hell. We are both so much wiser now but could the sickness grow in him again? And if it did, would I be strong enough to be the medicine for it, to fight it and defeat it, or would I run away again?

Only time will tell, and tell it will.

Our conversation two weeks ago, as Matthew was leaving after bringing me home, was really strange; strange but nice.

We stood together by his car, the door open to his hand, the seat waiting for him and one of his big feet still on my street.

There was a lot of looking at each other and a fair bit of silence as a lot of unspoken thoughts travelled between us without the words to carry them. I tried to say 'Thank you' again but he wouldn't let me get very far into that sentence. So I just smiled my gratitude and waited for him to say something. Eventually he did.

"So you will come over to see me? Bring Frankie? Sometime?"

"If you like." I was trying to sound nonchalant.

"What do you think?"

"About what?" I teased.

"About....agh, don't be trying to tie me in knots again. So when?"

"When what?"

He shook his head, but the smile didn't leave his eyes. "When would you like to come over?"

"Whenever you come for me."

"I'm here now," he joked. "Get your stuff."

I just laughed.

"I can't wait for Millie to see you," he said. "And Anthony and Monica. Mary too."

"This is starting to sound like a penny-peep show," I told him. "Like you can't wait to parade your trophy or something."

"Well," he laughed, "you'd have to admit it was a long oul hunt."

"So that's what it was then? A hunt? I was your prey, was I?"

"Aye, my wounded deer."

I was enjoying this banter and I could tell he was too by the grinning of him. Then he asked a question I have asked myself many times.

"Do you ever wish you could turn back the clock?"

I turned away to look down to the shoreline, just to give myself that wee minute to think. I wanted to say, "I wish to God I could turn it forward, just to see what is to become of the two of us." But instead I told him, "Maybe I do, but it would need to go back as far as the night of the harvest ceili, if you remember it."

"Aye, that would be a good place to start it again," he said. "But..."

I interrupted him. "There's not a lot of point though, is there? Thinking about what might have been. We're here now. It's surely more about making the best of it from here on, do you not think?"

That was when the words seemed to dry up completely between us. He just stared at me, as I at him, and I swear his eyes seemed to get a bit misty, as if some dust from the street had blown into them. He stepped out from the car and moved a wee bit towards me, then stopped and stuck out his hand and, strange though it may seem, we shook hands. The only other time I remember doing that with Matthew was in Strabane Fair when he hired me for Four Pounds Ten Shillings. This felt more like the shaking hands of two equals, two equals who found it hard to let go.

Matthew sat into his car.

"Promise me you'll write and tell me when to come for you."

"I will, I promise, but give me a while to get settled in here. I need to get to know how to work with Frankie, you know? And spend a bit of time with mammy. But I will write, I promise."

He drove away, slowly, waving out the car window.

I turned and went back inside, to mammy, to Mairead and Frankie and to Matthew's fiddle.

A couple of hours later I found myself thinking. This is the first time in so many years that mammy and I have sat and had a serious session of music, playing well-remembered tunes together from what seemed like a different age. It felt so good, the fiddle and the whistle, talking and listening to each other. They both sounded like they had a smile about them, a smile born in our family history, a smile in the face of the challenges we both have faced.

The voice of the whistle had never deserted my mother in all the silent sufferings of her story. Her tunes never let her down. Her well of music never dried up, the way I allowed mine to do for so long after 1922. Shame on me, that for all that time I let myself to be robbed, robbed of whatever it is that our music does to us in the deepest part of who we are. But now, thanks be to God, it is truly back in me and I am back with her. I am home and the music of my childhood rises again in me. As we say in Irish,

'An áit a n-ólann an t-uan an bainne'.

We always return to the 'home' place in ourselves, to the place where the lamb drank its milk, to the mother who fed it.

Chapter 52

Matthew Henderson

Millie tells me that there must have been a rat in the feeding house. I hadn't noticed myself.

"Looks like rat dung to me," she says. "Either that or some very big mice. They've been at the meal, but they couldn't get into the flour, thank God. You'll have to see if you can find the hole they come in."

So I do. I shift the bins that are against the back wall, the open ones that hold hen meal, the crushed corn for my cattle and the small spuds that we feed to the pigs. Sure enough, some rodent or other had gnawed away at the timber and made a bit of a gap. In no time the buggers would have got fed up with animal feed and found a way of invading the covered flour bin that Millie uses to store her baking materials. On my farm, like any other, if it's not one thing it's another.

"What are yous doing?" I call to the three or four cats that are lying by the back door. "Shift your lazy carcasses and hunt down a few of these rats about the place. Millie feeds yous far too well. You're just fat, useless wasters. I am going stop your grub until I see yous carrying some dead rats to me."

Not one of them lifts their sleepy heads to even look at me. They'll have my toe to their backsides later.

I am working to replace the damaged timber, thinking I have spent half my life fixing damage.

Back in the past, it seems to me I had separate compartments in my mind for things. Like these bins. One for family, one for the workings of the farm itself, then a place for church and mission meetings, then of course a good-sized space for my various neighbours in the community. It was a way I had of organising things, balancing up priorities.

Things have definitely changed.

All of those categories that had seemed important have faded a bit in my mind. They are still there but they are changed somehow, brightened by the light of what might happen with Sally Anne.

I dream. I dream when I am asleep. I dream now when I am awake and working. The day passes quickly and at the end of it I hardly remember the jobs I have done, the people I have talked to.

I look forward to going to bed. Then I can't wait to get up. There is a change in the whole tempo of the day.

Millie arrives sooner than usual. I wonder what's the matter.

"What brings you so early?" I ask her.

She gives me a funny look. I take out my pocket watch.

"Lord above, it's not five o'clock? Where'd this day disappear to?"

Or I'll be talking to Mary over at Kearney's.

"Would you not think of maybe doing that?" she says.

"Doing what?" I ask her.

"Doing...have you heard a single word I said, Matthew? I'm starting to think you are beginning to go like your mother, doting before your time."

"Sorry, I was thinking about something else," I confess.

"Aye, you don't say. It's becoming a habit."

"Not at all," I say, "just got a few things on my mind, that's all."

"Will you know your way home," she mocks, "or should I get Josie to take you up by the hand?"

How nice that Josie is the name she gave her youngest girl. Josie is 'the wee late yin' and, even at three years of age, the child puts me in mind of her uncle.

I would love to tell Mary about Sally Anne but I don't, not yet. Just in case anything puts a spanner in the works. It will be a better surprise for her when Sally Anne arrives.

For arrive she will and soon. Her letter has me well worked up.

'Dear Matthew,' she wrote,

if it is still alright I would love to take up your invitation and come over for a couple of days, maybe around All Saints Day, if that suits you. I would have to bring Frankie too, if you don't mind. If I could see a way to do this by bus or something, I would try to do that but it does not look as if that is easy. Am I being very forward in asking you to come and get us, please? Then you would have to bring us back after, whenever suited you. If you are not too busy on a Saturday you could maybe come for us on 2nd November and then take us back on the next day, the Sunday, or whenever you want rid of us? Don't be making any special plans, like taking me about the place, or don't be getting Millie to bake or anything. She can have a couple of days off and I can do whatever is needed. I was well practiced, if you can remember that far back.

I am looking forward to seeing the old place, but you will understand if it takes me a while to get used to it, for the memories, both good and bad, are still strong in me.

Yours sincerely,
Sally Anne

I immediately sent a reply, agreeing with her dates and telling her I would be with her on that Saturday in the afternoon. I didn't bother to tell her that that is the night of the harvest ceili in Castlederg. Somehow I don't think either of us would be wanting to dig up the distant memories of that particular event. I haven't been back to it anymore than a couple of times since 1922. Now wouldn't be a great time to be starting again.

She doesn't want a fuss and I can understand that. She doesn't want Millie about the place when she is here, maybe she is even hinting that I shouldn't tell Millie at all. Well, Millie will be able to work it out and, knowing how much she liked Sally Anne, I won't try to hide anything from her. I will even ask her to help me do a bit of a clean-up inside, get the bedclothes washed and brush out the rooms. Millie won't mind that at all.

Her husband, John, might mind of course. He will have all sorts of objections to the idea of my Catholic maid returning to my house. It won't just be about her religion either.

I can just hear him, in my imagination.

"It won't look right to the neighbours, Matt, and it won't be right either. You and her in the same house and her staying overnight."

"What are you worried about? Sure aren't there lots of rooms in the house."

"There may be, but there's corridors too."

"Sure if I hear her footsteps I can always lock the door."

"It's not funny, Matt. You would need to come down that night and sleep in ours, just to stop the tongues wagging."

John's, of course, would be well out in front with the wagging, I am thinking. Well, after twenty-four years of waiting, I know what my attitude will be.

"Let them wag, John. Let them wag!"

Chapter 53

Sally Anne Sweeney

Matthew arrives early in Ranahuel, an hour before I am expecting him. He is keen.

Keen and nervous. He talks too much and too quickly to Mairead. She is struggling to understand his Tyrone accent and those strange words and expressions that he throws into the conversation. I feel her looking at me for a translation as I get Frankie cleaned up and ready for the road.

The fiddle lies snug it its case on the kitchen table so it won't get left behind in my excitement. It is going home to Lismore. I have put a few things in my case, a change of clothes but I also packed the one American dress that I have kept. It's the blue one, not the red one, for it ended up in a garbage can in the hotel. The green one, that I had worn once at that dance, I gave to Caroline.

It's only going to be the one night we will be gone. I have packed some nappy towels for Frankie. He is making a bit of progress with the toileting, but you have to keep at him and remember to set him on his pot and keep him there till he does his business. I wonder how he will take to this long car journey. I wonder how he will take to being in a strange new house.

I wonder how I will too. It won't be strange or new to me of course, for every corner I turn in that house will whisper its memories to me.

I kiss mammy goodbye and I feel her eyes follow me out the door. Who can guess what she makes of this strange-tongued man from far away who is capturing me and the child and driving us away in his wreck of a car?

I try to relax and make small talk on the journey. Matthew is suddenly a lot quieter than he was in the house, as if he has reached the end of the string of things he had memorised to say and has run out of ideas. We travel miles with not a word between us. It is so strange. There are dozens of things I want to tell him, even more to ask him, but somebody seems to have put an invisible partition down the middle of the car between us. I survive the silence by fussing over Frankie, gooing and blabbering nonsense to him to keep him entertained. Then, I think to break the silence, he says, "Your foot is well mended up by the look of it?"

'It is," I say. "Just gets that bit tired if I'm on it too long. Your crutches were a great help."

"So you think you'll be fit for doing the milking and reddin' up the night?"

I give him a quick sideways look. Straight-faced he is, but he can't stop the quiver at the side of his mouth, that tell-tale sign that he is trying to take the rise out of me. I just play along.

"I'll be fit for it surely," I say. "You can burn the dinner."

On this narrow road near Doochary we get stuck behind a donkey and cart. The old fellow on top of his load must be as deaf as a doorpost, either that or downright 'thran', as Matthew has just called him, for he doesn't even look over his shoulder at us. A mile further up the twisting hill he glances back at us, guides his donkey into a narrow path and waves us past with a gesture that looks like he is swatting away a wasp.

The child gets cranky and tired and I sing a few songs to him to try to soothe him. The songs are all in Irish and I hope they don't annoy Matthew. It's a good test though, for I remember our first journey to Lismore in the back of his cart, when Joe and I were chatting in Gaelic and he told me angrily to stick to the English. This time his reaction is different. He passes the test.

"What does that one mean?" he asks, as if he had understood the other ones.

"Agh, it's just an old lullaby," I tell him. "'Close your eyes, my love; sleeping is natural,' something like that anyway."

"Nice," he says.

"It is."

Then, after miles of quietness between us, we both speak at the same time.

"What are..."

"Do you think...."

Giggles, then, "You go first."

"No, you go first."

"Alright," he says. "I was going to ask, are you nervous about this?"

I smile and wait for an answer to land in my head.

"I am. Just what you would know."

More car noise to fill the space, until he tries to put my mind at ease. I have to listen hard, for this is a terrible car for rattling.

"Don't be. I mean, well....I am as nervous as you, maybe not as bad, but I understand. Mainly though, I am finding it hard to believe this is happening."

"You've had plenty of time to get used to it. It's your idea."

"I know, but that doesn't change the point. It is all so hard to take in, do you not think? You in my car, heading back to Lismore, after all I have been through over the years. Yourself as well, I mean."

"Yeah," I say, thinking how easily I drop back into how the Americans would say it. "It sure is a strange one."

"I know," he says. "I want to nip myself to see if it's real. Then I am scared to, in case it's not."

I look at him and smile. "You've turned into a great romantic since back then. You must have had plenty of practice. Or maybe a few good teachers."

I am fishing in the murky waters of the past and we both know it.

So he tells me about the girl called Alice. He tells me in great detail and I think to myself, 'But it was all so long ago. He must have rehearsed all this hurt so many nights on his pillow to be able to recall it all so clearly, God love him.'

"You were badly used by her," I say.

"I was, but there was a part of me that thought that I deserved it, know what I mean?"

"No, I don't. You didn't deserve to be left like that, near enough standing at the altar. And her not even having the courage to tell you herself. It must have hurt you so deep."

Those are the words that come out of my mouth but, while I do mean them, of course I do, there is a big part of me saying, 'Thanks be to God that she found another man and left him, otherwise…'

"What I am trying to say is, there was a sort of justice in it, after how I treated you."

"Matthew, I don't want to hear anything like that from you again. You don't have to be putting yourself through purgatory all the time. I have told you that what is behind us is behind us. So will you please try to forget about then."

He says nothing, stares ahead, his grip on the steering wheel tightens. My train of thought has still open track ahead of it.

"What I mean is, what happened then is all gone with the tide. This is now and we have both had our fair share of grief. It's not because we did something to deserve it, right? Just because life is like that. Just because we were a bit daft maybe. Nobody goes through this life like it's plain sailing. We are here now. I am here now. I am with you in this car. It is strange alright, but it is true. You are taking me to your house, but the reason can't be because you want to make it up to me for the past. It must be about now, about you now, and me now."

'Jesus, Mary and Joseph,' I thought, 'where did that homily come from?' I have said what needed to be said and I take a quick sideways glance at him to see what effect it has on him. He looks solemn, as if he is pondering all this.

It is another good while before he speaks again. Frankie stirs on my knee but stays asleep. Below us to our right as we drive, the railway track runs beside a beautiful stretch of water. Lough Finn lies as if asleep, cradled by those mighty hills behind it.

"You are right, Sally Anne," he says, "and I do not want all that happened back then to spoil today, or to spoil any time we are together. But at the same time, it did happen, we can't deny that. I just don't want anything like that to come between us again, that's maybe why I am dwelling on it too much, you know what I mean?"

"That I understand," I say.

****

We drive up the lane to his farm in Lismore. Beyond the farmhouse ahead of us I see the land sloping up steeply towards the Donegal hills. The hawthorn hedges along the lane, now bare of leaf, are far taller and more straggly than I remember them being. Through a gate on my right I catch a glimpse of the old fort. I have such mixed memories of it. It has stood there for centuries and no doubt will hold its ground for many more. I can't properly see the house ahead until we almost are at it. Somebody could do with taking a billhook to those bushes. The same with the wee garden I used to look after in front of the farmhouse.

Not much in Henderson's street has changed, as we swing into it. It's as if time has stood still, but I have a strange and instant reaction now, as my mind leaps back to my last time here.

I start forward in my seat, staring out at the surface of the yard. In my mind's eye I have a sudden flashback. Joe's lifeless body lies there on the gravel. I want to tell Matthew, "Don't drive over that bit there, that's where Joe died. Steer round it."

He stops the car, turns off the engine and sits in silence for a bit. Can he hear the battering of my heart against my ribcage? He must. I try to get control of myself and breathe deeply. I look around his yard. All the same buildings are here, but looking like they haven't seen a lick of paint since I saw them last. There is a blue tractor in the shed that would be new and one or two bits of machinery lie in a tangle beside the back wall. The collie dog yaps from the doorstep, its tail excited at Matthew's return. He gets out and comes around to open my door.

"I see you are finding this hard," he says quietly. "Here, let me lift Frankie off you."

Thoughtful, I think, as I set foot on the gravel and take my first step along this street of memories.

The kitchen is a bit different. A big, black, iron range stands where the hearth had been. It must give out some heat. Likely great for cooking on too. Against the wall opposite, the same old grandfather clock stands like a sober guardian of the kitchen. That must be its only role now, for I notice its hands are stuck at a quarter to nine. I suppose it is right twice in the day. I wonder when it gave up the ghost.

"Will I make us a cup of tea?" I ask. It's like an echo from twenty years ago. It is not that I want tea, it's that I need to be doing something, something ordinary to offset the extraordinariness of what is happening here.

"Aye, if you like. Millie will have left in stuff for us to cook, if you want to have a look."

"Will I start now?" The maid in me is slow to die, I think. "You have a great range now, I see."

"Not at all," he says. "Time enough."

We look at each other across the kitchen floor.

He's holding tight to the sleeping child, as if it is a sort of shield, something to hide behind. He has been so good with Frankie but right now I want to tell him to put the boy down. 'Hold me instead,' I want to say. 'I am feeling lost here, where I need to be feeling found.' I am hoping he can hear my heart but, if he does, the sound is being muffled by his own struggles. Then, when he speaks, there is a catch in his voice.

"Welcome back, Sally Anne."

I break.

I cannot help it, trembling at first, the lump rising in my throat, then the sobs start. The tears pour from me and the moan that comes from my throat is like the sound of a cow as she's calving. I cannot put words on this feeling and I cannot keep it down, I cannot control it. All the years of bitterness and resentment and regret and loss seem to erupt in me and no amount of embarrassment will stop the outpouring. I hold myself tightly, for the agony in me is fierce at this moment.

In a split second Matthew has set Frankie gently on the sofa and has me in his arms, his hand holding the back of my head close to his chest. My own arms, crossed over the pain beneath my breasts, release themselves without my permission and find their way around his waist. I have never been hugged like this before, never. Years ago our embraces were flirtatious, full of fun, playing on the edge of desire. This hug is nothing like that. His strength is enormous and I feel that I am being compressed into his body, that mine is no longer my own somehow, that we are joined. Joined in long suppressed relief and searing bliss.

God bless wee Frankie, for he never stirred through this, despite the noise I was making. It is an age before we release each other from the intensity of that embrace and it is a silent age. My mind is trying to put thoughts in order, but the English is letting me down badly. My own language has the most beautiful and natural word for what I am feeling at the end of this clasping of each other, this emotional washing. It is the word *'suaimhneas'* and, while it mainly means 'peace', it has an extra sense, that of 'security'. I feel safe now, safe and at peace with this man who once broke my heart. As Caroline would say, "It's unreal."

Matthew breaks the silence between us eventually.

"You need a cup of tea after that," he says. "I'll make it, if you want to take your things upstairs."

"Alright," I say, gathering the case. "Will I leave the fiddle here?"

"That'll do. Leave it for now. And let Frankie sleep there as long as he wants."

As I am going out the door into the hall way I stop.

"What room, Matthew?"

He looks at me for a second, a flicker of a smile playing in his eyes, before turning away.

"Whatever one you like," he tells me. "There's plenty to choose from. Just don't be going up to the attic."

I leave him to his teasing.

'No attic banishment for me from now on,' I think. 'No more the maid.'

Chapter 54

Matthew Henderson

We will have the whole evening to ourselves, once I finish the milking.

My cows have never been more interesting. I feel a great sense of affection for every one of them, as good a herd of Shorthorns as there is in Tyrone. Something about today makes them all the more special. I am still milking by hand of course, though I have heard that a few farmers in the east of the county have invested big money in new machines to speed up the process. I could be doing with the same machines this evening for, appreciate them as I do, these beasts are dragging the process out tonight. The faster I want them to move, the slower they seem to get. The quicker I want to get finished milking each one of them, the more they want to hang around and enjoy my company. They are all so slow to let down their milk tonight. Maybe they sense I'm in a hurry.

The last cow, and she is always the last cow, is a beast called Molly. Molly has a character all of her own. She can be great one night and as cantankerous as bedamned the next. I can tell from the start that she is in carnaptious form. She won't stand in the right place, she won't stand still, she shuffles herself away from where I have plonked the three-legged stool and bucket. She turns around and looks at me as if to say, "What is the big rush tonight, boss?"

Frustration sets in with me.

"Stand at peace, ya stupid...."

That only makes her worse. The chain around her neck starts jangling as she shakes her head about in protest.

"Look, Molly," I growl, "If you don't work with me here you can carry that elder o' milk with you to the morning."

With that she lashes out with the foot nearest me, connects with the metal bucket and sends the milk splashing everywhere, including all over my trousers. A gallon or so of it seeps away into the straw and flows down the groop with all the other muck.

"Enough!" I rise from her. "That'll do."

Fifteen minutes later I have finished for the day. It's nearly seven o'clock and I am pleased to have got everything redd up so soon. I give my hands a bit of a wash at the outside pump and head for the back door to take off my wellington boots before dinner. My trousers are soaked and filthy and my old torn jacket is tied at the waist with a bit of rope. I have looked better.

Pushing open the kitchen door I am greeted by a scene like something from a picture book. The table is set, properly set but not with the normal kitchen-ware that Millie would always be setting out for me. This looks like a set of delft that has been in a glass cabinet in our house for years and years. Red roses painted on a cream background. I have a feeling it was a set given to my parents for their wedding. I haven't seen it used since a Christmas when my mother was still in her prime. There are shiny glasses and a jug of water. Two cooking pots sit on the table, the steam rising from them. There is a lovely aroma of cooked bacon in the air.

On the floor a child is crawling around after a ball that has seen better days, one I likely played with myself, wherever it came from.

But it's not really the wain nor the table that my attention dwells on.

On the other side of it, there stands a woman in a gorgeous blue dress, a woman with her hair put up in a modern style and a face that looks as radiant and beautiful as any man could ever wish for.

Where has my teenage maid from long ago disappeared to? Where has the tired and bedraggled woman that I didn't recognise beside the Scottish boat gone to?

"Lord, Sally Anne," I say. "You've knocked the breath out of me altogether. Look, this is Tyrone. You're not allowed to step out of some American fashion paper into my kitchen without warning me, alright?"

She loves my surprise, I can see that. I watch her turn her head away, trying to hide a wee self-satisfied smile of pleasure. Doesn't stop her giving me my orders though.

"Would you hurry up and go and wash yourself. This dinner is getting cold. Go on with you," she says, avoiding me and laughing as I follow her around the table. "Get away; you're filthy."

I do as I am told. I run upstairs to the bathroom, give myself a good scrub. The cut-throat razor needs a good sharpening on my leather strop before I do a very close shave, close but careful. I don't want my face to look like it's been in a fight. Then to my room to get changed into something decent. The good suit it has to be. If she is going to try to look special tonight, I can only do my best with the clothes I have. Thankfully I have a clean white shirt and a dark blue tie to go with the suit. I usually only wear this outfit to a funeral, or when I go to church the odd time. My hair gets a dollop of Brylcreem to lift it back off my face and the black shoes get a quick shine with an old sock. I glance in the mirror on the landing. "Good Matt, you never looked better," I tell myself.

She thinks so too, by her smile as I arrive back in the kitchen. Dinner is great. Sally Anne could always cook. The bacon is fried with onions; boiled turnip and spuds in the two saucepans. Between bites though, both of us are up and down to keep Frankie under control for he is one curious youngster. It is noisy. There is laughter and instruction, crying and compliments, and I am still trying not to pinch myself.

Later we get Frankie up to bed in what was the twins' room, beside mine. He takes a bit of pacifying in this strange room and a different cot that I had put together, but we take it in turns and eventually Sally Anne's stories put him over into dreamland.

"Would you like a drink?" I ask her when she comes back down.

"What have you got?" she says, coming to me and snuggling against me as I stand in front of the range.

"I think the only thing in the house is a bottle of whiskey. I wouldn't be a big drinker. It's not something I would usually have but someone gave me this for a favour I did them. Do you like whiskey?"

"I can rise to it," she says. "Put a drop of hot water in it and a bit of sugar. I remember my father used to give us *poitín* that way if we had a cold or something; it tasted great like that."

"Are you sure? You don't have to drink. I just felt like I wanted to celebrate, that's all."

"I'll drink to that," she says.

So we sip hot whiskey and sit together on the couch, telling each other the stories of our lives.

She has mentioned her father. It strikes me that, while she likely knows a fair bit about my father from her time here before, I know very little about her's. So I ask about him. It is lovely to sit with my arm around her shoulder, the whiskey hitting us and raising the honesty and intimacy between us as she tells stories about the late Sean Ban Sweeney. Fifteen minutes later, I feel that I have known and admired this man all my days. I also have a growing pride that now, even as she snuggles more tightly to me, it is me myself who is replacing him as the most important man in her life.

Later Sally Anne is trying to smooth out a wrinkle on my suit, running her hand over my thigh in a nice innocent fashion. Out of the blue she brings up something that I had forgotten all about.

"Do you remember that night that Joe died?" she says. "You took a while to come out to the yard with Anthony and whenever you did you had put on your good suit. I always wondered about that. Was it out of respect for him or something? I just couldn't think why you did that. Do you remember?"

"Aye, I do remember. I remember right well. And didn't you ask me about it when you wrote that first letter last year?"

"I think I did, yes. I was always curious about it. So...?"

"So...what?"

"So why did you?" she asks again. "Maybe you had no reason."

"I had a reason alright, but it was nothing to do with Joe or the fact that I had just shot him."

"What then?"

"You won't believe this when I tell you," I say.

"Try me."

"Right." I get a bit flustered. "That night I had been sitting thinking what an idiot I had been to let Victoria and her Englishman turn me against you. I honestly was sick of them, sick of myself too. I started to think how much you had meant to me since you arrived here. That and the fact that it was coming near the time for you to go back home. I was getting desperate to hold on to you, to get back to where we had been before. It may seem totally daft to you now, but I had made up my mind to put things right with you that night. I was going to ask you to forgive me."

"And you put on a suit to do that? Did you think I would have been more impressed because you were dressed up? That must be the Protestant in you."

She is smiling at me, not mocking me but close to it.

"There was more to it than that," I tell her.

"Go on then, what?"

"I was going to ask you...look I didn't want you disappearing out of my life for ever and I had come to think how much you meant to me, so, I was going to ask you to stay."

"To stay?"

"Aye, to stay and to marry me."

There, it is said. The rabbit is out of the bushes. Her mouth is wide open as she jerks forward from me and turns to stare in amazement.

"You were going to propose to me that night, when I came back from Joe's?"

"I was. It was just a terrible bit of bad luck that I shot Joe instead. My whole life hinged on that moment of madness. I might have been married to you all these years, instead of trying to live down the grief of having killed my friend."

She is still staring at me, the expression on her face is one I would give a fortune to be able to capture.

"Married to me all these years?" she repeats. Then, with a cheeky toss of her head, "What makes you think I would have said yes?"

"You likely wouldn't have, would you?"

"Likely not. I was still mad at you, remember."

I want to ask the next question, the obvious one.

'How about now?' I begin, but she jumps in on me.

"Matthew, before we talk any more there is something I want to tell you about."

"Alright, fire away."

My question will keep.

"When you hear this you might want to change your opinion of me, so I need to warn you about that first."

She seems very concerned about this, serious in a way she hasn't been since I picked her up yesterday morning.

"Nothing you could tell me..."

"Stop and listen," she says. "Remember when I wrote to you back after Easter time, just after you had sent me the fiddle?"

"Aye, and that reminds me. You need to play me that tune tonight, remember?"

"I will, but stop interrupting me. In that letter I told you that the fiddle had meant a great deal to me because I had been through a very tough time recently."

"Aye. I read that. I wondered what was wrong."

Sally Anne's head goes down and the light that has been shining from her all evening seems to go behind a cloud.

"What's the matter?" I say, taking her hand and pulling her back beside me.

She tells me about a man she met, an American. She doesn't spare me the details. As the tale goes on she gets more and more upset and I am dabbing her tears with the handkerchief I had stuck in my pocket upstairs. She tells me of a trip on a lake on some sort of house-boat, about a lot of drinking and then about...I find myself heating up inside at what I am hearing. She was seduced by some rich, bastard, American...and then he turned out to be married and humiliated her in front of her cousin and all the women she was working with. It is a shocking story to have to listen to and I am so sorry for her.

She goes on to tell me how much my fiddle meant to her, in healing all that pain that she was going through. Also about her friend Caroline, a black girl, and how she helped get Sally Anne straightened out. I will never meet this Caroline but I want to thank her, for she was an angel in the right place at the right time.

"I'm glad you had that Caroline," I say. "Seems like a good person."

"She was. But me? You must think I am nothing but a dirty tramp."

She cowers away from me to the furthest corner of the couch.

"I don't think that at all," I say, not strongly enough.

"You do. I can tell it in your eyes."

"Nonsense. I think of you exactly the same as before. It doesn't change anything for me."

"But that can't be true," she says. "I am second-hand now, soiled goods, you know what I mean? I can't be your…"

"You can't be…don't talk nonsense, Sally Anne. You are even more precious to me now that you have told me this."

"No!" She shakes her head. "How could you think that?"

"Well, you trusted me, for a start. You wanted me to know. You weren't hiding anything. But also, what it does to me is sort of…," I am trying to think how to put this. "It reinforces what I want to be for you."

"How do you mean?"

"I mean…look, you don't need me to tell you this. Everything inside me just wants to be with you, to be looking after you, all the time, not just for the odd weekend. No more Bobs. Nobody else, ever. Alright?"

I reach for her hand. She takes mine and slowly comes back to me.

"This whiskey must be going to my head," she says, "for I am starting to hear things I have wanted to hear all my life."

"Do you think I deserve that tune now?" I ask some time later.

She takes the fiddle from the case and tunes the strings.

"I take it you'll be wanting Eleanor?"

"I'd rather have you, to be honest, but go ahead, play Eleanor."

So she does and the years roll away. I close my eyes and I see oul Tam sitting by the fire, my mother in the armchair, the twins as wee girls and above all Joe Kearney with his eyes near popping out of his head. We're all gathered in this kitchen to marvel at the fiddle tunes of my maid from Donegal. Now it's just her and me.

"The fiddle has come home," she says.

An hour and a few more tunes later we go upstairs. I wanted to carry her but the stairs are too narrow. We stop on the landing, beside my bedroom door. She leans against me, head down. I am suggesting nothing here, it must be her wish.

"I remember one night up in the attic," I tell her. "For some reason I had to sleep up there in the box-room. You were just on one side of the door, a couple of feet away from me and I was so tempted to go in to you."

"I remember it too," she says. "I heard your breathing. I stood behind the door. Maybe at the start I was scared you were going to come in to me. Then after a while I was annoyed that you didn't."

"Imagine if I had. We could have ended up having to get married."

"I know," she says. "We could have had a whole string of children by this stage, maybe even grandchildren."

I laugh at the thought and she joins in.

"Talking of children, do you want to check on Frankie?"

"I do; come with me," she says.

She takes me by the hand. It feels so...so family, I suppose, to be led into that bedroom and stand together looking down at a sleeping child. Sally Anne's case stands beside the wardrobe. She goes and picks it up, turns slowly and gives me a shy wee smile that says, 'Lead on, I am coming too," and she follows me to my bedroom.

Chapter 55

Sally Anne Sweeney

Last night we got our own back on the wasted years.

Frankie's timing was perfect. The two times he cried he woke both of us up.

Matthew carried him to our bed and I went downstairs for a bottle of milk to soothe him. He lay between us till he slipped back to sleep. I took him back to his makeshift cot, so my man and I could make the most of being awake at that time of the night. I love his strength and his gentle energy and I love him with a love I have never believed a person could be capable of. It is an emotion, yes, a feeling as deep as the sea. But it is far more. It is a knowing that I belong, a soul-deep understanding of the rightness of me being with this man.

'*Is suaimhneas agus beannacht é*', a peace and a blessing, like God has finally smiled on me.

During my years of solitude in Ranahuel I imagined myself cursed, destined to be without love. It was maybe a self-imposed sentence, but nobody did anything to free me of it. I lived like a nun on that hillside. Then, in America I fell for the bewitching flattery of that man. What I thought was release from the curse turned out to be an even worse calamity.

I am awake early this morning. Maybe it is the maid in me, rousing myself for work. Maybe the motherly instinct with Frankie next door.

"Matthew," I whisper, though I think he may still be asleep. "You have mended me. The same beautiful man who destroyed me has fixed me."

He wakens.

"What did you say?"

"Nothing," I say and nuzzle into his back.

He raises his head to take in the light, the angle of the dawning morning through the half-opened curtains.

"What time is it?"

"Time for more," I say. "The cows will have to wait now."

"You'll bring me to ruin, lass," he smiles, pulling me over on top of him. "The farm will be away to hell and the neighbours will know right well what is happening here. I can't get out of bed for my hungry, wee, Donegal Catholic."

"Ha ha," I laugh. "And what if your hungry wee Donegal Catholic has a baby for you?"

"Oh Lord!" he says. "I never thought of that. Too late now though."

Later we do talk about that very subject. He is back in from the morning work and we are at breakfast, Frankie on Matthew's knee, slobbering porridge all over him.

"This idea of a baby," he says.

"It's not an idea…I mean, it's not a plan," I say. "But it could happen. I was just saying what if it did?"

"If it did I would love it," he tells me. "But could it happen? You being in your forties?"

"You think I'm past it, do you?"

"After last night I know you are not past it," he laughs.

"What would you do if I got pregnant?"

"Same as always. Do the milking first, then maybe…"

"You know what I mean. What would you do?"

He thinks for a minute.

"Sally Anne, whether you get pregnant or not you and I are not going to be apart any more, right? So…"

"What are you asking me, then?"

"What am I asking you? Well, I think we will need to look into getting married, won't we? I don't know if it is possible or what. With the religion thing. What do you think?"

"I think that is the dullest proposal of marriage I could ever have wished for," I tell him.

"Sorry. Aye, I suppose that is what it was."

"If we could ever get married you have to realise you would be marrying Frankie too. Would that be alright?"

"It would. Another wee Prod about the place sure…"

I see the twinkle in his eyes, thanks be to God. I don't rise to the bait.

"So after you take me home this evening? What happens then?"

"I come back here."

"And I might never see you again?" I am baiting him now.

"Not until you want to come and live with me."

"Married or not?"

"Married or not!"

"But, Matthew, you know it is a terrible thing for a Catholic to be living in sin, especially with a Protestant. Would you ask me to do that?"

"I wouldn't want to put you in a bad position with your church, no I wouldn't, but would it be any worse than staying in my bed last night? Will you have to confess that?"

He has me there. I don't think he realises how big a problem this is for me, my love for him and my need to be with him, against the hold of my faith. I need to turn it back on him. He must have issues with his church and his community as well.

"I will have to think about what I confess," I tell him. "You are lucky you don't have to worry about that. You just have to worry about your family and what they will say. Then there is your friend, Mister Sproule. Once he hears about me being here and staying with you he will be mad. You'll have to listen to him."

"He knows already. Don't you worry, I can handle John," he says, but I sense a shadow of doubt in him about that.

"Can I tell you one thing that worries me?"

"On you go."

"Right, I am back home with mammy and Mairead and you are here on your own again. John Sproule and your relations and your minister hammer away at you. 'You can't have any more to do with that wee fenian. You must honour your dead parents, your ancestors. Imagine a Catholic sleeping in your bed. You're nothing but an adulterer. Give her up, Matt! We are going to put a stop to you going back anywhere near her.'"

"I can handle them," he says.

"How? How will you answer them? They'll put a fierce amount of pressure on you. 'You can't be bringing up that wee orphan in your house. You can't let her rear him as a Catholic. Your da would turn in his grave.' I can hear them Matthew. I can just see that cousin of yours, the Belfast one, Victoria."

"What about her?"

"She will be on the warpath again. She treated me like dirt back then."

"You have nothing to fear from Victoria. I haven't heard from her in years."

"Well, if not her, then dozens like her. All those people. They'll wear you down."

"Sally Anne," he says. "Listen to me, just listen now and believe me. I have been through years of despair, years of the community talking about me. You were likely the first thing they talked about. 'Him and his Donegal maid!' Then I was the fellow that shot his best friend. People shunned me after that. Then there was the mockery I had to take over Alice; the man who got stood up at the altar by the bank manager's daughter. 'Who did he think he was?' After that I got into trouble with the law smuggling. Name in the papers. A criminal, a traitor to the Unionist cause. I was fined for that. Next I did a while in gaol in Derry for smuggling a bull that broke into my field. I was the laughing stock of the country. So I am well acquainted with being an outsider among my own people."

"I'm sorry." It's all I can think to say.

"I can understand why you might fear that I would bend to pressure from people like John, especially after me listening to those sort back in 1922. But believe me, girl. I have never in all my life felt so much happiness and love as you gave me last night. I would walk a bed of nails every morning to make it our everyday way of life, for both our sakes. So nobody is going to talk me out of it, not this time. I give you my word on that."

"And I believe you," I tell him and we hold each others hands across the table as if our lives depended on it.

We are still sitting like that when the door opens and Millie and John Sproule walk into the kitchen.

Chapter 56

Matthew Henderson

I have just left Sally Anne at her home in Ranahuel. I have that long drive ahead of me. I won't be able to sneak back over the Border tonight for I am going to be well after the time I am meant to be back. But I won't be bate. I have a torch and a pair of boots in the back, so I will park the car at the top of that lane that leads up to Gortnagappel bog and walk over the mountain to home. I know it like the back of my hand by now. That way I won't have any trouble with late-night 'B' Special patrols or Customs men. I can always get the car home tomorrow.

It was bitter sweet to be leaving her. On the one hand, I have this great feeling of comfort that she and I are together, together in understanding and love and purpose for our future. On the other, it is going to be a very long eight weeks until I see her again.

We have left it that she and Frankie will have November and December with her mother and Mairead, then I will come for the two of them and she will live with me and be my wife in all but name. She wants me to come back and have Christmas with her folks in their cottage, sort of as a farewell to her family and her home and to mark her and me leaving there to be together.

During this time apart we are both to try to work out how we can get married, for we both want to do things right by the church and by our families and neighbourhoods. So, she will see her priest and I will talk to my clergyman. On top of that, I am to see about using a registry office, wherever I can find one, to get us all the certificates and have everything above board.

This Sabbath day has been one of the strangest I can remember. All the joys of the night before…well, they will never be forgotten, of course, but a sick wain and a session with John did put a bit of a dampener on it, that's for sure.

Earlier Millie had been so delighted to see Sally Anne. There were big hugs and both of them cried. It was lovely to see their warmth, but it was such a contrast to the sour, angry face still standing at the door. They weren't right finished their greetings when poor Frankie decided to spew up his breakfast. Maybe Lismore porridge was too heavy for him but up it came. I was holding him on my knee at the time so I got the worst of it. Standing there with my two arms stretched out to try to avoid the deluge, his boke running down my shirt and him screaming, I looked at the stern face of my neighbour and realised he was thinking, 'A judgement of God on you Henderson!'

As soon as Sally Anne and Millie got Frankie cleaned up, they took him out to see the animals. Then John launched into me.

First of all, it was the verses from the Bible about adultery and fornication. What could I do but listen?

It was on the tip of my tongue to say, "So you've come to cast the first stone, have you, John?"

There would be no point though. He would still have cast it anyway. I would just have to try and roll with his punches and see if I came out safe on the other side.

I tried to think about something different as he ranted on. After a bit I realised he had moved on from the moral side of things to describing me as a traitor to my faith, to my family, to my neighbours. This got me. He meant my Protestant neighbours, of course.

"My neighbours?" I said. "And who is my neighbour? I seem to remember somebody in the Bible asking that same question?"

That stopped him in his tracks for a second.

"Aye," he said. "It was the people asking Jesus, in the parable of the good Samaritan. Why?"

He would be well versed in it, so he would.

"Because, if my memory serves me right, the person who was a good neighbour to the man who had been robbed wasn't even the same religion as him. One a Jew, the other a Samaritan."

'Put that in your holy-roller pipe and smoke it!' I thought.

"So?" he protested. "What has that to do with you and this... this woman?"

"It has this to do with it," I told him. "Her faith, or religion, or whatever you want to call it, has nothing to do with you. It won't keep us apart, just as it didn't keep the good Samaritan from helping somebody who wasn't his religion."

"The two things are completely different, Matt, and you know it."

"I don't see how. It's the principle of the thing. You may have hatred in your heart against..."

"The things are not the same. The Samaritan and the Jew weren't in bed with each other."

A fair point.

I had no answer to it. That didn't stop me arguing though.

"Look, John, you and I have been friends for years and we have helped each other out manys a time. You have your views and I have mine. They don't have to be the same. I respect your right to be the way you are. I am not trying to change you. What gives you the right to disrespect me and try to interfere in my private life?"

"God does. You were once a child of His, before you turned away and set yourself on this path to destruction. It is my duty to..."

"Right, now you have fulfilled your duty. So leave it at that."

"Will you let her go then?"

"No, John, I won't and if you want to know my plans you can hear them. I will bring Sally Anne back here to live with me. As soon as we can work out how, we will get married, alright, so you'll be grand; we won't be living in sin."

"She is still a papist. You can't marry one of them."

"Who says?"

"Your Bible says, that's who. Your whole community says. You can't go against what has been our Protestant way for hundreds of years. You don't marry out! Your neighbours won't stand for it."

"My neighbours again? What business is it of their's?"

John took a step up close to me, straining up on his tip-toes to look me in the eye.

"If you go on with this you will not be long of finding out whose business it is."

"What is that supposed to mean?"

"Look, Matthew. You have a farm to run. Who do you think is going to buy your calves off you? Same with that house of pigs out there. What about your milk, if the creamery stops sending the lorry up to you?"

"Is this some sort of boycott you're imagining?" I asked him. "An Orange threat to bring down my farm?"

"Doesn't matter what colour it is. You turn against them? Why should they not turn against you?"

"Agh, what nonsense you are talking, John? Look, your bigotry offends me and always has. Just because the woman I love is a Catholic. Why don't you go home and read that Bible you claim to follow and see what gives you the right to condemn people like Sally Anne just because they have been born into another church."

"Another church? It's not a church. It's the anti-Christ."

"Agh John, sure don't they pray to the same God as us? The same Jesus?"

Our argument stopped at that point as the women came back into the house. John rose from the table and stormed out past Sally Anne, nearly knocking her and Frankie against the door as he left. She gave me a look, as much as to say, 'What did I tell you?'

He sat in his car for a while, but the smell of the dinner had him back in at the table with us in no time and him eating like he hadn't seen food for a week.

"Powerful spuds them," he said, through a mouthful.

After eating Sally Anne and I took Frankie for a walk down the back lane to the march ditch and over to Kearney's. Frankie was loving it, high in my arms and looking over the stone walls and hedges at all my animals. 'E-i-e-i-o' I sang again. Crossing the ford I was glad to see Mary and Liam's car in the yard ahead of us.

It was a lovely thing to watch, that meeting of Sally Anne with Joe's folks. Mary wouldn't have had much memory of her, but Anthony and Monica are still as clear as a bell and greeted her like a long-lost daughter. Straight away their chat went into Irish. I didn't understand a word of it, except for the bits that Sally Anne wanted me to understand and gave me a quick translation.

They had a good recounting of stories from back in those early days, happy stories mostly, by the sound of it and the laughter. Then the tone changed and I sensed that they had moved on to the subject of Joe. The conversation faded to a hush. Not much was said, but, in the quietness, a great deal was meant.

I watched the glances between Monica and Anthony during this silence. It felt strange to be completely on the outside of the conversation that developed next between them. Monica seemed to have something she wanted to say to Sally Anne who sat quiet, giving me occasional looks which had just a tiny hint of pain in them. Anthony joined in at times, his tone as always more gentle. I noticed Mary's eyes go to this dialogue as well and I wondered what was being said. After a bit Mary rose abruptly and went to make tea for us.

I wanted to know what Mary thought about Sally Anne's return, so I followed her.

"Don't think I've ever seen you so happy looking," she began. "It's a great story."

"It is. A bit hard to take in."

"And she is going back home today? That wasn't a long stay."

"Aye, but she's not that long back from America and she has her mother and all."

"She's going to find it hard to settle at home after all this, isn't she?"

I knew she was teasing me so I told her the truth.

"I'm going to be bringing her back," I said. "Come Christmas."

"That's a great plan," she said.

"What was it your mother was saying to Sally Anne there?"

Mary didn't answer straight away, wouldn't meet my eye. I waited.

"Mammy likes Sally Anne, So does daddy, even more....and you know they think the world of you."

"So?"

"Well, they are just worried that... well, like Sally Anne stayed at yours last night. People talk."

"Agh, not them as well?"

"Sally Anne told them you have asked her to come back at Christmas. When the penny dropped with mammy what you were asking her to do, well, you see it is such a sin in our church to be living in sin like that. She was just worried for Sally Anne. For both of yous. It's not right. It won't go down well around here."

"She knows that, Mary. I know it. We will be trying to have a wedding."

"Aye but...it's near enough impossible, isn't it? And there will be all sorts of questions."

"Are you against it too?"

"I'm not against it. Sure I lived with yer man back in the day, but how is she going to get round the priest?"

"Don't know, " I said. "She'll talk to him anyway."

"And you, yourself? Have you any idea how hard this is going to be? You could lose some of those friends of yours."

"They wouldn't be great friends then, would they?"

"And how are you going to get round your folk, your sisters and all?"

"Don't know yet, but where there's a will there's a way."

"Where there's a will there's always trouble as well," she said.

It's only now as I drive over these dark Donegal hills that it strikes me what Mary meant by that comment. If Sally Anne and I marry and, whether we have children or not, this changes how I pass on the farm. It changes what I will probably write in my final Will and Testament. I think that is what Mary was saying. It is a long time ahead of me. Mid-forties is far too young to be thinking about wills. I have likely got enough legal problems to be working through long before then.

Legal problems and family problems and problems with the people of my community, her community and friends as well, by the looks of it. This is only the first day on this new path I have decided to walk and already I have had lectures from both sides of its fences.

On the drive to Ranahuel we talked about her chat with Monica. I could tell it had affected her deeply. I hoped to God it hadn't put her off our plan.

"They don't hold with the idea," she said.

"Of you and me?"

"No, not that. They are all pleased about that. Just that we would live together. I am going to have to face people in the neighbourhood. What will folk say and all that. Especially what will the parish priest say. He could make things very difficult for me, receiving Mass and all."

"How did you answer them?"

"Just said that we want to be together and we want to get married as soon as we can."

"Did that pacify them? I wouldn't want to hurt their feelings. You sure it's not because of the religion thing?"

"Well, it is the religion thing, but not because you are Protestant, more to do with stepping outside church rules, living in sin. It is such a terrible expression that, isn't it?"

I couldn't agree more, but it is the churches that are forcing our hands, forcing us to break their rules. That is the way I see it anyhow.

In times past, I would have worried about these challenges, turning the pros and cons over in my head until I am sick of the whole business. I have no doubt at all that earlier in my life I would have fallen at the first fence. I would be thinking of a way out of the situation, some sort of compromise, a way of keeping in with my neighbours but holding on to Sally Anne at the same time.

But last night happened. And, if ever a man needed anything to put a bit of steel into his backbone, what happened between her and me last night has given me enough back-bone to see this thing through, whatever it takes.

Christmas can't come soon enough.

Chapter 57

Sally Anne Sweeney

Mairead is finding it very hard to understand me. As someone whose marriage went on the rocks very early, she is afraid for me. It is understandable.

In my case, though, I will have no fear of Matthew taking to drink. Nor do I have any worry about him gambling. He has had twenty years to be looking at other women and I believe him when he says that, apart from that Alice, he hasn't bothered with any one of them, so I do not fear him being unfaithful. He loves his farm and he loves to work, so I have no fear of going hungry. Before this past weekend, I did have a deep concern that, despite his generous attention to me, he could be easily swayed back to the thinking of his own people. That fear had a hole blown in it by how he handled the argument with John Sproule. I witnessed how much John had gone back into his box by the time he and Millie left us on Sunday. He looked the picture of resentment, a great contrast to the quiet joy in Matthew. I was so proud of how he put his arm around me as those two visitors were leaving. The gesture said, 'See this woman? She and I are together, like it or lump it and there's nothing you can do to separate us.'

I must go and talk to Father Devine. I have left it a week, just to get my head straight on what I need to say to him, what to ask and what to answer to his arguments. My guess is that, in all his time as a priest in our parish, this will be the first occasion that he has had to deal with anyone asking about marrying someone who is not a Catholic. We do have a few Church of Ireland families living in the Rosses, but as far as I know they tend to marry their own kind. They get on well enough with the rest of the neighbourhood, they trade with us, fish with us and we help each other with anything that needs help. They come to our wakes and we go to theirs. There are no problems. But they keep themselves to themselves as far as things to do with religion are concerned. And that applies to love and romance as well.

My old bike clatters down the hill. I push against the breeze along the twisting lane to the village. I am pedalling slowly towards the Parochial House. I happen to look through the window of our little shop and there he is, laughing loudly with Bríd Mhicí Jinny. Bríd could entertain a nation with her yarns and today she has got the ear of Father Devine. I am not going to plough in there and demand that he come and talk serious with me about a mixed or any other brand of marriage, so there is nothing for it but to wait outside for him.

Twenty minutes later he drags himself out of the place and stops to light his pipe, shoulders hunched against the November weather and head down into his top coat. I watch from the shelter of the pub's gable opposite, hoping he goes straight home so I can follow him.

Not a chance. He turns in my direction and I have to sneak behind the pub. He is making straight for its door. This is not a good omen for the conversation we need to have. I do not want to be talking to him after this, with his quick wits and his temper on edge. It would not go well for me, I am sure. This will have to wait until another time. I get on my bike again and wobble my way around to the front of the pub.

My good Lord but isn't he waiting for me by the door.

"Sally Anne Sweeney! I thought that was you hiding round there," he says. "What's wrong with you anyway that you would be hiding away from your priest?"

That is me on the back foot right away, but I have to go through with this now.

"I was waiting to speak to you, Father, but then I saw you heading to the pub and I didn't want to get in your way, so I went round..."

"You didn't want to get in my way, did you not? Do you think I am some sort of alcoholic that would tramp over you to get a drink? This is the one day in the week when I come here. Sure come on in with me and I'll get you a wee half as well. You look as if you need a drink. Come on now. Set that thing down and follow me in."

What choice do I have? I follow in behind him. He goes to the bar and is greeted by two local fellas who look like they have been carved on to those barstools, so at home do they seem to be. I slink past their backs, trying to draw as little attention to myself as possible and take a seat with my back to the bar-room, so that at least I will be speaking to the corner of the place. This is to be a mistake but I don't know that yet. He will be speaking over my shoulder to anyone who wants to listen.

Father Devine plonks a glass on the table in front of me.

"Whiskey, I am guessing?" he says. "You wouldn't be a beer sort of woman, would you?"

"I am not a whiskey sort of woman either," I tell him, "but I'll drink it with you if you listen to me."

"Listen to you, is it? This is a funny place to be doing confessions, now isn't it? I haven't seen you for a week or two, have I? I haven't seen you since you came back from...", his tone takes on an edge, "back from your weekend in Tyrone, eh?"

How does he know about that? Did he prise it out of our Mairead? No, surely not. Mairead is no great friend of his and she would have told me if he had.

Ah, the letters. I remember. Bríd Mhici Jinny has had the kettle going and has had a nosey after the steam did its job. The system is working for his reverence.

I think I have hidden the shock of this revelation fairly well. I just stare at the table between his drink and mine. If I start in to ask him about marriage, here in this bar, I know that he is going to throw a fit. The whole parish is going to hear about it. They won't be needing any insider information from Bríd Mhici Jinny this time. The very seagulls will know of it. So I decide to play dumb, say nothing and hope he will drop the thing. I can talk to him later in the privacy of the Parochical House when I get the chance. That is my plan.

It is doomed from the start.

Father Devine goes off on a whole homily about women who flaunt their disregard for his authority, who think they know better how to run their lives, who deliberately place themselves in the way of temptation and debauchery despite his best endeavours to keep them pure. I realise I am his one-person congregation. His voice rises. I take a quick glance around. Connie, behind the bar, is all ears, peeking out through the beer mugs, his face twisted by the bevelled glass.

"You must, must....you hear me, must have nothing more to do with that man, Sally Anne."

"Bí ciúin, a Athair, le do thoil," I say, begging him to quieten down.

"Ah, now you want me to be quiet about it, do you? Do you have any idea how humiliating it feels for me as your priest, to hear that you have deliberately disobeyed me? You have challenged my authority and gone ahead on your own path of evil. I will not be quietened by you. I will expose sin wherever it rears its ugly head, whether I am in the pulpit of the house of God or in this public house, for God is everywhere. He is not restricted to His church. And He saw, yes lady, He saw what you were up to last weekend."

"I never heard you were hearing confessions here, Father," I say quietly. "I don't think it is very fair of you to be going over this, in front of these men."

"You don't think so, do you not," his voice getting louder again.

I want to run out of here. I want to have nothing more to do with this man. He hasn't an ounce of the grace that the last priest I talked to had for me, the one in Cape May. I know I have done some wrong things of late, but I have also fallen in love and something inside me says, 'Love is stronger than this. Love is worth having this fight about.' I take courage from that thought. I will not be brow-beaten by a man, a priest even, who thinks it is alright to attack me in such a public way, a man who won't show me the respect that I am owed as his parishioner.

"I will chastise you in front of whoever I like," he is saying. "Now, you need to appear in a confession box on Friday night and you need to make a full confession of your sins, you hear me? And you need to be ready for penance. You need to swear to me that you will have nothing more to do with that... that heretic."

'That heretic'?

Is this the time?

I think it is the time. I take a deep breath.

"That heretic is going to be my husband, Father."

He stares at me and through me, as if maybe looking into the pit of hell and me dancing on the rim of the cliff just above it. The stare lasts for long enough and the bar-room is hushed behind me, waiting for him to erupt.

"Your husband? Your husband is it? That will be over my dead body, you stupid woman..."

I don't know anything else that he spews out of his mouth at me for I am on my feet, knocking back my chair so roughly that it falls over with a rattle. I am wound up tight by his attitude and maybe the whiskey gives me false courage. I speak strongly to him.

"I wanted to talk to you to ask for your advice, Father, for your help. I wanted to do it in a private place where it was just between you and me. You have used this chance to humiliate me in front of my neighbours and I think that should be beneath you, a man in your position. I won't listen to any more of it. If you want to chastise me, which is your right, you will not do it in public like this. You will have to come to my home and talk to me there."

I turn on my heel and leave him spluttering there at the table. The two drinkers are looking at me as if I had grown horns, horns or wings maybe. Connie behind the bar catches my eye and winks at me with a curl of a smile around his mouth as he pulls another pint.

I find my bicycle and ride back up the hill to Ranahuel as fast as I ever have done, the wind at my back now.

****

It only takes two days for Father Devine to take up my invitation. He drives into our street and Mairead immediately starts fussing about the place, tidying and driving a couple of hens from our doorstep. She then grabs Frankie and takes refuge in the safety of the bedroom, leaving mammy and me to face the music.

This time the priest goes straight to the point, turning down my offer of a cup of tea and standing beside the chair I have pulled out for him, rather than sitting down. He likely thinks he looks more imposing if he is towering above me.

"You stirred my temper yesterday, Sally Anne. I could barely believe my ears with the stuff you were coming off with. You have obviously no shame at all in you. Not an ounce of shame."

I say nothing, just poke the embers in the hearth and throw in a couple more peats. I won't meet his eye, not until he apologises, and I have a feeling that this is as close as it is going to get to an apology.

"That is what made me so mad. The fact that you seem so confident of your own course. You have set your will against the church, against the family that reared you, against your own people here in this parish. You have decided that you know better than God in these matters."

"Better than God? I don't know how you figure that out, Father."

"'Figure that out?' 'Figure', is it? Listen to yourself woman. Are you trying to sound like some American movie star? You were only gone the guts of a year and listen to yourself. That's where you get your new, modern values from. America! You are ruined. Ruined in your chastity and ruined in your devotion to God and the church that you were raised in. That is where this is all coming from."

"You didn't answer my question though."

"What question is that? You have a right cheek on you questioning your priest."

"I don't mean to be questioning Father. I asked you how you figure out that I know better than God. I would never want that to be so."

"But that is exactly what you are doing. The church has clear teaching about relationships between our people and those outside of our church. It has clear principles about inter-faith marriage. You have decided that these teachings don't apply to you."

"Well, would you believe that it was exactly this that I was going to ask you about two days ago when I went to see you. I just didn't....I didn't get around to it."

"Right then. What did you want to know?"

"I wanted to know...look, Father, Matthew Henderson and I, we were in love over twenty years ago, when I worked over there on his farm. Back then, he treated me with respect. I know there are a lot of bad stories about what happened girls over in the Lagan and Tyrone in those days, but he didn't take advantage of me. I was well treated."

"Well treated is one thing. This is another. But what did you want to know from me?"

"I want to know...you see, all this time later and after my time in America, we both know that we are meant to be together. We want to do it right, be a married couple. So how do we do it?"

The priest stares at his boots and shakes his head, long and slow, before he replies.

"I had a premonition about this. When I met that man last summer in Kincasslagh and brought him up here. I could see where this was leading."

"Could you, Father?"

"I could, I really could. And this is the North you are talking about. Bad enough if you were to be marrying a local fellow, one of those Stewarts from the Point or whoever. But a Protestant over there is a special breed of person, Sally Anne. I know this, for I did a short period as a curate in a parish in Antrim. They are a race of people unto themselves, believe me. How they are going to take to you moving into the house and hearth of one of their own is anybody's guess. How long before this man of yours...."

"Stop, Father. I have no fears about my man. We have both made our mistakes in the past and we have learned from them. And as far as his people are concerned, all I ask is that they judge me for who I am as a person, not the label I bring with me."

"Label? It is not a label, it is who you are. You are a baptised Catholic, a Catholic in your very blood and bones, you're not some sort of blank page that you can decide what to write on. Catholic is who you are and who you will always be, you hear me now?"

"Father, I have no intention of being anything else. Catholic is what I will always be, as you say, but surely that does not mean that I have to be denied marriage to the man I love?"

"Alright, you want to know how you can be married? You can only be married to a Protestant if the wedding takes place in the Catholic church that you belong to, with me as your priest officiating and with two people to witness it. Your man would have to agree to that. He would also have to sign an agreement that any children of the marriage be brought up in the faith of our church. And you, Sally Anne, you would have to agree to try your best to bring him into our faith. Convert him. Those are the conditions"

"That is very harsh," I tell him.

"You may think it is harsh but it is the law of the church that has been there this past forty years. It's called 'Ne Tempere.'"

"He might agree to be married in our church, but if we ever had a son I can't see him agreeing to rear him Catholic."

"Fine, I can understand. But then I cannot marry you and neither can anyone else." The priest sits down to underline his victory.

I wonder should I bother to continue this argument. He has the weight of centuries of religion behind him. I will never shift him. I might be able to bypass him though.

"I have heard that people can get married in a registry office Father. Is that right? A civil marriage?"

"You may have heard that but it is not a marriage, Sally Anne. It is a sham. The church cannot recognise it as a proper Christian marriage, for no sacrament was involved."

"That is very disappointing, isn't it, Father. That two Christians who pray to the same God can't be married unless one of them gives up his identity, his way of believing. He has to give up the right to rear his own children the way he sees fit. Is that how it is?"

"That is exactly how it is."

"And if he and I go ahead and get married in a registry office in the north and I come back here for a weekend, you will refuse to give me Mass on a Sunday morning? You don't see anything a bit unfair about all that?"

"Nothing unfair about it. You would be making your own misguided choice and I can see that you are starting to realise what a terrible mistake it would be. An absolute disaster. To turn your back on the church that nurtured you..."

I won't hear any more of this. I want to shock him.

"So maybe I will just get married in Matthew's church in Castlederg."

He looks at me in shock.

"You would never do such a thing! Never! You would have to turn, convert. I cannot see you doing that. Betraying the people who reared you. You would never think of..."

He is interrupted by Mairead bringing an unsettled child into the middle of us. Frankie is squirming in her arms and she is not making much of a fist of holding on to him.

"Sorry," she says. "I can do no more with him, Sally Anne. I tried to pacify him but he's the divil himself when he gets it into his head."

I take the boy from her for a minute.

"Here, Frankie," I say, going to the press for a cup, "what is the matter with you at all? Do you want a wee drink, do you?"

Father Devine, if he is annoyed by the interruption, gets over it quickly and comes behind me, some sort of a sweet in his outstretched hand.

"Would you like one of these, Frankie?"

Frankie absolutely would like one of these and has it grabbed out of the clergyman's hand before he has a chance to change his mind. Thankfully it is a soft candy kind of bar. He won't choke on it, but what on earth is the priest doing with such a thing in his pocket?

"What do you say to Father Devine? Come on, say 'Thank you Father,'" I encourage him. To no avail.

"We haven't made much headway with manners yet," I tell the priest as he sits down. "We haven't made much headway with any sort of words to be honest. The boy has had such a bad start to his life it is little wonder he is away behind."

"I understand that. He has plenty of time sure. What is he now? He can't be two yet?"

"He's coming up to it, January."

"And what are your ideas for him, in the midst of all your....your plans?"

It is a fair enough question.

"He will come with me to Tyrone," I say.

"Will he now? But no matter where he is, you'll be rearing him in his Catholic faith, right?"

"Likely we will, yes," I tell him, giving a much happier Frankie back to Mairead and nodding to her to take him back to the bedroom. She does, with a resigned shrug of her shoulders. There is a silence now between us as I weigh up how to put my next line of argument. The priest interrupts me though.

"Need to be going soon here...," he begins, but I must have my say. I know that I must take this debate out to the bitter end.

"Father, I have listened to your rules. I have heard your arguments. I might be more inclined to follow them if I did not have two things burning right here in my heart."

My voice has a quiver in it, a shake of emotion, a sense of dread at what I am about to confront him with. But I won't stop now.

"What two things?" he asks. There is tension in his voice too. It has soured a bit from the more soothing tone he had as he saw me floundering under the cart-load of his arguments.

"The two things are these. I love a good man. A Christian man. He loves me. We have waited for over twenty years, both him and me, to know this and to realise that we have wasted half our lives apart from each other. He and I have lain together as man and wife, I admit to that. And, to make that right, we want to be married, so we can continue as man and wife. But we won't be bullied by the church into doing it in a way that would make one of us inferior to the other. We are equal and will marry as equals."

"This is outrageous," he blasts at me.

My mother sits forward with a jerk that is so out-of-character for her. She looks at him with as much fear as you would ever see in her eyes.

Father Devine pauses to blow his nose into his handkerchief before continuing. "What gives you the right to reject my authority, to flaunt your sinfulness in the face of your church?"

"Well, I'll tell you, Father, and it is the second thing that is burning inside me. You might not want to hear it but…"

I turn from the hearth and meet his eye.

"Many years ago, when my father lay dying in that bedroom, he talked to me about certain things that had happened here in the past. He told me a story about my mother, a story that she could never tell, of course."

I look at mammy and she glances at me from the settle bed where she is resting. There is nothing I can read there that says either, 'Go on and tell it, daughter,' or 'Don't be bringing up those terrible things of the past.'

"Daddy told me why mammy had such a fascination with that island out at the Point, *Oileán na Marbh*. Every Sunday when I was small we used to go out there and play in the sand, paddle in the water. But mammy had her own wee routine. She would leave us on the strand and climb up on top of the island and just sit there and look out to the sea. Whiles she would play a slow air on her whistle and we would hear it from down below and we would think, 'There she goes again, that sentimental old tune that she seems to associate with this place.' If we asked my father about it he would always have some way of explaining it that satisfied us.

But when he was readying himself for death that time he explained to me the background. I don't know if you know anything about it Father, for it was before your time and it had more to do with the Annagry parish and the priest there at the time."

"I know nothing about this," he says.

"Well, what happened was this. Years before, my mammy had been with child. Daddy and her had been friendly, all their lives they were friendly, so everybody blamed him. The priest did his best to persuade daddy to marry her. Daddy refused because he hadn't been with her, not in that way. He ran away to Scotland, for the whole place had turned against him. Nobody knew the real father and of course mammy couldn't tell what had happened. Whenever the baby was born it didn't survive. It died at birth. So my granny, Maggie Dan, went to her priest, to see about getting the baby buried. The priest turned her away. He wouldn't even come up to the house to see my mother. She was a fallen woman... and her couldn't say a word. The baby was a bastard and, worse than that, it was an unbaptised bastard. So do you know what his answer was? He told my old granny, "You can just bury it yourself!"

Bury it yourself? My granny was livid with him. She was so hurt and distraught. Mammy was just after giving birth. She had no idea what was going on, or that her baby would never feed from her. Granny was looking after her. Where would they bury the wee corpse? Who would do it? The church stood solemnly in the village and protected itself from scandal. And the village followed the church's lead. It did nothing. When my mammy needed help, the church's answer was, "Bury it yourself."

So Frank Sweeney, my grandfather, an old man, came and took the baby early in the morning and walked to Carrickfinn, to Oileán na Marbh. And he buried my baby brother there between the rocks, with not so much as a pebble to mark where that baby lay. It was as if he had never been born. He had no name put on him. He was a nothing, a puff of wind. But my brother was a human being Father. He had the right to a Christian burial, didn't he Father, as a child of God, a human being like the rest of us, except that he died before he could get a breath into his wee lungs? He had a right, didn't he, Father?"

The priest thinks about this. He can see my point and I can see that he does. But he can't bring himself to open his mouth to agree with me. Not a word. His silence speaks louder than anything he could tell me anyway. I won't let it rest until he sees clearly the connection.

"And, you see, Father, I am that baby's younger sister, and I have lived, and I have rights as well. I have the right to marry. I have the right to marry whoever I want. I have the right, with my husband, to rear any children we might have in whatever way we want."

"You do not have..."

I will not hear any more hypocrisy from him. My voice rises.

"And no church that refused to give my brother a Christian burial has the right to deny me a Christian wedding, does it?"

"You can have a Christian wedding," he says, "but only on the terms laid down by your church."

"Thank you, Father," I tell him, "but your terms are every bit as Christian as the reasons why my brother was denied a Christian burial. They are a nonsense. You can see my point of view on that, can't you?"

Father Devine, to his credit, argues no more.

I persist though. I want to know if there is any spark of human sympathy in this man for my situation.

"What would you do if you were in my shoes Father?"

He stands up slowly, making a drama out of it for my benefit, and takes a few steps towards the door.

"Many years ago, Sally Anne, I had a choice to make. I could follow after a girl I liked and let life take me on the course of the normal man. Or I could listen to the call of God on me to follow Him and enter the priesthood. It was not an easy choice, but I choose the life of the church. This choice you have to make is not an easy one either. You ask me what I would do in your shoes? Same as I did in my own shoes. Follow God's call on your life."

"And if God's call on my life is to be with the man I love?"

"It can't be though. God would never ask you to go against the teachings of your church, would he?"

I let this seep into me for a second. He remains standing, hand on the half-door, waiting for a yielding. In me there is a realisation that this is an argument I will never win. I am banging my head against cast-iron bars. These dogmas have been forged over many centuries; they come echoing along the marble walls of the Vatican Palace, from the first furnace of the faith. But I desperately want to touch some humanity in this man. I need some spark of understanding, of sympathy.

"Father, can I ask you a question, a personal one?" I say, deliberately taking a more humble tone.

"You can try," he says.

"You mentioned a girl you liked. Have you ever had any doubts about your choice?"

It's a far more courageous question than I could ever have imagined asking my priest. He takes a very deep breath and puffs it out through pursed lips. I can read in him a battle between continuing in his priestly role or opening himself up to me, even a little bit. I gentle the question a degree further.

"You never ever had a single regret about it?"

For once I see a smile half-forming on his face. It doesn't last long though, as the clerical instinct gets his lips back under control. But it had been there. His eyes flick up to the Saint Brigid's Cross hanging above the door.

I try again.

"Have you ever thought about her over the years?"

His eyes come back to mine.

"Now, now, Sally Anne," he says. "Remember who I am. And remember why I am here."

"I know, I know. I am sorry, Father. I just wondered. I suppose I am desperately longing for somebody to understand me, you know? This is a very lonely place I am in at the minute."

"I can understand that, of course," he says.

"And I know that what you say makes sense, about me and Matthew and all, but it is not just about the rules of the church is it? I mean, surely sometimes the rules of the church must make you wonder about things, do they not? Like what happened when mammy's baby had to be hidden away from everybody and buried secretly, with no blessing from the church on it? Surely you must have some sympathy for that, Father?"

"Sally Anne," he says, opening the door, "if you are asking me as a man for my gut feeling about that, then of course I have sympathy, of course I have. Any man would. But it is not fair to judge the priest at the time. He was only following the practice of the church. He had no choice."

"Yes, I understand that, but I still think he had a choice."

"No, No. He could not do..."

"He had a choice as a man, Father. Not as a priest, I get that. But he had a choice to show some sympathy, or human decency, you know what I mean?"

"Yes, of course and I am sure he did that. But his hands were tied by canon law, the rules of the church."

"And you, Father? Do you not think it strange that the laws of the church are at odds with human compassion? How can that be, that what your church orders you to do stands against what you would want to do as a basic human instinct, let alone a Christian duty, to show compassion and understanding and mercy? It must be a dilemma for you, Father, is it not?"

To be in this moment of confrontation, at this deep level of intensity and honesty is something I never imagined and yet to feel the sense of calm strength that I have, it is all very unusual to this ordinary maid. How on earth have I elevated myself to this level of debate with a professional clergyman who has debated these things since his youth?

"It is a dilemma, I will agree with you there. Do not think I am unaware of your point." Another long exhaling of breath, then, "Look, Sally Anne. No matter what I feel in this matter….and as you have probably realised I do have a degree of sympathy for you, otherwise I cannot believe that I have listened so long to your audacity in probing me in this manner, but at the end of the day I am a servant of the church. I must, no matter how awkward I feel or how debatable the merits of the case, I must hold to the teachings of the faith. That is my role and my duty. I cannot vary from it, not even for individual circumstances like yours."

"I understand that Father. But I just wanted you to know that when I marry Matthew Henderson I am not doing it to spite you or the church. I am doing it to honour the love I feel for him and to honour my own faith in God. After all, it was Him that brought us back together again."

"We will say no more now. I will pray for you, that you will see the error of your ways and turn back in repentance to your church."

"Will you not take a cup of tea?"

"Thank you, but no, I should be going."

He is about to leave without putting the usual blessing on us. I can't have him forgetting his duty as a priest, no matter how distracted he is.

"Will you not say a blessing, Father?"

He turns, an apologetic incline of his head acknowledging his absent-mindedness.

"Go mbeannaí Dia sibh. Slán agaibh."

What a feeling I had in me as he drove away quietly. Relief, amazement at my courage, bewilderment as to what this cutting away of my past has done for me.

What would my father have made of that conversation? Would he think I was very bold, very fool-hardy? Or would he put his hand on my head and say, *"Maith thú, a iníon!"*

This is a night I will toss and turn and find no answers. Nor will I find the strong arms of my big, Protestant farmer to hold me and make everything alright. Not in this bed. But it is coming.

Chapter 58

Matthew Henderson

For the first time ever, I haven't been able to rely on Millie to help out with the milking. John has put his foot down.

"I am sorry, Mattue," she told me. "it's because he knows you are going to Sally Anne in Donegal. He won't hear tell of me helping with the cows so you can go on being a...I don't know the big word he had for you.... 'rip-er-bate' or something. I would do it but he would be mad at me and I be scared of him then."

"Don't you worry about it," I told her.

"But don't be telling Sally Anne," she said. "I like Sally Anne."

"And how will you feel if she comes here to live with me?"

"Would she, do you think?"

"I am bringing her back with me on Boxing Day," I told her.

"What, to stay here? But you don't be needing a maid again. Sure I can help you?"

"No, Millie," I told her. "Not to be a maid. To be my girl."

"Your girl? But she's a woman now?"

"Alright then, to be my woman."

I watched her mind turning this over, puzzled.

"And are you for marrying her?"

"I hope so, if we can work out a way of doing that."

"Oh aye, I know," she said, "for she's a papish, John said. He would have no time for them wans. But I always liked Sally Anne."

"I know you do. Me too," I told her.

"What will you do about the milking then? Will you just come back early?"

"I'll see, maybe I will have to. I will have a word with Mary Kearney, see if she can do it, or Liam. They'll likely be over next door for Christmas."

"They be very good to you, the Kearneys," she said. "And Sally Anne, they always liked Sally Anne, didn't they? Joe especially."

"Aye, Joe especially," I have to agree.

"Joe would be glad if you bring her back here and marry her. I never thought that would be happening," she said. "Joe would have married her too, I think. But you can marry her now for Joe is..."

"Just houl your horses there," I told her. "It hasn't happened yet, maybe won't happen for a good while. There's things to work out."

"Aye, like who she gives that wee boy to."

I smiled to myself. Trust our Millie to think of that. What a pity she never has had any wains of her own.

"She is going to bring wee Frankie too," I told her. "He is going to live here as well."

She took that in slowly. Then, "Oh boy," she said. "You are going to have a wee family ready-made, the three of yous. Maybe Sally Anne will have a few more and it will be just like when I was wee and there was mammy and daddy and Emily and you and Jane and me. That would bate everything, wouldn't it Mattue?"

"Indeed it would, Millie."

****

It isn't the grandest Christmas dinner I have ever had, I will admit that, but for me it is one of the happiest. It feels sort of like a wedding dinner. I am about to take my bride-to-be home with me. It's just the timing of things is a bit through-other.

In spite of the weary light finding its way to the table, in spite of the steugh of peat-smoke choking the room, in spite of the humble surroundings of this simple cottage, every bite of duck that I put in my mouth is a celebration. I have to tell myself to stop grinning.

I am the only one who is feeling like that, though. For the Sweeneys it seems more like a 'last supper'. The meal is quiet, solemn. There are few words from Sally Anne or Mairead and of course the mother doesn't speak. Only Frankie is his usual chirpy self. I sense a hush between the sisters. Maybe it is understandable. Mairead is about to lose a sister. The house is going to go back to being the quiet place it had been before Sally Anne's return.

I try to keep some chat going.

"Where'd you buy the duck?" I ask.

Mairead and Sally Anne look at each other, unsure of which should answer the question. Mairead's head goes back down to the eating, leaving the answer to Sally Anne.

"Seamus got it for us," she says. "Do you remember my friend Ailish? She worked in Tyrone that time as well? No? Well, she lives not that far away. Her man is Seamus, Seamus Gallagher. He works away in Scotland but when he comes home he takes his gun and goes up into the hills to shoot rabbits and whatever he can shoot."

"Great," I say. "So he shot a few ducks and gave yous one?"

"He did."

"That was more than decent of him."

"It was." Then after a few seconds she continues, "Is it alright for you?"

"'Course it is," I say, "It's very good. So are these spuds."

That ends the chat for a while. I try again.

"Do you remember telling me that the smell of your Donegal turf was different to what we had in Tyrone?"

"I don't remember that," she says. "Why? Do you think now I was right?"

"I do. It definitely has a sweeter scent than ours."

"Sorry it's so smokey," she says, waving her hand as if to stir some air into the space above the table. "It's just the way the wind is today. And it's too cold to be opening the door to let it out."

"I know," I say, "I'm not complaining. It's the same with our fire at home."

More silence.

At the end of the meal I try to help with washing up but I am shooed away. I am only getting in the road anyhow. I go outside to find a place to relieve myself. It is windy, fierce windy, and it seems to have risen since I had arrived about noon. I turn my back to it and watch the sky as the watery light is closing down on us, the sun sinking below the mountain behind. When I arrive back at the door Mairead is standing outside waiting for me.

I don't find her face friendly, not like her sister's. Maybe it is just the way she is all the time, a bit soured with the world.

"I wanted to say to you that Sally Anne is a bit nervous about all this," she says to me.

I nod. I have sensed the same, of course I have.

"It is just such a big step," she says.

"It is, I know that. It is for us both."

"Yes, but she is leaving her home and her mammy. You are in your own place."

"I know. Don't worry about her, Mairead. She will be..."

"I know you will look after her, Mr Henderson, but..."

"Matthew," I tell her. "You need to call me Matthew."

"*Maitiu*," she says, using the Irish way of saying it that I have heard from Sally Anne away back. "But what I was going to say is, she would need to be married to you. It's not right, in our church anyway, likely in yours too. If it was around here, people would turn against her very quick. The priest would be on at her all the time. She needs to get married. Would you not agree to coming here for a wedding with our priest, would you?"

"I will do anything that Sally Anne asks of me, Mairead. She hasn't asked me to do that, for she knows I wouldn't ask her to make the kind of promises that your priest wants from me."

"What's to be the end of it then?"

"If I knew that I would tell you. What I can tell you is that I will do all in my power to take good care of her and to make her happy and, if that means getting married in a byre, then I will do it."

"Alright," she says, turning back to the door. "I hope you don't mind me..."

"I don't mind, in fact I am glad that you want the best for your sister, like I do," I tell her. "And thank you for allowing me to have Christmas dinner with you."

"That's alright," she says. "It is a nice present you brought. We needed a new lamp for the old one is leaking oil."

"That's good then," I say.

I sleep that night on the settle bed in the kitchen. I feel really bad about it, for there are only the two small bedrooms at the end of the house and I must be sleeping where one of the women would usually be. They must be very squeezed in those wee rooms, the three of them plus Frankie's cot. But Sally Anne insisted that that was what was to happen.

I am sitting on this wooden bed which is covered with a thin mattress, likely stuffed with straw or hay, I would guess. The pillow is decent though, soft as any feather-pillow would be. I have stripped off my shoes and my outer clothes and I am just staring through the foggy gloom of the kitchen. The bedroom door opens again and I can just about make out Sally Anne's figure, a pale night-gown floating towards me like a ghost.

She stands close in to me and takes my head in her hands, pulling it in tight to her stomach.

"I thought you were a banshee there," I whisper.

"No," she laughs, "more like the ghost of all your Christmases to come. Are you going to be all right out here on this hard bed?"

"You could always stay and soften it for me."

"Not tonight. I need to sleep in the bed I was born in, for one last time. You understand that, don't you?"

"I do, and sleep well. I can wait one more night," I tell her and we kiss, quickly and hungrily, before she shimmies silently back to her bedroom.

'That has to be the shortest honeymoon in history,' I think. I don't mind though, for the rest of my life stretches out in front of me, open and bright, like the view you have from the top of Bessy Bell mountain. I find it near impossible to get over to sleep. Partly it is due to the hardness of the bed, the lumpy mattress. Mainly, though, it is my imaginings of the future with Sally Anne.

What Mairead has said to me weighs heavy on me. Aye, for sure I do want to sort out some plan to be married. I go over in my mind the brief conversation I had with the minister of my home church about the matter. He was nice enough but, to be honest, he wasn't offering me any encouragement about a wedding. He had no solutions. He wouldn't hear tell of my suggestion that he could take part in some sort of ceremony with the local priest.

"It doesn't work that way Matthew," he told me. "If he is going to be involved in it, you will have to agree to his conditions and it will have to be in the chapel."

The stupid thing about it is that, for all I know Sally Anne and me may never have any wains, so the notion of raring them as Catholics won't come into it. We will have Frankie, of course, but, as his mother in Scotland was Catholic, I have no problem with him being brought up Catholic if we get around to adopting him.

What is so annoying about the whole thing is that it is all these people on the outside of Sally Anne and me who are making such a big issue of the thing. It doesn't matter two hoots to me, maybe a bit more to her but not enough to stop her coming home with me. She knows she will be able to keep going to Mass and I will take her to it, as I used to do when she worked at Lismore and I will go the odd time to the Methodists. It is our personal business so why is it everybody else's too?

These thoughts are not helping me sleep. I try to think of the farm, of Liam Coyle milking my Shorthorns in the morning. I smile as I remember the time the black bull nearly put an end to our friendship. I still have to explain that whole story to Sally Anne, that and a whole lot more. So much to be telling her about the missing years. And so much living and loving to enjoy, making up for lost time. And thinking of that, I seem to fall into a dreamy state of half-sleep.

Chapter 59

Lismore
Castlederg
Co Tyrone
N Ireland
16th January 1947

Dear Caroline,
    I am so sorry that I have not written to you in a long time. Please forgive me. It has been very busy with a lot of exciting things happening that have changed the path of my life.
I think that in my last letter I told you how, when I arrived back in Ireland, I had so much help from my old friend, Matthew, the very one I told you about who had broken my heart in the past. I will not take time to tell you all the details but he and I have come back together. It is a great feeling, to be in love with him again and not be separated. It feels to me as if years ago a tune that was being played by the two of us, a song that went completely off key and faded into nothing but a painful noise, yet now it is ringing out again in the most beautiful harmony. I know you love your music. I remember the joy of those songs in your church. I remember feeling a stirring in my heart and tears in my eyes at the passion and the strength of those tunes. This is how it feels again with my man. We are in harmony after years of silence. And the music feels like that happiness I felt in your church in Cape May, that is the only way I can describe it and I know you will 'dig' what I mean.

(See, I haven't forgotten all those different words you taught me.)

I also have a child. Don't worry though, I did not give birth to this boy. He is the son of my late cousin, you remember the sad story of her death. Her boy, Frankie, is now with Matthew and me, and we are living back in his house where I was a maid in my youth. How strange is that? We intend to adopt Frankie but there are some obstacles. We are not married yet and we need to be before we can adopt the child. The churches here are very strict and neither Matthew's nor mine want to help us get married. It is so sad and makes us both very angry. I wish we could escape Ireland and go to Cape May, for I am sure that lovely minister in your church would have great craic marrying us. I don't think it can happen though.

We could have something called a civil marriage but that likely would not be enough for the people around here. They need to see us on our knees to them at the front of their church, begging forgiveness for living in sin and then taking our vows in a sacred building.

I live on a farm, with lots of cows, pigs, sheep, hens and any other farm animal you want to name. It can be hard work and not at all like anything you have ever worked at, I am sure. But I love it, for I am out in the fresh air with my man and the child, getting weather beaten and rough skinned. It can be a bit lonely though, for there is only the one family nearby who are happy enough to be talking to us. Some others shun us, even Matthew's own relatives. I hope that in time we can win them round, but I can't really do that unless I get a chance to talk to them, but they are not for talking. I know you understand all this because of what you went through with your white boyfriend. You wonder how some people can be so twisted and hateful, don't you, especially those who claim to be so devout in their religion.

You must write and tell me about things in Cape May, especially the hotel. What is happening there now? Is Roisin still working you hard? I must write to let her know that I will not be going back to work there at Easter. Also tell me how your parents are getting on. They are lovely people.

I send you much love, dear Caroline. Please write soon. I am lonely.

Your friend,
Sally Anne Sweeney

Chapter 60

Matthew Henderson

The business of the farm must go on, in spite of our feelings of being left on our own up here, ignored by neighbours and old friends.

I haven't spoken any more than ten words to John Sproule since Sally Anne arrived. Even then it was mainly me talking, him with a dour stare on him, paying me little heed, crabbit as be-damned .

Millie has been up a few times to see Sally Anne. On one visit she cried and said that John had forbidden her from going to the Kearneys, to help them the way she has been doing for years.

"He said that, now one of their own kind is living here, she can do it."

I was shocked by this and my first instinct was to drive over to him and give him a piece of my mind. Millie is his wife but she is my sister first. Sally Anne stopped me though.

"Let the pot simmer," she said. "There'll be a time to tell him to catch himself on. I don't mind helping Anthony and Monica. Anyway, Mary seems to be coming around the place a lot more of late."

"Aye, I noticed that too," Millie said. "Maybe her and Liam will come back there to live. Take over the farm, for Anthony is not fit to do a hand's turn now."

Millie could be right too. I would be delighted to have them there all the time, from the point of view of morrowing during busy times on the farm. And there's no doubt that the older folks need full-time attention now.

Our Jane and her man drove over from Drumquin one Sabbath afternoon, their wee Austin 8 packed full of wains. She and Sally Anne had a grand time of remembering and laughing. There was not a hint of a problem between them. I just wished that the twins could have been together for the occasion, but Millie was likely away at some meeting with John.

Tommy, Jane's husband, has always been a very canny, peaceable sort of man. As we say around here, 'he doesn't rise much stour.' He sat in the corner chair with a couple of the wains on his knee and said very little. He didn't seem to have any grudges against either me or Sally Anne and that was nice. We had a bit of a chat about the price of cattle and the like, not a lot of conversation, but it was a pleasant enough afternoon right up until he was in the car and about to drive out of the street. He wound down his window and put his head out as if to speak to me. I moved forward to hear him, for as I say he is such a quiet-spoken man.

"Do the right thing by her, Matt," he whispered and was gone before I could assure him that I had every intention to. Afterwards I was kicking myself that I didn't ask him if he would be a witness whenever we get it all arranged, for I can't see John rising to it.

I didn't tell Sally Anne for I didn't want to put a dampener on her day, but it grated with me that I needed to be hearing such advice from somebody like Tommy.

A few days after that, I took Sally Anne and Frankie for a drive to Omagh. The idea was to visit the Register's Office there to ask about procedures. The two folk we saw in that place were solemn types, but more than helpful.

"This is not something new to us; we do mixed marriages more often than people imagine," the gentleman told us, "so don't be nervous about it, because we won't be."

That was nice to hear. Sally Anne was worried all the same.

"But if we do it here," she asked, "will we be as married as we would be in church?"

"Every bit as married, as far as the State is concerned. No difference at all there. In law, I mean," he said.

"But does the church agree with it," she asked, 'that we are properly married?"

"You'll have to ask your church that one. I can't answer for anyone but the State. But if you are worried about your friends and neighbours, well you can just bring out your official marriage certificate and show them. We find that satisfies most people."

It was good of him to try to put her mind at ease but I did realise that, coming from her background, she will want the church to have something to do with it all as well and that is fine.

Anyhow, we set a date in May for the wedding, Friday the 9th. So many weeks of notice had to be given, application forms had to be filled out, we have to bring birth certificates and make sure we have witnesses organised for the event.

I tried to put Sally Anne's mind at ease on the drive home. We stopped in Newtownstewart for fish and chips, just to make the day a bit more special.

"This is just the first step," I told her as we sat eating beside the river. "Once we have the marriage certificate, we can approach my minister and the priest in the town and ask them to have a service for us, in their church. They won't have any grounds to say no, for we aren't asking them to marry us."

Sounded simple enough to me.

"I would like it to be in Kincasslagh. The Kearneys are the only folk who know me in this parish," she said, "nobody else."

"Aye, that is alright by me," I told her. "We'll just have to ask your priest. You'll just have to ask him, I mean, for he doesn't like me."

"Nor me," she laughed. "I lectured him too much. He likely thinks I am a mad woman."

"Aye, well I suppose even he can be right sometimes," I told her.

****

Three of my year-old bullocks need selling to make room for this year's crop of Spring calves. I load them into my cattle trailer, a small one I had made myself for towing behind my tractor and drive down the hill to the Friday market in Castlederg. This is the first time I have been in the market since Sally Anne and me took up living together. It is to be an experience I won't forget in a hurry.

When my beasts appear in the ring and the auctioneer mentions my name and asks for a bid there is a murmur of antagonism around the shed. The atmosphere in the place seems to go stagnant all of a sudden. I sense dozens of eyes coming at me, some dull and unsmiling, others flaming with anger. Snarling lips on a few faces, curses from behind hands, shaking heads. It reminds me of one occasion in this market a long time ago, after I had been in prison. The same sort of smell dirties the place and it has nothing to do with cow dung or calf skitter or pipe smoke.

"Come on now, gentlemen. Three fine Shorthorns here, as good bullocks as you will see in this ring today. Who is going to open the bidding now?"

Not a soul, by the looks of it.

I follow the auctioneer's eyes as he looks for big Norman McKinney. Surely my animals will get a bid from him? The sons, Sammy and Jimmy, stand beside him, their twin sneers pinning me like darts. Then the three of them do something I had never seen in this place before. They turn their back on the ring, slowly and deliberately, obviously trying to make a real scene out of it. They had clearly planned this and they are not alone either. A number of others who might be buyers or sellers, I don't know, turn away from us as well and start talking loudly among themselves. Almost everybody ignores the auctioneer. I do see a few men who don't join them. These would be men that I know would kick with the other foot and maybe a few farmers from other areas that wouldn't know me at all. They have no notion what is going on; it's not their quarrel. They just stand and stare around at the others. Nobody puts on a bid, not one. The young auctioneer has no idea either what is happening and tries his best to get a sale moving, until his old father steps up behind him and takes charge. He is longer in the tooth and can read what the under-current is here.

"Shift Henderson's cattle on there," he calls to the cattle drovers. "Let's get some other bease into the ring."

I can do nothing but shake my head and leave the ring. I hear one angry voice calling after me, "Ye may just try an' sell them tae yer friends in Donegal," followed by a few cheers.

As I am going round the back to find my animals John Sproule follows me. I hear him cough behind me and turn.

He just stands and glares at me, silent as a tomb.

"What did you think of that, John?"

He takes a long time to reply, staring me out sort of.

"Nobody wants your bullocks, that's what I think," he says.

"But my good Lord, why not?"

"You shouldn't need to ask that question...and don't be taking the Lord's name in vain."

"Is this to do with Sally Anne?"

"Maybe, but I'd say it's more to do with you."

He clears his head of mucus with a snort like an oul sow and spits on the ground, then turns away.

"John," I shout after him, "I have to sell my cattle somewhere. People know that. What am I meant to do?"

"You shoulda thought of that," he says over his shoulder.

"So, if I can't sell cattle in this market, I'll just have to take them to Strabane market next week?"

"Aye well, you could try that."

He disappears into the shed again.

I don't think I have ever been so mad. The Fordson crawls back up to Lismore with those three bullocks in the trailer behind it, the black reek of burning diesel belching up into the naked trees. What sort of community turns on one of their own like this, refusing to do business? I feel like I have been punched in the guts. And, if I am suffering this sort of pain, how is it going to affect Sally Anne? At least I know what I am up against here. She only has a vague sense of it, mainly from her time over here in the past. That time was in the middle of the independence war, as Britain was trying to hold on to the six northern counties and Ireland was fighting to break away. Twenty-five years ago and how much has changed? Very little. The old antagonism runs very deep, but I never expected that what I have done in bringing Sally Anne to live with me would have this sort of outcome on my business. Maybe I have been naive, maybe I should have seen it coming but today has opened my eyes. My own second cousin turning his back on me in public, and him the dealer who usually buys my stock? Unbelievable. What on earth am I going to tell Sally Anne? Maybe I'll just say something like, 'It was a very slow market today and I wasn't getting a good enough price, so I just brought the bullocks back. I'll try Strabane next Tuesday."

It's all I can think to do.

As I near the top of the last rise before home, I see a bicycle flying down the far brae towards me. It seems near enough out of control, the man on board with his legs stuck out like some young gulpin, his coat and scarf streaming out behind him.

"Who under God is that?" I think to myself. "Is he going to hit me or miss me?"

The rider gets the bike under control just where the brae levels out and slows as he nears my chugging machine which has just about made it up the steepest part of the hill. Suddenly I see the flash of a white collar at his neck. Lord above, if it isn't Reverend Moore, my own clergyman. He stops and waits for me, very wise, for he can see that if I stop on this slope I will never get moving again.

"You'll soon need a new tractor, Matthew," he calls as I pull up beside him.

"You're not far wrong there," I say, "for I have the guts pulled out of this one on that hill."

He hears the cattle roaring in the trailer.

"So you bought a few animals?"

'I did not, your reverence," I say and I go on to tell him my sorry story of the events at the market. "You wouldn't believe something like that could happen in this countryside, would you? I have farmed and traded with these folk all my life, they are my friends and now that I have Sally Anne they turn against me."

"Well, that's the point, Matthew. As we talked about last time, you are now in a perilous situation, living with a lady to whom you are not yet married. You can understand these people's reaction. You have stepped outside the boundaries of loyalty," he says. "Loyalty to the clan. People see these things in very black and white terms. To them you are a traitor, you have to understand that."

"Are you standing up for them? Are you taking their side against me?" I ask him angrily.

"No, I absolutely am not. I am just trying to explain to you how those kind of people see things. I have seen it before..."

"I know how they see things," I tell him. "I used to see things the same way myself. Better if you could tell me what to do about it. How am I going to go on living and farming here if they keep up this madness? I have to eat and I have to provide for Sally Anne and Frankie."

"Well, yes, but you need to address the marriage situation. In the meantime, let me see what I can do," he says. "Maybe a quiet word to some of these stirrers, or their community leaders, what do you think? You have any names for me?"

I can't be passing on the names of the McKinney clan; that is just not something you would do.

"Look, it is a problem I have brought on myself. I have to come up with a way of changing their thinking myself. I have no idea yet what that way is, but I need to talk to them, get them to see my view of it."

"That is brave of you," he says, "and of course the other thing you must do is to have a proper wedding so that they would have one less nail to be hammering into your cross."

"That's the problem though. You said yourself, we can't really do that, not in a church way anyhow. We have this ceremony in Omagh coming up in May, just the registry office thing. But those sort of men will not pay any heed to it. They won't even know it's happened."

"Then we have to let them know," he says.

"How do we do that?"

"Well, a couple of possibilities. You could invite me to come to your registry office wedding and say a prayer of blessing over you, then we can invite a photographer from the local paper, the one the Protestants read. These people will see a picture of you and Sally Anne and your minister in his round collar in the paper. That should satisfy them, surely? Or you could come to church together on a Sabbath morning and after the service I will do a blessing for you."

These sound like good ideas and I am pleased that he has given me a choice.

"Aye, we could talk about this, her and me. Give me a few days and I will let you know," I tell him. I rev up the engine again. "And thank you. You have calmed me down a good bit before I go in to her."

He gives me the thumbs up and takes off down the hill again. I never even asked him what he was doing up our road in the first place. Likely exercising. These clergymen. If he'd come up to me of a morning I could give him his fill of exercise. He could dig drains for a day in the low field, for the rushes down there are getting out of hand. Or he could take into ploughing the fort field for me, twisted round all day in the tractor seat like a corkscrew till his back is screaming at him. And he could be making up his sermons as he is doing it, for there's not much else to be thinking about.

Chapter 61

Sally Anne Sweeney

I could not work out what had happened to Matthew at the fair that put him in such bad form, nor why he had landed back with the three bullocks he had been determined to sell. It is really the first time he has looked anything other than cheerful since Christmas. I watched his dark mood for as long as I could stick it. What had so distracted him?

In the end I sat him down at the table and drew the reason out of him.

"Remember we promised each other there would be no secrets between us, Matthew? You owe it to me to tell me what has annoyed you. It is written all over your face."

"Aye, but this is just farming stuff, business. It shouldn't concern you at all."

"It does concern me. If it is to do with you, it is to do with me too. No secrets, remember."

So he tells me of the boycott. He says it with a solemn bitterness.

This place!

We sit quiet for a minute or two, hands held across the table. Frankie trying to clamber up on to my knee. This is the first time since I arrived that I have seen Matthew's head go down. It's not like him. I know my duty here, to try to lift him again.

"There must be another way," I tell him. "There must be something you can do to beat them."

"It's not about beating them," he says. "We have to live among them. To beat them only makes them worse. They come back again to try to make their point and the whole thing boils up."

"Well what then? Have you another plan? You have to be able to go to market."

"Aye, and come Tuesday I will. The only thing I can do is take them to Strabane fair. The people up there don't know me and they don't care. I can sell them for as good money as in Castlederg. It's just the bother of it all and the waste of a day. It's just this feeling of..."

"I know, but don't let it get on top of you. I'm here for you."

Then I think to myself, 'And me being here is exactly the reason he is in this fix. Should I be here at all? Better for him if I'd stayed in Ranahuel.'

It must show on my face for somehow he reads my mind and gives me a knowing smile.

"Aye, you are here for me alright, Sally Anne. I wouldn't change the last two months for anything. Now, before I go back out to work, bring the wee man upstairs with you so the day is not a complete waste. We could both do with a bit of comfort, a bit of cheering up, eh?"

"Matthew Henderson," I laugh, taking his hand. "This farm is going to go down the drain and it won't be because you couldn't sell your bullocks."

****

Tuesday morning.

We are both up very early. Matthew wants to leave in good time to get to Strabane fair as soon as he can. No loving this morning. No lying on in bed together. I want to make him a decent breakfast so he won't be hungry before he is back.

He gets himself dressed and ready while I cook in my nightdress. Downstairs he comes at a gallop and knocks the bacon and eggs and potato bread into himself in no time.

"And you'll be fit to do the milking and keep an eye on the wain at the same time? Don't let him near Molly's feet for she's the divil for kicking. She could hurt him bad if she…"

"I know, I know. You seem to forget I was your milkmaid back in the day. Go on with you now."

"Aye but I didn't have Molly back then. Right, I should be back in the middle of the afternoon, if all goes well," he says. "Wish me luck."

I do and he gives me a quick kiss.

I sit down to eat my own breakfast while Frankie is still asleep.

I am barely started when Matthew storms back into the kitchen. He has the look of a wild man about him.

"I'll need you out here, Sally Anne."

"What is wrong?"

"The trailer has a flat wheel. The bullocks are gone. I need you to look for them while I pump up the tyre."

"What do you mean, the bullocks are gone? They can't be gone. Weren't they in the shed since Friday?"

"They were. I threw them hay last night. Unless I didn't close the gate right…no, it can't be that. I threw the hay over, I remember. The gate is lying open now."

We are out to the street. Matthew is looking very confused, his brow wrinkled in annoyance. There is no sign of the animals in the yard, nor in the lane to the road.

"What in the name o' God has happened?" he keeps saying.

I run to look down the back lane for any sign of our bullocks. In the soft mud I see the marks of cattle. It might be them or it might be hoof-prints from earlier. I run back and tell Matthew.

He has the pump ready at his feet and is starting to blow air into the tyre.

"I'll look at it in a minute," he says. "You'd better check inside and see if the wain is still asleep."

I do as he tells me. No sound from upstairs so I'm quickly back to him, my working clothes pulled on over my night things.

He has not made much head-way with the tyre. I see that he is stretched out on the gravel under the trailer.

"What's wrong," I ask him.

"I'll tell you what's wrong," he calls out from underneath. "Some bastard has stuck a knife in this tyre. On the inside of the thing too, so I wouldn't notice it. Likely the same hound that let the␣bease out of the shed."

"Oh, Matthew," I say, my hands to my mouth. "I am so sorry. This is all my..."

"Wheesht Sally Anne," he says, pulling himself up to his feet. "Enough of that. We need to find the bullocks first. The tyre can wait. What was the dog doing that we didn't hear it barking last night?"

"I did hear it," I tell him. I sleep more lightly than Matthew, maybe more conscious of the need to hear the child next door. "It did bark a while but I imagined it must have come across a fox or something."

"Pity you didn't waken me," he says, "but too late now. I was sleeping like a log."

I take him to see the tracks I have noticed down the back lane.

"It might be," he says. "They're fresh alright but maybe yesterday when....Listen, you take a look down there, I'll take a scoot around the roads and see if I see any sign of them. I'll take the car."

So I am left to myself in this search. I follow the lane and the deep foot-marks of some animals, all the way down to the ford over the burn. This stream wouldn't have stopped them of course, and I cross by the stepping stones and on into Kearney's street. From here they could have gone west, up the hill towards the bog, or right, along Kearney's lane to the road. If that's the way they went then Matthew will maybe come on them somewhere. I hope they haven't run too far, for not only will it take a lot of work to fetch them back, they will have run themselves into a sweat and will not be looking their best for the market.

I am in two minds here. I could follow my instinct and climb to the Gortnagappel bog, a dangerous place for cattle on the loose, with its deep bog-holes. But, back in the house wee Frankie might have wakened up and be screaming for me. The motherly instinct takes over, but before I run back home I find tell-tale hoof-marks on the lane up to the mountain. They are fresh and I can't imagine them being made by any cattle other than ours. Matthew will be pleased that at least we know where they likely are.

Frankie is screaming, indeed. He takes a bit of consoling, but a cuddle and a bottle of warm milk soon has him sorted. Matthew arrives back with no news of finding the cattle. I tell him what I have seen.

"I think they are on the mountain," I say. "Do you want me to come with you? I could leave Frankie with Monica?"

So that is what we do. The child cries as I leave him in Kearney's kitchen, but Monica will find something to amuse him. We take Jess up the hill and walk for ages. The moss is soaking wet at this time of year, the heather and whins at their lowest ebb and what scrawny bushes there are are bent towards us by the fierce winds that blow over these Donegal hills. Sometimes we are crossing areas where the soft peat glar is halfway up our boots. It is tiring to trudge through it. In this season, it feels a very bleak wasteland. Apart from a few greenish whin bushes, the scene is a flat spread, the colour of a potato sack, brown and dirty beige but slashed with black gashes where turf has been cut in the last few years.

"I just hope and pray they haven't fallen over the edge of a peat bank," Matthew says. "Or into a bog-hole. We'd never get them out alive."

Thankfully we eventually see all three animals in the distance, all above ground but at the furthest end of this huge stretch of bogland, a stand of wind-bent Scots Pine trees beyond them.

"We have to be very careful here," Matthew tells me. "We'll work our way around behind them and come at them from the other side, keep the dog close and quiet. No rushing them, for if they take off they could end up mired in one of those swamps or upside-down in a hole."

We take it very easy, doing our best to gentle the bullocks in the right direction and keeping them on the higher hard ground. Jess works great for us, staying behind us unless Matthew sends her off to the flank.

We walk apart by several yards. I look sideways at my man, the patient vigour of his body, the steady swing of his long legs through the dead rushes, the dogged angle of his stubbled chin, his brow lined with tension, brown as the bog, his eyes cold-blue and focussed.

I remember the teasing we did of each other in this very place. Those carefree days of first love. I remember thinking then just how perfectly he fitted in this landscape. He does still, even more so.

Somehow we get the bullocks down off the mountain and into the lane towards home. It has not been easy, it has not been quick. At one point I have to take a very long run to try to get ahead of them, climbing over stone walls and fences, to stop them running through Kearney's yard and out their lane to the main road. It is after eleven before we have them safely back in the shed, and Matthew still has a burst tyre to repair.

He is quiet.

"It won't be today you go to Strabane," I say.

"No, they've made sure of that, the buggers."

"Who are they, do you think?"

"I could guess but I might be wrong, so I'll not slander anybody yet."

"There's always next week, Matthew. We can try again; Strabane I mean?"

"I have to be better prepared for next week," he says. "I have to make a plan."

"Can I help?"

He is far away, thinking deeply as he starts to remove the trailer wheel.

"You might," he says, "but I don't have much of a notion yet what I'll do. When I have I will let you know. You did well up on the hill today."

"I did nothing."

"You were beside me," he said. "And you can still run like a hare."

"Thanks very much."

"So maybe run down to Kearney's now and fetch Frankie."

"Yes, I hadn't forgotten," I say turning to go.

"And Sally Anne. If you are talking to Millie in the next day or two, make sure you tell her about this handlin'. And make sure she knows that we are going to do the same again next week. Strabane or bust on Tuesday, for I won't be made a fool of in Castlederg until I sort out how to handle the neighbours."

Chapter 62

Matthew Henderson

The plan forms in my head bit by bit over the next few days. It is a scheme with a fair bit of risk involved in it and, if it goes wrong and backfires on me, it could make the killing of my friend Joe a small matter by comparison.

To my mind, the people who let my bullocks out of their shed and punctured my tyre in the middle of the night are bullies and cowards.

I despise them, but I am sorry for them too. Sometimes these people know no better, they've never been shown a better way. At the same time, cowards and bullies have to be told that that is what they are, cowards and bullies.

Bullies have to be taken on. To run away from them only encourages them, so my father would have taught me when I was a wee lad and having trouble at the school. He himself was no coward. When the Kaiser's army started to bully its way around Europe in 1914 he joined up to try to put a stop to it.

"Don't be afraid of a bully," he always said to me, "for he only feeds on your fear and grows stronger. Deny him that. Stand up to him and show him what you are made of."

I am a son of James Henderson, I remind myself. In my head I have heard the echo of his wisdom on many occasions and this is another one of them.

Some of that wisdom I have tried to share with Sally Anne during this week of planning. When I talk her through my scheme she seems scared to death of the idea. She is full of 'What ifs,' her eyes wide as saucers at some of my notions. That is no bad thing, for the more she challenges me the more I think about the rough edges of this idea. Aye, of course there are problems and things that I might not foresee in what I am thinking to do. Her questions force me to change bits of it, make the plan a bit more water-tight. To be fair to her, even though she is hesitant about it and worried sick about what might happen if it goes wrong, she is prepared to trust me and back me up one hundred percent.

What it is to have a woman behind you, I think. I have lived forty-six years without that support. Millie was fine as someone who could keep the basic things running in the house and on the farm but she was never a person to think things through with, or help with an idea. Now, to have the strength and love of Sally Anne as my foundation is a wonderful feeling. It puts a new level of confidence in me, where before I would have been the sort of man who could be swayed by self-doubt, like ripe corn in a storm.

A good while ago, I shed the talking bird that seemed to sit on my shoulder and chirp at me, 'What will people think Matthew? You can't be doing that, what will the neighbours say?' Maybe that is why I ended up in prison after the smuggling thing. But this is a different type of courage that Sally Anne inspires in me. It is not so rash, so reckless. It's a more sensible courage to do the right thing and take on anyone who wants to try to stand in my way.

"But how sure are you that these men will come back tonight and try the same nonsense?" Sally Anne asks me.

"I'm not sure at all," I tell her. "It's just a hunch. If they don't come, well, so much the better. I can go to Strabane and sell the bease. But my guess is that they'll want to keep the pressure on me. Last week was so easy for them. They'll not be expecting any difference tonight."

"So what is it you want me to do? I want to help but..." she says.

"First thing I would like you to do is to bake a cake."

"A cake? Are you serious? What has a cake to do with anything?"

"Just wait and see. But we will need a cake if this goes to plan," I tell her.

"What kind of cake?"

"I don't know. Did you see any fancy sort of cakes in America? This has to be a good one."

She thought about that for a second.

"I did... and I ate some of it too. It was amazing. Caroline's father made it for Independence Day," she says. And then the interesting line, with a great grin spreading over her face. "It was red and blue with white icing in the middle."

"Now you're talking," I say. "You ate a red, white and blue cake, did you? And you didn't choke on it?"

"I didn't, no. It stuck in my throat a bit, but I got it swallowed."

"That's great," I say with a grin.

She stares at me for a bit.

"But if you think I am going to feed you red, white and blue cake you can think again," she says with a frown.

"Ah no, I wouldn't be on for fancy stuff like that. Just put plenty of nice sweet cream on the top and in the middle, right?"

"I can try, master," she says. "Anything for you, master."

****

Monday night, tenth of March, 1947.

My make or break night. My future as a farmer in Lismore and as a member of this community hangs on how tonight turns out.

In many ways it reminds me of the night I was to be attacked by Kevin Duggan and his gang of rebels, twenty-five years ago. The main difference is that I have had time to plan it all out. Time to come up with a better scheme, a well-thought-out one.

It's half past ten. I could have a long wait tonight. As I squat down on my three-legged milking stool behind a couple of creamery cans, I start to wonder. Is this a better plan or is it every bit as mad as what I did on that dreadful night? That night I was inside, looking down at the darkened yard. Tonight I am on the street itself, squinting out into the wintery gloom from between these sturdy milk cans. It is bitterly cold. The clouds are high and wispy, blowing across the half-moon at good speed and leaving just enough light in my yard for me to make out the buildings opposite and the trailer, reversed up to the gate of the shed as it had been last Tuesday night. I can just about make out, in the far corner of the yard, the opening to the back lane, a dark, shadowy hollow. In 1922, the danger came from that art. Tonight, if I am right, the danger will come from behind me, from down my lane to the road. I have the shelter of the feeding house behind me and I am well-coated-up against the weather, a warm scarf around me and a cap pulled down over my ears.

My dog is not in the yard tonight. I have her fed to the back-teeth and she is now cosied up in a soft bed in our front room where she can sense no disturbance in the yard behind the house. The last thing I want is for her to be barking and spoiling things. She can have the night off, all to herself.

Sally Anne can't though. She is awake and will stay awake all night, or until events unfold. She understands the small role she has to play…later. I have no doubt that, as she sits in the darkness of the kitchen, she will be saying the rosary or praying to whatever saint they have in her faith who looks after daft farmers and their crazy plans, maybe to the saviour of lost causes. She cannot be putting on a light. The house must seem to be asleep. My fingers are well and truly crossed that Frankie doesn't decide that this is a night for raising the roof, as he has done a few times when the teeth were bothering him. He is a good sleeper most of the time, to be fair to him, and he needs to oblige me tonight by staying quiet.

At my feet lies a coil of rope, good sturdy rope that I would use normally for leading my bull or securing a load on my trailer. I have tested it well, putting all my weight on it. It has held me fine. It will do its job when the time comes. One end of it I have tied tightly to the gatepost across the lane. It is attached to a point about nine inches from the bottom of the post and well hidden by a sheaf of hay. The rope runs across the lane to where I am hiding, itself hidden under a light skiff of loose gravel.

The only other gear I have, and this is the one great unknown in this scheme, is a weapon.

My old shotgun!

I have not held this gun since storing it away in the roof space above the attic in 1922. I have had a dread of guns since that terrible night. More than that, I have never needed my gun since. The weapon has been lying there, safe and undisturbed ever since. For me to climb up there and get it, bring it down and clean it, take it up the mountain to where I could test-fire it and not be heard....well, it took a lot out of me. I had to keep it hidden from Sally Anne till the last minute of course. She near had a fit when I brought it out. It took some explaining to her about how I planned to use it before she settled down.

In preparation for tonight's ambush I had driven to Strabane to make a couple of purchases; some cake ingredients for Sally Anne and a few new cartridges for the gun. I also called at the auctioneer's office, more for a chat than anything else, just to let him know that I would likely have bullocks in the fair on Tuesday morning. You never know how news filters back into a community. Millie knows as well, so likely her husband does too. And, if he knows, I am fairly sure a few others within his circle will know too. It is not something I want to keep a secret, not in any way.

I am well settled down to wait for the night to unfold. My pocket watch, when I bring it out for company, can just about be made out in the flitting veils of moonlight. I wonder how Sally Anne is? Is she still with me in this escapade? Are her misgivings being stirred into serious rebellion by the ghosts of what she saw when she ran into my street back then, the sound of gunfire ringing in her ears, the name 'Joe' screeching from her as she cradled his dying head?

I have asked too much of her, I know I have.

Those memories deserved to rest in peace without being dug up so bitterly by tonight's re-enactment.

Should I go to her? Check if she is alright? Should I abandon this madness now before it can go wrong? Aye, maybe I should. My doubts are beginning to swamp me. I could end my days in prison if this goes astray, leaving Sally Anne all on her own here on my farm and me not even married to her yet. My family would turf her out of the place, send her packing back to Donegal and, if they didn't, I know exactly who would. The wider community, the wider family circle, the staunchly faithful of the tribe...they would delight in my fall, they would welcome the chance to set the Henderson farm back on a firm and faithful foundation. I would have no say in the matter, no way of protecting the woman I love and the wain that we are growing to love and who might, for all I know, be the one who takes the farm on from me in the future. What on earth am I doing to be putting all that in jeopardy? No, this is the daftest thing I have ever done. Who do I think I am? John Wayne in some Wild Western movie or....

Footsteps grating on the gravel!

My heart nearly explodes through my chest!

No way back now. I either do this or freeze here, let it happen as it did last week.

It all plays out in a blur of speed.

I can just about make out two shadows moving across the yard, quickly and as quietly as the gravelly surface of the street will let them. I think I can make out their heads glancing around. I am well hidden, deep in the shadow. As they reach the shed door and start fiddling with the bolt that holds it shut, I lift my shotgun. I aim at the night sky.

Bang!!!

It is a huge explosion of noise in the sleepy silence of that enclosed space, my four-sided farmyard.

Both figures react the same way. They drop, as if hit by the shot. It is an instinctive reaction. I hear a screamed oath from the floor. In a split second, though, both are on their feet, scrambling madly in a stooped sprint towards the lane again.

My gun goes down for a second. My hands grab the rope. As the two figures reach the lane I pull the rope tight with a massive jerk. It rises at exactly the right time, catching the running figures around the ankles and sending them sprawling. I grab the gun again. My move after them is every bit as fast as theirs. One of the two is quicker to his feet than the other, who seems well dazed by the fall. As the bigger one makes another mad dash for freedom, I grab the smaller one by the scruff of the neck and hold him firm.

The lad squirms and flails at me, swearing like a trooper. I still have my shotgun in my right hand. I stick it in his back.

"Stand still or I'll pull the trigger and you'll end your days on my street, full of lead," I tell him through gritted teeth.

"Don't shoot! Don't shoot!" he begs. "Please don't shoot!"

"You stand still and do as you are told and I won't shoot, alright. Make any more mistakes and I will! Don't give me the excuse."

"Alright, I won't," he says. "What do you want me to do?"

"Just stand there and shut up," I tell him. "You're Jimmy, aren't you?"

"How'd you know that?"

"I just know things," I say. "I know you and Sammy were here last week. I've been watching you. I knew exactly when you'd be back. I wondered if your father would be stupid enough to try this lark again and, sure enough, he was. So now, son, the boot is on the other foot."

"What are you going to do to me?"

"Well, I haven't decided yet, Jimmy. That depends on big Norman a bit. You see, he knows that in this very yard I have already killed one man. He was a fellow called Joe and he wasn't that much older than you."

"Don't be killing me, please don't be killing me. I'll do anything you ask. Please."

I am sorry for him. He has pished himself. I can smell it. I hold him well away from me, my gun still in his ribs. At the far end of the lane I can just about make the shape of a big lump of a car parked across the lane entrance. The running figure has reached it and I hear snatches of shouted conversation, mainly swearing.

"Right," I say, "tell you what I want you to do. You and me are going to walk out this lane and meet your father. Him and me need to talk. He needs to start listening to me and that's something he has never done in his life. We are related you know, Norman and me. Some sort of cousins. Does it not strike you as odd, Jimmy, that your daddy has you up here in the middle of the night, a cold windy night that you should be asleep in your bed. And what has he brought you up here for? To let a couple of bullocks out of a shed? His own relative's bullocks? Maybe stick a knife in a tyre? What sort of a stupid racket is that son, eh? To his own cousin? Can you explain that now, can you? You are an intelligent lad. You had a good schooling down there in Erganagh. You know what's right and what's wrong. So what are you doing in my yard at three o'clock in the morning, just pure mischief, eh?"

All this as I am marching him out towards his father by the scruff of the neck, gun jammed against his kidney. As we approach the car I notice that Norman has taken guard behind the vehicle, his head just about popping round the rear window to keep an eye on what he can see of us in the faint moonlight. I'm fairly sure that Sammy is hidden behind the car as well.

"Norman," I shout, "how are things with you?"

"What the hell are you doing to my boy?"

"What the hell was he doing in my street?"

"You let him go, you daft bastard! You hear me, let him go! You coulda killed him, him or his brother. Are you mad altogether?"

"Aye," I say calmly, "maybe just a wee bit mad, but it'll pass. Once you and me have a bit of a decent conversation it might just pass."

"What do you mean, decent conversation? I am not talking to you, Henderson. Not till you let Jimmy go."

"And I am not letting Jimmy go until we talk, so we're stuck. And let me tell you Norman, I don't mind either way. I can stand here until the morning. I can stand here with my gun in Jimmy's back until the RUC drive up to check if there has been any trouble on my farm tonight, like there was last Monday night. And you can explain to them what you and your boys are doing up here."

This is a bit of a bluff of course, but it just comes into my head at the time and I think it is quite a useful bit of bluff.

Norman is thinking.

It takes a while but I can wait... and I have the gun.

Jimmy speaks.

"Da, do what he says. He's already killed a man, he says. I don't want him shooting me. This was a bad idea anyway."

"Shut your mouth, son," Norman gulders at him. "Let me think."

"Jimmy is right, Norman; and he would need a change of trousers here for... Look, let me be fair about this. I want to end this and I want to end it well. I want to talk to you, but I don't want to be doing it at three o'clock in the morning on the side of Lismore hill."

"What do ye want then?" Norman is coming around, starting to see things my way.

"I want you to put Sammy in the car and drive up my lane to my house. I'll bring Jimmy with me, right behind you. No messing about now, for Jimmy is still feeling this shotgun in his back. And when we get to my house Sally Anne will have a cup of tea for yous and maybe something to eat and we can sit around my table like friends, like family, Norman, and I can explain to you some of the things that are on my mind, alright."

He seems very unwilling to do this, very suspicious of what I might be after. He needs a bit more encouragement.

"I know this is a surprise to you and I don't blame you for not just jumping at the invitation, but the way I see it, Norman, you and me had the same great-grandfather, our fathers were first cousins. We shouldn't be at loggerheads over anything, never mind over a woman that you have never met."

"You have no right to be living with a woman like that," he says.

"Like what? You haven't met her. Wait 'til you do before you make judgements on her. So what I am asking you to do now, is come up to the house, sit down at my table and eat the cake that she has baked, have a cup of tea, have a chat, then go back down to your place and have a good think about life and how short it is and so on. Alright? What do you say lads? You want a bit of cake before you go home? Jimmy? It's going to be better than a gun barrel in your spine, isn't it?"

"Aye, come on, da," Jimmy begs.

"It's maybe a trick," I hear Sammy mutter.

"Shut up while I think," Norman growls. Then to me, "What trick have you got up your sleeve?"

"No trick. Honest to God. I swear it. What do you think I am going to do to you? Poison you or something? I am genuinely saying, come for a cup of tea. It'll warm you up if nothing else. Fifteen minutes and yous can all be on your way again. What do you say?"

"You put that gun down and we'll think about it."

"I will put the gun down when we get into my kitchen. You can understand why....I am not the one who started the trespassing last week, nor tonight. I'll set the gun down when we get the tea."

"You've no choice, da," Jimmy says. "Just do what he says."

"Good for you, Jimmy," I tell him. "You'll love this cake too."

Norman jumps in the car. It sinks a bit on its springs with his weight until Sammy evens it up by getting in the other side. I wait for him to move off up the lane and follow with my 'prisoner.' Into the street and sure enough Sally Anne has the lights on in the kitchen and in the yard. She is standing at the back door, a torch in her hand. Maybe she was for coming to see if I was alright. Her face reflects her struggle to be welcoming to these guests, while she must be sick inside with terror at what is going on and what could still go badly wrong. I have put her through some ordeal tonight, not as bad as poor Jimmy here but very distressing for her all the same. And it's not over yet.

Chapter 63

Sally Anne Sweeney

As that grand big car creeps reluctantly into our street, my heart seems to be a sparrow trying to break out of my chest. In all my life I have never felt fear like this. I don't know yet if Matthew is lying in a bloody heap in the boot or the back seat, or whether his plan has worked and he is safe. The car eases to a halt not far from where lane meets street. Nobody gets out yet. Although I can clearly see the car itself in the spread of the yard light, I can see nothing inside it. The windows seem well steamed up.

If I have been saying prayers for the last four hours they are nothing to what I am saying now.

"Jesus and Our Blessed Lady, let him be alive and alright! If I stay away from his bed from now until we are married, will you please let him be alright. I couldn't bear to lose him a second time, and us both so happy now."

These are silent prayers of course. I wouldn't want this man or any of his kind to be hearing me in the deathly silence of this street.

Before long I hear the shuffle of feet coming from the lane and the sound of Matthew's voice, low and consoling in tone.

"Just relax now. Don't worry about a thing. You are going to enjoy getting cleaned up and getting a cup of tea in a minute. Your daddy and your brother will be grand."

He comes into view, the light picking up his shape and throwing a huge shadow against the barn wall beyond, like some kind of a four-legged monster from a children's picture book. He has his hand up at the collar of the tall figure ahead of him, seemingly pushing him forward against his will.

"Come on into the house, the pair of you," Matthew calls into the car as he passes it. "No tricks, no messing about now, for I still have Jimmy at the business end of my shotgun. Just do as I ask you and he doesn't get hurt."

That is what he says, but he doesn't sound very menacing with it, more like a father chastising unruly children. I stand aside as he ploughs on past me into the kitchen.

"Come on in behind me, Sally Anne," he says urgently. "I don't want them grabbing you to even matters up. Come in quick and get the tea on."

I do as I am told. I don't say a thing. The low tension in his voice now is like nothing I've heard from him before. He may be on top in this feud at the moment, but I can tell he is taking nothing for granted.

"Leave the door open. Norman and Sammy should be coming behind me. Here, Jimmy, I want you to sit at the far end of the table there. You like cake, eh? You want a bit of Sally Anne's lovely cake? We'll get you some cake as soon as your father comes in."

Jimmy very stubbornly starts to do as he is told, Matthew watching him like a hawk. The dog has started yapping in the front room, disturbed by the voices. Matthew continues barking orders too!

"Sit down now. No! Don't be going on around the table! No! I told you...sit down there! Now!....Good lad. That wasn't hard, was it?"

Then to me he says, "Jimmy had a bit of an accident with his trousers out there. Do you think you could get him an old pair of mine? And let Jess out the front door before she wakens the wain, would you?"

"I will," I say. Ó *a Mhaighdeán bheannaithe*. The shake in my voice, like an old woman. "You want those trousers now?"

He nods. I go through and let the dog out, then run upstairs. No sound from Frankie, thanks be to God. He has slept through the gun-shot and Jess's yapping. I am back down in the kitchen in a matter of seconds, a pair of well-worn trousers in hand.

I am greeted by the sight of two more men standing close in to my range, taking whatever heat they can from it. Big lumps of men they are, all three of them. Matthew is no dwarf at over six feet but he looks a small fellow beside these three. How on earth has he managed to capture all three of them tonight and then persuade them to come peaceably into our kitchen? The gun in his hand has helped of course. I just hope it doesn't have to be fired again tonight, or any other night. This farmyard has seen enough of gunfire in its time.

I stop at the hall door, unsure of myself, not knowing how to react to this nightmare situation. The visitors have their eyes fixed on me. I feel like a fox must feel just before the hounds tear it to shreds. But I have my Matthew and he has the gun, otherwise I think I might flee from this scene as fast as I could run.

"Sally Anne, this is my cousin, Norman. These are his two sons, Sammy here and Jimmy; those trousers are for Jimmy. You want to slip into the toilet through there and change? Go on, you're welcome; those must be getting very cold on your legs by now."

As Jimmy comes past me, I stand well away from him but hand him the fresh trousers. He grabs them from me with an angry gesture, not a word from him. I think 'dour' would be the word Matthew would put on him. Not the most mannerly fellow, I am thinking.

Matthew continues, his voice still full of strain.

"And Norman, this is my friend, my intended, soon to be my wife; this is Sally Anne Sweeney. Sally Anne hails from Donegal, as you might have heard. She was a maid here on the farm away back. It has taken me over twenty years to find her," (he gives me a smile here), "and talk her into coming back and getting married to me, so you can see why I take it ill if anybody tries to put a spanner in the works, know what I mean?"

Norman says not a word, just stares at me with a look that is full of menace. I stare him back, straight up into the eyes, as Matthew has asked me to do. I do my very best to appear as open and friendly as I can, though inside I am absolutely churning with fear.

"*Cad é mar.....*" Oh Lord, I nearly lapsed into an Irish greeting in my panic. That wouldn't have done. I settle myself.

"How are you, Norman? I am pleased to make your acquaintance," I say and stride across the floor towards him, my hand out to him. "I hope you'll take a cup of tea from me."

I get glared at from a great height, the son writhing beside him like a dog with stomach cramps. It takes all the courage I have to stand there, look up into his big flabby face and still keep my hand stretched out towards him.

'God help me. Give me strength,' I pray in the ferment of my brain, my heart doing double time at the very least. I stay there, my arm as strong as my intention to break something in this man.

"I have a cake to cut for yous, but shake my hand first, Norman, for any relative of Matthew's is going to be a relative of mine and I don't want us to get off on the wrong foot. You'll take a piece of cake, the lads as well?"

My hand is still there, right in front of his stomach, insisting. And my eyes are still at his face, not a flinch in them. Will he break first? I daren't back down.

"In my part of the world we always shake hands with folk, whether they are complete strangers or folk that we see every day. That is how we are," I tell him. "I'm sure it's the same around Castlederg too."

Matthew watches intently from beyond the table, the shotgun limp in his hand. It is of no use to us now. You cannot force civility from a man by threatening him with violence. That part of the night is over. This monster of a man is in my kitchen. It has to be about hospitality now, it has to be about drawing some sort of basic human response from him, a man who is steeped in prejudice and dominance, whose first instinct is to suspect, to fear the stranger rather than shake her hand.

I am just about to give up and lower my hand. It has been held out to him for a full minute, I am sure of it.

Then he breaks. His body seems to slump, his chest lowers and his hand comes up towards mine, almost creaking like some rusty mechanical thing. He takes my hand, very briefly but firmly enough. It is a huge, brutal hand this, rough as the bark of a tree.

Settle down, my heart. Breathe Sally Anne.

My eyes are burrowing up into his, looking for a softening, for some shadow of vulnerability. I don't know that I see it, but he has shaken my hand.

Then he speaks, the first word since they entered the house. Not to me directly, just into the quiet of the room.

"You say yous are going to get married?"

"We are," I say, as warmly as my weariness will allow me. Matthew supports me now. I can hear pride colouring his voice.

"Aye, we are. We are going to Omagh for it. The Registry Office. Has to be that way first, for the churches can't seem to...but Reverend Moore from the Methodists is coming with us, so...." He breaks off, unsure how to end a sentence he has started without knowing what it was he wanted to say.

"And your crowd?" Norman turns to me, making space to let me in to the range. I have gone to the hob to put the kettle on again. "I take it they aren't too keen to be marrying you to Matthew, him being a Prod like?"

"Agh no, Norman. You know what they're like. They'll wait until they can do nothing about it and then they'll likely agree to give us a blessing or something."

His mouth twists into a dismissive snarl and he shakes his head.

"Those bloody people," he says.

Jimmy appears back in the kitchen, Matthew's old trousers fitting him very snug, just an inch or two short in the leg, his own damp pair in his hands. I feel sort of sorry for him, a fellow of about seventeen and him wetting his pants. Matthew must have terrified him altogether.

"Here son, sit down here," I tell him. "There's a plate for you. You'll like this cake I have made."

"Why are you doing this?"

Fair play to you, Jimmy, I think. That is a courageous question and I am glad of it.

"Why not, Jimmy," I say. "You had a bit of a shock out there tonight. The least I could do was ask my man here to bring you in after for a cup of tea. You must be very cold, cold and wet and maybe hungry...at four o'clock in the morning. It's not a great time to be out roaming the roads."

In all my life, this has to be the most uneasy conversation I have been part of. I should be on a stage somewhere. I can sense the ebbing and flowing of these men's emotions. The Sammy one seems to be the one most on edge, bristling with resentment. I keep an eye on him. He hasn't relaxed yet, like his father and brother have. As it happens I am right in my suspicion.

Matthew has been standing, gun in hand, watching and listening to me, allowing me to try my hand at charming the father. Now he steps forward to the table, pulls out a chair and sits down opposite Jimmy.

"Have a seat, Norman," he says. "It's as cheap as standing. Here." He pushes a chair towards Norman with his feet.

I have the tea ready. I set the cake on the table between them.

Then I hear the sounds of Frankie crying upstairs.

Matthew and I look at each other. This wasn't in the plan. There's nothing to be done about it. Manys a more experienced parent would be content to just let the child cry, I suppose. We are not that breed of parent yet. My instinct moves me, without thinking, towards the door. Matthew nods.

"Aye, you'd better go and pick him up," he says.

In some ways it is a huge relief to be out of that situation, even for a few minutes. But I don't want to leave Matthew too long on his own with those three. I leap up the stairs two at a time, rush into the bedroom and pick up Frankie.

"*Bí ciúin anois, a leanbh*," I try to soothe him as I carry him out to the landing and downstairs.

I come back into the kitchen to a very different picture.

Sammy stands in the middle of the room with the gun in his hands. He is pointing it directly at Matthew.

How in the name of God has this happened?

There is a fire of hatred burning from the young man's eyes. Even his father and brother are staring at him in dread.

"Put the gun down," the father says.

"I am putting no gun down, da. This bastard has made a cod of us tonight. He's going to pay for it."

"Put the gun down, I tell you!"

Frankie starts to scream. I feel like doing the same myself. I make as if to escape back into the hallway.

"You stay where you are, bitch," Sammy cries after me. I freeze, stock still.

Matthew moves behind me. "Here, Sally Anne, give the wain to me. He'll be alright now, don't be worrying. Hush now Frankie, it's alright son."

Then to Sammy, as he takes Frankie from my shaking arms, "Put the gun down, son, don't be scaring the baby. You don't want to be doing something you'll regret now."

Lord above, but isn't my man the calmest, coolest person? Not a sign of worry on him and him at the wrong end of his own gun. How has it ended up in the hands of this mad young fellow? Matthew reads my mind.

"I just set the gun down to get plates," he explains to me quietly, apologetically. "Sammy here fancies himself as a bit of a hero."

"Aye, well you were the one thinking you were the hero earlier on, so it's time you got a bit of your own medicine."

"Put the gun down, I tell you," the father tries again.

"Here," Matthew says, making a quick decision and giving Frankie back to me. He turns and takes a determined step towards Sammy, "Come on Sammy. Why don't you just give the gun to me? Come on now."

Sammy brings the gun up level with Matthew's face.

"You stop right there, you fenian-loving bastard."

"Come on now son, don't go making a fool of yourself," Matthew continues taking another step towards him, his arm outstretched.

My heart is in my mouth. What is he doing?

"I am going to fire! I'll kill you if you take one more step!"

Matthew looks him in the eyes.

He steps forward and...

I shield Frankie, covering his ears.

Sammy pulls the trigger.

Click!

No bang!

Just a dull click.

What happened the bang?

Matthew reaches quickly up and wrenches the gun from the fellow's hands in one aggressive twist. He pokes Sammy in the belly with the butt end of the weapon, a good thump sending him backwards into a chair.

What just happened? I look at Norman and the other fellow. Norman has his arms lifted up in the air in a sort of panic pose, the beads of sweat sitting out on his brow as if he's just come in out of the rain. Jimmy's hands are on his head, his mouth and eyes wide open as a gate.

Matthew sets the gun in the far corner and turns slowly to us. He puts his hand in his coat pocket and pulls out a small tube of a thing.

"I took this cartridge out of the breach at the start of the night," he tells us, "just in case. It was a good call, wasn't it, Sammy? Mind you it wouldn't have done any more than scare the wain, for if you could read this wee label on it, you'll see that it's a blank."

There is a stunned silence in the kitchen.

"You mean..." begins Sammy.

"You know what a blank is son?" Matthew has a strange wee smile on his lips. How does he seem so relaxed here, so in charge?

"You were never armed in the first place? The gun against my back didn't even have ammo in it?" Jimmy says. "You sly bastard."

"Norman," says Matthew, "you're going to have to clean up these boys' language. There's no bastards here lads, no fenian-lovers, no bitches except the dog that was in the front room. Now, sit back up at the table, Sammy, and have a cup of tea and a slice of this cake. Your da looks as if he could use a cup, eh Norman?"

Norman hasn't spoken yet. He seems to be in some sort of shock, dumb-struck. He stands shaking his head, his two arms twitching as if they have a mind of their own but have no strength to act.

He flops down on the chair and grabs a cup.

"Matthew Henderson," he says, his voice quiet and quivering. "I have to hand it to you. You are one cool customer."

"That's alright then, Norman," Matthew says, coming with the teapot. "Here boys, take a cup there. Cut them a slice of cake, Sally Anne. Give Frankie a wee bite too for he looks hungry."

Frankie becomes the focus of attention as I hold him in one arm while trying to slice the cake with the other.

"So this wain?" Norman says. "Is he your's or what?"

I look at Matthew. I just get a smile.

"No he's not my wain," I tell him. "This is Frankie. His mother, God rest her, was a cousin of mine in Scotland."

Matthew takes over. He knows what bells to ring with these boys.

"The wain's father was killed in the war. He was called Frank as well and he was a Protestant, married to a Catholic." Matthew gives me a questioning glance. I nod, he is on the right track. "Frank was a service man, like my father was. He was in the Navy, lost at sea near the end of the war. Fighting for his country against them bullying Nazis. So Frankie here, he is all on his own. A war orphan, if you like."

"And yous are keeping him?"

"We are," I tell him. "Soon as we are married, we are going to adopt him. He'll be Frankie Henderson then."

Norman shakes his head and grabs a slice of the cake, stuffing it into his cave of a mouth. The sons follow suit; they love their cake, these boys. Norman downs his tea and I offer him more.

"No, I am grand, missus," he says before he can check himself. Then realising what he has just called me he tries to apologise. "I mean...sorry, I didn't mean 'missus', not like that."

"It's alright, Norman," I tell him. "I'll answer to that for now, but, if you want to come down to Omagh on the ninth of May, you can see me becoming a missus in front of your eyes."

God but haven't I got a glimmer of a smile out of him.

"Hurry up boys," he says rising. "We're for home."

The boys, as he calls them, follow him out the door like well trained sheep-dogs. Not a backward glance. Not a word of apology, not a 'Thank you,' a 'Goodnight'. Nothing.

It's very cold and I close the outside door behind Matthew as he sees them to their car. I have no fears for him. He has quenched this fire with the greatest skill I could ever have imagined.

He comes back in to me a few minutes later.

"Get to bed, Matthew," I tell him as he holds me. "You have to be up in a couple of hours to drive those bullocks to Strabane."

"No I don't," he says. "I can sleep on as long as I want."

"How come? What about Strabane? Why have you changed your mind?"

"Just," he says. "Castlederg market on Friday will be grand."

"You think?"

"I know," he says. "And I have a buyer too. Big Norman has offered to buy them off me."

"Are you serious? He offered?"

"Well, maybe not offered. But when I asked him if he would deal with me on them he didn't say no."

"He didn't say no? But he didn't promise either? Can you trust him?"

"I hope so. He shook my hand on it anyway, so I hope he is good to his word."

"He shook your hand? That's great, Matthew."

"Sure he shook yours too, earlier on, didn't he? You had him wound round your wee finger Sally Anne. I was nearly getting jealous."

I just laugh at him as he paces about the floor, reliving the night, smiling to himself. I feed some milk into Frankie and he falls asleep again.

"You want a drink, Matthew? A proper drink? Celebrate?"

"Nope," he says. "I want Frankie in his cot and I want you in my bed and it is going to feel the greatest night ever."

I laugh at him.

"Another of those 'greatest nights ever'," I say. "You're going to have to start a diary."

Chapter 64

Ranahuel
Kincasslagh
25th March 1947

Dear Sally Anne,

    I am very pleased for you and your man that you have set a date for the wedding. Thank you for the invitation. Of course I will do my best to come. I will have to think about getting new clothes for it. I will have to get some of the neighbours to sit in with Mammy. I haven't told her yet about you getting married. I wonder what she will make of that when I tell her.

Ailish tells me that Seamus is going to drive her over. That is really good of him so I will see if they can give me a lift. She is pleased that you asked her to be a witness.

We will have to leave very early for Seamus says it's half a day's drive to that Omagh place. I know you said it is a civil wedding but I don't understand. Does that mean you are properly married or do you have to go to church too, for the sacrament with a priest? It will be a new thing for me to see this, likely for you as well.

Everything is as normal here. Mammy is grand. She doesn't seem to have missed you or Frankie one wee bit. It has been a long time since she has been out to the Point, to Oileán na Marbh. Once the weather picks up I will to try and get young Stewart to come for us in his car and take her out there a run.

I had a visit from Father Devine. He had some news to pass on to you about Frankie and the baptism. When I told him you were planning to get married in May he didn't say much. That was a surprise in itself. Maybe he knows when he is beat. He wrote this note for me to send on to you. You can make of it what you will.
Le grá,
Mairead.

****

March 47

Dear Sally Anne,

I was just talking to your Mairead and she tells me that you and that man are for having some sort of civic wedding there in the North. It is your right to do that but it is also my duty to remind you that this will not be recognised by the Church as a Christian marriage. That is the first thing I have to say to you. It is not too late to change your mind and come back here, away from that sinful situation you have put yourself in.

The second thing I have to tell you is even more important. I wrote to a priest in St Columnkille's Church in Glasgow. He is an old friend from seminary days and is now high up in the administration of church matters in the city. I had asked him to contact the various Catholic churches in the Gorbals to see if he could find out if there is a Baptismal record for that child you have in your care, the boy Frankie Wilson. He found no trace of any such record. (Nor, by the way, is there any record of a marriage between his mother Nuala and a man called Frank

Wilson). The boy, it seems, has never been baptised. This is a terrible situation for any child and I must insist that you contact the church authorities where you are currently living and have the boy baptised. Failing that, I will do it myself, if and when you come to your senses and return to my parish.

Yours in Christian duty,
M Devine (Parish Priest)

Chapter 65

Matthew Henderson

I stand in Castlederg market shed, my head held high and my heart beating like a snare drum. A few neighbouring farmers have acknowledged me, to be fair, but none have done much more than that backward twitch of the head and the tilting up of the chin that is the customary way around here of saying 'Hello, I see you there, how are you doing?' It is just the quiet way farmers have in our countryside, a piece of our local dialect which doesn't need any words to pass between two people. The head-gesture says it all.

I see John Sproule away at the far end of the shed but he keeps his head turned away from me, talking to one of his cronies in that capturing way that he has. I haven't set eyes yet on any of the McKinney clan. I hope they don't disappoint me. In this public forum, it is vital for them to be here and signal some change in attitude towards me. I will be badly annoyed if their courage deserts them and they stay away today.

Business is brisk, as the auctioneers like to say. All categories of cattle are making excellent prices. It is a good market. The babbling of the auctioneer's voice, rising and falling in that sing-song style he has, his stuttering words tripping over themselves and reminding me of the ratchet wheel on my potato spinner, clickety-click, clackety-clack.

"How much am I bid? How much am I bid? Ah, a bid, a bid of a tenner, a bid of a tenner, here to my right, a bid of a tenner, who'll make it eleven, now. Do I see eleven, anywhere in the shed, come on now men, the best of a cow, do I see a-bid, a-bid, a-bid? I see eleven, thank you over here to my left, from a Killeter man I think, any advance on eleven, a fine animal now, reaching its prime, great milker, do I see ten shillings more now?"

My three bullocks are next into the ring.

No sign of big Norman. He has chickened out on me, I think.

Did I so humiliate the great bully, the biggest buyer in the cattle business, that he can't show his face?

The auctioneer begins his patter again and I scan the crowd of farmers and dealers for any interest. At least nobody is turning their back on me. That is a start. Nobody is snarling at me from the ranks, no smart comments, just a wall of blank stares, indifference.

Nobody is bidding for my cattle.

The auctioneer is doing his best but I sense a growing frustration in him. Maybe he hasn't been filled in on the background to this affair. He is innocently doing his damnedest to get someone to raise their hand and make a bid, any bid.

Just about to give up. I see him looking up into the crowd to try to find me, to get a signal from me about what to do. I raise my hand to draw his attention, but, just as I am about to shake my head to signal the withdrawal of the sale, I hear a shout.

Some of the men part near the back of the crowd. The auctioneer glances that way too and pauses in his chatter.

I see the head of big Norman above the other heads. You couldn't miss it.

"How much is bid for these bullocks?" he shouts up at the auctioneer, still pushing his way in. A man on a mission.

"Nothing yet, Norman. Will you bid?"

Norman bids.

He bids generously too and I sense a murmur go through the ranks of farmers. Heads turn in my direction, curious stares, eyebrows raised. I ignore them and listen as the auctioneer tries in vain to get a higher bid. He needn't bother. Once Norman McKinney has put on that sort of money, nobody else is going to try to out-bid him. I don't give two hoots. I would have been happy enough with less. But the significant thing is the signal, the nod of acceptance again that Norman's bid has brought about.

The hammer slams down.

"To Norman McKinney of Erganagh."

I try to catch Norman's eye to give him a wink of thanks, but he is not looking anywhere near me. I don't exist. That is fine by me. I would rather have this distance than any false cordiality.

Afterwards, in the Ferguson Arms, Norman is in his usual spot at the corner of the bar. I am in two minds about whether to ignore him or offer him a drink, as would be the usual custom after he has bought my bullocks. I don't want to embarrass him by forcing the issue. But old customs die hard and I sidle up beside him.

"Can I buy you a drink, Norman?"

He turns and looks hard at me, as if weighing me up. I don't meet his gaze, mainly because I take the chance to greet one or two other men nearby, farmers I would know from the district. It's just a finger raised in recognition, or another wag of the head. I get some wary looking gestures in return, hesitant, eyes flicking between big Norman and me, as if waiting for some sort of signal.

"Aye, a bottle o' stout," he says. "Good turn out the day."

"There was," I say, gesturing to the barman for another couple of bottles of stout. "I was starting to wonder if you were about yourself."

"Oh aye, always about. Just got held up on the road."

He turns away to continue whatever conversation he was having with his friends. I wait for the Guinness, surveying the old sepia photographs on the wall beside me. I notice one in particular.

'Electric Light for Castlederg 1920/21'.

I give it a wry smile. I remember it well.

Hopefully a bit more light has dawned in the place today.

As the bottles arrive in front of Norman, he picks one up, raises it and says "Cheers, Matt."

"Cheers!"

"Three fine bullocks."

"They are, aye."

"And thon's a brave wee heifer you have at the hoose," he says with a bit of a smile, just the slightest hint of raunchiness in it.

It takes me a second to realise what he is telling me here. I just return the smile and hold the bottle up to him again.

Enough said.

I move on along the bar.

Chapter 66

Sally Anne Henderson

The night before our wedding I slept in Kearney's. It was Monica's idea and, when she invited me to do this, I felt very honoured.

"Look, Sally Anne," she had said, "your poor mother will not be at your wedding so I want to stand in for her."

"That's lovely of you," I said.

"Well, the way you have been living with Matthew for the last few months...it's not good at all. So getting married from his house just doesn't seem the right way to do it, to me anyway. Will you not spend your last night as a single woman with us? Then get dressed and ready here, away from Matthew's eyes, and leave from our house for the wedding?"

It was all the more special that she offered this for she wasn't going to be able to come herself, on account of her health. So that is what I did. Monica helped me dress as best she could that morning. Her eyes told me that she was very happy for me, delighted to be doing this. A taxi collected me on the Kearney street in the morning and I couldn't help the feeling that Joe was maybe hiding in the barn, looking out at me in my finery through the broken boards in the wall.

Our wedding took place in a room that looked far more like an office than a church.

An office desk gave up its normal role for the day and became our marriage altar.

Two officials guided us to a line of chairs in front of it, before sitting themselves down behind the desk. I had Ailish beside me and Matthew had Jane's husband, Tommy, on the chair to his right. The others had to stand behind us.

My sister looked very nervous as she stood against the side wall with Seamus Gallagher. Maybe it was because she had Frankie in her arms and she was scared he would make a scene and want to come to me. Liam and Mary Coyle had their whole family with them, Josie, the youngest one squirming about in Mary's arms. Jane and her children were there too, Millie helping to pacify them and probably glad of a role that would distract her from the fact that her husband couldn't bring himself to attend a wedding service that wasn't being held in a proper church building. To be honest, I did not mind a bit that he had stayed away.

And, to be fair to John, he did offer to do the milking for Matthew on this special day, one less thing to worry about. Matthew's older sister, Emily, had thought it was too far to drive from Belfast. That was fine; I don't really know her anyway. My only regret was that Anthony and Monica were not there.

The Methodist clergyman stood up at the side of the 'altar', waiting his turn to do a prayer and a homily.

Earlier today, when I met him for the first time, just outside the register's office, I had called him Father Moore. The Protestants all thought this was very funny and the laughter sort of broke the tension a bit. He took it all in good heart; he said he had been called worse. He put my mind at ease with his calm, matter-of fact chat.

And then he introduced me to his wife.

I knew, of course I knew, that Protestant clergymen could be married, but to shake hands with the wife of one of them for the first time, and right before my very own wedding, was the strangest feeling. I wondered why he had brought her. I didn't know whether it was the done thing or not, but just as we were milling about, getting ready to go into the office, I found out what I think was his reason. This lady, Mrs Moore, ten years younger than me maybe, and a very attractive woman, took my arm and held me back for a second.

"Sally Anne," she said, "you look beautiful. I really like this dress; it's a lovely shade of cream and it suits your figure so well. And these flowers are so nice. I always loved Easter lilies."

"Thank you."

"And listen, I just wanted to say, enjoy the day and don't be nervous. I know exactly how you are feeling."

How could she? Did she just mean getting married or what? I waited. This needed an explanation.

She went on, so quietly and in such a strange lilting accent that I strained to hear her. "I am from County Limerick, you see. A village called Adare. A bit like yourself, I married into a very different way of life up here in the north."

I stared at her, trying to take in what she was telling me.

"Yes," she went on, "Peter was a Belfast boy. We met in college. It was a big shock for me coming up here. Then he decides he wants to go into the church and be a minister. That was an even bigger change."

Now that was something to be hearing just before my own wedding. Mrs Moore was smiling secret encouragement to me, but all I could think was, 'Well, I am not marrying a Belfast man; and my man is staying a farmer, or I am for Donegal again.'

At the same time, it was nice that she had wanted to tell me this about herself.

The wedding service itself was very formal of course, but without the solemn atmosphere you would have had in a church. We gave them all our forms and certificates. We read the vows they had printed out on card for us. We held hands and Matthew gave me the ring we had chosen in Strabane. We signed on the dotted line, followed by Tommy and Ailish. We were pronounced man and wife. I said it in Irish in my heart, just to make sure.

I was married to Matthew Henderson.

Reverend Moore read a section of the Bible, all about love, as I held Matthew's hand. He said a prayer and then talked for five minutes, a dark blur of a figure through my tears. They were probably very nice things he had to say, but I could only think of the long painful journey behind me, of my long-dead saint of a father, of poor Joe Kearney who also looked down on us today from his heavenly chair in the gallery and of my silent mother who may never understand my life.

A final short prayer from the clergyman, an 'Amen' and that was it over.

Then the hand shaking, the smiling, the kisses and the congratulations.

Out to the street, laughing in a subdued sort of way, me hooked on Matthew's arm.

A breeze had risen since we went inside. A thoughtful gust seemed to come around the corner at exactly the right time and blew clouds of spiralling cherry blossoms from two fine trees that stood on either side of the path. We were covered in pink confetti without ever planning it. Some of the pictures that our photographer put in the local paper for us show this shower of petals. It felt like a special blessing on us, a very natural one.

****

Later, the whole crowd of us are back at Lismore. The house is filled with laughter and noise. There are ten children altogether, including our wee Frankie, who seems a bit mesmerised by all this company. They take some watching, these wains, but Matthew and Tommy and Jane take them out to the fields to let off some steam. As Mary helps me with the food we have prepared together beforehand, Liam drives over and brings Anthony and Monica. It is a lovely time for them and we share tears of joy at the closing of the circle.

The food is spread out on a couple of tables. People, and there are twenty-four of us in the house, start helping themselves from various platters and going off to eat wherever they can find a space to sit down.

On a sudden notion, I take off my apron and leave the kitchen. I head out to the byre where John Sproule should be finishing the milking. Sure enough he is just pouring the last bucketful into a can. His back is to me and he doesn't hear me come in behind him, with the sound of the filling milk.

"Thanks for doing this, John," I say. "We appreciate it."

He gives a start of surprise, then freezes for a second before resuming his pouring. Not a word, not a nod, nothing. Why is he still stubbornly refusing to acknowledge me? Am I not a person, like he is? I cannot let this go.

"And, when you have that done, I want you to come in with me for a bite of food."

Nothing.

"We have a lovely meal ready there for you, John. Millie helped with it, there's nothing in it that you shouldn't eat. Nobody will try to feed you anything against your will," I say with a bit of a laugh in my tone, just so he knows I am trying to be light and friendly in this invitation.

"Will you come with me?"

He stands upright at the end of his task, still staring straight ahead, as if to turn and look at me will be a betrayal of his principles. I want to look him in the eye. I want him to see me in my wedding clothes. I want to bore in through this facade that he wears around himself and find some kindness in him, no matter how long it takes. It is my wedding day. What better day to appeal to him?

"Look John, you and Matthew have been good friends for years and years. You have been a great help to him in his life and I am sure you would say the same about him. You have needed each other. That is how life should be, especially in places like this. I do not want to be the cause of that friendship going down the drain, do you know what I'm saying? It will mean the world to Matthew if you can just come in for a minute or two, just eat a plate of stew and have a cup of tea. Come in and shake his hand even, same as he did to you when you married his wee sister. It will mean so much to her as well. I don't mind what you think of me, or what objections you have to my religion. I don't care about that, for you are entitled to your opinion, but I do care about you turning your back on your friend, do you know what I mean?"

He stands thinking for a good thirty seconds, no turning around yet. I take the initiative. I walk around in front of him, keeping my distance as you would with a ram that you are not sure of. I stand in front of him and slowly he brings his eyes from the far distance to focus on me. They stay on me too.

"Will you not come in with me?"

"Who all is in there?"

It is a quiet, subdued question.

I tell him. I end with, "And Reverend Moore and his wife are there. I'm not sure if you know them, the minister in Matthew's church? He did the wedding."

This brings a flicker of interest.

"The Methodist clergyman? He did the wedding, you say?"

"He did. He did a homily or a sermon, whatever you want to call it. And he did a prayer and a blessing and read from the Bible. We are married now John, properly married, and that is how life will be for Matthew and me from now on."

I think this surprises him. He is thinking about it. The tide is turning my way.

"And he'll likely say a blessing on the house at the end of this. You have to come in, John. Will you come?"

He looks at his clothes, his working overalls and wellington boots.

"I can't go in like this," he says.

"You can surely," I tell him moving forward to him. "Nobody will mind at all. Sure they know you have been doing Matthew's milking for him."

"It wouldn't be right to go in like this. I look wile dirty."

"Is there not something in the Bible about people looking at someone on the outside, but God looking at their hearts?"

Lord above, how did I think of that one? It must have been a text on one of those religious pictures that used to hang on Matthew's landing before I shifted them up to the attic. It sort of has the desired effect on John though. He gives one of those cold smiles of his that you think might crack his jaw.

"Imagine, you a Catholic telling me what my Bible says."

"Ah ha, John. Did you think only Protestants can read, did you?"

The tone is so much better now in this conversation, but he still hasn't moved to come with me, though I wait for him at the byre door.

"But here's the thing," he continues, "in the gospels it talks about a man who tried to get into a wedding in his ordinary clothes. But the master saw him and threw him out into outer darkness. How do you answer that one, eh? How do you answer that one?"

"John, I am no expert in these stories in the Bible. You are way ahead of me there, but believe me, nobody is going to throw you out of our house, not tonight, not ever. I want it to be an open house, like it was back in the day, when Matthew's folks were alive and all sorts of people were welcome there, from a beggar like oul Tam to a wee maid from Donegal. So come on, just give your hands a wash and take the boots off at the door. You'll be grand."

To my surprise and delight he makes a sudden decision and stomps past me to the pump in the yard. I wait for him as he scrubs his hands. I bring him a towel from the scullery but he has them wiped in his hair. Nothing beats the old habits. Boots off at the door and he follows me in.

Matthew looks at me like I have just walked on water. He goes to John and their handshake is as warm as you could wish for. Millie is so pleased she has to wipe away her tears.

After we eat and before Seamus and Ailish and Mairead leave to drive all the way back to Kincasslagh, Matthew takes out his father's fiddle and puts it in my hands.

"Before we start any dancing," he says, "I want to read out a telegram that arrived here yesterday. You were away in the town, Sally Anne, so I thought I'd keep it as a surprise for you today."

He takes the sheet from his inside pocket and reads solemnly.

'Wishing you and your new husband all the luck in Ireland. Congratulations Sally Anne Henderson. Love from all at the Windsor, Roisin and Caroline'

How lovely. I can't believe they have done this. It has made my day complete.

Matthew continues.

"And now I want my wife to play my favourite tune. It's a tune that has stayed with me ever since our first go at this whole love thing, many years ago, so I think it deserves to be heard again, now that we are married. Away you go, Sally Anne."

So I play our tune with all the feeling I can put into it. Monica hums along in a different key but I don't mind at all.

"That's for you, Matthew, and for all the years ahead," I say at the end.

Then it's into a few reels and the place goes berserk for half an hour, dancing into the hall and right up the stairs and out into the street. Mrs Moore turns out to be a great dancer and a great caller, as she organises everybody in the street for 'The Waves of Tory' and 'The Walls of Limerick', before it breaks up into a free for all.

To end the evening, Reverend Moore quietens everybody and suggests that we all say the Lord's Prayer together. A wile man for the praying, as Matthew said afterwards. He leads off and, as the thing gets going, I am hearing it in both English and Irish. The Donegal ones are in their native language, because, of course, they learned the prayer *as Gaeilge* at their mother's knee. The Tyrone ones, including John, are saying the prayer in English, led by the minister. Mrs Moore, though, as I tune in to listen to her, is praying in Irish with me. '*Agus maith dúinn ár bhfiacha, mar a mhaithimidne dárbhféichúina féin.*'

'And forgive us our trespasses as we forgive those who trespass against us.'

And, when Matthew and I go to bed tonight we will love each other as man and wife for the first time, maybe even in both languages.

Chapter 67

Matthew Henderson

It takes us until August to get the baptism service for Frankie settled. My new wife and her priest in Kincasslagh were sending letters back and forth to each other for weeks before she finally got her way and persuaded him to agree. I have to give Sally Anne her dues; she is not easily put off when it comes to something she has a principle about.

I suppose it was understandable that she wanted Frankie baptised in her own parish, and by Father Devine. At the start he did not seem keen at all, despite his earlier note that had sounded so urgent about the thing. I think he expected Sally Anne to just roll over and have the local priest here in Castlederg do it in St Patrick's. That would have kept me out of her local picture in the west and would have been easy enough for her to organise. But easy is not something my wife has much time for. It had to be St Mary's, Kincasslagh, the home place.

We talked about it often. I needed to know why she was insisting on going back home for this. After all, Frankie's connection with Kincasslagh was very faint. I knew right well, though, that is wasn't about Frankie; it was about her.

"Father Devine was my priest for years," she said. "Himself and me have had our disagreements in the past but I still respect him and I want him to be the priest who baptises our child."

"But he's not our child," I argued. "The adoption hasn't come through yet. He will be but..."

"I know all that, but that isn't the point. Look, Matthew, we got married more on your side of the fence than on mine. It was your clergyman who blessed us, not mine, not my church. I just want Father Devine to stand in front of us, in the church where I grew up and I want him to know that we are properly married and that our child, when we get him adopted, will be brought up in my faith."

"Sure you could write and tell him that."

"I could, but that isn't the point."

"What is the point then?"

"The point is that I want him to...I suppose I want him to see it for himself, not just know it from a letter. My neighbours too. I want him and them to see you, standing beside me as my husband,

and accept it. And I want to ask him to pray a blessing on our marriage. I think he owes that to me. I think you do too."

"Fair enough," I told her. "I can understand that."

"You don't mind?"

"Of course I don't mind. We always said this would be done as fair as possible, so I will take you to your church and I will stand beside you."

"And you will go along with the vows and all?"

"What vows?"

"The vows that he asks us to make. To bring up Frankie in all the ways of the Catholic faith?"

"Ah right," I said, "but surely he can't ask me that, me not being a Catholic? I can promise not to stand in your way but I don't know anything about bringing him up in the traditions of your church. I have to leave that to you."

"Well, maybe," she said, "but I'll have to write to him to see how that works. Usually it is both parents and the godparents who have to promise. Maybe he will be alright with just me and Mary and Liam doing it."

"I hope so."

"I will ask him about that anyway. And are you happy that I ask him to do the blessing on us as well?"

"I am," I tell her. "Sure what harm can it do?"

"Don't be so negative about it," she said. "What harm? It's meant to be a blessing for us and you're worried about what harm it could do. I remember one time when I worked for you. It was after I had gone to hear Mass in the cemetery at St Patrick's and you said it was all mumbo-jumbo. Is that what you still think?"

"I never said such a thing," I protested, but in the back of my mind I did remember something about it. I also remembered how angry it had made her.

"You did. I will never forget it, for it offended me a lot that you thought of our prayers and blessings as if they were some sort of pagan ritual. Mumbo-jumbo!"

I needed to set the record straight on this with her.

"If I said that, Sally Anne, I can only say that I am sorry. And if you wonder do I still think like that....no, I don't. I may not understand it, the Mass and all, but it is your tradition and I respect it, for I respect you."

"And you won't have any problem with Father Devine praying over us? Blessing us like, maybe even in Irish?"

"Well if it's in Irish, sure we can't go wrong for I won't understand a word of it. You will have to tell me after what he said."

She laughed. "I could be telling you anything under heaven and you would have to believe me."

All that was settled between us then, but it wasn't settled with Father Devine, not yet. It took a meeting with him before Mass, in the vestry of the chapel, to sort it out. He had shaken hands with me when we came in, no smiles but civilly enough, considering how antagonistic our first meeting had been two years ago. Now he was explaining the service to us and to Mary and Liam Coyle. When he finished that and was sort of dismissing us so that he could get himself ready for Mass Sally Anne wasn't for budging.

"And when the baptism is over, Father, is that when you want to do a blessing for Matthew and me, for our marriage? Or will you have that done already?"

She spoke in English so that I could follow the discussion.

"Now, Sally Anne," he began, "you will have noticed in my letters that I made no such promise."

"I did notice that, Father," she said, very casually, "but I just thought you hadn't mentioned it because I should take it for granted that you would want to bless us."

"Take it for granted? How do you mean?"

"Just that you would not want to miss the opportunity to say a blessing on us here in my home parish, after Matthew's minister having blessed us over in Castlederg. You would not want to be leaving the thing so lop-sided like."

"Hmm, I see," he said, his back to us as he scuffled around at his desk getting his notes and prayer book organised. "What sort of minister would that be now?"

I thought I should add to the chat to support Sally Anne.

"He's Reverend Moore, he's Methodist. He even came up to the house after and said a prayer for us. The thing is, Father, I want to be as fair as I can to Sally Anne. I never want her to feel that my church accepted her and blessed her marriage, but her own church held back on it. I never want her to feel any pressure from me or my folks that she should convert from her own faith. So if you could see your way to blessing us, here in front of Sally Anne's own folk, now that we're married and have the documents to prove it, that would mean a great deal to Sally Anne... and to me."

"Would it now? Well..."

We said no more. The priest was thinking hard. We both sensed that he was coming round, that we had said enough by way of argument. We wanted to let him think about it. At the same time Sally Anne wanted him to promise her this, before we went into the service. Then it would be too late.

He took Sally Anne's hand in a nice fatherly way and said something to her in Irish. By the tone of it and by the wee smile lighting her eyes, I could sense that he was promising to do as she asked.

As we sat and knelt and stood and sat and knelt during the Mass, my mind wandered. I was far away and far back in time. I started remembering my father for some reason. It was an unusual memory to be dwelling on right now, for it involved the time of my first adventures in the whole business of love.

I was maybe about fifteen at the time. I was just starting to notice girls. Back then, the first girl I noticed as a girl was likely my glamorous cousin, Victoria. At that age it didn't matter too much that she was my cousin I suppose. I was a bit in awe of her and her Belfast way of going on. She was funny and flirty and brash, and she ruled my affections far too much to be healthy. The thing about it was that I only saw her for a couple of weeks every summer when she would come to stay on our farm. Then, when she left, it would be back to porridge for me.

Porridge wasn't so bad though. My neighbour was turning out to be a very nice girl too; Mary Kearney, of course.

During my childhood I was always caught between her and her wee brother. With Joe, I was the leader of the devilment we got up to as lads. When Mary was around, however, I became a junior partner in things. She was the boss, Joe did what she said and I tagged along. We would work in the fields together and the craic would always be great. We had our rows and fights but we always made up. Mary was a Tom-boy and the best of fun to be with.

Then, when she was about fourteen, I noticed her starting to change. The shape of her. The legs became interesting to stare at when she'd be working on the peat-bank above me and the wind would be playing tricks with her dress. The way she would look at me changed. Her whole confidence grew. She could twist me round her little finger, for I became devoted to her. We'd be playing hide-and-seek in the hay. Mary was quick and light on her feet and, though I was as big as her, I could never escape her. She would catch me behind hay-rick and land on top of me before I could escape. I will never forget the first time she kissed me in that position, her knees on either side of my chest, her hair hanging down around my face and her lips slobbering all over mine. I would protest and struggle like mad to get up and get away.

My father started to notice that I didn't always run away from her as fast as I could have done. I sensed him watching me the odd time, making wee funny remarks at my expense.

"She has you again son. I think you are enjoying that too much. Looks like you are waiting for her to catch you."

We had a lot of fun. Maybe she was experimenting, enjoying the discovery of her power to make a fellow fall for her. And I certainly did. She had me eating out of her hand.

We both went through a rough patch shortly after that time of innocence. Our fathers left us to fight the Kaiser. Anthony came home crippled for the rest of his life, but he left my father behind. While I grieved the loss of my daddy, Mary grew bitter at the wound that had stolen so much life and joy from her father.

Later, as she grew up even more, our closeness faded and we drifted apart as naturally as you would expect. At one time we became more like enemies, with all the bother in the country.

The thing that got me thinking about this today was that, here we are in a Catholic Church in the west of Donegal and here is the same Mary Kearney, standing between Sally Anne and Liam, standing as god-mother for our soon-to-be-adopted child. I started to wonder how my father would feel about this situation if he could be here now. My old sparring partner supporting my wife and our wain. All three of them Catholic.

And, as I think back on my father's attitude to his neighbours as a Border farmer and to his example to me in the years before he was taken away from us, I can never think of one single instance when he was anything other than accepting of other people. He was always generous and opened-hearted to folk of a different church. He never joined any organisation that would have been a stumbling block to his relationships across the community. He always stood up for the rights of others to think differently, to worship differently, to vote differently. It was just how he was. In some ways, I wish that I could have known him in his early years to see what had shaped him into this moderate man that I knew.

Never once did he rebuke me or warn me about my infatuation with Mary Kearney. She was never 'the other sort'. I have no doubts that he would have had the same view of Sally Anne.

Today, as this service drones on in a language that I do not understand, I think of him and I am proud of him. I hope he would feel the same way about me. I think he would.

I have become my father's son.

Father Devine moves to the baptismal font and nods to us to join him. Sally Anne, carrying Frankie on her right, slips her left hand under my arm and lifts her head.

We approach her priest. Father Devine has a sort of watery smile on his face.

So have I.

Epilogue

Frankie Henderson

This is my eighteenth birthday.

My parents told me today that I am adopted.

This is a total shock for me. It will take me a while to get used to it all. I had no idea.

I am ginger haired. This should maybe have made me curious. You see, neither of my parents are, nor my cousins in Drumquin.

Today they told me all about my birth mother. She was a second cousin of my....of my adopted mother, so we are a bit related by blood. My father is not, but I do not love him any the less for this. He has been very good to me. He will always be 'my da'.

My actual parents were Scottish. I would 'nivir hae' guessed. They lived in Glasgow. I am not sorry I was reared on a farm instead of in one of the biggest cities around. I am told that my birth father, who may have been ginger for all I know, only saw me once in his life; that was when he came home for a short while during the Second World War. He drowned soon after that when his ship was sunk by a German torpedo. I intend to find out all I can about that ship, about him too. I wonder if there are any old photos of him in Scotland? It is a strange coincidence that both my birth parents were victims of drowning. My mother drowned as well, as a result of an accident when walking beside the River Clyde. Her name was Nuala, Nuala Quinn. I wonder what she was like. I have my father's name, Frank(ie), but he was Wilson.

Matthew and Sally Anne, my mother and father, (for that is what they will always be), sat me down after dinner today. We did no work in the afternoon, just sat around the table and talked. They had all this to explain to me and they did it as best they could.

They also told me the story of their lives. It is a crazy story, like something you'd read about in one of my mother's novels. I am so glad they eventually saw sense and got themselves together and married. From my point of view, from a selfish motive of course, I could not be more pleased that they did, for it meant that they could adopt me back in 1948.

I love Lismore farm, the land that I will take over when my father passes on. I hope that won't be for a good while yet, for he is only 62. I have always felt that this farm is in my blood and my bones, but now, now that I know I was a Glasgow baby, I am not so sure about where that notion comes from. There is no better feeling in the world than to take my girl for a walk across our fields and up to the top of the hill behind us to look across our land and down to the Derg valley below.

I love it too when she comes with me and we climb the ancient fort in our front field; ('*lios*', as my mother always calls it; she insists on me trying to speak Irish at times, just to keep it alive in the family). I wonder did my da ever bring his maid up here when he was trying to court her. On these occasions, I am thinking about the crops in the fields below us, or the animals I can hear from all around the farm, while my lass is picking flowers and making a necklace for herself. Then we will lie together in the middle of the bluebells as the light dapples down on us through the sycamore leaves. We never seem to run out of things to talk about and, if we do, we are content to just stretch out and hold each other, her eyes a story waiting for an ending.

Our area is as pretty a place as I have ever seen…well maybe west Donegal, where my mother is from, is nicer. That is one place I love going over to; the beaches and the mountains are unbelievable, but there the land wouldn't be as good as here.

Lismore and Castlederg have had their share of political bother over the past six or seven years. Being right on the boundary between north and south, the area suffered during the IRA's border campaign which only ended earlier this year. The violence in a lot of border communities only divided people and did nothing to bring about the aim of getting rid of partition.

While that was all going on, from 1956 till now, we have music in the house near enough every week. If the violence was separating people, the music sessions in our kitchen were bringing them together, people from both sides of the house. Religion was never a bother to any of us. My mother's fiddle playing was the main thing to bring folk in. She is a great encourager of young ones who are interested in our tunes. Myself, well she had me on the fiddle for a while but I could never really take to it. There was a man called Beattie used to come over to the sessions. He was from Drumquin but the distance did not keep him away. He played a banjo very well and I sort of fell in love with that instrument, that and the guitar. As a result, my father bought me a banjo for Christmas when I turned 11 and the Beattie man got me on to the technique of it. The fingering is the same as the fiddle and my mother and me could play lots of tunes together.

Now that I am listening to the new music on the radio and seeing 'Thank Your Lucky Stars' on the television, I would be interested in learning to play the guitar properly. I love the songs of The Everly Brothers, Elvis Presley and The Four Seasons. There are some good bands coming up across the water too, the Beatles, a new band called the Rolling Stones and the like. To me, that is the future of music and I aim to be involved, if I am good enough. I do a bit of singing already; my mother tells me I am pretty good at it, but then she would, wouldn't she?

I was at St Patrick's Primary School in Castlederg. I left at fourteen and came straight on to the farm, which was a great relief, for I could never be doing with the master in that school. I'd far rather have the open spaces of the land and the songs of the thrushes and blackbirds during the quiet mornings, the cooing of the pigeons and the creackin' of the corncrakes at night, all that as well as our own music in the house in the evenings. Our neighbours, the Coyle family, would come over to us regularly for these nights of music. None of them play anything but Josie is a great singer, mainly of Irish folk songs. I am working with her though, trying to get her to learn some of the pop songs from the radio. If I can get a guitar soon we could perform together.

Josie is a year older than me, but that hasn't stopped the two of us getting together. She is the nicest girl in Ireland and I hope I can keep her, not like my oul father who lost his girl for twenty years before he found her again and married her. Am I ever glad he did, for if he hadn't I'd likely be working in some dirty oul factory in Scotland. Mind you, I am even more pleased for my mother for, according to daddy, she was the one that got it all started again by writing him a simple letter, a letter he still keeps in the back of his bible. I have read it too, a precious piece of our family history.

If Josie and me ever get married, and that is what I am working towards eventually, it will make a lot of sense, with the two farms marching on each other. We might even get around to knocking down a few of those stone walls and making the fields a bit bigger.

But that is all for the future.

In the meantime, there's plenty of work to be done here on the farm, plenty of tunes to be played, plenty of songs to be learning with Josie. And of course, there is always the thought of walking up to the peace and quiet of Gortnagappel bog, herself beside me, the larks warbling in the clear air above us, her white hand in mine and a soft smile of promise in her apple-green eyes.

Glossary of Ulster Scots dialect phrases.

A lock o'	A lot of
Bairns	Children
Bease	Cattle, Beasts
Bate	Beat
Boke	Vomit
Carnaptious	Contrary, quarrelsome
Clabber/Glar	Muck
Crabbit	Angry, annoyed
Cutty	Girl or young woman
Dake	Dyke
Dander (or danner)	Short walk or stroll
Dour	Grumpy, serious, unpleasant
Dwamle	A weak turn
Fornenst	Opposite
Ejit/gulpin	A foolish person, idiot
Gerning	Complaining
Groop	Draining channel in a byre
Gulder	Shout
Hoose	House
Houl your horses	Stop (Hold back on something)
Ither boodie	Other person
Mair	More

Morrowing	Farmers helping each other with farm tasks
Nivir hae	Never have
Rare *To rare up at someone* *Rare boys* *Raring Frankie*	Rare can have several meanings—— To rise up in anger Strange fellas Rearing the child
Rodden	A rough lane or track
Scunnered	Annoyed, disgusted by
Sleekit	Underhand, devious
Skellyin'	Glancing
Skitter	A derogatory or abusive term
Steugh	A smokey atmosphere
Stour *'He doesn't rise much stour'*	Dust. The phrase can be applied to a person who is reticent, shy or lazy.
Oul banger	Old car
Thole	To put up with something
Thon wan	That one, that person
Thran	Obstinate
A wee scoot	A short journey, (or a little pour of tea!)
Wains	Children
Wheen	Several
Wheest!	Be quiet!
Whins	Gorse
Wile	Very

Glossary of Irish phrases.

An áit a n-ólann an t-uan an bainne	Where the lamb drinks its milk.
An bhfuil tú go maith, a iníon?	Are you well daughter?
An Trá Bán/ar an Trá Bhán	The white strand/on the white strand
Agus ná lig sinn i gcathú, ach saor sinn ó olc'	And let us not fall into temptation but deliver us from evil
Bean dhubh	Black woman
Bí ciúin a Athair, le do thoil	Be quiet Father, please
Bhí tú ag rámhaillí'	You were raving (delirious)
Bosca ceoil	Accordion
Breac	Trout
Cad é mar atá sibh	How are you?
Cad é mar atá an saol i Rann Uí Thuathail?	How is life in Ranahuel?
Cailín óg amaideach	Silly young girl
Camán & sliotar	Hurley stick and hard leather ball
Caoineadh	Crying
Caonach	Moss
Coinleach glas an Fhómair	The green stubble of autumn
Créatúr	Creature
An chrotach	The curlew
Go mbeannaí Dia sibh. Slán agaibh.	God bless you. Goodbye.
Fear gorm (fear dubh)	Black man

Foinn mhall	Slow airs
An fháinleog	The swallow
An fhuiseog	The lark
Gabh mo leithsceál	Excuse me
Gabh sábhála Dia muid	God save us!
Galánta	Lovely
Geansaithe	Jumpers
Grianstad an Gheimhridh	Winter solstice
Halla Naomh Muire	St Mary's Hall
Is ola le mo chroí é an Ghaeilge a chluinstin ag na stócaigh sin	The Irish that I hear is a pleasure, the conversation flows easily.
Le do thoil	Please
Le grá	With love
Lios	Fort or rath
Lon dubh	Blackbird
Maith thú, a iníon	Well done, daughter
Ní thuigim	I do not understand
O a Mhaighdeán bheannaithe	Oh Blessed Virgin
Seanachaí	Story-teller
Slán anois a sheanchara, agus ádh mór ort	Goodbye now, old friend and good luck
Spioraid an fhoinn	The soul of the tune
Stad a leanbh	Stop child!
Is suaimhneas agus beannacht é	It is tranquility and blessing

Tá tú ag déanamh gnoithe maith agus do chailín aimsire féin agat.	You are doing so well you have your own servant
Tchí Dia mé	God bless me!
Uisce beatha	Whiskey (water of life)

ABOUT THE AUTHOR

David Dunlop was born and raised in the north of Co. Antrim. He spent many years in education, both as a teacher and as a school leader; in those roles he exercised his passion to bring together young people from across the various political and religious traditions in Ireland, north and south, so as to encourage a shared understanding of their history and culture. To that end he wrote and directed several stage musicals which had historical and cross-cultural themes. These shows drew on his experience of performance in various musical genre. Music is an enduring theme in his writing, as is his interest in language and dialect.

"A Maid Again" continues the story of the fictional characters, Matthew Henderson and Sally Anne Sweeney, the two main actors in "The Broken Fiddle", published in 2016.
"The Broken Fiddle" was, in turn, a sequel to "Oileán na Marbh - Island of the Dead", published in 2014.
A further novel by this author is "We, The Fallen" (2018), a more modern story set in Ireland, France and Germany against the backdrop of the 2016 Brexit vote.

All of the above novels can be purchased online through the usual websites, from selected outlets in Ireland, north and south, or from the author by direct contact.

email- dadunlop50@gmail.com   Twitter- @dadunlop50

Printed in Poland
by Amazon Fulfillment
Poland Sp. z o.o., Wrocław